THE VALEDICTORIAN

THE VALEDICTORIAN

David James Elliott

IGUANA

Copyright © 2022 David James Elliott
Published by Iguana Books
720 Bathurst Street, Suite 303
Toronto, ON M5S 2R4

The Valedictorian is a work of fiction. Names, places, events, occurrences and incidents are either products of the author's imagination and/or used in a fictitious manner. Any resemblances to actual persons, living or dead, or to actual events is strictly coincidental.

Publisher: Meghan Behse
Editors: Paula Chiarcos and Rachel Brodie
Front cover design: Ruth Dwight, designplayground.ca
Front cover image: Stefano Pollio, Unsplash.com

ISBN 978-1-77180-512-4 (paperback)
ISBN 978-1-77180-513-1 (epub)

This is an original print edition of *The Valedictorian*.

Part 1

Chapter 1

"The day after you die, yeah, that's the one you need to watch out for. The day of the actual event, there's a lot of drama and things to do, time moves fast, and the script you have in your head works well. But when the sun goes down, they turn off the teleprompter, load all the lights and microphones onto the cart, sweep the floor, and turn out the lights. There's only you and the darkness on that big empty stage. Yeah, what are you left with when the moon and stars come crashing down around your ears and your ride home doesn't show up the way they all said it would? There you are, outside the barbed wire wishing you were back inside. Back anywhere for that matter. On that cold and lonely morning, the horror of it all starts to work on your gut. You see the outline of the real problem for the very first time. Suddenly you're not so sure about settled stuff anymore."

A thin spectre with silver hair hopped up onto the coffin of a young man who was receiving his first and likely last application of makeup. He was in the visitation room being prepped for his close-up. Pamela, the able and attractive beautician who was dotting the i's and crossing the t's for him, was totally engrossed in her work. John had a thing for her. He enjoyed watching her work. She had beautiful precise hands. He felt safe around her, even gregarious. She was oblivious to him, but he was used to that. He carried on talking to her as if they were old friends.

"Did you see that poor little old guy sitting in the chapel all by himself? I know. What a mess. It broke my heart to see him that way. There he was, looking at his casket and sighing. Oh yeah, he wanted to send his order back to the kitchen. You know, most people have opinions about death, strong prejudices they inherit from their families and, damn it, some pretty clear expectations too. He wasn't where he expected to find himself and he was pissed. You see, we all bought that line about an out-of-body experience. If you can still see your body, you're really not dead. The ball is still in play. Got to be some way to jump back in. But that's not the way it works. The day after you croak, you can go back and forth on that point for quite a while. Most people move on, but not everyone. It makes you think, If I had known about this, would I have done things differently? I would have listened.*"*

He chuckled to himself. "The old boy could've used a few pointers. Speaking of which, Pamela, I think you've gone way overboard on those eyebrows, but hey — what do I care? I could've used someone new to talk to as well but, unfortunately, he didn't speak English. Too bad. Gestures don't cut it on this. He started yelling after a while and then he left. I hope he finds what he wants. Don't laugh, Pamela, everything's possible on Madison Avenue. You could live your whole life on this one magical block. It's got a Montessori, the U of T prep school, a Buddhist temple, frat houses, a treatment centre, the Granite Glen, Flannerman's, schools of both philosophy and psychotherapy, and the pub. If you can't find your heart's desire here — you're in deep trouble."

John hopped off the casket and started to limber up by doing a series of stretches. He intertwined his fingers and raised his hands, palms up, over his head. He held the pose for a full minute before he relaxed. He shook the tension out of his arms and, placing his hands on his hips, began to turn left and right vigorously while his feet remained firmly planted on the floor.

"Peter and I are always on the lookout for a new pal, as you well know. It's one of the rare points on which we agree. Ordinarily, Peter and I would not be friends. He's by way of being a bit of an aberration. Does that sound harsh? Oh, he's a nice enough man, but maybe not so good at picking up on the subtle clues you get from other people when they've had all they can take. You know, little things — an angry tone of voice, a look of horror, even running out of the room — those things escape his notice. I can never get him to see the big picture. Always a little too preoccupied with whatever is going on inside his head at any given moment."

John put his hands on his calves and tried to touch his knees with his nose. He carried on grunting as he spoke.

"Actually, Peter's head would be a good place to start talking about him. He made a lot of money in real estate and put it all into cryogenics. That's right. When he croaked, they cut off his head and put it in the deep freeze, right beside the lasagne. He left some moon-faced rodent in charge of his money. It's in trust, waiting for Peter to sort out this death thingy and drop by the office. He's hanging around waiting for them to thaw him out, clone his ass, or some other Buck Rogers thing. He figures that, since he got out of his old body, there has to be a way for him to jump into a new one. It's hard to find a flaw in his thinking."

Feeling refreshed, he returned to Pamela's side. She was finished and the client was beautiful. All she had left to do was remove the collar of tissue paper she'd placed over his suit coat. John prattled on as she packed up her tools.

"He goes by the lab every day; after all, it's in the basement of the Granite Glen Nursing Home. He needs to make sure the temperature gauge on his

cryotank is at absolute zero. He didn't have any family to look after his affairs. He lived alone, worked alone and, you guessed it, he died alone too, which is why he hired that nice young lawyer who drew up all those legal papers. Peter sets great store in that young man's integrity. It would never occur to Peter to ask a few awkward questions before signing on the dotted line. People are exactly what he needs them to be. But as you and I well know, Pamela, a few deft strokes of the pen and there go Peter's millions. Never trust a trust account. But I look on the bright side — Peter won't have to worry about waking up with an ice-cream headache.

"He and I are what you might call restless spirits. The phrase carries more than one meaning. The thing you discover — to your fury — once you are no longer living but not quite dead is that you cannot rest. I remember my first night, putting my head down on the pillow. I shut my eyes, and nothing happened. I felt like a sick child waiting for the morning, trusting that I would feel better when the sun came up. I knew somehow that if I could fall asleep for a few minutes, I'd wake up in a better place."

He looked at the young man in the coffin and made a face. "What I could have used was a drink."

Chapter 2

Arthur Cardel lay motionless under his fine white linen sheet. Sleep was life's ultimate disappointment. It brought sweet relief from pain, but it made time pass in an instant. Waking landed on wanting and produced a steady despair that made heavy club-footed progress throughout the hours of illumination.

The light of day that found its way through his shuttered windows dragged a potent mix of sorrow and panic back into his consciousness. He groaned and rolled onto his side, away from the light, away from the beckoning day. He pulled the covers over his head and dialled the number again. Four rings and the voice.

The sheets wound around his body like a shroud, and all that he could feel was the stifling warmth of the bed and the hot moist air of confinement. He was *mummified* — there was a word that had a new meaning for him. Six months ago, his life made sense. He was a young man on the rise. But this morning, nothing made sense. He dialled the number again.

"Pick up, you heartless bitch. I need you."

He could hear his younger brother, Dale, laughing and banging his way through the house. "Where's Arthur? I want to play with Arthur. Mommy, wake him up."

Arthur wanted to play, but then he thought about Linda, and something predatory deep inside him, something wounded, shrank back into the shadows. He went with it.

———

Sally Cardel had wisely put off the moment of confrontation until after her husband, Gerry, left. She had a sick feeling in her stomach. Arthur had agreed not to spend the morning in bed, and yet, here it was ... 10:00 a.m. She knocked on his door. "Arthur, are you up?" She gently turned the knob and found, to her surprise, that it was locked.

"Arthur." There was a long silence. She heard life stirring.

"What," said a fed-up voice, followed by more silence.

She waited a minute, listening for movement, and then she rapped again — harder than she intended. "Arthur, get up."

"I said I was up. Leave me alone. Damn it, I'm not feeling good. I need to sleep."

Sally felt a wave of shock move through her body. She felt as if she'd been shoved toward the subway track. She looked down and saw Dale standing next to her. The little boy was confused by the look of distress on his mother's face. He grabbed her leg, hoping to be picked up.

"Arthur, we agreed. Get out of that bed now and come get a cup of tea." A hard object hit the inside of the door with considerable force. Dale ran crying down the hallway to his bedroom and slammed the door. Sally stood there in the silence, shaking.

Arthur sat up in bed listening for the sound of her reaction. Throwing the book had broken a bond. He felt an ache in his gut that sucked the life right out of him. He seized his pillow and wrapped it around his head as if he was trying to drown out an unbearable noise. "I can't stay here. I have to get back."

———

The eastbound subway pulled into Spadina Station at 8:04 a.m. The car was crowded with commuters of every size, age, and nationality, all of them going somewhere different on the same train. Nobody seemed to mind. Greg Bass was hanging on to a ceiling-mounted handrail and listening to his iPod. He was reviewing the playlist for this weekend's gig. His band, Pataphysics, was playing a benefit at Hugh's Room. This was the best venue they had ever landed and he was excited.

Greg was dressed for work in a dark-blue suit with a hint of pinstriping. He wore a London Fog topcoat that he had owned for decades. His expensive leather shoes were shined to a high gloss. He strode out of the subway car and followed the phalanx of commuters up the escalator. Descending on the other side were a line of rather young and inebriated Roman senators in togas. They looked happy and sleepy in equal measure.

He emerged into the bright sunlight of an early December morning. Toronto had yet to have a frost; the temperature still hovered in the high single digits. The air felt cool and clean on his face, and he could still detect the faint smell of algae from Lake Ontario.

A woman walking behind Greg snuck an admiring look at him. He was fit, forty, and had a full head of thick blond hair that he kept fashionably long. He looked like a subdued rock star on his way into court, ready to face the tabloids and a drug charge, someone whose face you would recognize from an album cover. It was an affectation that served him well on weekends, when he fronted his band.

Greg, as always, was thoroughly engrossed in his music. His thoughtful countenance sometimes seemed impassive and oblivious to his surroundings. Toronto sidewalks boast something to delight you, and something to disgust you, in every walking mile. Greg watched it all from a vantage point where cool drinks were served under a canopy. He passed a long line of young mothers pushing strollers, marching in lock step on their way to daycare. A vagrant wrapped in an old blanket and a winter coat was sleeping on the front lawn of the apartment building next to the school. No one seemed fussed by this. Some of the kids waved at this man as they passed. Apparently, this was an arrangement that worked for both parties. *I wonder if the kids think he's hibernating?*

Greg felt a cold shiver in his bones as he passed the sleeping man. *God I hope he's not one of ours.* Turning off Spadina and onto Lowther, he spied a familiar face. A youngish woman in a bedsheet was being handcuffed and placed into the back seat of a police car. Darlene had been partying with the clients and had forgotten about court.

He felt it would be impolite to wave. They'd been friends but they weren't exactly on speaking terms these days. They shared a client list, but their relationship, if such a word could be used, was more cops and robbers than project manager and subcontractor. It hurt him to see her in distress. She had an impressive run of sobriety once, but alas it was only the once and it was difficult now to remember her in good health.

Turning left off Lowther, he caught sight of the Punanai Centre. It was a formidable red-brick structure built big, solid, and square. It faced directly east and got the full force of the morning sun. An elevated patio sitting six feet above the sidewalk ran the length of the northern portion of the building and was surrounded by an imposing thick black metal fence. This was where the counsellors gathered at the start of shift.

The building was originally constructed as a private home. In the centennial year, it was reborn as a seniors' residence and carried on business in that vein until the early nineties. It was supplanted when they built the swankier Granite Glen up the road. No one knew what to do with the building, and after a few false starts, it took up its current role as a treatment centre. The distinguishing feature that lingered to the modern day was the scale of the place. Senior citizens in 1967 were considerably shorter than today's adults. All the handrails, sinks, and counters seemed impossibly short, and there was no money to fix it.

As Greg mounted the front steps of the centre, he heard an enormous blast of sound that overpowered his iPod. He took off his earphones and looked around him. The boys at Theta Chi were wearing bedclothes too and obviously enjoying some very satisfying designer drugs. They'd gathered to greet the dawn. The stereo was cranked to the max and they were howling and dancing on the balcony. Maybe it was their way of saying thank you and farewell to Darlene.

Mike Sage and the mononymous Kaiser were standing on the sun porch watching the fun while they smoked. The music was unrecognizable to anyone over twenty, but it was definitely dance music. It was irresistible. The juxtaposition of tweaked dancing adolescents in their finery and conservatively dressed addictions counsellors, each viewing the other from their respective solitudes, while the music incited them both, was just too funny. Without missing a beat, Kaiser began to sway in time with the music. Mike, who was naturally kinaesthetic, began to move his hands in small counter-clockwise circles. Kaiser mirrored that move, and pausing to make eye contact, invited Mike to do a sidestep. In two or three beats, both men looked like dancers in a chorus line. Greg's face beamed with delight at this magical, spontaneous moment. The kids across the way waved and cheered.

The heavy oak front door opened, and Reg Topping emerged with an unlit cigarette in between his lips. He was a heavily muscled man who walked with difficulty, assisted by two stout ash canes. Reg was good-looking, with a crop of thick dark hair and an intelligent demeanour that he emphasized with his choice of glasses. A look of outrage crossed his face when he saw Kaiser dancing. "What is that awful sound? Oh look, the circus is in town."

Kaiser looked up at his adversary and saw an opportunity to score some points. "Are we embarrassing you?" he asked, as he continued the dance.

"In more ways than you'll ever know." Reg shook his head in disgust and turned his back on them to light his cigarette. Kaiser stole a look at Mike and Greg, both of whom were pleading for restraint with their eyes. A little grin and a twinkle in his eye told them their plea was in vain.

Kaiser began to dance faster and faster. "I can't control myself ... Jesus ... help me!"

Reg rose to the bait, and in a measured but angry tone said, "Hey, Baryshnikov, knock it off. Look around, boys. These houses go for three or four million each. Do you see anyone else dancing in the street this morning? Well ... do you?"

Mike, Kaiser, and Greg all pointed in unison to the frat house as they gave way to laughter. Reg stepped out from behind the pillar onto the sundeck and saw the dancing kids for the first time. He felt a flush that made his knees buckle.

Kaiser still knew all the cool dance moves, but he wasn't fit enough these days to do them for very long. He was gasping for breath but determined to hide it. "Someone tell Doug. I got the dancing plague. I can't stop!"

Reg glared at Kaiser and sensed that anything he did or said now would simply invite more bad behaviour. Kaiser loved to trump embarrassment with outrage, and he would keep escalating until the cops showed up. Reg tried to let his silence and his body language speak for him. He walked back to the far end of the sun deck to smoke his cigarette in peace. But then he gave himself away. He did a quick quarter turn, hoping to see a look of support from either Greg or Mike. Kaiser saw this moment of vulnerability and smiled. He did one more victory jig and then he grasped the railing to get his breath back. His face was beaming.

The police car that was taking Darlene to the lockup stopped in front of Theta Chi for a minute and flashed its lights. The music stopped and the mice ran back inside.

Greg felt a moment of dismay as he put his headphones in his pocket. *We were just having fun.* He turned and entered the building. *What is it with those two? They used to be friends. Now the whole world is their battleground. What the hell have they got to fight about?*

———

Reg needed a moment. A run-in with Kaiser shared a number of features with being chased by a wolf. There was a potent cocktail of emotions that all of Kaiser's victims shared: anger, fear, shame, and an overwhelming desire to respond in kind. Reg caned his way into the counsellors' office. He would be safe from Kaiser in there. Mike Sage was already back at his desk taking a phone call when Reg sat down next to him. Mike had a sour look on his face. Reg assumed it was the conversation he was having. It never entered his mind that Mike might be angry with him. When another call came through, Reg was only too glad to pick it up. "Good morning, Punanai House."

It was a woman. "I'm not sure I called the right place … I got this number from the internet … I'm not even sure what it is I want to ask…"

"My name is Reg Topping and I'm a counsellor here." Reg's voice sounded thoroughly professional. "Do you have a family member who needs some help?"

"I'm calling about my son, Arthur. Arthur Cardel, after his grandfather."

"What's your first name?"

"I'm Sally."

"What has Arthur done that has you so worried, Sally?"

"Arthur is driving us mad. He's never given us any trouble before. He's always bright and loving, but he went away to university in the fall and when he came back for Christmas … he was different. I don't know my own son anymore. He never comes out of his room. I can't even talk to him."

Reg selected a pen from his coat pocket. "Does Arthur drink or use drugs?"

"No, never. Well at least we've never seen him take anything. He's always been a perfect child. His younger brother, Dale, idolizes him. This is why his behaviour is so frightening."

"Forgive me for asking, but has he ever had a mental health problem?"

"No. He was the school valedictorian last year, for heaven's sake."

Reg was starting to warm up to Sally. "What makes you think he may have a problem that requires our help?"

She sighed. "I don't understand what's happening. One day, Arthur is going off to Queen's to study medicine, and the next time we see him, he's dark and depressed and angry all the time. He hounds his father and me for money. He threatened to leave school if we don't give him some…" Her voice rose in grief and anger. "But he won't tell us what the money is for. He's up all night and sleeps through the day. Something is so terribly wrong. And the friends, what do I want to say about them, the mysterious new friends? He's on the phone with them at all hours."

Reg needed to know if Sally had enough steel in her to call Arthur on his behaviour. Most parents didn't without a little coaching. That's why they called. "How does that make you feel?"

"I don't know what to do. I hate feeling this way. I want our old life back."

"Do you think Arthur would talk to me?"

"Let me try," she said, setting the phone down.

Reg let his eyes wander around the office as he waited. The day staff were all settling in at their desks checking emails before the morning census meeting. *These guys really are my own little sitcom. I could pitch this as a TV show. Mike the under boss: tough as nails. Never backs down. Always looking uncomfortable in a suit and tie. In a TV show, I'd give him intuitive superpowers. Then there's our resident rock star Greg: He carries that damn guitar around with him wherever he goes and gets that otherworldly look on his face when he plays it. I don't know why Doug and Mike let him get away with that. He's a ladies' man even if he does have two kids and a wife he goes home to every night. Then there's Paul: He'd steal the show. Photographer, philosopher, and stand-up comedian all tightly wrapped in a cool, calm exterior. Never flies off the handle or says the wrong thing unless he's bored. God, I wish I had his sangfroid. Then of course, there's Kaiser: international man of mischief. We don't even know his first name. A human tornado in a designer suit—*

His reverie was interrupted when the office door opened. One of the clients, Aaron Johnston, walked into the middle of the office with a tablespoon in his right hand. Aaron was prickly.

Reg pointed at his phone as he looked across the room at Paul. Seeing that everyone else was busy, Paul beckoned Aaron over to the filing cabinet where the medications were kept. "You looking for something?"

"I need my Buckley's." He thrust out his spoon as if this were proof of his peaceful intentions.

Paul heard the siren cry. "What kind of alcoholic *are* you?" He looked down at Aaron's hand. "A spoon? A real man drinks his Buckley's out of the bottle and then wipes the spout with his sleeve and passes it on to the next guy."

Aaron's face radiated turmoil. People were always making fun of him. "They told me to bring a spoon."

Paul smiled kindly at Aaron. He felt sad that his joke had misfired. "I know. I was trying to get you to smile. You feeling okay this morning, Aaron?"

Aaron poured himself a spoonful of Buckley's, drank it off and made an awful face, and then left the room without saying another word.

"I can see the headline now," Paul said with a dramatic sweep of his arms. "Local comedian dies the death. The stage opened and swallowed him whole." He pantomimed plunging a dagger into his heart. Reg and Mike did their best to ignore him. Paul danced a little jig over to the filing cabinet and returned the bottle to its place. He looked into the faces of his fully engaged colleagues and sighed. "Tough room."

Reg caught Paul out of the corner of his eye, sword-fighting his way back to his desk. At least this time he hadn't borrowed one of his canes as a prop.

Sally was back on the line and her voice returned Reg to the problem of reluctant adolescents and their inherent dislike of doing the right thing. "I can't get him to come out of his room."

Reg adjusted the phone against his ear. "Okay, he's stalling. What we need to do is set up an appointment. But here's the problem: Arthur has to make that appointment himself."

"I'm his mother—"

"When wives and mothers make appointments, the client never shows up. Always some emergency. When Arthur gets up, you need to talk to him."

"He doesn't listen to me…"

"We need to do what my old professor called 'cutting the baloney thin.'"

"What in the world?"

"We don't want to overwhelm Arthur. We want him to take a small step in the right direction."

This was one of Reg's favourite ploys, and his rich tenor voice glowed with confidence. Sally, for her part, was squirming in her chair. She had to get to her feet and walk around the room to stop these horrible words from separating her from reality and sanity. "We're going to make the step seem small by threatening him with something larger. So you'll say, 'Arthur, I need you to make an appointment with the people at Punanai.' He'll make another excuse. So then you'll say, 'Fine, but your father and I will not give you any more money until you make the appointment.' Then he'll get angry and make some threats of his own. But don't get angry. Be matter of fact and say, 'Well, it's up to you.'"

Sally put her free hand on her forehead as she fought to keep the horror she was feeling out of her voice. She shut her eyes, hoping against hope that this would help her master her feelings. It didn't, and it couldn't. She knocked over a water glass that skittered across the kitchen floor. "I don't know…" was all she could manage.

Reg knew where she was and spoke into that darkness. "If your son is an addict, he'll be desperate for money, and if the only way he can get some is to show up for an appointment with us, then that's what he'll do."

"This works?"

Reg had practised the real odds out of his voice; it didn't give him away, but his face was a different matter. His brow was furrowed. This was risky, but it was the right thing to do.

"Oh yeah. Either way, you have a solution. If he comes to see us then we can get to work on him, and we have a good success rate with young people. If he refuses, then you'll have to ask him to leave."

"I'm not going to throw my own son out of the house!"

Reg's voice was all oil and ball bearings. "Sally, I haven't known you for more than a few minutes and I've asked you to take a step that most mothers would never dream of. But here's the thing — Arthur is not your only child. If you let Arthur stay in the house and use drugs, Dale is going to pay a heavy price."

Chapter 3

Getting together with Peter at the funeral home was the highlight of John's morning. Peter's ritual was to read the paper, check on his head, and then visit for an hour or two before he disappeared again. There was a funeral in progress when John arrived, and to his great surprise, he recognized the father of the deceased standing in the receiving line. They'd worked together on the lighting and sound crew at the Tarragon. He couldn't recall the family name, but the father's first name was Owen.

His son was obviously goth. Well, that's what the kids called themselves. He and all his friends dressed like vampires. All wearing the same kind of dark, paramilitary clothing. All having the same deranged poodle-clipper do their hair.

"It's enough to break the stoutest heart," said Peter. "His only son. Full of promise. And still in university."

"I can't get over these kids," said John. "They look pretty tough going in, not so tough coming back out. Don't any of them own a suit?"

From the receiving line by the front door, the mourners were invited to enter a small alcove where the deceased lay. When they finished paying their respects, they were ushered back through the visitation room, where they were encouraged to sign the book of condolence before entering the chapel. The kids all looked cool and confident as they lined up to view their friend for the final time, but when they came out of that confining space, they couldn't hide the fact that they were frightened children. They hugged and reassured themselves until they were once again certain that this was a one-in-a-million fluke. They were not buying this death bullshit.

"This is the first time they've seen death," Peter said grandly. "I remember my first time. It felt as if the ice had given way beneath my feet and plunged me into cold water. That was when my beloved Aunt Mary went to her reward. She would take me to the movies when it only cost a quarter. The first film we saw together was The Jazz Singer, and the last was Bringing up Baby. She loved that film. Cary Grant and Katharine Hepburn." Peter got to his feet and began to wave his hands in great distress as one young woman, possibly a sweetheart, lost control of her emotions as she made her way out of the viewing area. "Oh dear, look at the young people. Still streaming in and streaming out with tears streaming down their faces."

"I give them credit for being able to cry. That at least gives me some hope for them," John said. He didn't quite mean it, but he had to interrupt Peter before he gave him a complete history of the movies from the last silent film until his dying day and beyond. He'd done it before. He had the whole thing committed to memory. He still went to the movies. Sitting all alone in the back row, absolutely riveted. Not John though, he preferred the legitimate theatre. He thought it glorious to have someone to talk with after a play was over. John once devised a small role for himself in The Sun Also Rises at Soulpepper and brought Peter along. While he enjoyed the play, he was too moved to speak about it afterward. He sat there blubbering and showing John the palm of his hand. Not much of a dialogue, but it was a review!

John was made aware of his ongoing displeasure with a look. He blathered on, hoping to avoid additional censure. "I wonder what kind of service we're going to get. Did you smell the pot outside when we came in?"

"I didn't smell anything. Are you sure it was pot?"

"Peter, my career was in addictions after I left the theatre."

"Oh, of course, John, I'd forgotten. This young man, he was a client of yours?"

"No, he never made it that far. His father and I were friends many years ago. It's a happy accident that I'm here today."

"What did he die of?"

"The kids outside said he overamped."

"He electrocuted himself?"

"It's slang for overdosing."

"What was he using?"

"Don't know, but what does it matter? They all do the same job in the end."

"Undeniably so. The proof is laid out over there in the box."

Peter looked around the room with the practised eye of the frequent funeral-goer. "That casket is not up to much. I don't think your friend made a lot of money. The floral tributes wouldn't be out of place at a cat's funeral. No doubt about it, these folks are hurting for cash. What did they bury him in?"

"A suit, I think."

"One they bought post-mortem by the look of it. I guess it doesn't matter since the deceased had the good sense not to hang around."

"If only people knew that the box doesn't do them any good. They'd be far better off spending their dough on a good suit. Still, there's no way to know that until after you die."

Peter went on. "The thing that really surprises me about funerals these days is how un-Christian they are. It's always so painfully obvious that none of the families have been to church in years. The minister rarely knows the deceased.

Why do people do a Christian burial when they don't believe in God? When was the last time that you saw everyone pile into a car and go to the gravesite? These days, a paid stranger pretends to know you and what your life was all about. They invite the family to gush, and then they all repair for sandwiches, leaving the deceased alone in a box. It's not much of a send-off."

"We're a fine pair to be discussing this," said the thin ghost, eager to regain control of the conversation. "What would they make of us? I wonder how they would feel if they knew we were here watching them?"

The fat ghost ignored him. "We were all told that if we didn't take the plunge, we would regret it. They always pointed to the single people in the community in those days. They were losers. Funny looking for the most part, and to be pitied. Queers, lunatics, and perverts mostly." Peter's round face lit up as he slipped into parody. "'The things men get up to,' my mother would say while shaking her head. Those were in the days when people dressed up for church. My mother always wore a hat and gloves and frequently had a flower on her lapel. She got her dope from the women's group at church. That's where the secrets unravelled." Peter paused for a moment as if considering the dimensions of a kingdom he had lost. You could see it on his face: the joy of those childhood memories, the certainty of his youth and his beliefs. Not changing a quarter of an inch in an entire lifetime. After a moment, he took up a new theme.

"But the serious point about Christian marriage, or burial for that matter, is that it should be based in a mutual understanding of God. Do you see my point, John? If you believe in God, then you agree to live with a woman who shares these views, in a way that's congruent with both your beliefs. But why would you choose to do that if there was no belief in God underpinning it? I think that's what the problem is today. Marriage without a shared faith is a travesty. One, I think, that is amply demonstrated by the friends of the deceased assembled here in all of their splendour. Well really — look at them. They're awful." He got to his feet and walked down the centre aisle pointing to persons of interest as he went. "Look at the belly on that poor fellow. And this lady, dressed right out of the recycling bin. This is the fruit of the forbidden tree. In my mother's day, they wouldn't have let them in the building. Would have given them a quid to buy a pint and sent them on their way. Church was for respectable people, in spite of what the namby-pamby young minister had to say."

As Peter was on his feet and moving down the aisle, John had some hope that he was leaving and that he might be spared further insights. He was wrong. Peter seemed to gather strength as he strode toward the front of the chapel. "I saw an authentic ghost town once," Peter said. "The place was in wonderful shambles. When the gold ran out, everyone left. Because it was hot and dry all the time, everything was well preserved. The thing that caught my eye was a sign hanging by one hinge from a post outside a store: COOL WATER.

"Of course, there was no cool water there anymore. There hadn't been for a hundred years. That's why the sign was memorable. It promised the very thing that was needed in that parched place. But it was only a sign. It wasn't real anymore. That's what faith has become for these people. A sign swinging in the breeze. Look at them, all broken-hearted at the death of their son, sitting there weeping, not knowing what it means or what to do. How did it ever get to be this way?"

Chapter 4

The house manager's office was the antithesis of the counsellors' working area. Here, the first rule of heaven was order. Doug Moore prided himself on being able to put his hand to any file or piece of paper. He insisted on having his facts clear and documented before he offered a public opinion. The inside and the outside of the man were in alignment. Doug was a big man. Well built and thick through the shoulders. Now in his sixties, he still sported a thick mat of black hair and a face that should have hung below the forehead of a man twenty years his junior. He was always impeccably dressed and groomed. His hair was cut so frequently and to such a standard that newcomers to Punanai often speculated that he wore a toupee. His suits came from a specialty shop in Barrie, near Camp Borden, where he served for many years. They did custom work and they did it to perfection. Lots of men look awkward and unhappy in a suit. Doug's assistant, Mike Sage, was one of them. But not Doug. He was naked without a suit.

His other great asset was his stony face. He might have been a silent screen actor had he timed his entrance into existence better. Doug was the master of the stare down. He could stare anyone in the eye for half an hour or more and never show of flicker of interest in anything they said or did. He was a camera lens; taking in information and processing it instantly while remaining perfectly opaque.

But there were human touches, too, scattered here and there around the office. Pictures of a grandson playing hockey; a granddaughter's loving portrait of her grandpa, with his name incorrectly spelled in crayon; pictures of friends playing golf. Order was sacred here, but so was concern for the human creature. Punanai was famous for confronting people with their own nonsense. That is why Doug was such an obvious choice as commanding officer for this very last all-male bastion. The confrontational style of the house found its origins in the force of his convictions and personality. But Punanai was first and foremost a place of compassion and healing. This, too, flowed from the commander. He had a tender side, which was seen on rare occasions.

Doug was on the phone as Greg opened the door to say good morning. "That's what I'm telling you. Yes, right there in front of everybody. But look, someone came in and I have to get back to work. Yeah, yeah, we'll do that."

Greg leaned over the desk and took Doug's hand. "Good morning, boss, what's up?"

Doug was positively beaming. "Big night last night. We went out to see *Mamma Mia*. And before that, we went to the Mandarin for the all-you-can-eat buffet. It was wonderful. The perfect way to spend a Sunday afternoon."

Greg had a story of his own about a weekend gone right; his band had been howling on Saturday night. But before he could launch into his story, the door flew open. Reg was still furious with Kaiser. He elbowed Greg to the side. "Doug, do you have a minute?"

Greg drew his lips into a grimace. *This can't go on. This is getting in the way. One of these guys has to go. Is Doug being drawn into the drama too?* The great stone face he stared at offered him no clue.

Greg gave Doug a playful little wave and pantomimed the words *I'm leaving now* as he pointed to the door. Doug winked back at him as Reg began to unpack Kaiser's latest outrage.

———

Kaiser and Mike could have been mistaken for two black crows perched on a rail. They were sneaking a cigarette on the sun deck.

Kaiser noticed a spot of mud on the toe of his shoe. He took a Kleenex out of his pocket and began to clean up the mess. "Darlene got busted again."

"Good, maybe we won't have to toss anyone for a while."

Kaiser loved to tease. "She goes to your meeting, doesn't she?"

Mike shook his head. "She used to."

Kaiser poked at the old scandal. "Never a good idea to sell light ounces to Police Science students."

Mike remembered the stink. "She always seems surprised when she gets busted."

"Maybe that's what keeps it fresh for her."

Below them on the street, a couple was having a heated conversation in a vehicle parked in front of the centre.

"Could this be admission number one?"

Kaiser's face showed a sign of recognition. "Oh, I know this guy. I did his assessment. Oh crap. I didn't think that he'd show up."

"Not our boy?" asked Mike.

Kaiser waxed oenophilic. "This full-bodied mendicant opens with a bouquet of red algae bloom and hints of carcinogens in the well water. On the palate, a note of coywolf is heard baying in deep synchronicity with an undertone of weasel. The finish is vindictive and self-absorbed with a nicely protracted note of meth mouth and tooth decay. An ideal pairing with fraud, child abandonment, or vehicular mayhem."

"Get the corkscrew … let's have a go at this guy!" Mike smiled. "Look, the old lady is combing him pretty good."

Enzo and Debbie Carafalli were both staring straight ahead. They could not bear to look at each other. Their relationship, if one could still speak of such a thing, was a polite fiction. They were both angry enough to say something indelible.

Enzo felt himself to be the aggrieved party and his tone was toxic: "I can't believe you're making me come here. I'm not going in. Take me home. This is bullshit."

Debbie struggled unsuccessfully to keep the anger and disgust she was feeling out of her voice. "It's this or jail."

Enzo lit a cigarette. "It's not right. I shouldn't have to do this."

"You said you wouldn't smoke in the car."

"Fine," he said, and he threw his smoke out the window.

This was back to square one. He couldn't really think she was going to let him argue this as if it was for the first time while she was parked outside the treatment centre. She drew on her mothering skills and talked to him as if he was her son and not her husband. "I know, honey, but what else can you do?"

He heard the sound of the trunk opening. He panicked and blurted out what he had been pussyfooting around. "I'm going to need money! I can't stay here for three weeks with nothing."

Debbie's blood was up. She didn't need to think about what she wanted to say anymore, she was coming from a place of pure venom. "You're trying to make me feel bad again. We talked about that too. If I give you money, we both know what'll happen. You'll be out the back door of this place and into a crack house before I get around the corner."

He'd been outflanked and didn't know it yet, so he decided to brazen it out. "Okay … look, that happened, and I explained why it did. But we need to get over that and get on with what's in front of us."

Debbie had thought through and felt this moment a hundred times. For the sake of her children she had stuffed, pickled, salted, and freeze-dried her anger for a decade. It found its way to the surface at last.

"What's in front of *us* … did you say *us*? There is no *us* anymore. There's only you and your crack pipe. The rest of us are in the way. Oh yeah, and your little hottie. Didn't know I knew about that did you? You need to learn to pick up after yourself. *Animale. Bruto.* If you want to die like a dog in the street, I can't stop you. But I'm tired of your shit. I'm tired of lying to the kids about you and what you've been up to and where you've been. What do you say to a six-year-old when she's being tormented at school because her father's name is all over the front page of the newspaper? You wouldn't know because you're out making more headlines. I have to deal with it. I'm fed up. Get your friggin' bag out of the back and get up those steps right now. This is the future!"

Enzo was speechless. Who the hell did she think she was talking to him that way? When he looked at the mother of his children, he saw the worst kind of betrayer. He flung the passenger door open and made his way to the back of the car. He grabbed his bag from out of the trunk and slammed the lid closed with all his strength. The bang frightened Debbie, who stepped on the gas with the car door still open. She fishtailed down the street leaving her angry husband, the smell of rubber, and their youngest child's sippy cup in her wake.

Kaiser was enjoying the show. He waited until the incredulous man was halfway up the front steps before he spoke to him. "Do you remember me?"

Enzo Carafalli suddenly realized that Kaiser and Mike had been watching the argument. He was still shaking. He could have used a moment alone. But his crack addiction had taught him to always take the initiative. "Yeah, I saw you last week at the other place."

Mike wanted to lessen the adversarial tone. "Welcome to Punanai. When did you have your last drink?"

Enzo's focus was still on Debbie's parting words. *How had Debbie found out about Tina?* He was racking his brain trying to make sense of what she'd said. *What mess haven't I cleaned up? What did that mean? If Rocco found out he was doing his daughter and feeding her crack too, this could be fatal. That little slut had better keep her mouth shut.* A lengthening list of what-ifs was starting to unhinge him.

Mike asked him again, "Enzo, when did you have your last drink?"

The question struck him as being inspirationally stupid. How could they not know that he wasn't a drunk? He responded the way an important man whose attention had been dragged away from the newspaper by a fool's question would. "A couple of days ago." He looked at Mike as if he was an idiot. "You could have asked my wife, but she was in a foul mood."

Kaiser saw his opening. His tone was intentionally condescending. He was trolling for an even angrier response. "Does your wife answer all the important questions?"

Enzo was still reeling from the shock of finding out that Debbie had discovered his infidelity. How had he slipped up? Addiction was one thing in the Italian community, infidelity was a far more serious matter. Feeding crack to the girl who babysat your kids was off the scale. He was screwed. Enzo was a fighter caught on the ropes. He blindly tried to turn his rage and panic into punching power. He came out swinging. "I don't have to be here. I can quit on my own any time I want. I'm only doing this to get that dickhead judge and my wife off my back."

Kaiser had seen what he needed to see, and, as an experienced field commander, he knew when to exploit a tactical advantage. Enzo had been able to hide his real feelings at the interview. Kaiser could bide his time now. He knew where to take him when the time was right. "That's good to know. Relax. Take a breath." He smiled at Enzo and spoke softly to him. "So when was it, your last drink?"

Enzo responded like a petulant child: "It was Friday. I had a terrible weekend. Stupid rule. I don't even drink."

Kaiser held the front door open. "Okay, Enzo, why don't you put your bags down there on the bench and go have a smoke with the guys out back. I'll tell Doug you're here."

The young man made a great show of standing ramrod straight and flexing his muscles before he entered the house. His body language said that he was a dangerous man and not to be fooled with.

Mike smiled his trademark little grin. "I wonder how long he can keep that up?"

Chapter 5

Reg felt a little bit more settled after giving his grand-jury testimony to Doug. Something had to be done about that infuriating man. He was making everyone look bad with his nonsense. Part of him wanted to confront Kaiser face to face but he'd been asked to talk to either Doug or Mike and let them handle things. Reg shook his head. *They never do a damn thing. They must be scared of him.* He peeked through the portal in the office door to make sure it was safe to enter.

"Oh, hang on a second. He just walked in." Paul put his hand over the receiver. "Reg, you're wanted on line four, that lady about her son. She's crying."

Paul transferred the call and then picked up another call that was on hold. It was the beginning of the annual rush to get the family drunk dried out before Christmas.

"Reg Topping here, how can I help you?"

It was Sally. She was crying all right. "It didn't work. He's packing."

Reg carefully modulated his voice the way a hypnotist might. "Sally, I know it doesn't look or feel like it now, but you've done the best thing you could ever do for Arthur. You've broken the stalemate. Do you remember taking him to the dentist when he was a kid? This is the same drill."

Sally was still with him. She was a tough lady. "Are you a parent?"

Reg answered gently, as if he was a father talking to a child. "No. Does that shake your faith in me? Would it be better for you if I were?"

"People who don't have children can never understand. It's not as if I can ever stop. I love him to death. What am I going to do if something dreadful happens to him?"

"Look at it another way. What if you let him stay, said nothing, did nothing, suffered in silence, put up with his addiction, and pretended that everything was going to sort itself out? How do you think that would end? This problem is only going to get worse. We have hard choices to make here. If you lose your nerve something awful is going to happen."

"It's all happened so fast."

"Are you still able to listen?"

"I think so."

"Arthur has made his threat. So now we need to wait him out."

Sally turned and leaned the small of her back against the island in the kitchen. "What a day. When I woke up this morning, I thought I felt about as bad as ever I could; now I feel even worse." She laughed, but it was a very odd laugh. "And of course, you think we're making splendid progress."

"The only way out of this mess is straight through it."

"This can't be right. Oh, I wish Gerry was around."

"Who's Gerry?"

"My husband. He's useless. He gets mad and then clams up and runs off to work. He won't confront Arthur. He acts as if he's afraid of him. He gets mad at Arthur and then he gets mad at me. Like it's my fault. Like I let this happen. Like it's my job to deal with this. I'm so tired. Look — Dale is crying. I'll call you back."

Reg shook his head and loosened up his aching shoulder muscles. He couldn't keep his thoughts to himself. "Five bucks says we get that little prick in for an interview by the close of business today. That is one motivated mother. When her compassion morphs into something more useful, well … things will be different."

Reg dialled the phone, listened, and made a face. "Jan, it's Reg. I have a woman named Sally that I want you to talk to. A little of your magic wouldn't be out of place here. She's been stepped on hard."

Reg put the phone down and began to type furiously into the computer. Kaiser entered the office with his coat on ready to go home.

Mike looked up from his desk. "You're out of here?"

"At long last." Kaiser shook hands with everyone in the room but Reg. As he turned to leave, Reg stood up, looked Kaiser in the eye, and stuck out his hand. They shook. That was the custom. To do otherwise was unthinkable. The gesture said reconciliation, even though the body language said something different.

"Before you leave," said Mike, "a package came for you."

Kaiser was intrigued and a little afraid. What if this was something obvious from one of the bill collectors? They had so far failed to get his work address or phone number, but it was only a matter of time before they did. He didn't want anyone here to know how much trouble he was in. He sucked in his gut and held out his hand to receive the package. The address was handwritten. The ink had run and the postage had been paid in rather ancient ten cent stamps that covered most of the surface of the package. Kaiser didn't recognize the handwriting and there was no return address, but he was relieved to see that it didn't look as if a professional hand had mailed it.

He tore off the brown craft paper and discovered a box that had originally held three golf balls repurposed to hold a selection of dead bees and several dark pieces of honeycomb. This was a turn-up. He shook the box. A handwritten letter fell to the floor.

"Ah," said Kaiser. "At last. The dead bees I ordered."

"What kind of maniac sends you dead bees?"

"In this room or the larger metropolitan area?" That got a laugh.

"What does the note say?"

It was done in a red colouring pencil: DO YOU SEE WHAT HAPPENS WHEN YOU DON'T LISTEN?

"We have a mystery."

Paul took charge. "Mike, look up deranged beekeepers with more than four drunk-driving arrests living within a three-hundred-mile radius of the centre. Have it on my desk when I get back."

Mike looked at Kaiser. "What are you going to do?"

Kaiser placed the box of bees on the filing cabinet and dropped the wrapping paper and the letter into the recycling bin. He took the diamond stick pin out of his tie and used it to fasten a dead bee to his lapel. "I'm going to own my part in this, clean up my side of the street, and try to get through the rest of my life with as much dignity as I can manage."

"You're an example to us all."

"I know. Good day, gentlemen. Divide the rest of the bees up among yourselves."

———

Sally sat looking out the kitchen window. The bright sunshine was telling the world not to take all this crazy talk about winter too seriously. The kettle came to a boil and she got up to make a pot of tea. Dale came pounding into the kitchen carrying his fire truck. "Mommy, Mommy, look at me! I'm a fireman!" He just as quickly ran out of the room, leaving Sally with her thoughts. That was Arthur not so long ago. A delightful little boy full of fun and mischief. She thought about how she felt about him then and how she felt about him now. They couldn't be the same creature.

Dale walked back into the kitchen and looked at his mother. "You look sad, Mommy."

"I am a little bit," she said as she hoisted him up on her lap. He wiggled until he found a good spot.

"Why is Arthur mad at me? What did I do? He won't play with me anymore."

Chapter 6

It was an amazing bit of theatre. The poor little bastard certainly knew how to make an entrance. Even John didn't know he was there. He was sitting all alone in the front pew with his head down. People always leave those seats empty if they can. It's dangerous to sit at the front. No one wants to be too close to anything holy or dead.

After the prayers and the fuss and the gush were over, everyone got to their feet and started milling around. While the organ played Bach, people shook hands and hugged in the aisle as the herd slowly made their way up the ramp and out of the chapel, until only the solitary hunched figure remained. Someone undone by grief in need of a moment alone.

There was a roar of conversation coming from the reception area. Flannerman's had heaped the table to overflowing as usual with tiny sandwiches, sweets, and fruit. All of which was presided over by the lovely Pamela, dressed in a very smart skirt and blouse. None of which tempted the silhouette on the horizon.

John barked out, "Hey, monkey face! Why don't you go join the other apes and get yourself a banana?"

A young man got to his feet and turned sharply toward John's voice. It was the deceased, hiding in plain sight. He had a priceless look on his face.

"Can you hear me?"

"I can see you too, you ugly bastard," replied John.

That phrase broke the frame of the story. Kevin had been expecting some kind of heavenly annunciation for a day or two now, something familiar such as, "Be not afraid." Worse still, he had watched Franklin handle his former person roughly, heard relatives say horrible things about him and his personal habits, endured the cries of his loved ones and been unable to respond to any of it. He was part of the furniture now.

Peter got to his feet with a look of joy on his face. "Over here! We're over here. Welcome, my young friend, welcome."

They could have been dressed as mimes and Kevin would not have cared. He was thoroughly discouraged and beaten down. He began blurting out questions, all of which were pointless because they were the wrong questions to ask. He was so full of anxiety that he kept interrupting Peter, his obliging mentor who was trying his very best to answer the question he was being asked while a new question was thrust at him. The constant butting in very soon turned the stout ghost's altruism into distemper. It fell to John to restore order.

"Kevin, sit down and shut up."

"But you don't understand…"

"Kevin, right now we're the only friends you've got in this world, and if you can't behave yourself, well we're out of here, and you can figure this stuff out on your own."

Kevin looked from John's face to Peter's, and he realized they meant business.

"Everything that anyone ever told you about death is wrong," John said. "We don't have all the answers, but we're sure about a few points and these are things that you need to know."

There was a moment when it looked as if he might come around. But then his eyes darkened, and his lip began to quiver. "I can't stay here; I need to get into the other room. Those are the people I love. I'm never going to see them again."

"Knock yourself out, kid."

Kevin went rushing out of the chapel into the anteroom. They watched him run from huddle to huddle trying desperately to make sense of what they were saying, but more than that, trying to get them to acknowledge his presence. It made John sad.

Peter looked thoughtful. "Well, at least we tried. Let him try things his way. Let him pull their hair and knock over their water glasses till his heart breaks."

John tried to lighten the mood. "They have a four o'clock down the hall, don't they?"

"Yeah, let's go there. You don't suppose we could turn up two in one day, do you?"

"It would be a first, but who better than you and me to pull it off?"

Peter smiled. "A coup of that nature would make us the darlings of the next Grand Council."

John looked at him quizzically. "What's the Grand Council?"

"Our monthly meeting," said Peter, straightening his shoulders and rising to his full height.

"When did that pack of mutts become a Grand Council?"

"No complaints from you, John. You didn't come to the last meeting. We voted on it."

"A room full of clueless bickering spooks, that's the first thing I think of when I hear the phrase Grand Council. Say, why don't you take Kevin along to the next meeting? I'll sign a proxy for him. He can be my eyes and ears."

Chapter 7

Reg was still trying to sort out his feelings around Kaiser. That handshake that almost didn't happen. That was something new. He needed to talk to Mike, but he didn't get the chance. Mike pointed at the phone and held up four fingers. He heard Sally crying.

"Sally?"

"He's gone. He came into the kitchen and said, 'I'm outta here.'"

"Did he say where he was going?"

"No, he just left."

"This might be a good thing." Reg should have kept that thought to himself.

"Do you have any idea what you're doing? I don't even know you, and you're telling me to break up my family." There it was — the pushback.

"Sally, you don't need to agree with me or even stop being mad at me, but you need to listen to what I'm going to say. You're right. You don't know me and you don't know about addictions. But I do. I know exactly what I'm doing, and if there's ever going to be an improvement in Arthur, we're all going to have to go down this road together. And yes, it's going to be this painful every step of the way."

"What if he dies? What if he gets arrested or beaten up? What am I going to do then? All of this gets dumped on me."

The fourth corner piece of the family jigsaw puzzle was now in place. So far, the family boasted a young emperor, a middle-manager mom, a distant distracted dad, and a doting younger brother. The pieces were lined up on the chessboard, but how did they move? What kind of dance did they do when they were all together in one place?

"Sally, if we don't get Arthur in for an interview, then bad things are going to happen. That's what the disease does. It is relentless and remorseless. Stop for a second and try to get some perspective on this. You asked your son to make an appointment to see us. That's all. He's the one making a huge issue out of this, not you. Take a breath and wait to see what he does next. When he left, he didn't say where he was going. Am I right about that?"

"He never does."

"I'm only guessing here, but I'm thinking that if he had a place to go, he would have thrown that at you on the way out the door. He would've said something along the lines of, 'I'm going to live with Uncle Pat; at least he knows how to treat a person with dignity!' If he didn't have an exit line, then chances are he doesn't have a place to go, and that helps our side."

"This is a nightmare." Her sobbing had ceased. She was gathering her strength. "But I don't see what else I can do right now. I need a moment. I'll call you back."

Sally put the phone down and looked out the window. This was beyond being unfair and out of the blue. It couldn't be true. She remembered bringing Arthur home from the hospital. She and Gerry were so excited. That was the day Gerry had enrolled Arthur in Briar Hurst Prep.

The sound of the mail coming through the mail slot brought her back to reality. She went to the front door and picked up the letters from the floor. There were bills, flyers, Christmas cards, and a letter addressed to Arthur from the university. It was from the office of the registrar.

These have to be his marks. She left the letter on the table by the front door where he could find it. But the worms of doubt and fear were loose in her head. The answer to what was happening was in that letter. That envelope contained the truth that Arthur was trying so hard to conceal from her. She couldn't bring herself to open his mail, but she couldn't let go of the letter either.

He's going to tear this up to cover his tracks, she thought. *Where do I stop and where does he begin? Do I have to violate his privacy if I want to learn the truth? Do I have to violate his trust to keep him from harming himself? He's never lied to me before. It's not in his nature. Why is he lying to me now?*

She could see him folding the letter without opening it. Yes, because he knew full well what was inside. She could see him slipping it into a pocket. She tried to imagine the look on his face as he did it, but she couldn't. This was Arthur after all. He was incapable of that. But then she stopped and thought about the look on his face as he left. That face was capable of anything.

———

Mike had been listening to the call. "Not going well?"

"Au contraire, it's heating up nicely."

Mike tried to take Reg's emotional temperature. "Do you have enough energy to talk some more about your unbounded feelings of admiration for Kaiser?"

Reg's anger was gone for the moment. "Are you kidding me? What more needs to be said? I'm so fed up with that creep, I'm ready to get violent."

Mike walked across the office and sat on the edge of the desk. "Reg, Kaiser has been here forever. He's helped a lot of people. Sometimes he's difficult, but on every staff, you need at least one guy who's over the top. One guy who's really going to give it to the clients good. It's too bad he takes on the staff as well. But we need him. If we fired him, we'd have to go out and find someone else as crazy as he is. Before Kaiser, there was Matt, and before him, Bob. These guys don't grow old gracefully."

Reg was still calm. "That is the goofiest thing you've ever said to me. Why—"

The phone rang. "Arrggh. Interruptions." Reg was back into his cheerful telephone persona the moment he put the receiver to his ear.

The transition jarred Mike's sense of reality. *How does he do that?*

"Sally? He did, eh? Good. Bring him in at two. Yes today. You know where we are? Perfect. Have him bring his health card, we need that so he can see our doctor. You sound happy about this." He made a note in the appointment book. "Good stuff. See you then."

He hung up with a smile on his face. "Seems the housing market is pretty daunting for the young drug addict these days. Who'd a thunk it?" Reg looked Mike in the eye. "Let's go have a smoke."

It was almost noon. The men would be out of the morning session shortly. Until then, Mike and Reg had the sun porch to themselves. The sun had some power and it felt warm on Reg's face as he passed through the door. Below them on the sidewalk, a long line of young children toddled past the house unsteadily in their colourful new winter boots. They were on their way back to the daycare after a trip to the park. They waved and made faces as they passed.

Reg picked up the thread of the conversation. "Mike, you know I love you. I'd take a bullet for you. You're an intelligent, sensitive, caring individual. Which is why it blows me away when you defend Kaiser. I would think you'd be howling the loudest for his blood. After all the things he's said to you and about you, both in front of the guys and behind your back." Reg was disappointed when Mike didn't ask him the obvious question.

Mike took a long draw off his cigarette and looked off into the distance. He seemed at peace. "Reg, you're a counsellor. Shine your light on Kaiser. Have you ever asked yourself why he behaves this way?"

Reg started to heat up again as his reality was challenged. "You think there's a reason! See, that's where you start to go wrong. Kaiser says the first thing that comes to his mind and expects the rest of us to treat it as a revelation. God informs Kaiser, and Kaiser tells us. No wait, it's worse than that — Kaiser leaves it on God's desk for a signature and then drafts our marching orders."

The smart thing to do was let Reg vent his anger and wait for him to calm down. But Mike was feeling a little annoyed too. Doug had asked him rather pointedly why he was dancing in the street with Kaiser when he was supposed to be otherwise engaged. Both of these guys were floundering but only one of them knew it.

"Peel the onion. You get arrogance and ego on top. But what's below that?"

"Oh please, let's not get all psychological on his ass. Let's shoot the prick." Reg's voice became childlike and playful. "Come on you know you want to." He paused and changed gears. "Besides when you peel an onion all you get is tears. And I have no tears to shed for Kaiser."

Mike soldiered on: "He has to be right all the time. He can never be wrong. The only sports teams he backs are ones that are winning. If a team goes on a slide, he ditches them. First sign of trouble in a relationship and he's out the door and running. The answer to my question is *fear*. He's deathly afraid of a cave-in. And why not? He undermines structures all day long. Who wouldn't be worried about getting buried alive?"

Reg was surprised by this line of reasoning. He was so angry and hurt by Kaiser's snub that he had yet to work past his own feelings of outrage to the larger picture.

Mike watched Reg very carefully, weighing how his words were being interpreted. "Kaiser is working very hard at what he believes in, but it's a pressure cooker, and sometimes he loses his way. You get a lot of stress in this job, right? Try doing what Kaiser does for a week. Take on every juvenile delinquent, has-been, and never-will-be in the place. Call them all on their bullshit in front of a room full of men. Do it day after day and never back down. It's not an easy thing to do."

Being a prick is not that hard. I could do it in my sleep, thought Reg.

Mike ground out his cigarette on the fence and went looking for the coffee can that served as the ash receiver. "He takes enormous risks. It takes tremendous courage and tons of emotional energy. On top of that, these guys know how to fight back — all the borderline guys, the sociopaths — these guys know how to get inside your head and hurt you. They smell vulnerability. Kaiser deals with them all."

The look on Mike's face delivered the rest of it: *Can't you find it in your heart...*

The point was not lost on Reg. He did feel that. But he felt so much more. "Where does that leave me? Am I his understudy? His youthful ward? Are you suggesting that I should be back at the Batcave doing the ironing and freshening up the spandex? I'm done with his shit."

Mike's face mirrored the pleasure he felt delivering his next question. "What feeling does your defiance hide, counsellor?"

It cost Reg something to say, "There is a little edge of anger peeking out…"

Mike smiled as if he'd known all along. "There has to be a reason why his behaviour is bothering you today. Up until now, you seemed immune to his provocations. Why the sudden change? Is it him or is it you?"

Reg came straight from the heart, even if he kept a thing or two back. "I won't put up with people making fun of me. Cripples are funny that way. I'm good at what I do. I deserve respect. I can't stand someone misbehaving in a group. It drives me nuts. I need calm and order to do my thing. Anything else, and I can't function."

Mike knew this wasn't the whole story, but it was enough of the truth for him to make his point. "That's why you and Kaiser clash. When he sees someone who is calm, he feels helpless. The world you inhabit is not the world he lives in. He can't find a place for himself there. But what he can do is drag you off the mountain top down into the ravine where he lives — that gives him the advantage. His world, his rules, he wins every time. That makes him feel safe, when really he isn't."

"You make a good case. Does Kaiser know this?"

"I don't know. Probably he does. He's a lot of things, but he isn't dumb. And he'd rather die than admit how vulnerable he feels. My point is, when Kaiser gives me shit, he's fighting to regain control of his world. He's an angry child venting to a parent." Mike looked at Reg with a smile that said, *exactly as you are doing now*. "The clients have hurt him, they've put the fear into him, and this is the only way he knows how to restore order and hang on for one more day."

"You make it sound like one of those water traps for wasps."

"You mean the ones where they can get in but not back out?"

"Yeah. They climb on top of each other. It's cruel."

Mike thought the image was apt. "The new victim tramples the weaker ones until they all drown. Then a fresh wasp comes in and they fight until one of them gives way and gets crushed. That's Kaiser all right. He wants out, but there is no way out, and there's nothing for him to do but hold on to the top spot for as long as he can."

Reg was hoping for a snappy comeback to occur to him, but none was forthcoming. He stalled a little bit, waiting for inspiration to strike. Nothing could take the image of the doomed wasp out of his imagination. He wanted to move on. His thoughts took a lighter tone. "So to review, you're saying that he's a soul in agony."

"A drowning wasp."

"But are you saying we have to put up with his nonsense because he can't change?"

"He doesn't know how to yet. But that's different from saying he can't."

Chapter 8

Arthur Wilberforce Cardel was eighteen years of age. He carried a lot of muscle, as befits a young man in his prime, but he was beginning to show a slight rounding of the abdomen. He had thick, black, closely cropped hair. He wore an expensive black leather coat and designer jeans. There was a delicate silver cross on a thin chain around his muscular neck, which showed up brilliantly against his tight-fitting black T-shirt. A nice-looking college kid. Someone had put a lot of time and effort into his formation.

But there were signs of trouble if you knew where to look. Arthur had acquired the habit of touching his nose. He was restless and overly conscious of his surroundings. The dead giveaway was his endless preoccupation with his cell phone. That portal through which death and woe had entered his world. He kept looking at it, rubbing it, willing it to ring. Waiting for the miracle to come.

As Arthur eyed up Greg in the interview room, he got a slightly superior look on his face. He could handle this over-the-hill rock star. Arthur's youth, good looks, family connection, and obvious promise always made short work of fools.

Greg looked at his file. "So you're in pre-med?"

Arthur loved answering that question. "No, not yet. But that's the plan. I'm still in my first year." It all sounded like splendid modesty. A little flicker in his eye gave him away.

There's a dark spot on that apple. Greg looked up at his young charge and tried to take his measure. The paperwork in his hands was useless. Arthur had filled out the form with page after page of one-word answers and obvious evasions.

Greg's tone was calm. "So where does that leave us, Arthur? You're smart. You're pissed off at being here. And you've made a mess of the paperwork."

Arthur felt a hit of adrenalin. No one talked to him that way. His voice betrayed an anxiety he was desperate to hide. "What do you mean?" His throat was full of constricting sensations.

Greg took full advantage of his tactical position. He let an agonizing minute go by before he looked up from the notes again and spoke. He sounded like a kindly uncle. "Look, your family says your behaviour has changed. They say you're angry, desperate, secretive, and abrasive. This is very different from the way you were before you went to university. What I'm looking for is evidence of either mental illness or addiction. Your paperwork doesn't support either of those conclusions."

Arthur was churning inside. It was becoming hard to contain the urge to move. He hated being trapped in this chair and this conversation. His best game was using his youth and promise as a counterweight to any criticism. He wasn't accustomed to people calling his bluff either. His tone suggested that he was about to throw a tantrum. "So you're calling me a liar." That line never failed to panic teachers or parents.

Greg didn't raise his voice. "Not a liar; more of a saboteur."

Arthur couldn't work out the implications of Greg's last remark. Too much run chemistry in the brain. "There's nothing wrong with me. I'm fine."

"No drugs, no drinking?"

"No drugs. I drink a little bit but that's all."

Greg reached into the pocket of his suit coat and took out a plastic urine collection jar. He tried to hand it to Arthur. Arthurs's hands came up in a reflexive, defensive posture. He looked as if he had been offered a dead rat.

"Can you give me a sample?"

Arthur was stunned. He wasn't sure of his ground. "I don't have to give you anything!" He practically spat out the words.

Greg smiled and put the jar back into his pocket. His calm was infuriating. "No, you don't. That answered all my questions." He closed the file and put his pen on top of it. He pushed his swivel chair away from the desk and faced the young man. Arthur looked wary and frightened, ready to lash out in anger. Greg was as untroubled as the Buddha. He put his hands behind his head and leaned back in his chair. "Tell you what. I'll talk and you listen. Arthur, your parents are on to you. Your secret life is not a secret anymore. My job is to figure out what's going on with you. I know all about drugs and I know all about secrets. The only reason that you're here today is that your mother told you she wouldn't give you any more money unless you came in to see us. We told her to say that."

That came as a body blow. *Mom wouldn't lie to me. We tell each other the truth.* In his mind's eye he saw the book sailing toward the bedroom door, and he wished with all his heart and soul and might that he could somehow stop that horrible impact simply by wishing it. He felt an introspective moment of loss so profound that Greg's voice became an intrusion into sacred space.

"So you figured you could come in here and con us. You're not the first guy to try that. But the thing is, Arthur, this is what we do, day in and day out. We're hard to fool."

None of that registered for Arthur. He was still on the wrong side of that door.

Suddenly the quiet of the early afternoon was interrupted by heavy footsteps in the hallway and the sound of happy male voices. Greg looked at his watch. "The guys are out of their meeting. Go have a smoke with them and meet me back here in fifteen minutes. Ask them what they think of this place. Check it out. If you don't want to talk to me by then, you can go home." Arthur made a move to leave. Greg stopped him by holding out his hand. "Arthur, when you come back in, no more pretending."

Arthur was out of his chair and through the door in seconds. He wasn't sure why Greg had let him go. The guys were outside having a smoke break before returning to the second half of the afternoon session. The first part had gone well, and all the guys were in a good mood. Lots of happy faces.

Arthur's interior monologue was condescending. *Look at that poor old prick. Christ, if I ever get that bad, I'll shoot myself. How am I going to get out of this? I don't belong here. No one here is my age. All these guys are on welfare. I'll die if I have to come here.*

Doc knew when he was needed. He had more uses than a Swiss Army knife. He could do anything that needed doing. He talked to girls, stared down bullies, and put the fear of God into parents and teachers. He could talk when the wind had been knocked out of Arthur. He could act when Arthur's head was spinning. He could see and hear the lie in everything and everyone who stood between him and what he wanted. Doc craved stage time. He gave Arthur a playful punch in the arm as he strode manfully into the spotlight. *Take a breath. Take a breath. Breathe. Okay, you've been in spaces this tight before. That guy surprised you, that's all. Go back in there and politely tell him thanks, but no thanks. Don't argue with him. Tell Mom and Dad he was a jerk. Man, could I use a blast. I could sure use some loving from Linda right about now too. One little bump is all it would take, then I could tell that jumped-up old prick where to get off. I can't believe they charge money for this place.*

Arthur was standing by the fire door that led out onto the patio. A second wave of bodies came down the stairs and walked past him out onto the smoking deck.

Andrew Medved was in this second wave, and he was surprised to see Arthur standing alone in the living room. They'd been friends in public school until Arthur's father had taken a dislike to his family and forbidden Arthur to hang around with him. That still stung. Arthur had never even tried to put a patch on that wound or to tell Andrew he felt bad about it. Andrew had heard about it for the first time when the other kids teased him in the schoolyard. Arthur had told them but not him.

"Hey, Arthur, what're you doing here?"

Arthur was shocked by this chance meeting. He had no interest in talking to Andrew. One more lie wouldn't matter much. "I'm visiting."

Andrew smiled at his old chum. "Wrong time of day for a visit. Wrong day too, for that matter."

Arthur was flailing again, but Doc knew what to do. He modulated his tone, trying to sound as if this was two old friends getting caught up on the street. "What are you doing here?" he asked, not really caring what the answer might be.

Andrew decided to have some fun. "Delivering some auto parts." He smiled as he jerked his thumb in the direction of the other men. He cocked his head and said with a smile, "And the guy over there is researching a novel. Who do you think you're kidding?"

"Washroom," said Arthur.

Andrew smiled. "I'm pretty sure it's inside…"

Arthur turned on his heel. He found the washroom and ran some cold water over his face. He looked at his features in the mirror and hated the weakling he saw looking back at him. He took out his cell phone and dialled the sacred number furiously. Four rings and then the voice. He thrust the phone back into his pocket and put both hands on the sink. After a few minutes of silent prayer, he reached into his coat pocket and took out a folded piece of tin foil. He carefully opened it and examined it under the bright bathroom light. Exactly what Doc had ordered.

"No guts, no glory," he told the image in the mirror. He licked the inside of the tin foil clean and then balled it up and tried to flush it down the toilet. It floated. He wasn't going to reach in to retrieve it. He took a sip of water from the faucet and dried his hands and face on the paper towel. He fixed his hair, tucked in his T-shirt, and felt his sense of omnipotence returning. When he looked at his reflection again, he saw Doc. The guy the world wanted to see.

———

Jan Smith, the family counsellor, stood out. It was not simply that she was the only woman in the room — she would have been noticed no matter where she was. She was an imposing figure. Tall and thin with dark curly hair. Always well dressed. She rushed into the counsellors' office with her arms full of papers and her overcoat still on. "Did my three o'clock show?"

"Arthur's mother? She's on her way; stuck on the Don Valley."

Mike got to his feet and cleared a place for her to put her things down. He'd loosened his tie and rolled up his sleeves and — yes, there it was — he had a cigarette tucked behind his ear. Jan marvelled at him. If he could do this job in a jean jacket, he would be the happiest man on earth. Doug would never put up with that. He insisted that the staff dress better than gangsters on their way into court on RICO charges.

She looked around the room as she caught her breath. All the desks were covered with files and reports. But Mike was the only one in the room. "Where is everybody?"

"They're all teaching. They'll be down in a minute. I put a big pot of tea on."

Jan flung her overcoat over the back of a chair. Her perfume filled the usually scent-inert air of the office with a wily, feminine touch. "What a day! I've been on the phone since I got up. I didn't even get lunch."

Mike offered her a big mug. "King Cole, special blend, only for the elite."

She sat back in her chair and took a big sip. "Oh, that helps … but enough about me, what about you?"

"That thing I laughingly refer to as *the self* continues its slow decay."

Jan smiled. People said such crazy things in this office. It made coming here fun.

"Greg is talking to Sally's son Arthur right now."

"Did they come together?"

"No, we gave Arthur the one o'clock slot and scheduled his mom for three. We figured that would give you more to work with."

Jan put her tea down. "We're moving fast on this. Is there a reason?"

"The big panic is on. Arthur got the boot from Queen's. His mom opened his report card. Arthur's got some 'splainin' to do."

———

Arthur made an entrance this time, but then faltered at the place in the script where he was supposed to look Greg in the eye and say something Hollywood. The room was different. Greg had moved the chairs around and taken a seat by the window where the afternoon sun fell on his shoulders. He still looked too damn relaxed. "So Arthur, what are you going to do?"

Arthur wasn't there yet. "I know one of the guys outside, Andrew Medved. We went to school together." A feeling of connection tried to make its way to consciousness. Once upon a time, they really had been friends. Arthur remembered, but Doc had no time for sentimentality. He was loose and on the attack. There was a cocky edge to his voice. "I'm not going to be a fit here. Andy was really sick and creepy even back then. I'm nothing like any of those guys. I have a life and they don't, and I'll be damned if I'm going to waste any more of my time here. This place is for losers."

Greg thought for a moment before he spoke. *Andrew wants to go to med school; it's his dream, it's all he ever talks about.* He took a deep breath and returned to practical matters. "I'm going to lay this out for you. I'm not mad at you. You haven't burned any bridges. What you have done is make it abundantly clear that you don't want to do anything about your addiction today."

He never got to finish his thought. Doc grabbed Arthur and pushed him toward the exit. There was a triumphant grin on his face. "Great talking to you," he said. With that, he was gone.

Greg made his way from the interview room back to the office. Jan was on her second cup of tea. "How did it go?"

"Badly. I told him he isn't fooling anyone. That set him off. He left in a hurry. He's either going to come up with a story to tell his parents or despair and go on a drug run."

"Did you tell him about his marks?"

Greg eagerly helped himself to a mug of tea and sat down beside Jan. "No, what's up with them?"

"He flunked every subject."

"I wish I'd known that. You talking to the mother?"

"Soon as she gets here."

"I'll write this up, for what it's worth."

Greg gathered up his papers and went back to his office. He put them down on his desk and reached for his guitar. He strummed a few chords and looked out the window at the dying power of the December sun.

———

Jan helped herself to Doug's office. It was a large, warm, and well-lit space. Since he had gone for the day, she saw no reason not to use it. She had a lot of work to do with Sally. "It was good of you to come in. This works so much better face to face than it does over the phone."

The two women sat at Doug's desk. Sally got a funny, disdainful look on her face as she surveyed the room. "This isn't your office, is it?"

Jan grimaced. "Pretty grim isn't it? You can tell it's the men's house. They put a statue of a cowboy on a leather-top table and, well, they think it's so beautiful they could cry. You'd think they would at least notice the dust. Who knows, maybe they think that gives it all a more authentic western feel."

Sally didn't laugh.

"So what's happening with Arthur?"

The question made Sally squirm. "His marks came today. I shouldn't have opened them, but I did. I couldn't stop myself. I had to know. He failed every subject. He didn't attend any classes. They've suspended him."

"And he didn't tell you?"

"Not a word, he told us everything was fine at school. I've never caught him in a lie before. He and I have a bond. I talked to Reg on the way in and he told me that Arthur kept his appointment. But he did the same thing here that he does at home — he started an argument and left in a rage. I'm so worried about him. He was always so gentle as a boy, and thoughtful. He cared about other people. Now he's selfish and horrible. In his head all the time. Rude and distracted. What they saw in the interview is what I have to put up with at home."

"Sally, why didn't your husband come with you today?"

"Gerry is useless. He gets mad and leaves. He won't confront Arthur. He's afraid of him and I don't know why. So it all lands on me. All the men in my life are insane. All except for Dale, my youngest. He's so confused. He loves his brother, but now when he looks at him, he has hurt in his eyes. I'm so tired of all this. Why is this *my* problem?"

Jan was holding a large mug of tea at the level of her chin. It highlighted her eyes. They looked old, soft, wise, and inviting. "This is not your fault and it's not your problem alone."

"That's not the way it feels." A tear ran down Sally's cheek.

"Sally, the reason I asked you to come in here today was to show you how to protect your sanity. I want to put some resources into your hands that will help you cope with this. If we're not careful, this crisis will become the new normal for you and your family."

"I don't want to hear that. And I have to be honest with you here too. At first, I thought Reg really knew what he was talking about, but now, well now I'm not so sure."

"This is the sheer hell of addictions. We're not going to fix this the way we fix a broken leg."

"I don't care for the sound of that, either."

"When I properly explain it to you, you're going to like it even less. I'm going to teach you how to detach."

"Detach?"

"Sally, you're sane. You love your children and you see it as your job to protect them. You've spent the last twenty years of your life making sure they don't pull pots of boiling water down on themselves or stick forks into electrical outlets. Kids are curious and they experiment."

"You're a mom too."

"Oh yeah. I have two girls and a boy."

"Any addiction problems?"

"My youngest is showing all the signs."

Jan leaned a little closer to Sally. "Arthur is at the right age to leave home and become an adult. You have to let him do that."

"I did, but he is not making a very good job of it."

"Well so far I would say, he has a more of a flair for demolition than construction. The big knock against parents these days is that we overprotect our children and rob them of their independence. But young people learn by trying and failing. That is what we're going to do with Arthur."

"I don't follow you."

"The counsellors here are going to hold Arthur's feet to the fire. They're going to make him feel the full horror of what he's done to his family and the people around him. They're going to try to reconnect his head to his heart."

"But what good will that do, apart from making him miserable? He knows the difference between right and wrong."

"Sally, if Arthur can't experience despair, he's never going to recover. Your job is to love him while he finds his way in the world. That's what I mean by detaching."

"But what if—"

"Don't go there anymore. *What if* should be your friend."

"This feels like pin the tail on the donkey."

"Good, because that's exactly what you're doing. You've been blindfolded and spun around three times by your son's addiction. The son you know and love, better than anyone else in the world, has been hijacked. He's different now: mind, body, and soul. Now here's the hard part: Maybe you are too. You're going to lose your way with Arthur. You're going to lose a lot of arguments that you should win. He's going to put a terrible strain on you and the rest of the family. You're going to doubt yourself. But you need to know three things: You didn't cause this, you can't control this, and you certainly can't cure this."

A look of horror sat Sally back deep in her chair as her hand automatically came up to protect her face from another blow.

"You think you can fix this because you fixed everything else. But you can't. Pretending that you can or hoping that you will only prolongs the misery."

Chapter 9

The 96 Wilson bus ran between Wilson Station on the Spadina subway line and York Mills Station on the Yonge subway line. In ideal conditions, the ride took about ten minutes. In rush hour, when the roads were jammed with cars and trucks, it wasn't unusual for the trip to take half an hour.

On this December afternoon a gentle rain had begun to fall as the sun touched the horizon. The outsides of the bus windows were covered in road spray, which made them look silver and opaque. It was disorienting, claustrophobic. It was impossible to see out the side windows even after scrubbing off the fog inside with an elbow. At least it wasn't snowing.

A young woman had two infants in a stroller. Blessedly they were asleep, warm and dry under a thick plastic rain cover. Her stop was coming, and she prudently began to align the wheels of the baby carriage with the side door of the bus. People noticed what she was doing and gave her a little room. As she lifted the wheels of the carriage off the ground in order to line it up with the door, she bumped the leg of Arthur Wilberforce Cardel. When she turned to say sorry, Arthur gave her a push. "You bitch!" he yelled. "Who the hell do you think you are? Get the hell away from me!"

The startled babies started to cry. The young woman instinctively turned her back on Arthur to attend to her children. She needed a moment to find her courage and confront Arthur. "You leave me alone!"

Arthur shoved the handle of the stroller this time. "Get away from me, you cow."

There was a furious silence from the passengers. A middle-aged man standing near the back door removed his glasses and put them in his pocket.

The mother stood her ground. "You can't talk to me that way!"

"Shut up, bitch!" roared Arthur as he stood up from his seat and towered over the petite mother.

The middle-aged man wanted to punch Arthur. He knew this bus had a camera system. It was a black ball suspended from the ceiling that was about the size of a fully grown grapefruit. The man glared at Arthur. He then spoke in a loud voice that restored order. "Can I help you with that stroller ma'am?" The young mother nodded as she wiped the angry tears from her face. The man helped her off the bus and then came back on board. He stood next to Arthur, glaring at him, daring him to say something else.

Arthur's cell phone rang. He began yelling into it. "What time is it? I know it's five thirty, asshole, but is it five thirty in the morning or five thirty in the evening? I'm trapped on this bus, and everyone is staring at me. Some bitch just attacked me with a knife."

There was a meeting of the minds among the passengers. Those who could, moved away from Arthur. A few of the healthier males, who looked as if they might enjoy a scrap, formed a semicircle around Arthur, who continued to cower in his seat, frantically sending text messages. They exchanged some knowing looks. This was not as bad as it could be. The driver looked back to see what the commotion was, and the man nearest him gave him a hand signal that said drive. *This guy is nothing to be worried about. Fucked up on something. Serves him right.* The sighs of the passengers carried their singular thought toward heaven. *Are we never going to get to York Mills Station?*

An older woman with a cane found herself uncomfortably close to the action. She tried to tuck her handbag and her groceries under her seat. *Oh great. This idiot is going to get us all locked down. It'll take an hour for the cops to get here. If he lands on my bad leg, this could be a disaster.* The incessant whir of the ventilator stopped, and a second later, the lights went out. *Oh no ... the drivers locked us down. I knew it. This happened last week too. Now I'll never get home. I'll be locked in here forever.*

The bus driver spoke clearly and calmly with a South Asian accent. "We are all right. The bus stalled. In a minute, I will restart it."

Arthur filled the silence with a menacing voice. "Speak English, pygmy!"

These Torontonians weren't about to put up with that. The catcalls started.

"What's wrong with you men?"

"Why are you letting that punk get away with this?"

"Treating a mother and her children that way..."

"Make him get off and walk in the cold rain. This is only for civilized people."

Arthur was too afraid to look up. His fingers moved maniacally over the keyboard of his phone. The middle-aged man knew exactly what he was doing. He leaned into Arthur's personal space and spoke to him with a soft Scottish lilt that was incongruent with the sinister intent of his words. "Do you hear that? They want to throw you off. Behave yourself, sonny, or we are both going home with the knees torn out of our trousers."

The driver restarted the engine and all the lights came back on. Everyone was staring at Arthur. It was too dangerous not to know where he was and what he was going to do next.

Arthur was still fixated on his cell phone. He began yelling again. "What time is it? Is it five thirty in the morning or five thirty at night? Man, don't hang up; I'm coming over to your place. I gotta get off this bus. I need you to talk me through this. I'm freaking…"

The door to the bus opened. Arthur sprang to his feet and shoved a man carrying two heavy grocery bags as he tried to get off the bus. The man lost his balance and fell heavily onto the sidewalk. His groceries spilled out onto the pavement and under the bus. He wasn't hurt, but he landed hard in the filthy slush and then he was wet and very angry.

Arthur was running for his life. The bus had stopped on the southeast corner of Bathurst and Wilson. Arthur left through the rear door and then unwisely cut in front of the bus while trying to make his escape. He attempted to cross the four lanes that separated him from the north side of Wilson Avenue without looking. The passengers had felt a moment of relief bordering on joy when Arthur bolted, then a moment of concern when they realized he'd knocked a man over in his haste. Three seconds later, the mood changed again. Now the bus driver was yelling. He instinctively put his hands up to protect his face as the words "Look out!" merged with the sound of automobile tires squealing and the sickening sounds of a multi-vehicle crash. No one could see anything. The windows were impenetrable. The driver got on the phone. The middle-aged man had a dreadful moment. *Oh shit. He's killed himself. Why did I say something?*

―――――

Reg set the kettle to boil and put his favourite classical-music station on the radio. His apartment was always too hot in winter, so he stripped down to his boxers and covered his muscular frame in a thick blue terry-cloth robe. The apartment was tiny, less than four hundred square feet. Reg had to pay dearly for mobility, so having everything in one place was ideal. The bedroom could be made to give way to a living room, but only if he folded up the Murphy bed. Something that Reg contemplated only on state occasions or when Hy Campbell came in to do the cleaning. She owned the building and was the cleaner, landlord, and mother confessor to all her tenants.

Kaiser's apartment was on the main floor. By mutual accord, he and Reg had agreed to treat each other with respect here, even when they were feuding at work. On the surface, such an arrangement was ridiculous. But it was quite practical, founded on solid principles of need and annoyance.

The original plan was for the two men to share the two-bedroom apartment on the second floor. Hy called that unit the Cadillac suite. That would have supplied Reg with a ride to work every morning and someone to do the running around, and Kaiser would have finally had someone to talk to and do the cooking. But after a week of domestic bliss, the police had been called and Hy had quite wisely separated the two and reassigned them to their current units.

The temperature between the combatants could be measured every morning by simply looking out the window. When Reg was fed up with Kaiser, he would take the bus to work. When Kaiser was annoyed with Reg, he would honk the horn at him and wave as he drove past the bus stop several times to make sure his friend had not missed the point. On other mornings, they would drive to work together as if there had never been a cross word between them. When asked, Hy would simply shake her head and say, "Old bachelors."

This evening Reg was intent on preparing his secret pleasure. One that he didn't confess to in church. As the kettle was about to boil, he took it off the stove and poured the hot water into a white ceramic basin. He caned his way over to the fridge and removed a small bottle. In it was the secret recipe. He gave it a shake. One part Epsom salts, one part ginger root extract, one part apple cider vinegar. He poured a goodly measure into the foot bath.

His cat, Upset, saw his opportunity and made for Reg's lap as the tired counsellor eased his feet, one at a time, into the still too-hot liquid. Upset allowed Reg to look deeply into his feline eyes. They rubbed noses, and then they both sighed.

"Hallelujah, cowabunga, Cheektowaga."

Uppity, as he was known to his intimates, was indifferent to gospel. He wanted his stomach rubbed. He reasoned that if he rolled over onto his back, Reg would come through. He was right. Reg loved the power and elasticity of his body.

"Do you want Daddy to write some lovely prose for you? Maybe something about an overbearing jerk? Something spicy! Something naughty and inflammatory. Fodder for a lawsuit? Detraction spilling over into defamation of character? You would? That's great because now we have a plan for the evening."

———

Jan was finishing up with Sally when Mike knocked on the office door. Mike was always at his best in a crisis. He chose his words carefully. "I have some news for both of you. There's been a minor traffic accident. Arthur has been slightly injured and he's in police custody. Your husband has been trying to contact you."

Sally fumbled through her purse trying to find her phone, but it was hopeless. Her eyes were full of tears.

Mike saw what was happening and spoke very slowly and softly. "Arthur is at North York General. Your husband is on the way there now. Are you well enough to drive or shall I call you a cab?"

Jan gave him the high sign. "We need a moment, Mike."

The unfairness of it cut Sally's flesh from the bone. The absolute godforsaken hatred at the very heart of the thing galled her. The evil spirit that moved the sick, jackbooted monster through her life wasn't finished with her yet. It was on the move again, stalking her precious cub. A million years of instinct told her that she had to stand between it and him. She had to keep Arthur safe.

She wanted to say something, but now the tears were welling up in her eyes, and after a minute they said more than words ever could. Jan had made her point. Arthur had to fight the beast alone. But how was she supposed to stand idle and watch it happen? She couldn't abandon Arthur. Not while he was hurting, and certainly not when he was wounded.

Sally looked over at Jan. She hated the future. "I can't fix this, can I?"

"This may be the very thing we hoped would happen."

"No. Never hoped."

"This is a catastrophe without a fatality. Be grateful. Not everyone gets one of these."

Chapter 10

Andrew Medved was up early, which was unheard of for him. He'd slept badly. Not an unusual event at Punanai, where twenty-six prima donnas defied common sense and courtesy with pointless errands in the night. He had alternated between long bouts of regret and short fitful naps that left him feeling tired and empty. There had been one moment of peace and connection. He'd seen the face of a woman as she danced. Her eyes were clear and they sparkled when she smiled. He knew her. But as he reached out to take her hand, the image faded. His eyes opened and grew accustomed to the pre-dawn light. The feeling lingered longer than the image. Something essential that had been in his grasp now eluded him. He groaned and got out of bed.

As he made his way down the wide staircase to the main floor and the coffee corner, he was startled to see Arthur sitting with his mother in the living room. They both looked as if they'd spent the night sleeping in a car wash.

"What are you guys doing here?"

Arthur kept his head down and his mouth shut. Sally smiled a stranded traveller's smile. She was too polite to let Arthur's snub stand. "Well, we finished up at the hospital and police station and we thought there was no point in going home."

It was clear to Andrew that she didn't recognize him. But then, she hadn't seen him since Gerry had put the run to him all those years ago. He was nothing to them and never would be. Arthur was still wearing the clothes he'd worn yesterday. But whereas before they had been clean, ironed, and new looking, now they looked awful. His coat was torn, his jeans were smeared with dirt, and he was holding a crutch in his left hand. Andrew almost smiled. *Quite an improvement if you ask me.*

Andrew heard the front door open and looked over his shoulder to see Gerry walk in with a sour look on his face. This really was perfect. God's anointed all scuffed up, and Mommy and Daddy trying to frantically push the toothpaste back into the tube. *Gerry, the look on your face pays one half of what you owe me, you miserable old prick.*

The living room began to fill up. The guys were trickling downstairs looking for a coffee and a smoke. A few of them had chores to do. The smell of bacon was beginning to waft up from the kitchen and mix with the smell of fresh coffee. Any other morning this was the time to read the newspapers and slowly ease into the day.

The Cardels were a buzzkill. They were as uncomfortable with the situation they found themselves in as they were with each other. They had a lot to talk about and no idea how to get it done. A sleepless night had dumbed the whole family down.

As Andrew found a good seat from which to watch the fun, he noticed a painfully thin Black man dressed in mismatched clothes standing near the fire door that led from the living room to the smoking deck. He was having a word with Paul.

"I don't need any luggage. I'm here for treatment."

Paul was asking all the right questions. "You seem a little agitated to me. Are you feeling all right?"

"I'm feeling fine, my friend. Thank you for asking."

Paul kept pressing. "You were supposed to be here yesterday. What happened?"

"None of your concern, my man. Show me to my room. I'm tired."

Paul smiled from ear to ear. He always enjoyed a good round of Call My Bluff. "We need to sort a few things out first. Why don't you get yourself a coffee and then we can go sit down somewhere comfortable and get things settled."

"Settled." The young man parodied Paul's word disdainfully. "We don't need to settle anything, Mr. Minion. Your job is to do my bidding. I pay your salary. Mr. Man doing a woman's job."

Paul had to admire the delivery of that line. It was all he could do not to laugh. "Do tell!"

The man went straight to the mayor's office. "Do you have any idea who you're talking to?" He paused waiting for an answer. "I thought not. I am Charles Dorn. That's right. Mr. Charles Dorn. My friends on the street call me Chucky, but I can't for the life of me think why. You can call me Mr. Dorn. Got it?"

Paul was still amused, and his tone was perfectly friendly and familiar. "All right, Mr. Dorn, when did you have your last drink? You seem high and belligerent to me."

Dorn had nowhere to go but up. "How dare you doubt my word? You still don't get it, do you? Must be new in town. I am Chuck. The magic man. My word on the street is pure gold. When I do dope deals, they don't weigh the drugs or count the money — they don't have to, because I am there. The cops know enough to stay away too. You get it now? I'm the guy. I'm the one who makes it all happen. I don't pay for my drugs. People are so happy to have me around, they give them to me for free. They invite me into their mansions. It's always been that way."

Paul was quick to take the point. If wealthy people were glad to invite Charles Dorn into their homes, it made perfect sense that the Punanai staff should roll out the red carpet for him too, so as not to be outdone, as it were. "Well looking at you this morning, I can certainly see how we misjudged the situation. Grab a seat I'll be back in a minute."

Chuck started to strut. He walked over to where the Cardels were sitting quietly and looking horrified. He took them into his confidence. "The nerve of that punk, talking to me that way. Say, I don't suppose you have a smoke to spare, do you, frat boy?"

Arthur was genuinely terrified by Chuck. He couldn't give him a smoke fast enough.

Chuck checked his pockets for a match. "Got a light?"

Arthur handed Chuck his BIC lighter. Chuck took it and lit the cigarette. He looked ferociously at Arthur and seeing his fear, he put the lighter in his pocket. He gave him a wink. Arthur was too afraid to ask for it back. Another victory for the Chuckster. The best protest Arthur could muster was an appeal to the rules. "I don't think you can smoke in here; you have to go outside."

"Posh," Chuck said as he blew a plume of smoke into the air. "Those rules are for the children. They don't apply to me."

It took Paul a full minute to get Mike's attention. Mike looked harassed as he finally put down the phone.

"Mike, we have a gentleman out here with some swagger to his stagger. Do you want me to look up the number for nine- one-one?"

Mike got up from behind his desk and put on his suit coat. The look on his face conveyed power and menace. "Let me have a look. We don't want to get stuck for the ambulance tab again."

Paul chuckled. *He never takes my word for it. One day I'll say there's a drug-crazed lunatic with a gun looking for you in the living room, and he'll trot out and get himself killed.*

Mike blew into the living room like a storm front. Nobody smoked in the house. He measured his tone. "Mr. Dorn, put out that cigarette and come with me."

Chuck was not going to be trifled with by underlings. "Are you the manager?"

Mike was fighting a primal urge to punch Chuck. "Oh yes."

"Finally!" said Chuck in a triumphant tone, looking around the room as if to say *I told you so* to the doubters. He looked around for an ashtray and, not seeing one, he ground the cigarette into the carpet with his foot. "Now we're getting somewhere."

Mike looked at Paul, who was enjoying himself. They hadn't had a go-around this good in weeks.

"Hold up on that call." Mike then turned his attention to Chuck. "And you come with me."

Chuck didn't appreciate his tone. He was about to tell him so when they rounded the corner to an empty hallway. Mike backed him into a doorway. "Don't you ever come back to this house high again as long as you live, got it? Don't you ever talk to one of my staff that disrespectfully again, got it? You were supposed to be here yesterday, clean and sober, with your bags packed and ready for treatment. Now look at you."

Chuck stayed in character. "Have you any idea who you're talking to?"

"Wrong answer," said Mike. He reached into his pocket. "Take this bus token and get the hell out of here. Go to St. Joe's. And don't even think about telling me you don't know how to get there. If I get a call from them, I'll keep your bed open. If not, I'm putting you on the banned list. Got it? Either go to St. Joe's right now or stay off our property for the rest of your life."

Chuck was mortified by this outrage. He stepped right into Mike's personal space and tapped him painfully on the sternum with his thumb. "I want to speak to your boss."

Mike grabbed his thumb and gave it a twist. He had Chuck up on his toes. As long as he went in the direction that Mike wanted, he felt no pain. When he resisted his hand hurt like fury. "I doubt that very much. Out you go."

Chuck was beginning to see a familiar pattern emerge. A lot of people in this town had recently taken to seeing him to the door. But he played the hand he'd been dealt. "See if I ever set foot in this place again," he said as the door shut behind him. "I will tell my friends."

"Start a blog!" said Mike as he turned the key in the lock. He felt a hand on his shoulder and turned around. Doug was smiling at him.

"What's the banned list?"

Mike shook his head. "Invention in the heat of the moment. Chucky is so wound up this morning, he doesn't even know who I am."

From his vantage point by the front door, Doug could see both the living room and the sidewalk in front of the centre. He took in the temperature of both locations with a glance. He motioned to the Cardels. "Get Paul to settle them down. I'll keep an eye on Chucky."

Chuck didn't appear too fussed by what had happened. He was standing on the sidewalk enjoying the sensation of the morning sun shining on his face. It was as if he hadn't quite taken it all in yet. No man was ever so fully in the moment as Charles Dorn was when he was buzzed out of his mind. Why, by the time he'd made it down the front steps, he'd forgotten why he was where he was and couldn't remember what he had hoped to accomplish by being there. So he stood still in the weak December sunshine and rocked gently back and forth on his heels. He continued to proclaim his legend to the world. Passersby took his measure in a glance and wisely decided to cross the street. He waved to them. He was going to freeze to death without a winter coat.

Inside, Doug bellowed, "Kaiser!"

"What's up?"

Doug pointed through the window. "You remember my cousin, Chucky, don't you? He's out of it. He's never going to make it to the detox on his own. I'm going to drive him there."

Kaiser smiled. "For the Chuckster, anything. Let me get my coat."

Kaiser and Doug quickly corralled Chuck and got him into the back seat of the car. Most people would be alarmed if two burly men in suits forced them into the back seat of a vehicle, but not Chuck. It was warm there from the sunshine and smelled agreeably of leather. Chuck was happy to be going anyplace in such a fine automobile. He sat back and beamed as they drove off.

Reg had painfully caned his way around the fracas on the sidewalk. He joined Mike on the sun deck as Doug's car pulled away. "Where's the boss taking the guy from head office?"

"Reg, he's not from head office, he's a lunatic."

"That's a paradoxical statement."

"Say what you will about Chucky, he has some top spin. Can you believe the nerve of the guy — grinding out his cigarette on our carpet?"

"Oh, I don't know," said Reg. "Have you had a boo at our carpet lately? It's as badly worn as the road to perdition."

The two men made their way inside. Mike was heartened by the change in the Cardels' body language. "Well … will you look at that. Chucky seems to have turned the tables on young Arthur. Maybe all this fuss was a good thing."

Reg entered the office after he'd taken off his overcoat and straightened his bowtie. Mike was staring at a computer screen while Greg was looking over some sheet music. Without looking up from the screen, Mike said, "I'm going to get you to evaluate Mr. Cardel."

Reg was still feeling playful. "Happy to do so. He's a jerk. Anything else?"

Mike frowned and looked up from the screen. "He's back, and we need to do an assessment."

Greg chimed in. "Didn't he tell us to go jump in the lake?"

Mike smiled and stretched. "Yes. And a very refreshing dip it would be, this time of year."

"But, why me? There's so much other high-powered talent on the staff. That Kaiser fellow for instance, he's so full of … insight."

Mike returned to his screen. "Dorn was your admission. He went to detox, leaving you with nothing to do this morning. That makes you the most qualified assessor on the planet."

Greg looked up from his music. "You're going to have to start from scratch. None of the paperwork Cardel did yesterday was useful. I wonder if he dropped the acid before he did it. That would go a long way toward explaining some of his charming little quirks."

"He dropped acid and you couldn't tell?"

"It's one of the possibilities. If you get chummy enough, ask him."

"So to review, the client dropped acid during the interview, got hit by a car, got arrested, and spent the night in emergency with his mom. So our hopes for this interview are what, that he'll only smoke a joint this time, get run down by a bicycle, and spend the night sleeping in a stairwell?"

Mike waded in. "That was yesterday, and yesterday was a very long time ago. Much has changed. Jan wised up his mother. The TTC has a wonderful video of him raising hell. The cops have charged him. His marks came from school. So the airtight story he told us yesterday — well it's not so convincing this morning. He also has assorted bumps, bruises, a bail ticket, and, I hope, a new attitude. And he got to meet Charles Dorn. You're now perceived by the family as the reasonable one on the staff … so, in you go. I want to bring him in today if we can, but if you think he needs a trip to detox to sharpen his perceptions of reality, I can live with that too."

"Well, all right, but I'm not ruling out a cane fight."

"I have no objection to you beating the sweet love of Jesus into his apostate hide."

———

Reg ushered Arthur into the interview room and invited him to sit in the larger and more comfortable of the two available chairs. What with his obvious infirmity, this struck Arthur as being an odd choice. That was the chair that Greg had occupied yesterday. Being offered the power chair piqued his curiosity. *What is this guy up to? Are we buddies now because we both have canes? He's going to talk nice to me so I feel bad when he starts yelling.*

Reg offered a reasonable explanation. "Sit there, my friend. You have some writing to do. You look a little rough this morning, Arthur. Did you get any sleep last night?"

Arthur's face was white pressure points of contempt and red streaks of defiance. The way he punched the word *no* said everything that needed to be said. Any breach that Chucky had made in Arthur's defences had been staunched. His willingness to listen had evaporated. They were back to a battle of wills.

Oh, no thank you, young Arthur. Not another hour of one-word answers and hurt looks. Not today, my friend. You and I are going to beat the rug.

Reg stared at Arthur blankly for a full minute before he spoke. "I would love to draw a cartoon of you."

"Do you think I look funny?"

Reg made a face. "No, not that type of cartoon. Cartoons are visual and imaginative, and they let us see what's going on inside a person. The agreed-upon convention is that you can exaggerate certain physical features of the person or dress them in a way that suggests what's going on for them. In cartoons, you can tell what's happening to a person on the inside by looking at what's happening all around them." He paused, hoping for a nod, but when he didn't get one, he made his meaning clearer. "It's not like real life where we can't tell just by looking."

Arthur was squirming in his seat. Even he wasn't sure if it was the pain from his injury or his displeasure with his circumstances. He was annoyed that he couldn't get a reading on Reg. Every instinct told him to jab him and see what he did. "Are you going to be a jerk the way that other clown was?"

Reg's smile suggested that he agreed with Arthur. "You can't mean my esteemed colleague?"

Arthur started to nod without realizing it. "Yeah. The paunchy rock star. Worse than my parents. As soon as I walked into the room, I could see it coming. All concerned and full of shit."

Reg settled back into his chair. *He's putting me on warning: I'd better be nice to him or he won't like me.* "Well then, let's learn from what didn't work yesterday."

It was Arthur's turn to make a face. He looked as if he wanted to stick out his tongue.

This kid needs to be dragged across the front lawn in his best suit. Reg lobbed a softie at Arthur: "What did you want to tell Greg?"

Doubt vanished from the young man's face. Arthur was suddenly full of energy and sitting up in his chair. "Lies," he said, really punching the word.

Reg had to laugh. "What kind of lies?"

Arthur looked perplexed. "The kind of lies he wanted to hear. I guessed wrong, that's all, and he got mad at me. All I want to do is go back to school. What's so hard to understand about that?"

Reg kept him talking. "Did you enjoy university?"

"Oh yeah. It was a blast. I felt alive for the first time in my whole shitty little life. I could do what I wanted and say what I pleased. I was happy." There was a pause, and he lost all that energy. "Now I'm back with my folks. I fell asleep in high school and dreamed about having a real life — only to wake up back at my old grade-twelve desk." He perfectly parodied a nagging voice: "Be in at ten. Not too much television. Did you clean your room?" He blew out a stream of air. "It's as if I never left."

"University can be very liberating."

Arthur looked down his nose at Reg. "Did you go?"

Reg actually felt himself go on the defensive. "Yeah, I went to York in the eighties. It was Woodstock with an academic program. I thought I'd died and gone to heaven. They had a pub in every building, and all the girls kept their birth control pills out on the night table so you could tell they were ready for action."

Arthur countered, "My mom went to York."

Reg didn't miss a beat. "I remember her well; she was different from the other girls. Always kept her room clean and was back in the dorm by ten. Never too much television either."

Arthur wasn't accustomed to being beaten to the punch. "Now you're making fun of me."

Reg had to stretch. He got painfully to his feet and caned his way over to the wall where he rested his aching back. "Arthur, try to think of me as being you twenty years in the future. I've jumped into the time machine, and I'm back here this morning to give you a few pointers."

Arthur changed the subject again, back to a previous strand, hoping to make Reg forget his own question. "What kind of cartoon would you draw?"

"I would draw you in a suit of armour sneaking away on tippy toes from a battle."

"Why?"

"Because you are secretive, heavily defended, and avoiding something you need to do. Arthur, the reason everyone is on your case is because you're different. People who go off to university change. No surprise there. But, usually, it's a good thing. They grow up. Your parents say you've stopped talking to them. They're worried you're in deep trouble with drugs, money, or maybe even mental illness. That's why you're here. You and I need to sort this out."

Arthur actually managed to look unconflicted. "I'm fine. There's nothing wrong with me."

"You dropped acid yesterday in a treatment centre. You are not fine."

"Why can't you all leave me alone? I can take care of myself."

Reg looked down theatrically at Arthur's cane. "It doesn't look that way."

Arthur looked ready to bolt again. "This is pointless."

"Yes, it is. Are you still such a child that you can't even talk with an adult?"

He glared at Reg. "I can't talk to *you*. I want another counsellor."

"Arthur, don't be a wimp your whole life. Look me in the eye and tell me how it is."

The lack of sleep, the pain from his injury, the jagged aftermath of the acid, the vague feeling of guilt, and a strong intuition of impending doom were all working on Arthur. His brain wasn't its usual agile self. Worse still, Reg was a much better interrogator than his parents. He didn't get lost in the emotional mush the way Arthur's mother always did. He didn't get mad and leave the room the way Arthur's dad did either. Instead, Reg stayed on point and remembered what Arthur had said. Part of Arthur wanted to throw in his hand.

He heard a voice from off stage. Not Doc this time but a persuasive, familiar feminine voice. She spoke with an authority Doc would have loved to possess. *Hold your tongue. Toe the line. Think about us. Don't believe his lies. He's wearing a suit. We've talked about these guys. He can't be on your side. Soon, my love, soon.*

Arthur took heart and went on the offensive. "What would you know about girls? Look at you. You're a cripple. All you could ever get is a mercy fuck."

Reg said nothing. He gave Arthur a quizzical look.

Arthur leaned back in his chair and rubbed his hands on his chest and stomach. Doc hit the floor with his feet running. "I'm getting all I can handle. I have three girlfriends, and they all put out. They love the pre-med thing. Yup, playing doctor is what it's all about."

When Reg didn't react, Arthur took it up a notch. "Oh yeah, my parents buy this bullshit even worse than the girls. They all want a piece of the rich, young doctor. Makes it look as if they know what they're doing. Makes up for their own shitty little lives." Arthur was bouncing in his chair.

Reg nodded ever so slightly. Medical school was at the heart of this mess.

Still not satisfied, Arthur pulled out all the stops. "Is that how you ended up here, preacher? Wanted to be a big-time psychiatrist and lost your edge? So now you play headshrinker with the guys from the mission and tell them about Jesus. That must put the hot girls on your trail. What do you do for kicks, granddad? Do you get a face full of greasy chicken wings up at the strip club and hot sauce on your bowtie? Does your scrawny neck hurt the next day from staring up at the stage? I've had all those girls. They loved it too. They can't get enough of me."

Reg walked back from the wall and took his seat. He looked impassively at Arthur. The rant, though impressive, shed no light. It was smoke, nothing more. *Where's this bravado coming from? Does it serve a purpose? Is he trying to hide something? Is there a sexual addiction here? Coke addicts talk this way.* Reg went for the easiest piece of the puzzle. "So why did you drop acid yesterday instead of talking to us?"

"Because you're a pack of assholes, pointy head."

Reg was a glacial lake — stately, cool, and magnificent. "Thank you, Arthur. I see the problem now. I'm sending you off to the detox. I want you to sleep, eat, and relax while you're there. We'll bring you back in three days. We can do the paperwork then."

Reg gathered up his papers, rose to his feet with the help of his canes, and left Arthur sitting at the desk with a bewildered look on his face. Arthur threw his cane on the ground, but he couldn't make it turn into a serpent.

What the hell does that mean? I didn't tell him anything. Arthur bellowed his defiance down the hallway. "I'm not going to any damn detox! Do you hear me? Come back here, damn it. We're not done."

He got to his feet and began to prowl around the office. *What the hell does he know?* The worm of fear was feasting on Arthur's sleep-deprived brain. He reached into his pocket and brought out his cell phone. He dialled the number he had dialled a hundred times before. "Linda, pick up," he whispered, almost like it was a prayer. One that was being heard. One that could be answered. This time, next time, or the time after that. "Please. Pick up. I'm dying here."

Chapter 11

Reg needed a moment. All vipers know enough to put some distance between themselves and their prey while they wait for their venom to work. It was a lead-pipe cinch that this was all going to end up in Doug's office with lots of tears and recrimination. Reg spotted Greg sitting alone in one of the adjacent interview rooms strumming his guitar. He burst through the door uninvited and shut the door behind him.

"Why the long face?" asked Greg as Reg looked out the portal to see if he had been followed and then quickly lowered the venetian blinds.

"I'm a moose, you asshole."

"Oh, that's right, it was your turn to watch Arthur. Didn't go well? Not all warm and hinky yet?"

"Some progress, but shit mallard, this kid is tough. I'm sending him off to Eddington for a few days. Let's see if that doesn't knock him off his perch. Say, you're well-appointed in here. Do you share the biscuits with failures?"

Greg placed his guitar carefully in the corner. "Oh yes, anyone who's done an hour with slippery Arthur deserves at least two cookies and a cup of tea."

"What do you make of the kid?"

"He's behaving like a sociopath. You don't suppose he is one, do you? Did you get anything new out of him?

"Yes, I carefully built rapport with him around being a former bad actor at university, and he came back with a rant about his sexual exploits, and he then told me I couldn't get laid in a whore house with a fifty-dollar bill rolled up and stuck in my ear."

"He really is a new puppy, isn't he? Have you unburdened yourself with the larger minds yet?"

"Nope, I needed to talk to someone sane for ten minutes, that's all. I appreciate you giving me asylum."

"In which sense of the word? Are we talking political asylum, church asylum, or the psychiatric version?"

"Which ever one comes with these delicious cookies."

"Did he drop acid while he was with me?"

"Didn't get that one settled entirely, but he did tell me that he dropped it because he was entirely dissatisfied with you both personally and professionally."

"He might have offered to share. I could have played some Ravi Shankar for him while we discussed my failings. So what's your next move? You know how I love it when you supervillains unravel your mind-boggling plots."

Reg got to his feet and made his way slowly to the door. He opened the blinds and had a look down the hall. "I'm going to go all limp and helpless in Mike's office and let him ride to the rescue."

———

Arthur made his way back to the living room where his parents were stewing. He felt dizzy. He couldn't work out why. His breath was coming in short, sharp rasps and he felt weak. They had a look of faint hope on their faces. Arthur's scowl ground their hopes into the carpet, six inches to the left of where Chucky had made his mark.

"Now they're sending me to detox. What the hell do I need that for?"

Gerry finally had his issue. "Arthur, we don't use that word in front of your mother."

"From here on in, we fuckin' well do. This is fuckin' bullshit."

Gerry pulled the bail order out of his coat pocket while Sally hid her face in her hands. "Let's see about this." He unfolded the document. "Oh yes, here it is ... will attend the renascent treatment centre and follow-up program ... failure to do so will result in this order being rescinded. That means jail, Arthur. Is that what you want? You smart-mouth your mother or me one more time, and I will pull the plug."

The guys in the living room were done with the Cardels. There were murmurs. The living room was a sacred space. You had to behave. Mike sensed the darkening mood and shooed the Cardels into Doug's office. Doug wasn't expecting them. He was back from taking Dorn to the detox. He was looking forward to playing a Chuck Berry album and doing some paperwork.

Doug watched the Cardels troop into the room as if they were there to surprise him with a cake. But none of them looked particularly merry. This mess was getting too hot to handle. Any remark made in this kind of emotional heat could easily colour a decade of family dinners to come. *I am so glad we haven't taken a cheque from these people.*

Doug rose from his desk and wordlessly invited the combatants to take a seat at the conference table. Everyone spoke at once. Doug looked impassive, pretending that he was listening carefully, but there was nothing to hear. The babble went on for an agonizing two minutes. One by one, the Cardels realized how ridiculous they sounded, and they fell silent. Reg and Jan were to be commended. The family was ready to have the conversation.

Doug kept his suit coat on and took a seat at the table. "People, what are you doing? How can anyone help you when you talk to each other this way?"

Arthur, Gerry, and Sally looked at each other. They were exhausted, they were scared, and this was all being expressed as anger. Sally tried to remember what the family counsellor had suggested, but it seemed like such nonsense. Her head went empty. Gerry and Arthur were ready to throw punches. Mike wondered if Doug was going to break the log jam by making this crisis worse. He'd done it before. It was his signature dish and superpower.

Doug looked from face to face, going slowly and carefully around the table. He was going to make them do the work. "I honestly don't think we can help you."

Sally wasn't having that. "What? You provoked this crisis and now you want to bail? No way. I came to you for help and did what you suggested and now look at the mess we're in. This is all your doing!" Doug nodded at her to acknowledge what she had said.

Gerry whipped out the court order again, as if the mere sight of it gave weight to his words. "You have to take him. We have a court order."

"Actually, we don't," said Doug. "The court won't force us to take Arthur against his will or our better judgment."

Doc did a buck-and-wing. *What a gift. Cue the getaway.* "Mom, Dad, let's get out of here, these guys are bozos."

Sally and Gerry both looked at Doug with equal measures of curiosity and contempt. Was he a bozo? Was this all a con?

"This all comes down to a single point," said the great stone face. "All of you are pretending. Arthur, you make a mess of your life and then run home to your parents looking for a handout. You're a dishonest boy in a man's body. A very dangerous combination."

"A fat lot *you* know."

Doug ignored him and moved on. "Sally, you make it sound as if everything was fine before you called us. Has it been? How long has this been going on?"

Sally responded like she'd been slapped in the face. The hurt in her eyes was difficult to watch. *How can he say that? I'm not ... we'd never...*

"Gerry, when are you going to be a father to this boy? Why do you need a court order to talk to your own son? Is there a problem in this family? Can we start with something that basic?"

Silence — absolute, stunned silence. No one had ever spoken to them like this. Were their problems that obvious? Could an outsider see to the very heart of what confounded them?

Doug counted thirty steamboats and said a little prayer before he spoke again. He didn't have his facts straight and he knew it. This was dangerous. But it might get the truth out on the table.

"I want to back you guys away from the addiction issue here. You're too heavily dug in on that point. I want you to pretend that we're talking about a transmission repair."

"Now who's pretending? This is stupid," said Arthur, enjoying the conversation for the first time.

"Yes, it is," said Doug. "But we have to start somewhere. The issue here is, do we repair the vehicle or scrap it? That's the choice when the transmission goes. We're not going to play the blame game. It doesn't matter at this point who was driving the vehicle, who was in charge of the maintenance, or who suggested buying this particular make and model in the first place. None of that is important. Do we fix the vehicle or not? That's the issue."

"Arthur, you're arguing that the transmission is fine. Sally, you're convinced the vehicle was running well before we had a look at it, and now it's broken. And Gerry, you're holding up the warranty card saying we have to fix this mess even if you abused the vehicle." Doug counted to forty this time. He nudged the conversation one inch in the right direction.

"We can fix the transmission. But before that happens — Arthur, we need you to stop pretending there's not a problem. Sally, we need you to acknowledge that this problem was in full bloom before we got involved. And Gerry, we need you to take some personal responsibility for dumping this problem on Sally."

The Cardels exchanged furtive glances. They had been rumbled.

"Why did all of you allow this to become a crisis? Why can't you talk to each other? I'm not going to take your money until I see a winning hand on the table for this family. We don't operate that way. You can't buy your way in here. If you won't play straight with me, then there's nothing I can do."

The Cardels didn't know what the truth was anymore. They were bewildered. A year ago, the events of the past month would have been unimaginable. Doug was prepared to wait any amount of time for their answer. He had attacked them, and it remained to be seen if they would respond as a family or as individuals. The silence was horrifying as they worked it out. Did their best interests still lie where they used to? They couldn't work it out.

Predictably, Sally spoke first. She knew her role. She was tired, angry, and scared to death. She felt betrayed and put upon by her son, her husband, and now by the Punanai staff. She only got three words into her sentence before she faltered. Gerry made a show of trying to comfort her, while Arthur rolled his eyes in contempt. But what did Arthur find so awful? His mother's tears, his father's half-hearted embrace, or the whole spectacle of the family dictated to by a stranger?

Mike, who hadn't said a word or moved a muscle since the conversation began, was nonetheless hard at work, sweating the body language, dreaming with his eyes wide open. Inventing and imagining lives that fit the few facts at hand and the tortured faces staring back at him. The undisciplined dogs of his intuition were loose in the room using the past to foretell the future. Mike the Nose was picking up the scent.

Arthur is still defiant. Where's that coming from? This kid's not tough. Why is he turning his back on the people who love him? Sure, there's the whole drug thing, but that doesn't explain this. No, he's hiding something. Some person, some cause, some hope for the future has Arthur by the scruff of the neck. It owns him. This kind of crap is infuriating. Crazy people always believe something that isn't true. If you can figure out what that is, then their behaviour makes sense. A lie, a rumour going around, a fact misunderstood is all it takes. Arthur, what changed the world for you?

The long silence was working on Arthur. He looked into the faces of the two people he knew best, and he despaired. He couldn't ask his parents for what he wanted. They'd say no. They always said no, even when they could say yes. What he wanted would set their hair on fire. But he didn't care. He needed it. He wanted no part of the future they'd rammed up his nose.

The old anger returned. He didn't even try to supress it this time. It was loose and damn glad to be loose. They were the problem, not him! Why were they making a fuss? So he did a few drugs. So what? Why couldn't they leave him alone to find his own way in the world? Oh, they said they wanted to know, they said they'd accept his choices, but that wasn't true. No, they insisted on calling the tune. He had tried talking to them when he'd gotten home about what had happened. Well actually, he'd talked all around it, but then he had seen the looks on their faces. They were horrified the moment he went four feet off their plan. They couldn't abide the chapter headings he proposed. The rich prose that described what he really wanted would kill them.

He remembered Linda. The way she walked through a room that time in her green dress ... No, it was impossible. If he showed them who he really was, they'd stop loving him. He could live without their love now — he had his special lady — but he still needed their money, for a little while longer. They had a ton of green, and all he needed was a sprig. They'd give it up. He learned long ago that they always got tired before he did. They'd messed with him, and now it was only right that they pay up.

Mike turned his attention to Gerry while Doug continued his slow count to two hundred. *What are you all about, my frustrated friend? The Rosedale address says whatever you do, you do pretty well. When did the pretending start? Playing the waiting game until the damn kids finally grow up and leave.* Mike looked over at Sally and then back at Gerry. *Sally's not hard to look at. Oh merde. Does the kid know what his old man is up to? Oh, that would fit. And Gerry's afraid the kid is going to rat him out. Nah, too easy. For sure, Arthur knows that Gerry's not playing fair. Maybe he never did. That opens up some possibilities. "Daddy wounds" always get septic.* Mike fixed his gaze back on Arthur. Was *that* what that unhappy, tortured face was afraid to tell the world?

Mike next turned his attention to Sally. She still looked as if she had been punched in the stomach, but even that kind of rough treatment didn't diminish her. There was defiance in her eyes. As long as she was alive, this family had a chance. *And as for you Sally, what are you all about? I've only known you for ten minutes on the worst day you've ever had, and I'd still trust you with my life. How in the world did you end up with these two losers? You're the only one with enough sense to holler when you're in pain. They both want to move on. But they don't want to hurt you. Is that why they lie to you and pretend? Silence, silence, all this bloody silence.*

Doug had counted down to zero and resumed his line of argument. "All three of you have got some work to do." Doug focused his attention on Arthur's accomplices. He got to his feet, took off his suit coat and placed it on the back of his chair, trying to take the mood in the room down from its current war footing. "Sally has already talked to our family counsellor, but, Gerry, I need you to talk with her too. I want both of you to attend some Al-Anon meetings and do some counselling around improving your communication skills."

Who the hell does this guy think he is? I'm not having this. Mister you're asking for trouble.

"What about the courts?" thundered Gerry. The court order was his ace of trump, and he was devastated that it had not carried the day.

Megalomania, père et fils, thought Mike as he looked at Doug for a reaction.

"The court has the power to do whatever it sees fit," Doug said. "Look, you guys are treating us like we're the bad guys. We didn't come to you looking for help. If you don't like what we do here, or if you don't think that this is going to work, then go back to the court and tell them that the treatment offered here wasn't a good fit, and that you want to try something else. They'll change the paperwork for you in a second. The court wants your family to solve the problem, they don't care how you do it."

Doug's tone softened. "Arthur, you haven't slept in a while, and people never make good decisions when they're as tired as you are." Sally and Gerry looked over at Arthur waiting for an explosion, but it didn't happen. Arthur looked beaten. Doug sounded fatherly. "Arthur, you used yesterday, and so I'm going to send you to detox for three days. When you come back, we'll try one last time to assess you. If you still won't cooperate, then we're done." Sally looked at Arthur, wondering, *Why isn't he saying something?*

Doug turned to Mike. "Get Arthur a bed at the Eddington. I want to talk with Gerry and Sally alone." Arthur got awkwardly to his feet and followed Mike out of the room without saying goodbye. He was pissed, and his hip hurt like fury, but the prospect of three days away from all these pikers suddenly sounded pretty good. He knew that he was never coming back to this hellhole, but they didn't need to know that. He was so tired of being where he didn't want to be. He felt around in his pocket until his hand touched his phone. There was a way back and he was going to find it.

———

As soon as the door closed, Gerry let fly. He was furious. He needed to regain control, and by God, he knew how to do it. "Why are you picking on us when it's painfully obvious that Arthur is the problem? There's nothing wrong with us! We're decent, hardworking people. We're not your regular stock-in-trade." Doug looked at him in disbelief. "Don't look at me that way. I've sat in your living room long enough to know what goes on here. This ain't the Betty Ford Center. I got to have a smoke with Chucky, remember?"

Gerry looked to Sally for support and got none. She was staring straight ahead with a blank look on her face. Arthur's exit had cut deep. She knew exactly what Gerry was about to say. She hated this rant. It usually made it to the top of his playlist after about four drinks. "How do you people stay in business? If you worked for me, I'd fire you! You can't talk to paying customers the way you do." Gerry angrily pushed his chair back from the table and got to his feet to leave.

Doug loved venom because poison was real. "What else are we doing wrong?"

Doug's remark was intended to infuriate Gerry, and it had the desired effect. It flushed him from his cover. Gerry became so angry he lost the ability to weigh his words or measure their effectiveness. They came out as a mixture of bile and truth. Every angry word he spoke liberated another one from his deep store of resentments. He spat his contempt at Doug. "You prick … who the hell are you to sit there judging my family? You don't even know us." He looked to Sally for support a second time. She looked shocked now. She had seldom seen him this angry, and it frightened her.

Doug wasn't done yet. He had found the primary cancer. He gave it a poke to see how deep it went. "Why do you care what I think of you?"

Gerry snarled, "You got a smart mouth, mister! Have you got a boss too?"

Doug had the sheet music for this one at home. "I have more bosses than I know what to do with."

Gerry reverted to type. The silver-grey mane and high-end clothing were tools designed to prop up the double talk. He was corporate. Always in character, always in control, always thinking before he spoke. Well, maybe not this morning. He looked at Doug with a kind of authority, or maybe it was privilege, or even possibly superiority. It was clear that he couldn't leave until he put this runt in his place.

"Let me tell you how the world works." A mechanical arm deep inside his brain reached into the library and grabbed the needed disc and spun it at forty-five rpm. "In finance, the word comes down from on high announcing a new product — usually something pointless and derivative, something maybe even a little dishonest. It's got *loser* written all over it. But the minions pick up the phones and sell it. They do what they're told. That's how guys like you keep cashing paycheques." He looked at Doug expecting to see anger or fear written on his face. No sign of that yet.

There was a heavy emphasis on the first word of his next sentence. "*But* then someone important gets screwed and he makes a call. All the clerks can do is quote the policy and pretend they don't know it's a cheap rip-off. The next call goes to their boss and then to his boss, all the way up to the top of the food chain. Where it lands on my desk. It's a simple matter. If I can make money out of him, we get on the phone and I tell the clerks, 'Settle with this guy.' If I have all of his money already, I say, 'Read the fine print.'

"It doesn't matter if the guy has a case or not, or that the doughhead signed the agreement without reading it. That's never the issue. What matters is who is making the complaint. That's how it works. It's all about ongoing relationships. Right and wrong don't mean a thing. I can get on the phone and demonstrate how this works for you."

A wave of pure pleasure coursed through Gerry's frame. He had put another weasel in his place.

Doug saw the look of triumph in Gerry's eyes. *So there you are. I knew you were hiding in their somewhere.* With his first task now accomplished, he wisely took his tone down two notches, from confrontational to familiar. For the first time he was sure of his ground. "So what you're telling me is, you want to drop off your defective son for service. That's not how this works. Gerry, you can go over my head and maybe even get what you think you want. You could easily spend a hundred thousand dollars today, but that won't help Arthur."

Gerry was stunned. *This guy's not even fussed.* He looked over at Sally to check her reaction. She looked vacant. *Can't she see what's happening here? What's at stake?*

Sally knew it was time for her to bail out her mate.

"All right, Doug, I need your help on this. Make me understand what exactly it is you're saying. All I'm hearing is bafflegab."

"Arthur has turned your world upside down and given it a good shake. The things that should matter and hold a family together have no power here. This is a moral inversion. Right is wrong and wrong is right. Arthur is going to abuse your love and your desire to do the right thing in order to get what he thinks he wants. That's why what you expect us to do isn't going to happen. This is *Arthur's* problem. You can't fix this. You need to let him go. Let him take his lumps. Let him grow up. He needs to experience the consequences of his addiction. He won't recover until his deluded belief in his drug of choice is smashed by a personal experience."

Sally and Gerry looked at each other and then back at Doug in wonder.

"If you think that anything you do or don't do at this point is going to help him with his addiction, then you're deluded too. Your task is to learn how to love him while you watch him wrestle with his demons. The more you meddle in this, the longer he'll stay sick."

Gerry's knuckles were white. *Why is she listening to this crap? Can't she see what he's pulling? Oh Lord, she's buying this shit.*

"Gerry, you can't buy your way out of this mess. And Sally, stop treating Arthur like a child. Kick him out of the family. Let him try to live whatever crazy fantasy is in his head."

Where is he going with this? He's my son. He's not some vagrant we picked up hitchhiking on the highway. I'm not kicking him out. No way!

"I'm sending him to the Eddington detox. It's a mighty rough place. There's no pretending there. It's straightforward madness and addiction. Let's see how he makes sense of that."

Sally wasn't finished with Doug yet. "Doug, you're wrong about some important points. Our relationship is not as bad as you're making it out to be. There have been more good times than bad, and a lot of love. And this problem really has come to us out of the clear blue sky. Arthur didn't even smoke cigarettes three months ago. You're making it sound as if this drug business has been going on for years, and we've been ignoring it. That isn't true, and it's wrong of you to pretend that you know these things when you don't. We're out of our depth here, I'll admit that, but we are still very much a family and still very much in love. So back off on that point and we'll get along just fine."

Doug knew enough not to say another word. Sally was ready. Doug looked over at the angry, brooding figure of Gerry. *I know how you feel, Sally, but what about you, Gerry? I have yet to hear you say anything real. You poor, dumb bastard, you're still trying to win the argument, not solve the problem.*

Chapter 12

The ZiggZagg was a private club. The rules were strict. If you caused trouble, out you went, no exceptions. And no, you couldn't tear the place up on Thursday and come back Friday with a box of doughnuts to apologize. Once out — never back in.

There was a lot of money made in this club. There was a bar, and a band with big dreams — but no bass player. People who tried the sandwiches thereafter stuck with the pickled eggs. The waitresses all had criminal records and boyfriends who kept them on a short leash. Mostly, they were too old to dance anymore. Lots of unwanted lines showing, even in the bad lighting. Still better looking than most of the regulars. Not a lot of choice on the mixed drink menu, either. Why would there be? It all came out of the same bottle this time of night. This was a booze can, and no, they wouldn't let you run a tab.

The location was durable. They'd been at it here every night for three months. The cops knew what was going on, but they put up with it. They were happy to have all their bad eggs in one basket, safely tucked away from the suburbs and the sleeping taxpayers. Made it easier to keep an eye on things. The detectives knew where to go when they needed to talk with someone in the middle of the night.

Dan and Bill ran the place. They already had the next location scouted and rented. Another industrial unit in a dying plaza. Lots of parking, no houses nearby, and a landlord getting sweated for the mortgage payment by the bank with no legitimate tenant in sight.

Peter and John were at the ZiggZagg hoping to watch someone die. The older the spook, the nastier the disposition. There was another near miss last night. People were hitting up drugs in the can. Some of them carried guns. Peter and John wanted to be up close and personal the next time someone took their leave. People were overwhelmed by fear at the end. It was hard to detach and split focus to take in all the subtle details of your own passing. Peter and John weren't looking for a light when they died. They had other things top of mind. That's why they were making enquiries. They wanted to know why they got left behind. Did the light always show up? Did they simply miss it in all that racket?

They tried to figure this out first in hospitals. People died there every day, but they took their own sweet time doing it and most of them simply moved on. It was easier for the boys to hang around funeral homes — to meet the few who didn't. But they didn't know anything either. That got them to thinking: What about someone who died violently, unexpectedly, oh, and of course, not in a state of grace ... what did the light do about them? That's what they were at the club to find out. They were convinced that knowing how the light worked would give them an invaluable edge.

The bar was busy this Thursday night. Full of millionaires for the moment. It was the triple witching hour. The welfare cheques were out, and poverty was laying low till the hurly-burly was done. The kids had finished their exams at York and Humber, and had enough money left for a little celebration before heading home for the holidays. The working guys were here too; Thursday was payday and a few of them had their Christmas bonuses. None of them looked as if they would be ready for work on Friday. The night was young, they had cash, and the girls were looking very sexy.

Peter and John had taken a position in the parking lot outside the club. They caught a ride over with Norman the barman. He lived at 46 Madison. They were eyeing up the prospects. Looking for the next guy to make the wrong move.

The university kids arrived on foot. They always parked their cars a few blocks away from the club. Hell, they must have had the cops completely buffaloed. The science of urban camouflage. The cops wouldn't know what to make of a York University parking sticker in the window of a Camaro parked two blocks away from a booze can in an abandoned industrial plaza at 2:00 a.m. Beyond shrewd. But it made the kids feel safer to walk half a mile to the club. Why put the wheels that Daddy was paying for at risk? The regulars were too far gone to take that kind of precaution. They needed the drugs a little more urgently, and they had lost their sense of shame. Hell, they would smoke the evidence right there in the courtroom with their whole family watching, if they could only wiggle out of the handcuffs.

The party girls were standing outside, flirting and smoking, trying to entice the men to invite them inside for a drink. They had to make enough money to jolly up the holidays. Their kids were at home asleep with a sitter, so they wanted to be quick about this.

Peter and John had set their hopes on a man who called himself Israel. Ghosts imagine themselves to be the best eavesdroppers in the world. John overheard him telling someone over the phone that he used to be a boy soldier. Peter heard him say that there was a deportation order waiting for him at the police station. He didn't have a long-term future in Canada, and he knew it. He was trying to organize a little travelling money. His scam for the last two nights was to hotshot people and then rob them. Peter and John figured that he was either going to kill someone or get knocked off himself. Either way they would have a chance to see the light up close. They were convinced that apostate Israel was about to come to grief.

Israel was dressed well for the hustle. The first thing they noticed about him was his smile. He had gorgeous teeth. They were so big and white and perfectly formed that you would swear they were dentures. His face was clean shaven and his skin tone was perfect. Not a blotch or a blemish. He could have been an aftershave model. He told people he was studying to be a nurse, and he dressed the part. His pants were pressed, his shirt was ironed, and he didn't have a hair out of place.

Israel was talking to people in the parking lot. He was eyeing up a young kid with short black close-cropped hair wearing an expensive black leather coat. He'd had a little too much to drink about five drinks ago. Eric was out of his league. He had sucker written all over him. He had a tag on his coat: HIGH. MY NAME IS ERIC.

Chapter 13

"Eric," said Israel with a look of real joy on his face.

Eric was confused; he'd forgotten about the name tag. "Do I know you?"

"Me? Good heavens, no. I am a student at Humber. I am studying the nursing. What are you taking?"

Eric was trying to place the man. "History. I'm at York."

"No, I meant what drug are you taking? This afternoon has been my last exam. That is why I am here. I want to celebrate, but I need to get organized."

Eric was intrigued. "How do you mean ... organized?"

"Well, let me tell you. This is a good place to buy heroin if you know what you are doing. The problem is that the dealers always try to cheat people our age. They cut the drugs. What works best is for two people to team up. We buy a single dose of the drug and make sure of its potency before we buy what we really need. I usually bring a test kit with me, but tonight I have forgotten mine. Do you have one?"

Eric shook his head. "No, I've never even seen one."

"That's too bad. They're very useful. It's one of the advantages of being a nurse: I know how to use such things. I brought twenty-eight hundred with me." He flashed the money in a roll. "Were you going to spend a lot this evening? We could buy in bulk."

Even as drunk as he was, Eric sensed the come-on. "I don't have that kind of money and I don't know you."

"Which is fine, thank you for listening. Do not worry, I will find someone."

Israel left Eric standing in the parking lot and entered the club. The bouncers gave him the once-over, but they knew who he was and let him in. He was on their list of possible troublemakers, but they didn't want to talk to him about it. They needed to get this settled. Eric tried to follow Israel into the club, but the bouncers stopped him. "Hey buddy. Are you a member here?"

"I didn't know I had to be a member to get in. The guys at school never mentioned that."

"This is a private club."

Israel seized the moment. "Gentlemen, this is my new friend, Eric. Could I bring him in as my guest?"

The bouncers continued to glare at Eric.

"Give them ten each," whispered Israel.

Eric did as he was told. The bouncers grunted and made way for them. "He has to sign the book."

"Yes, I will show him where, thank you."

They walked to the guest book. Israel spoke softly. "They do not check documents, so sign anything you please but be sure to remember it while you are here. And Eric, if you are planning to change your name then take that ridiculous name tag off your coat."

Eric thought this was hysterical and signed the name of his high school physics teacher.

"Come, I will show you where to sit. I still need to find my new best friend."

The ZiggZagg was rocking. The band sounded almost plausible and the no-smoking rule that applied to every other club in the city hadn't caught on. The room was filled with a grey haze. The two hopefuls paused by the entrance, waiting for their eyes to adjust to the smoky absence of light.

Eric felt that he owed Israel a drink, at least, for his help with the bouncers.

"Can I buy you a beer?"

"Good heavens no, I do not drink alcohol. It is forbidden. A Diet Pepsi would be good."

"You don't drink but you do heroin?"

Israel smiled at his new friend. "Theology is an active complication in my life."

Eric liked his answer. He made his way to the bar as Israel found a table on the periphery of the club where they could see everything that was going on but stay out of sight themselves. The beer was twelve dollars, and the Diet Pepsi was eight. Eric placed the drinks on the table. He was delighted that everyone was smoking; he lit himself a Marlborough.

Israel nodded toward the other side of the room. "Do you see that man over there in the blue blazer? He is the fellow I tried to buy from last time. I do not trust him. He agreed to sell me the drugs, and then when I took out my kit, he told me to find someone else. The problem is that I do not see the fellow I generally deal with. I hate making a new connection, especially when I want to buy a lot. It adds an unacceptable element of risk."

Eric was warming up to Israel. "How did you know that I wanted heroin?"

Israel smiled. "I did not, that is why I asked. The way that you dress gave me some hope. You at least looked as if you might be interested."

Eric took a big swallow from the bottle.

Israel was shaking his head. "This is not a good night. Too many people for a Thursday. Why are they all here tonight?"

"It's getting close to Christmas."

Israel gave him a puzzled look.

"Everyone gets some time off at Christmas."

"Canadians are very complicated. They confuse me."

Eric started to feel even more comfortable with Israel. Had his first intuitive hit been wrong? Perhaps this guy only struck him as being odd because he was foreign. Maybe something could be worked out. "The guys in my dorm wanted me to buy some junk. They all kicked in. Now that I know you a little better, maybe we should team up for a buy." Eric was drunk enough to think that saying it made it so.

Peter moved in a little closer when he heard that.

"Partners then. Very well, you stay here while I have another look around. See if you can spot someone you know. If there is no one here who I feel safe with, then I am going to go. There is an all-night card game at Tony's Sports Bar, a couple of blocks from here. I know some of the people. We can try our luck there if we have to. Let me check this out. I wish I had brought my kit. I really should go home and get it."

When Israel left, a thin young woman approached the table. "Are you lonely?"

"I'm here for a quick beer and then I'm off home, another time perhaps?"

She nodded and quickly found another man sitting at a table alone.

Peter was getting excited. "How does he get them into the washroom?"

"I don't know, but grab a seat and we'll find out shortly."

Israel returned with a smile on his face. "We are in luck. I found a man and he is willing to give us the Chinese price if we buy twenty-eight grams. He will give it to us for one hundred and sixty a gram. We need to have forty-five hundred dollars, and I have twenty-eight hundred. Eric, do you have, or can you get, seventeen hundred in the next hour?"

"That's over an ounce. An ounce is a lot. I have the money, but how do we know we won't get ripped off?"

"That is the problem, we don't know. This would be much safer if we could test the drugs. Do you have a car? I only live a few blocks from here. If I had the kit, we could do some very good business."

"Yeah, I brought my car."

"Good. Let's work with what we have. I need a little hit to pick me up. He gave me a quarter gram to try. Let's shoot it up and see what we have."

"How pure is it?"

"He says forty-five percent, but he is a liar. Do you have a syringe?"

"No, I was going to buy it and leave."

Israel gave Eric an older brother smile that worked better than messing his hair. "I can see why you get cheated. Well tonight, my friend, is your lucky night … you get a free sample in a clean needle administered by a trained health practitioner. Let's go to the men's room."

Eric gulped his beer knowing that it would be gone if he left it on the table.

Two men entering a cubicle would have caused a stir in most clubs, but not the ZiggZagg. Eric sat on the toilet and examined the baggie. "This is the same stuff I used last night; the bag has the same black dot in the right corner."

"What a thing looks like and what a thing really is can be very different. A black dot is not a trademark you can rely on," said Israel as he pulled a new needle, still in the plastic wrap, from his backpack and handed it along with an alcohol swab to Eric.

"What ever happened to dirty needles?"

Israel stayed in his buttoned-down character. He fired a ferocious look at Eric. "I am a nurse," he said with mock solemnity. "You are going to do this right, at least while I am around." He gave it all away with a wink and a little smile.

Eric was getting excited, and his breaths were coming short and sharp. Eric watched as Israel cooked the heroin with a spoon and candle and drew the dark, foaming liquor through a gauze filter into the needle. Eric was impressed with his technique.

Israel held the syringe up to the light. "Can you do a quarter gram?"

"Easily," said Eric with a grin as hung up his overcoat on the hook and rolled up his sleeve. "This is the same stuff we've been doing for weeks. I did twice that much last night. This will take away that sick feeling." Eric tied off his arm and wiped the injection site with an alcohol swab.

"So this will be a nice little taste," said Israel. "Do you want me to do this?"

"Please," said Eric. Israel adroitly found the vein, flagged the needle, and injected the drug.

The rush was incredible. Good things come in sharp needles. Eric looked up into Israel's eyes to say thank you, and saw too late the cold, evil stare of a constrictor.

"Surprised?" asked Israel.

Eric slurred his words. "What did you give me?" He tried to get to his feet but then slumped over, semi-conscious.

"Too much of a good thing for sure and perhaps a valuable life lesson about trusting strangers," he said in English that was suddenly no longer accented.

Israel frisked Eric and relieved him of his valuables — including the car keys. He only found a thousand in cash but he figured the rest would be hidden in his car somewhere. It usually was.

I hope his wheels are worth stealing, he thought as he pulled the needle out of Eric's arm and released the rubber tourniquet. He slapped Eric gently across the face. He was out of it. "I'd hoped for better things from you." Israel applied the tourniquet to his own arm and coolly injected what was left of the dose he had prepared for Eric. "Waste not, want not," he said to his now-silent partner.

Chapter 14

John could feel Peter's hot breath on his neck as he peered over the partition into the stall. This is what they had come to see. But now that it was happening, right before their eyes, they lost their focus. They forgot all about the light. Eric was a nice kid. It was hard to see him this way. They listened, hoping to hear the sound of him breathing and panicked when he started to snort. Israel pulled back his eyelids to check on him. Maybe he did know something about nursing. Eric was in a coma. Maybe he was going to die.

But then Israel split, leaving Eric sitting on the john with his head tilted back against the wall. He was puking white stuff that got all over his shirt. His lips were blue. He looked dead. Peter and John were both screaming. The calm, cool, detached scientific scene they had worked so hard to bring about got trampled in the moment. It always did.

A guy in a top hat came in to have a whizz, but he didn't notice anything. In desperation Peter kicked open the stall door so that the man could see. Eric moved a bit and fell off the toilet which made an awful racket. He hit his head on the floor with a sickening thud as his legs slid out from underneath the washroom partition.

The pisser looked around and shouted, but no one heard him either. He zipped up and zipped out the door. A minute later, everyone was packed in the can. The bouncers were furious. This was three nights in a row, but now they knew who the prick was. Israel had been on their radar. Bill, the older of the two bouncers, wordlessly took charge. He flung Eric over his shoulder and took him out the back door of the club. He gave him the Heimlich manoeuvre in the parking lot. Eric spewed some nasty looking stuff. Bill had obviously done this before. He wasn't going to give him a chance to puke in his car.

There was a moment of pure panic in the club as Bill dragged Eric out. Someone yelled that the cops had shown up. People started flinging their dope on the floor until they realized that other people were picking it up. That's when the fight started and, pretty soon, the whole building was in an uproar. Dan, the younger bouncer, paid no attention to the melee. He was looking for Israel. When he was satisfied that he wasn't in the building, he bellowed for everyone one to shut up. They did. Nobody messed with Dan. He told them that the fun was over and that they should all sit down and have a drink on the house. Those orders were followed.

Bill and Dan had been expecting trouble. The overdose set them in motion. They both had their assignment. Israel was begging for trouble by being so predictable. Three nights in a row in the same club: hotshot, rob, and steal the wheels — that was just plain dumb, desperate, and greedy. They were not going to let anyone get away with that. The ZiggZagg was making big money. But more than that, they did not tolerate thieving addicts.

They had a pretty good idea of where he'd go. Dan headed for his vehicle, unaware that John was hanging on to the scruff of his neck. There was an eerie calm about the man. He put on an FM station and drove very slowly around the deserted industrial plazas with his lights out, listening to the beautiful music.

Dan didn't seem at all upset to John, who was wondering what he was going to do, of course. John assumed that because Dan was calm, he was only going to beat the guy up or yell at him. Then John heard him say, "There you are." Dan stopped the car and parked.

Across the street and barely in sight, Israel was walking up and down the plazas with the remote entry clicker in his hands, looking for Eric's car. He kept looking back over his shoulder as if he was watching for the cops. Dan got out of his vehicle and started to follow him. He stayed close to the buildings in the shadows. That was smart. Israel was looking for a light, not a predator moving in the darkness. At first, Dan moved very slowly so that John was able to hang on to him. He was stalking his prey. He kept his distance until Israel found Eric's car.

When Dan saw the lights of the Camaro flash, he began to run on tiptoe. He moved the way a big cat does. When he squeezed through a hole in a hedge, John was brushed down his back. As he instinctively put his hands up to protect himself, he lost his grip on Dan completely. By the time John reached the car, Israel was already on the ground. His head was at a very funny angle. Dan had broken his neck.

The silly bugger had been listening to his iPod. He still had one of the earpieces in. It made him look sad and ridiculous. If the light did show up, John didn't see it. Even if it had, John wouldn't have cared. He had completely lost interest. He thought that he was over his horror of death, but suddenly he felt sad and dirty. Like he didn't have to be here, didn't have to see this twice. Why was this happening?

John was winded and had to sit down on the curb. He sat there looking at Israel. Attempted murder, murder full on — all of it done by people who didn't give a damn. No anger, no passion, simply a business arrangement. He was horrified. At first, he was drawn to Dan's calm. Now it repelled him. Dan went through Israel's pockets and retrieved Eric's belongings. He pocketed the cash and loaded the lifeless Israel into the back of Eric's car. He drove it back to his BMW where he off-loaded Israel into his trunk.

Dan simultaneously wanted to make this as difficult and as easy for the cops as he possibly could. He made a call on his cell phone. It took a few minutes for Norman the barman to walk the two blocks from the ZiggZagg to where Dan was waiting. He and John sat there in the darkness, listening to the violins and cellos on the radio.

Norman drove Eric's car back to the university. Dan carefully placed Eric's wallet on the floor beside the driver's seat. They parked the Camaro in a handicapped spot, left the engine running with an open beer in the drink stand, and trusted York's finest to connect the dots.

Dan dropped off Norman at the club with instructions to order Chinese food for the staff. As he drove away, he shouted to the corpse in the trunk, "This one's on you, my man." On a whim, he dropped Israel off outside Tony's Sports Bar. "Let them take the heat," he said with a laugh.

John went back to the club and watched the desperadoes eat Chinese food and laugh until he hated them all. When the Open Window Bakery truck brought the bread the next morning, John couldn't wait to slide into the cab with the detestable little driver and wait for him to make his way back to Bloor and Spadina. He was finished with questing for one night.

The papers said that the body was discovered by someone on the night shift. Israel was in the morgue for a week before they figured out who he was. His real name was Richardson, and he was from Detroit. He used to be an auto worker. The nursing stuff was all a hustle.

Peter had learned about it from Franklin at Flannerman's, who performed the entry-level embalming job that the city favoured for its indigent cadavers. He said that the cops did a drug test after they found the needle marks and figured hey, what the heck, another lowlife. No one claimed the body.

Any fool could see that the more important job was to stick with the kid who got robbed. He was the one who was supposed to die. Peter got a hold of his belt while he was lying on the bathroom floor and had been hoisted up over Bill's shoulder along with Eric when he took the boy outside. When Bill gave the kid the Heimlich manoeuvre, he barfed right through Peter. Thank God it didn't stick. All three of them ended up in Bill's aging Jeep. He drove three blocks to the fire station and rolled Eric out onto the sidewalk across the street. Then he drove to the convenience store and made a call from the pay phone there.

Bill watched from his car as the lights in the fire station came on a minute later. The firemen knew what the deal was. They picked up Eric, got him walking and gave him some oxygen while they waited for the ambulance.

Eric kept on puking up that awful-looking white stuff and he pissed his pants, but he didn't die. He didn't even come close. No light, no answer to the burning question. Israel knew his way around a needle. He took him right to the edge.

Who wouldn't get a little mushy? It must have been the funeral that afternoon. Hell, this kid could have been one of the mourners. He was the right age. When the ambulance arrived, the paramedics administered an opiate antagonist and a minute later, Eric answered the bell. They told him he would need another shot or maybe two. He refused to go to the hospital, so the cops were called and when they arrived, they placed him under arrest to make him go.

They handcuffed the kid to a gurney in the emergency ward. His cold urine was starting to irritate both the insides of his thighs and Peter's nose. He didn't look quite so slick lying there. The doctor told him he had a concussion, as if he didn't know, and that he couldn't sleep for the next twenty-four hours. We at least have that much in common, thought Peter.

They were about to uncuff him when a call came over the radio about his car. The officer on the scene was instructed to find out what Eric had been up to and where he had been before the ambulance arrived. This was impaired driving for sure and possibly something worse. While Eric was dissembling, another call came in. A body had been found very close to where Eric had been picked up and there were obvious signs of violence and drug use. Detectives were on their way. Eric was hip deep in something, and they were not going to let him go until they found out if he was a victim, a witness, or a killer. Peter could tell by looking at his beady eyes that Eric was struggling to come up with a story. But there was no innocent reason for being where he was at that time of night. When the detectives showed up, he took one look at their hardened faces and despaired. He turtled, played the good little boy card, and asked them to phone his parents, which they were only too glad to do. He tried to shield his eyes from the annoying neon lights. They were making his headache worse. It was awful, helpless, knowing that the worst day of his life had just begun. And knowing, too, that all they would give him for the pain was a cold compress. He was ripe corns in tight leather shoes all right.

Peter had seen enough for one night, so he started scouting around for a ride home. He made a bad choice based on something he overheard an orderly say and ended up in Halton Hills for two days. Still, he thought it was nice to be back in the country to see all the snow.

Chapter 15

The cops uncuffed Eric only after he agreed with his distraught parents and the attending physician that he needed to go someplace safe. He wanted to go back to campus. His elders insisted on sending him to a detox. That suited the cops. They didn't want him to go home and tamper with evidence. They were eager to get back to the station and see what the science had to say about his account of the events. The doctor was clear that there was no medical reason for him to continue to occupy valuable hallway space in the emergency. Returning home with his parents for the weekend wasn't an option after what had happened the last time. They were still mad about that.

The bump on his skull wasn't bothering Eric as much as the turmoil going on inside his head. If he'd known the whole story, he would have been even more worried. That would come later when the cops finished reading the mystery novel that Bill and Dan had written for them. The detectives came back with a search warrant for his vehicle and his room in residence. They wanted to know what if anything he knew about a dead guy found not two blocks away from where he had overdosed. The deeply bewildered look on his face matched his story. The cops gave him a ride over to the Eddington and he was admitted shortly after 7:00 a.m.

Eric was assigned to the same bubble at the detox that Arthur found himself in. The bubble was the first rung on the ladder whether you were planning to get drunk or stay sober. They could keep you for up to seventy-two hours. The stakeholders who lived for one week a month here accepted this place for what it was, a damn significant step up from the homeless shelters. If you could land a space in detox you were safer, better fed, and far better prepared to resume your addiction when the next cheque arrived. Very few people in detox were there because they were in danger of going into life-threatening withdrawal. They were simply waiting in line for some sort of opportunity to turn up.

The Eddington was the roughest place in the city. The staff was first rate and the facility, while a little under decorated, was otherwise up to its task. The problem was the clients. This was where the wild men came when they wanted to get out of the rain. There was a maxim that people in the know used for the addicts in a detox: "First they sleep, then they eat, then they relapse."

Eric was assigned one of the twelve plastic coated couches — all of which smelled faintly of urine and powerfully of disinfectant. The couch smelled significantly better than the ragbags occupying the couches all around him. There was a hum coming from these guys that was more complicated than any high-end cologne. There were notes of mildew, body odour, everything that could cling after it was spilled, and, holding it all together, a sharp edge of despair.

The walls were made of transparent plastic, and a bored attendant watched them without the faintest flicker of interest from a gondola above. Eric wondered if they got the same smell up there.

Two cots down from Eric, a very thin man of about fifty lay sleeping. He was exhausted after a drug run that had lasted for ten days and produced a rib-cracking seizure. He had been given a snoot full of benzodiazepine. He moved often enough so that you knew he wasn't dead. He appeared as yellow and lifeless as a fallen leaf.

Arthur was beginning to feel some real pain and soreness in his hip and leg from the accident. The painkillers they had given him at the hospital were off the menu here, and the Tylenol he was allowed to have wasn't dulling his pain. He complained to the staff and they gave him a bag of ice.

Eric and Arthur had a lot to talk about. Addictions, guilty secrets, meddling parents, assorted bumps and bruises, and run-ins with the law. But there was no one to make introductions. The sorest point for both of them was the loss of their cell phones. Their parents had bought them calling cards, but it wasn't the same. You had to line up to use the pay phone, and there was always a crowd of scary guys hanging around listening to what you said.

Eric and Arthur were out of place in the Eddington family portrait. They were twenty years younger than the regulars, and being young, they were intimidated by the older men. They felt a quite natural impulse to form a subgroup. But they were wary of each other too. They had been eyeing each other for a couple of hours when the thin man on the cot broke wind. His bowels had restarted the process of peristalsis after a long prorogation. The sound and the duration of the flatulence simultaneously reduced both young men to tears of merriment. That got them talking.

Eric and Arthur found a good place to sit. There was a large east-facing window that got the morning sun at the far end of the bubble. There were some leather chairs pushed up against the wall that people used for family visits. It was a deserted spot this time of day because all the regulars were lining up to go outside for a smoke. They fought, gossiped, squabbled over the phones and, lacking everything but the desire to feel something other than what they were experiencing, they milled around and went in and out like house cats all day long.

Eric was still feeling a little dizzy from his bump on the head and the loss of a night's sleep, but he was grateful to be sitting up, at long last, with natural light to deal with instead of LEDs. Arthur was simply another half-drowned sailor in his lifeboat. At least he didn't smell of feet and street. For his part, Arthur was intrigued by his new friend. His face was calm and accepting, which made him somewhat of a rarity around here. Everyone else went back and forth between angry and demanding.

"I thought about going to York, but my parents insisted that I go to Queen's. They want me to be a doctor," said Arthur with a sigh as he shifted about trying to find a comfortable position for his hip.

"Why so sad? That would be great. You could write your own prescriptions."

"I lost my taste for it. Too many super-brains in medicine. I don't fit in with them. What about you, what do you want to do?"

"Well until last night I was doing it. I was living the dream. I was brought up in Woodbridge. You wouldn't know about that. Parochial school, lots of rules, and 'Why the fuck you wanna go to school when you could work with Pop and your brother Tony in the business?'"

Arthur laughed. "Halfway through that sentence you got an Italian accent. Where did that come from?"

Eric was pleased. "Mom, Italian; father, English … that makes the bambinos *Italio-Canadesi*. Capiche?"

"I thought my home life was complicated."

"It wasn't so bad. Mom and Pop met in Italy. Dad was going to be a priest and make a lot of old ladies in London very happy, but then Mom kind of put the kibosh on that. She gave him the eye, Gina Lollobrigida style. Pop's family was Anglo-Catholic and they were not too thrilled with Mom, even though she brought them a basket of perfect plum tomatoes from her garden. 'Won't last' was the verdict on both sides of the family.

"Dad couldn't live in Italy, Mom couldn't live in England, so next thing you know they're in Woodbridge. They make sense together. They love each other and home is kind of magic for them. They have the family and the grandkids and their friends. But for me, that's not what I want. I'm all about the drugs."

Arthur's ears pricked up. He felt a moment of real hope. *Finally, someone who gets it. Maybe I can really talk to this guy.*

Eric loved an audience, especially when he got to play the bad boy. "Heroin is an Italian thing. You gotta know people. There was a bunch of guys at York in my dorm, and they knew all the right people. They made it so easy. It was a dream come true. One day I'm sitting at the cousins' table for family dinners, and the next thing you know, I'm a scholar making my mom ever so proud and smacking up on the weekend. It was perfect. But I think for the next year or so, I'm going to be a very good boy again. We make jokes about it. We say, 'Whatever you say, Pop.' Capiche?"

A promising narrative had gone off the rails. "What are you talking about, dude?"

"It's the heroin. It's the love of my life. It's the nature of the thing. Once you've tried it, and you find that you can't do without it, well ... your path in life is decided. From time to time you get into difficulties, and that's when you have to go on a diet."

He gave Arthur a worldly look and leaned into his space. "Being Italian has its advantages. Everyone in your family is an expert on everything and willing to invest hours of their time on your reclamation. So as not to go crazy, you say, 'Whatever you say, Pop.'"

Arthur smiled and repeated the phrase to himself. It resonated. That's what he'd been feeling for years. He adjusted his leg, hoping for an improvement.

Eric soldiered on. "So I do what everyone else does when they get caught. You say you're sorry. You go to the meetings, you smile at people, you save your money, drink bottled water, go the gym, and wait for the whole thing to blow over. But remember this, my friend, this love is never over."

Arthur butted in with what was on his mind. "Have you been to treatment?"

Eric was on a roll. "Smack is like you were born in the desert eating rats, and missionaries come and take you to New York where you see live theatre, drive a Lincoln, have two girlfriends, and only have to work eight hours a week. It's beautiful. They serve you only the finest food and wine and it never rains on the weekend. I can never explain that to my parents. Pop thinks he knows what love is because of Mom, but he doesn't know the half of it."

Eric's face looked wistful; he was suddenly aware again of the pain behind his eyes. While he'd been talking about the good times, he'd felt the good times once again. "But then you get caught. They send you back to the desert, and the next thing you know, you're back to chasing rats and drinking rainwater. In the evening, you hit a stone with a stick to keep yourself entertained, but really you're not all that grateful for being home. You remember your love. You remember Broadway."

"I feel as if we should be bursting into song."

Eric's eyes came alive. "You want to go back to New York. That's where your real life is. So you lie, you say you enjoy the desert, how good the dry air is for your skin, you do a good job, catch a lot of rats, drink a lot of rainwater. On the outside it all looks very encouraging. It matches up in their heads with the stuff you said about being sorry and confused. But that's not all that's happening. Every day your resistance to the drug drops, and then one day when they're not looking, bingo, it's back to Broadway. Oh, they'll catch you again. And they'll be madder the second time. But my friend, they're going to be mighty tired out, surprised, and disappointed by the time they get you by the scuff of the neck again. If you can't be with your lady all the time, you gotta enjoy the time that you do spend together. Capiche?"

Arthur felt a jolt of excitement. He couldn't believe his luck. Eric spoke his language. He was saying out loud what Arthur had been muttering to himself since he got back to Toronto. The distance between them began to shrink. But he was wary. He started slowly, carefully unpacking his story, trying hard not to give too much away. "I get the lady bit. I met a woman at Queen's. Oh man … she's really something. She was teaching psychology. So sexy and so crazy. On our first date she took me for a drive in her father's BMW M6 convertible. A sweet ride. You know the car? A five-litre V-ten front engine, ninety-two mil bore, seventy-five mil stroke and a double overhead cam. All power."

Eric was smiling and nodding. *There's money there. I wonder…*

Arthur misread Eric's body language as encouragement. "Her dad was out of town. He's some kind of fucked-up cash machine. She drove me to this stretch of country road that was really hilly, farm road — you know, the kind that is just gravel and mud. She was wearing this killer black miniskirt and her legs, well I don't have to tell you, they looked even better than the car. It was almost dark and we'd done a line. And we flew. I couldn't look at the speedometer. I swear we were airborne half the time. I was scared and happy all at once." There was a gear change in Arthur's head. His face changed from elated to sad. "But then it got weird."

"Dude, it's not weird already?"

"I'm going to tell you what she did next, because if I don't tell someone soon I'm going to go nuts, but you can't tell anybody. Capiche?"

"Whatever you say, Pop."

"So Linda pulls over to the side of the road and turns off the engine. We're sitting there with the top down."

Arthur could still see the wild look in her eye, could hear her breathing hard. It was the first week of September, and it was still hot and dry. The sun was going down. Someone nearby had cut hay, and the air was full of its intoxicating smell. "I was hot, you know from the drugs and the drive, and my heart was beating hard. And then Linda told me to take off my pants. Right there on the side of the fuckin' road. We had dope in the car and if the cops came by we were done. But you know ... I did what she told me to do. She climbed over the stick shift and got on me right there in the passenger seat. Then she fucked me. I don't mean we had sex; I mean *she fucked me*. Like a quarterback calling the play." He checked out Eric for a reaction.

"Dude, you're letting the side down."

It cost Arthur something to say more, but he had to. "That was just the start. She took me to New York, if you don't mind me borrowing your phrase. I'd been pulling my pud in the shower thinking I was getting it good for years. That whole first weekend all we did was sex and cocaine. She ordered me around, bought me new clothes, made me light her cigarettes, and spanked me when I was bad. One night, she brought her girlfriends over and they took turns while she filmed us. I failed my whole first term. Spent the last two and a half months stoned out of my mind."

"Dude, I can see that I'm definitely going to have to spend more time with you and your new family. You said she was your teacher? Bet she gives you an A after all your *homework*."

"No, dude, she went on stress leave the weekend after we met. I went over to her place to help her move some books and I haven't been back to the dorm since."

"So what's the problem? Why are you so fucked up? You should be down on your hands and knees right now thanking God you got a chance to go to university."

"I don't know. I screwed over my parents and the school pretty good. But I'm not even sorry about that. What's got me freaked out is that now Linda isn't returning my calls. I stay high and do every crazy thing under the sun for three months and I don't even get a parking ticket. I leave all that behind me and come home for Christmas and what happens? I get arrested, run over, detoxed, and now they want me to send me off to clown college. Where's the fairness in that? There's definitely something wrong with the universe. All I know is ... I gotta get back to Kingston."

"But, Arthur, the large brains and the big mouths here have it that you're going to Punanai."

"What can that pack of idiots teach me?"

"So what's the plan, Arturo?"

"I'm going to get a good night's sleep. Have a big breakfast. Then I'm going to throw my bag out that window and leave through the fire door. I have enough money for a one-way trip to Kingston."

"Give me your phone number."

"They have my cell downstairs."

"This is your first escape, isn't it? This is a detox. They get more two-hour stays here then they do at the no-tell motel. You don't need to jump out a window. What were you going to do … throw your crutch out first? Go downstairs, ask for your stuff back and leave. It's so much more dignified."

"They'll let me go?"

"They can't stop you. If you don't believe me, go sit in the living room for twenty minutes and watch the traffic come and go. Pay cash for your bus ticket and the bail guys will never know. Make sure you don't get into any trouble in Kingston. If they catch you doing that, you're definitely screwed and going to jail. They call that a breach. Tell your parents you got scared and went for a walk to think things out and forgot to come back. They don't want you in jail, so they won't rat you out."

"Man, I need that phone. My whole life is on that phone." Arthur got to his feet and tried walking in circles as a way to lessen the pain in his hip. It helped. "But what about you? Are you really going to get cleaned up?"

"Hell yes, dude, I'm caught. Look, the older guys I hang out with have been doing this dance for years. This is like being a crook and going to jail. It's inevitable. It's a game we play. They watch us and know what makes us tick, but we watch them pretty close too, and we know what makes them go. It's all about playing the game."

"Isn't any of this real?"

"Tell them what they want to hear. And believe me, what they really want to hear is the bullshit. About how sorry you are, how you want to change, how it wasn't really your fault, how you got all confused. And how you really appreciate their help. Try to get misty in the eyes when you say that part."

This was too much, too soon, and Arthur was confused.

"I mean sure, there's something wrong with us for using dope and bailing on life. I can say that much. But these guys, they got a few bedbugs and hickeys too. Saving us makes them feel important. They'd rather try and fix us then look at themselves. My dad got talked into being a priest when he was a kid so that a lot of old ladies could talk loud and proud in church. If he hadn't gotten lucky and met my mom, where would he be? I'll tell you where. He'd be talking the same nonsense to a room full of people who didn't know the first thing about him. Hoping that by saying those words he could keep the awful feelings in his gut out of his head and far away from his dreams."

Chapter 16

John decided to give himself a bit of a brush-up before he went into the meeting. There was an elegant three-sided mirror in the men's shop in the mall that he favoured for this purpose. He gave himself a critical once-over, hoping to judge the effect of his appearance on his audience. Tall and thin with a flash of thick silver hair. That was what first struck the eye. His face was long and symmetrical, and it wouldn't have strained credulity to describe his features as classic. He had transformed this face countless times, sitting alone in the dressing room, applying makeup, trying to match the face in the mirror to the lines written on the page. Certainly, the face of a lover, but it could, with some art and time, become that of a healer, a villain, or a madman. Acting demands attention to detail and endless rehearsal with or without an audience. In his solitude he was reduced to having to give himself notes.

"The very moment I set foot onstage," John began, as though teaching an acting class, "the audience takes in all the subterfuge I have been obsessing about for months. In the twinkling of an eye, they make a decision on that whole body of work. The human animal is a quick study. I am one of the few who understand and accept the finality of their judgment. Which is why I can bring anything I imagine to life upon the stage."

He turned to examine his profile. From the back he looked asymmetrical. His head was far too large to be adequately supported by his girlish shoulders. This was a defect that only the guillotine could put right. He remembered his first director's words: "What cannot be transformed must be camouflaged, or in this case, hidden under a tarp."

John had seldom worn this particular suit. Toward the end of his life, he had suffered from ascites and could not bear any tight-fitting clothing, especially items that constricted his windpipe or belt line. This suit had found a place at the back of his closet for that reason. However, post-mortem it had fit him a treat, even if the pants were bell-bottomed.

Thank God they buried me in pants, *he thought.*

He addressed his image in the mirror as if it belonged to a patron, one who had paid full price for a seat and deserved a prologue. "The Grand Council of the

Undead — tell me then good people of the audience, what do you picture when you hear those words? Do you immediately imagine eight ghosts standing around talking smack?"

His sneer was the final word, done to perfection.

"This is what I have to put up with: half-crazed losers who can't even get dying right. I am expected to attend this august body once a week."

John did a spin and passed effortlessly out of one presentation of self into another.

"What kind of fool chooses the store display window at Holt Renfrew on Bloor Street as the site for a meeting? I hate meetings, any kind of meetings — always have. When I'm around these clowns I want to stick pins in my eardrums." He brought his hands up to his ears to emphasize the point and then thought better of it. He dropped out of character and turned his attention to examining his chin. "But owing to a lack of cultural events for mobility-challenged ghosts in the middle of the day, and the fact that Peter is unbearable when he doesn't get what he wants — I don't see how I could turn down his gracious invitation to attend."

He grew reflective. "Ghost history is oral history. It has to be. It's physical torture to try to write anything longer than a sentence or two. The best of them have failing memories. The rest of them are delusional. They claim to have secret powers and special insights, but it's all the worst kind of social climbing and self-serving nonsense.

"The other problem is that all of our history is recent history. Rosa is our oldest member. She died in 1940. She cleaned houses around here. She was a big pal of Walter's before he went bust. She's not quite a poltergeist yet. She can still put a sentence together, and sometimes if you look her in the eye when she talks to you, you could swear that she knows what it is she's trying to say, but you would be wrong. She spends her days butting into other people's conversations. You got it … she's always the first to arrive and the last to leave.

"Ah, and then there's Maddy. Dear, sweet Maddy. A child in a woman's body. Next to her is Jack. Nowhere near right, that one. Not to be trusted. He's got psycho-killer whack job written all over his pockmarked face, but since we're all dead anyway, what the hell? No big mystery as to why he didn't want to move on. There are warrants out for him.

"Then there's Barry. He's giving the presentation this afternoon. I hate Barry. I hated Barry before I knew him. When I met him for the first time, I realized that I had never known real hate until that special moment, when the back door to hell opened and out popped Barry with a terminal wedgie and a Kick Me sign pinned to the back of his shirt by frustrated fallen angels. Demons wouldn't waste their spit on this pompous, mewing mutt. Unsuitable even for the fires of hell. Who

knows, maybe his mom loved him for a fraction of a second before she put her glasses back on and got a good look at him. I figure when she saw him, she got right out of bed and shot his father.

"Finally, there are the Bailey brothers — Fergal and Declan. Bad enough to be born identical twins but worse still to die in the same traffic accident. I don't think any force of nature could ever pry those two apart. I wonder sometimes if that's the best or the worst thing that could happen to a person. It would be a useful situation to find myself in."

Finished with the mirror, John began to strut through the fashionable mall, pretending that the passersby were extras on a Warner Bros. backlot.

"Most of the preliminary conversations at these things are about transportation. Human beings are creatures of habit, at least Monday to Friday. People get up at the same time, wash and dress the same, and take the same route to work every morning. That's why we look at people the way the living look at a bus schedule. I don't know who the first ghost was who figured out that we could get a free ride by grabbing a hold of a human, but that insight changed our world. It's too hard to get around on our own. We burn too much energy.

"It's easy to grab someone by the scruff of the neck — but that's chancy and often leads to disaster. Peter calls it bull riding. We don't have any mass. Almost anything can knock us off our perch. Chance bumps, wind, someone opening the bus window, a moment of inattention, or a subway door closing have all brought us to grief. Office buildings with sealed windows are the worst. When the wind gusts outside the building, one of the doors will pop open unexpectedly to equalize the pressure and" — his hand fluttered up over his head as he spoke — "out and up you go into the wild blue yonder.

"Declan told us he got caught in an updraft on Bay Street and ended up being carried out into the Toronto harbour. That was in the winter, and it took him forever to find his way back to shore. He finally found a seagull asleep on the water. He was lucky the bird came ashore; it could just as easily have decided to head for Buffalo.

"It's bad when you're in the middle of a journey and your ride takes off without you. Then you have to gamble. It's all pure chance and observation. If you see a bus driver, he might take you to the subway. But he might be on his way home too. You don't know. I've had to leap from shoulder to shoulder a dozen times to get three blocks in the right direction. When things go wrong, they really go wrong.

"The button hook changed all that," he said as he continued his history lesson. "All the ghosts carry them these days. Mostly we make them out of shoelaces and belts — if we were lucky enough to be buried with them. Choose well before you go into the box my friend: A linen shroud may make you look cool and humble for your last close-up, but it's a pain in the ass when you get here. You gotta dress for the weather.

"Worse still are the bastards at the funeral home, the ones who bury you with the back cut out of your suit coat and no pants. The tail-end view of a ghost is not a pretty sight, and it doesn't improve over time — no one will ever take you seriously at the Grand Council of the Undead if your tail feathers are on prominent display. Ask my pal Barry, he knows all about first impressions — and no, he never turns his back on the group!" He chuckled at his own punchline.

"Jack was the first one in our group to use a button hook, and it was his seminar last year that revolutionized transportation in the city. He was the first one to figure out that you were safer and spent much less energy if you made a loop out of something on your person and then popped it over the head of your ride like a bridle. It allows you to ride piggyback in relative style and safety."

John stopped outside a flower shop. There was a lovely white lapel flower that would have looked striking, but alas there was no way to attach it. He smiled sadly, cleared his throat, and resumed his walk.

"It all keeps coming back to the problem of the mass. A human body with all the water evaporated out of it weighs only a few pounds. When you get rid of the mineral content, you are down to something with the same weight as a black fly. We are as dry as a bone and lighter than air. That's why people can carry us around from place to place and never know we're along for the ride.

"Oh yeah, did I mention open flame is a no go?" he asked his invisible tour group. "Rosa told us that we burn faster than spiderwebs. She swears that's what happened to poor Albert — he got too close to the man roasting chestnuts outside the museum. Went in for a sniff and never came back. I have my doubts about anything that she says, but I'll let some other poor fool settle that fine point of metaphysics.

"Most of the ghosts spend their time mapping the city. What else have they got to do? It's an adventure, going off on a voyage of exploration every morning. They lay hold of someone and see where they go. Then we memorize their face and their address. The best ride in the city is someone in a motorized wheelchair. That is comfort written large. Sitting there with them under the blanket on a cold day wheeling your way through traffic. Cargo carriers on bicycles are good too, but you have to watch the age of the rider. The young ones are reckless, and more than one spook has found himself airborne after some off-road antics.

"We never go on airplanes because the pressurized cabins make us so dizzy that we wish we could die. Fergal once said he wanted to get home to Newfoundland, so he jumped into the baggage compartment. It worked a lot *better than being inside the jet because they don't pressurize that space. Don't know why, but that's the way it is."*

John paused outside of the meeting room and looked around.

"But back to Barry. He fancies himself an intellectual. He reminds me of a German shepherd. Have you ever noticed the look of wonder and delight on the face of a puppy playing fetch? Every time you throw the ball is the first time. That happens to Barry every time he opens his mouth. The wonder of his mental process continues to amaze him even after all these years."

John entered the display window and made a place for himself on a stack of wooden crates. He nodded to his fellow conspirators and prepared for the meeting.

He's going to talk to us about the light, *he thought.* His mind grappled with the inherent flaw in the ghostly explanation about the properties and purposes of the light. It reminded him of the joke about the young praying mantis who brags about having sex with a big, beautiful female. If you really had sex with her, Jack, she would have bitten your head off — liar! If Barry knew what the light was, he wouldn't be here would he? *John glanced around the faces in the meeting.* I do believe I'll take this opportunity to raise that very point with him. Shit, here he comes, walking sideways toward the lectern — let the bullshit begin!

Chapter 17

Arthur collected his phone and split. In spite of what Eric had said, he still expected a big scene with the staff. But it was millionaires' weekend, and all the homeless guys had their cheques and were living large. Well at least until the money ran out. The Eddington staff was far too busy with the frequent flyers to worry about a fresh-faced kid who really didn't need to be there. Bodies that were aching to have a seizure were piling up in the hallway of St. Joe's Emergency Department. They were glad when Arthur asked for his phone back; they needed the bed. They should have phoned his parents, but they hadn't even had time to read his file yet. Detox is a busy place, with lots of special people milling around making threats and demands.

———

The bus terminal at Bay Street was jammed. Arthur could see a phalanx of students with wheeled suitcases rolling toward the bus station. The line waiting to board stretched around the block, and Arthur wondered if he could even get a ticket. He was in luck. He got a seat, and an hour later, he was looking out the window as the powerful Greyhound roared effortlessly down the eastbound 401 to Kingston.

In southern Ontario, the December landscape is rendered in shades of grey. The sky was heavy with fat, billowing, low-hanging, ashen clouds. The farmland and pastures were sombre, as if they had both bled the last of their lifeblood out, and then turned to face the sky, waiting for death.

The woods were grey, the highway was grey, the dust clinging to the windows was grey. The sun was only days away from its lowest ebb of the year. Where had the summer gone? What had happened to those gorgeous days of light and warmth and subtle colours? To those long evenings he had spent on the deck with Linda, drinking white wine and listening to the summertime orchestra of birdsongs? Arthur tried to push his seat back into the reclining position, but it would go no further. His hip was still sore, but at least now he could take the painkillers with codeine. He thought about Linda, beautiful, elegant Linda, sitting in the afternoon sun on her chaise lounge. *What seemed further away*, he wondered, *Linda or that late-summer afternoon?*

Did any of that really happen? Was such a summer dream even possible? And what about Linda? Was she as ephemeral as a summer's evening? No, she was real. She was brooding somewhere, in someone's high tower, looking out a window at the world at rest, wondering when her love was coming.

Arthur was excited. Being a fugitive for the first time was invigorating. He felt a little sorry for the students returning home for Christmas. He used to be one of them. Would they have to say, *Oh, Mommy, thanks for the new jeans, and, Daddy, thank you for the new computer!* That phase of his life was over. That reality as unwanted and unloved as a boarded-up gas station on the old highway.

He was returning to something far more durable. Linda was his pole star. Bright enough to outshine everything else in the heavens. Cold and distant at times, but hot and breathtaking at others, and always showing him how to orient himself. Whatever possessed him to leave her bed? He felt such a sense of distance. Every mile that brought him closer to her fanned his ardour and churned his memory. The dinners, the walks, the talks, and the sex. Oh, the sex. Arthur never thought something that wonderful could ever happen to him.

The thought jarred him out of his reverie and back onto the bus. Enchantment was giving way to irritation. This was all so wrong. This silence. This bloody all-knowing, all-powerful silence. It cut him.

Where the hell is she? Why isn't she returning my calls? Is someone her age going to answer the door in a bath towel when I get there? He didn't want to think about age. He was eighteen and she was thirty-two. When he was twenty-five, she would be thirty-nine; when he was thirty, she would be forty-four; and when he hit forty, she would be fifty-four … five years older than his mom now. A shiver went down his spine. He felt a moment of despair. How would it feel to reach that age? Would it matter? What they had was beautiful. That could never change.

They had been playing a dominant-submissive game for months. This separation had to be her way of saying, *See, I told you, you can't live without me.*

He dreamed of burying his face in her lap and hiding there until his doubts and fears passed overhead the way storm clouds do on a summer's evening.

A girl his own age was giving him the eye. Why not? He was a good-looking guy. Fit and full of vigour. Of course, the crutch made him irresistible. Hobbled by a varsity sports injury, a hero in need of some TLC. A crutch was a wonderful icebreaker. Arthur ignored her. She couldn't take him where he wanted to go.

The bus arrived on time at the terminal. Arthur gathered up his kit and followed the procession of young people shuffling off the bus. The next heat of eager replacements was waiting to fill the still warm seats. This bus was headed home to Montreal for Christmas. The students were in a party mood.

Arthur knew his way around Kingston. The bus took him down Division Street past the military college and onto the campus. He wanted to call ahead, but he was running out of minutes on his phone, and he was worried about cell phone records showing that he had been in Kingston. His fingers had dialled the number before he could think it through. He heard the phone ring. If it got past the third ring there was hope. No luck. The machine came on with the voice of his love. Her inflections, her crisp and clear diction: It was all so perfectly Linda.

Anyway, he still had his key.

When he arrived at the front door, he felt a bad vibe. The papers and the mail were piling up. He collected them and opened the door. He punched the passcode into the alarm system and cautiously announced his presence by calling out, "Hello…" in a tone that would awake a sleeper, but which wouldn't startle anyone. No answer. The oldest paper was from three days ago. He opened the fridge and found that it had been cleaned and straightened up. Alice the maid had been in.

The garbage had been taken out and the dishes done and left to dry on the rack. The kitchen smelled a bit like a swimming pool. He steeled himself against the worst possibility and resolutely walked into the bedroom. It was pristine, as if it was being staged for a real estate open house. Linda was not lying there dead in the bed; she had left in an orderly fashion. He redialled her number to see if he could hear her phone ringing. He couldn't. He turned on the computer and went into her email. She hadn't been online for two weeks. Her last reply was the day after he left. Something very odd was going on here.

Could she have ended up in a detox too? They'd been hitting the coke pretty heavy for a couple of months, but she had not been showing any signs of slowing down. She was always pumped and ready to go. He checked her answering machine. There were fifteen messages, the limit. He knew most of them were from him. He couldn't remember her access code. He felt stupid and angry with himself. He didn't know what to do. It didn't seem right being here without her. Suddenly he had a moment of pure panic: the dope. Where was the lacquered box?

If Linda had cleaned up, which was highly unlikely, she would have put it away. But what if Alice had found it? He went to the closet and opened the shoe drawer. His hands were shaking. He felt around until his fingers found the familiar shape. He shook it. It had some weight. The box was made of wood. It had an unmistakable Japanese aesthetic. It was square and brown and lacquered with a little lock that any child with a paperclip could open. The pattern on the surface would not have looked out of place on a room divider. There were flowers and rocks and trees and something that looked halfway between a serpent and a dragon. He smiled and turned the key to have a look inside. Linda had been to see the candy man. The box was full. He thought about doing a line but stopped cold. *No. I'll wait till she gets back.*

He ran his fingers over the top of the box tracing the image of the garden. He carefully put it back in its proper place and on a whim, took one of her sweaters down off the hanger. He remembered her wearing it on the day he left. He closed his eyes and drifted into her perfume and her body smell, still clinging to it, taking him back to where he wished he was right now. He lay down on the bed. The trauma and travel pushed him firmly back into the pillow.

———

The morning broke clear and cold. When Alice opened the door, she noticed that the alarm had already been turned off. And there was only one paper outside; there should have been more. *Why don't they cancel it when there's no one home? A pile of newspapers screams, come on in and rob us.*

Her intuition told her someone was here. "Hello," she said in exactly the same tone that Arthur had used the day before. The word jarred Arthur back to consciousness. He'd slept through the night on top of the covers. "Linda," he said with a hope that was not supported by reason. "Linda, is that you?"

"No," said the familiar voice, "it's Alice. Arthur, is that you?"

Arthur was on his feet. He flung Linda's sweater back onto the bed and left the bedroom. He was so glad to have someone, anyone, to talk to.

"Alice, where's Linda?"

Alice wished someone else was here with her. She shouldn't have to be the one to tell him. She hoped her face wasn't giving her away. She was more than a little afraid of Arthur. Linda had been fine until he showed up. The people who pick up after you know more about you than your confessor does. "Didn't anyone tell you?"

Arthur felt sick. "Oh God. Tell me what's happened."

"She's fine now. She's in the hospital; she's been there for a while. The doctor wanted to talk with you. I left you a note. Didn't you see it?"

"Where?" His guts were churning.

Alice went into the kitchen and returned with the note he had failed to see. "Here it is. There's the number. You need to call them."

"What's wrong with her?"

"They wouldn't tell me, but they need to talk to you."

Arthur went to the house phone as Alice hung up her coat and went into the kitchen where she set the kettle to boil. He was going to need breakfast. This was going to be a very tough day for him.

Arthur got the answering machine at the clinic and he left his message.

"Get a shower," said Alice. "I'll cook you some breakfast."

Arthur knew that the romantic thing to do would be to run out the door, but he was eighteen, he hadn't eaten in twenty-four hours and he was famished. He did as he was told and jumped into the shower.

A blast of hot water changed his focus. At least she wasn't dead or in the arms of an older man. He shaved and put on some of the high-end clothes that Linda had purchased for him. He wanted to make a good impression. He didn't want to be dismissed as a kid.

When he entered the kitchen, the eggs and bacon smelled as delightful as cologne. He was so hungry. Alice was setting the table when he sat down.

"How could you miss my note? I left it on the fridge."

"I didn't eat anything last night. I was exhausted."

"When did you get back?"

"Last night. I came on the bus."

"I had been trying to call for days and all I got was the damn answering machine."

Alice brought the frying pan to the place she had set for Arthur.

"When did she go into the hospital?"

"The day you left she had a doctor's appointment."

Arthur tucked into the eggs. They were perfect. "That's right she told me about that." He tried to speak but the eggs were burning his tongue.

Alice was buttering the toast. "Well, they found something and sent her straight to the hospital. She phoned me from there and asked me to come by and pick her up a few things and straighten the place up. You two left it in quite a state."

Arthur kept attacking his eggs and trying to recall the scene. Yes, the place had been a divine mess. Sex toys and sexy clothing everywhere. He blushed a little. What did Alice think of him? Up until now he had always played the innocent student with her, but it was clear that she had known all along.

"So she's fine."

"Don't ask me. I don't know. If she was fine, she'd be sitting here talking to you. All I know is, they have her in the psych ward."

The psych ward? "When you said she was sick, I assumed you meant an infection or a broken bone."

"Finish your eggs and I'll drive you over there."

Chapter 18

Alice drove to Dr. Irvin's office. It was in an old building a few blocks from the hospital. Alice and Arthur parked the car and crowded into the claustrophobic zinc elevator. The building was full of businesses that didn't require a prestigious location. There were accountants, landscapers, builders, and several doctors and dentists.

Arthur hated everything about the building: the potholes in the parking lot, the sad and grimy doughnut shop with the streaked windows, the dull lights in the corridor, the smell of wax on the floor, and the steady drone of dead air circulating. This building hated life. He was here to receive a death sentence. All of these people around him, working away in their offices, were ghouls. They all made their living off death. They had hardened their souls to pain and disconnection for so long that they had nothing left to feel with. Arthur ached in his core. Some evil force was pumping air into his vital organs and paralyzing them.

Dr. Irvin was a ferociously intelligent man of sixty. He stood five foot eight with a medium build. Running and yoga had kept him fit and trim. He possessed a kind of animal vitality. He was the kind of older man who scared the hell out of Arthur. When Arthur had imagined Linda's new boyfriend answering the door this man would have fit the bill. Everything about him — his intelligence, his vigour, his air of confidence, and his profession gave him a kind of moral authority. It occurred to Arthur that this is what his parents had in mind for him. He was relieved when the doctor addressed him as an adult.

"Mr. Cardel, I wanted to speak with you before you saw Linda. She's changed since you last saw her." Arthur squirmed in his chair. "She asked me to speak with you. She wants you to know that she's sorry for what happened. She should have informed you that she's bipolar."

The calm and reasonable tone of this discussion filled Arthur with dread. His voice squeaked when he spoke. "Bipolar?"

"It's a mood disorder. It can be managed with medication, and Linda had a good, long symptom-free run until our present troubles. I had her off work on short-term disability this summer while we readjusted her meds. When she came in two weeks ago for her follow-up, I had no choice but to send her to hospital."

"Is she going to be all right?"

"She's making a very good recovery. I have hopes for her. But, Mr. Cardel, you are simultaneously a part of the problem and a part of the solution with Linda."

"What do you mean?"

Dr. Irvin underwent a subtle shift from professional to personal and then back again. There was something about this next question that engaged both sides of him. He had some exposure here both as a man and a healer, and the duality was painful. His face read as conflicted. Later in the day when he reflected on the experience, he would realize that he didn't want to know what Linda and Arthur had been up to. Somehow this dalliance diminished her in the order of things.

Dr. Irvin got to his feet and walked across the room to the table where he kept the medical supplies. He leaned his back against it, hoping that this would make him appear less threatening. "Linda doesn't remember very much about the last three months. As near as we can tell, she went off her meds shortly after her last visit, and after that, things get fuzzy for her. I need to tell you before we go any further that anything you say to me about this matter will be kept in the strictest confidence. You saw and heard things that I need to know about in order to help Linda. You're not obligated in any way to speak with me if you don't care to. But if you want to help me help Linda, I need to ask some uncomfortable questions. Can you help me, Mr. Cardel?"

Arthur hated the sound of this. *Linda is sorry? She's never been sorry in her whole damn life. What kind of crap is this? She's not on medication and she sure as hell isn't crazy. This isn't right.* Arthur decided to play along with the doctor and find out as much as he could. "What do you want to know?"

"Linda's system was full of cocaine when I admitted her. She was dehydrated and seriously underweight. She recalls doing the drug but can't remember how much she was using or for how long. Do you know?"

Oh crap. Arthur's run chemistry was starting to simmer on the stove. He heard a long line of betrayers: teachers, guidance counsellors, cool kids at school, all saying the magic words that always led to trouble: "You can tell me."

This conversation was heading for trouble. He endured a moment of panic, a moment that should have empowered his alter ego. But Doc never made it to consciousness. When Arthur looked into Irvin's face searching for clues, he had a change of heart. Something deep in his gut said it was safe to trust this man. "We used the drug a lot, but she seemed to be fine with it."

"Did you use every day?"

That escalation made him wary, but he went along with it despite his misgivings.

"Yes."

"Could you give me a dollar figure of how much you were spending?"

"Well, she paid for everything, but it was certainly five hundred a day for the both of us."

"Did you do any other drugs?"

"We smoked pot in the evening to calm down after the cocaine."

"I suspected that was the case, but it's good nonetheless to have some clarification. How much pot did you smoke?"

"Two or three joints between us, not much really."

"Any drinking?"

"No, we had wine and beer with meals and cocktails in the evening but no heavy drinking."

"Okay, thank you. That was helpful. Arthur I can tell you're still a little bit wary of me. I understand why you are. But there's one more area, a little more personal, that I need to ask you about. Linda has some pretty substantial gaps in her memory, and they frighten her. She worries that she may have done something inappropriate. Arthur, were you and Linda in a sexual relationship?"

Arthur felt fire in his face as the full weight of playing the fool pressed down on his shoulders. There he stood in borrowed clothes, found wanting by the real adults, just another dumb kid playing with fire. His voice wouldn't serve him, so he nodded and blinked.

"Thank you. When the memory is not so accurate it's useful to have a reliable witness. Arthur, what you and Linda did is your business and your business alone. But how Linda feels about what happened, now that she's back on the medication, is very important, and it's my business to help her sort through these feelings. Linda thinks she may have produced a video with you and some other people she met in a club."

Arthur took a breath. The horror of the situation was coming clear to him. "Dr. Irvin, are you saying she's nuts? I love this woman. She's my whole life. I would do anything for her. She knows that. Every question you ask makes it sound more and more as if she doesn't remember me. How is that possible?"

There was not a trace of judgment in the doctor's eyes. "It's possible. It's a feature of the disease. We only remember what we can bear to remember. Arthur, I want you to see Linda when we're finished here. But I need to warn you. She's not the same woman you said goodbye to two weeks ago. She's having a hard time sorting out what was real and what was imaginary in your relationship. She's focused now on strong feelings of guilt around dating a student. She could lose her job at the university. If you could let her know that you're doing well, that would help, and I would be grateful."

Alice was reading a magazine in the waiting room when Arthur finished with the doctor. She searched his face for clues. He looked a little shocked. *How in the world did Linda and this child end up in the same bed? She really must be crazy or more self-indulgent than anyone ever dreamed. No one could think that this had any chance of going anywhere.*

Alice remembered the day she had come to do the cleaning and seen the sex toys and the lingerie spread out all over the house. It was all so out of character. If Linda had been overhauling a car engine in the living room, she couldn't have been more taken aback. Linda was always on top of the housework. Alice sometimes thought Dr. Dickens brought her in to be a little company for Linda. That first morning when Linda told her she had met someone, Alice's heart had jumped. Finally, a nice man. Finally, her life could begin. Then she was introduced to Arthur. She couldn't believe her eyes. Who was this boy? Now look at him. Not much of a homecoming.

"Do you want to go over to the hospital?"

"I think I better. Can you drive me?"

"Yeah, let's do that." She put her arm around the boy and gave him a little hug. He responded in kind.

Arthur was only vaguely aware of being in the car. He was sleepwalking. Alice had to tell him twice to put on his seat belt. What he wanted, what he had come so far to retrieve, was now in the hands of strangers. Strangers who looked at him with resignation in their eyes.

Arthur felt his gut tighten as they entered the hospital parking lot. It was a familiar sequence, Alice fishing for a credit card, taking the ticket, and finding a space, but this ritual brought him no peace. Arthur was feeling an urge to strike out. The energy in this place was pernicious. He didn't want to be here. As they entered through the large revolving door, he began to see people in wheelchairs and people rolling IV stands along with them as they walked. His gut tightened even more. He hated hospitals. The very smell of them made him sick.

Dr. Irvin's nurse, Gina, was waiting for Arthur at the nurses' station. She was a tall, dark-haired woman with eyes that watched and loved the world. As the leader, she was dressed in a quite fashionable skirt and blouse that set her apart from the other nurses who wore pantsuits and sweaters. Only the plastic card hanging from the lanyard around her neck identified her as a member of the staff. Alice made the introductions with some difficulty. She had a look of deep distress on her face. She surprised Arthur by saying, "I can't stay. I have work to do." The look on her face told him that she had to get away before she lost control of herself. But was she trying not to laugh? Or cry? Arthur quite rightly wondered for a second how he was going to find his way back to the house. It took him a moment to realize that he wasn't going to be sleeping at Linda's tonight.

The staff were watching this performance from behind the desk at the nurses' station. Linda had been in and out of their care for years. They were prepared to do whatever was necessary to put her feet on firmer ground. The task today was to get rid of the embarrassing boyfriend. But they were unprepared for this piece of deviltry.

Alice's departure put a strained silence into the air. Everyone stood motionless as she pushed the elevator button. Arthur wondered if they were waiting for her to leave so that they could finally talk freely. In the silence, the nurses looked back and forth between Arthur and each other. Arthur's appearance rewrote the conversation they were prepared to have.

Where did she find him?

He's just a kid!

I was expecting someone older. A gold digger should have a creepy moustache and a big, beautiful smile.

Linda, Linda, Linda, what kinda shit are you inta?

The eyes had it. This frightened child was no gold digger, no heartbreaker, and certainly not the villain they had been expecting. How had these two ended up together?

Gina stayed on point. She had given out a lot of bad news in her time. No words were going to be necessary. All she had to do was get this kid into the chapel. The nurses kept exchanging looks, one of them even giggled. Gina heard it without reacting and started moving Arthur down the hall. "We have a little chapel room off to the side here. Linda loves it because it's full of growing things. She wants to visit with you there." Gina got Arthur's feet moving while his brain struggled to find something to hang on to. He needed more time than Gina was prepared to give him.

The chapel was welcoming. The walls were painted grey, and thick beams made of dark wood gave it a very rustic, Elizabethan look. There were windows everywhere that filled the back of the chamber with light. The room smelled agreeably of moist topsoil. A wide windowsill ran all the way around the room and it physically groaned under the weight of every kind of plant imaginable. The space looked and felt as magical as a garden in a children's story. Arthur looked past an older woman in a wheelchair as he searched the room for Linda. When he didn't see her, he looked at the woman again.

Linda looked off-centre, more like a scarecrow or a life-sized doll than a person. Someone in a hurry had dressed her. She was wearing clothes that didn't suit her. They were dull, formless, and worst of all, something had been slopped on the lap of her housecoat. Where were the crisp blouses and skin-tight miniskirts she had been wearing since the fall?

Her forlorn expression produced a stab of pain in Arthur's chest. Someone he loved had been disfigured and dumped here. It wasn't only the frumpy clothing or the absence of makeup; Linda's visage had the same lifeless expression that mannequins possess. The Linda he knew was a familiar pattern, as lively as a fiddler's jig, but now, she was inert. She had been pumped full of the wrong kind of drugs. The thought struck Arthur that she was a light bulb. He had only ever seen her turned on; this was what remained when the filament melted.

She looked distracted when he came in. As if she was trying to recall some poem she had committed to memory ever so long ago. Some special private song that piped her dreams and held them safe below the realm of consciousness. When she turned to meet his gaze, her eyes were empty.

Gina watched a look of pain and sorrow wash over Arthur's face. He was halfway home.

"Linda, look it's Arthur, he's come to see you."

The counterfeit looked up at Arthur in an uninterested way. Her face seemed troubled but also put out by having to make the effort. She couldn't quite place him. She held out her hand rather formally and introduced herself as if this was some unwanted social obligation. She was moving at three-quarter speed. Arthur couldn't get past her eyes. They were so different. They used to remind him of wasps dancing from flower to flower. Now they were dull and waxy.

What the hell have they done to her?

"I'm so glad that you have come. Please have a seat and we can visit for a while."

Arthur was praying that this was all an act. He wanted Gina to leave so that Linda could drop her mask and outline her plan of escape. But Gina had her orders and she wasn't going anywhere.

"Arthur, you were in one of my classes, were you not?"

"Yes," he answered.

It took forever for her to form her second remark. It sounded as if she was waiting for a question to be translated at the UN before she answered it. "Did you enjoy it?"

Arthur didn't know what she was taking about.

She opened a tin of sweets and offered him one. "The class, I mean."

Arthur looked at the box in wonder, as his mind moved at speed to the lacquered box in her bedroom. "I only heard you lecture once."

"That's true … I had forgotten. I only gave the one lecture last term. I went on sick leave after that." There was an exceptionally long pause as she worked something out in her head. Gina had her figurative Geiger counter out. She was carefully measuring the number of rads that Arthur was absorbing. There was a look of mounting disbelief that was hard to watch on the young lover's face. "Arthur, I feel foolish asking this, but did you rent a room from me for a while? I've been ill, and I get confused very easily. I'm having a hard time separating daydreams from things that actually happened."

Arthur shut his eyes. This was a leap off a bridge in the dead of night.

Linda brightened a bit. "You're going to be a doctor, aren't you? Someday you may end up here. Wouldn't that be exciting?"

A single tear rolled down Arthur's face. He was talking to a stranger. He had to know the truth. He went straight to the heart of the matter, directly to the memory that was more sacred to him than any other. "Linda, do you remember taking me for a ride in your father's sports car?"

A look of fear and concern passed over her face, his question had connected her to the memory, but in an instant the look of turmoil subsided and was replaced with a wan smile. "Daddy doesn't let me play with his toys. Besides, it has a stick shift. I could never drive it."

Gina had shown Arthur what she wanted him to see. He was practically radioactive. It was time to end the interview. She got Arthur by the elbow and started to move him toward the door. "Linda, I need to get Arthur in to see the doctor. Say goodbye now."

She rose to her feet in a dignified manner and offered her hand to Arthur once again. "Please come and visit me again soon. I so enjoyed our talk."

Arthur grasped her hand with both of his. He looked directly into her dead eyes. When he said, "I love you, Linda," it sounded as empty as one person clapping in a disappointed theatre.

She smiled like a young girl and reframed the statement in her mind. "Why, I love you too, Arthur. It was so nice of you to come."

Gina eased Arthur through the chapel door leaving Linda to her book. Gina wrapped her arms around the sobbing child in the hallway and held him until his grief found words. Arthur's eyes were awash in tears and his mouth overflowed with ropes of saliva. "She doesn't know me. How could that be?" Gina took him back in her arms and rocked him gently while the tears did their work. "It's all right, Arthur, it's okay now. Let it all out. I'm here."

Gina sat with him for an hour. Arthur was coming around, but he was still groggy. She didn't have the heart to boot him to the curb.

"Where are you staying?"

"I don't know. I really need to get back to Toronto. I'm out on bail and I'm not supposed to be here. But I couldn't stay away. I had to find out what had happened to Linda. Now I just want to go home. I've never felt this awful. I don't know what to do next. I feel dead inside."

"You're not dead, you're in shock. It'll pass. I'll give you a ride wherever you need to go."

"I need to go to the bus station, but I don't have any money for the fare. I'm going to have to phone my parents."

"Do you want me to talk to them for you?"

"No, it's better if I do it."

"All right. I need to make a phone call too. I'll meet you back here in five minutes."

Arthur thought about the things he had left back at the house. He snorted. He didn't want them anymore. They felt dirty. In fact, he never wanted to see them or this godforsaken town ever again. He felt so deeply exposed and ashamed. Linda had an excuse — she was nuts. What the hell had he been thinking? How could he have been so wrong about what was happening? What did these people think of him? What were they going to say five minutes after he left?

A man in a grey sports coat and dark blue trousers was talking to the nurses. They pointed at Arthur and the man came over to where he was sitting. He was beefy enough to be a cop. Arthur felt a stab of fear. *Oh shit, here we go.*

"Excuse me, sir," the man said, as he came into his personal space. "Can I speak with you for a moment? My name is Bob Dickens. I'm Linda's father. Gina told me you'd been in to see her today. I was wondering if we could talk for a minute?"

"Sure, I guess we could," said Arthur, feeling very relieved he wasn't talking to the police.

The older man pointed to some plush-looking armchairs at the end of the hall. "We might as well be comfortable. Do you have to be anyplace soon?"

"The nurse" — Arthur corrected himself — "*Gina*, is going to give me a ride to the bus station. I need to get back to Toronto."

"I thought you were studying here at the university."

"I was, but I've made a mess of things."

"I can certainly see how you would feel that way this morning. Arthur, I've been going through Linda's accounts, and she's been spending money faster than a drunken sailor for months. I'm not overly concerned about that. It's all paid for by my company. The doctor says that this happens quite often in these cases. She's on the mend. What I'm concerned about is you. Arthur, you were her student. She was in a professional relationship with you. It's possible that criminal charges could be filed against her. Arthur, did Linda put you up to this?"

Arthur stared at him. "Put me up … what?"

"It's an awkward question, I grant you, but I feel that as her father I need to, well — clean up this *mess* — but that's not the right word, is it? What I need to do, and I hope it helps everyone involved, is bring this chapter of our lives to an end with as much dignity as possible."

Arthur looked at him blankly.

"What do you need to get on with your life?"

Arthur thought about it for a minute. What he wanted was the wild excitement of that September night. That special feeling of being the sole focus of Linda's attention. The hot sex, the roar of the cocaine as it blew reason and responsibility out of his life, as if he was a mere sheet of newsprint in a subway tunnel. That feeling of immortality and invincibility that he had experienced as hammer blows to his heart. The warm glow of the pot easing the jitters as they came down from the high and held each other in their arms. That was what he wanted. How in God's name could he explain that to the man in the grey sports coat and dark blue trousers? A father, whose only goal was to sweep him out of his daughter's life with a cheque book. Another trivial expense that he could charge to one of his companies.

Arthur sat in silence until his thoughts ran clear again. He knew what he had to do for the first time in days. "Mr. Dickens, I want to thank you for coming down here to make sure I'm all right. I want about a million things right now, but I can't have any of them. I came to this town to become a doctor and I'm leaving in disgrace. So I'm just going to ask you for what I need. I think what I need is going to be the best thing for everyone. Could you lend me enough money to get a bus ticket back to Toronto?"

Dickens suspected that Arthur was still in shock. "I would be happy to do that, son. Before you go, could I ask you to do us one big favour? I had my lawyer draw up a paper saying that you agree not to pursue Linda or the university for damages. It would go a long way toward helping her get back on her feet and into her professional life." He moved in and spoke in confidential tones: "The university knows what happened, and without this, they could never take a chance on her again. Can you do that for us? For Linda?"

Arthur smelled hush money, a big wad of it. He hesitated. Was the Linda he loved the Linda he'd known? Or the scarecrow waiting to have another bash at the straight life? He didn't know, but he did know that it wasn't his call to make. He signed. Let them take her off life support. He didn't have the heart for it.

Six hours later, he was back in downtown Toronto. Same head, same heart, same hands, but the tragic lover was now reading from a different script. It was a desperately cold night. The wind was whipping off Lake Ontario, and Arthur was dressed for the fall, not the winter.

Arthur examined the change in his hand for the umpteenth time. No matter how often he counted it, it never became a larger sum. *Dr. Dickens is a cheap prick. The guy owns a BMW M6 convertible that he never even drives, and he gives me a bus fare one way out of town and enough money, if I go for the deals, for dinner tonight at Harvey's and breakfast tomorrow at McDonald's.*

Arthur sat in the waiting room in the bus station, staring at the coins in his hand. He'd put off thinking about his final destination all the way back to Toronto. The horrible choices kept spinning in front of his eyes as if he was watching a slot machine. What to do? He called his mom. Gerry answered the phone but was too messed up to talk with him and predictably handed the phone to Sally.

"Mom, it's me. I'm okay."

"We were worried. You left the detox. Where did you go?"

Eric's words had been committed to memory. "I couldn't stay there; I went for a walk to calm down and sort things out. I know what I want to do now. I'm going back to the detox to see if they'll let me back in. If they won't, can I come home tonight? I haven't been using. You can tell that by looking at me."

Sally was trying to do the right thing but lately she had been getting too much good advice. It was choking her. The pros all said that she had to let him feel the pain, but her heart couldn't cash that cheque.

Before she could speak Arthur took control. "Mom, I know you're struggling with this. So am I. I'm going back to the detox. I don't think I could bear to be home tonight. If they let me back in, the problem is solved. If they won't let me in, I'll call you and let you know what's happening." Sally hung up the phone and screamed.

Chapter 19

The people at Eddington made him stand outside and phone every half hour to check on availability. It was their farcical way of maintaining order. You couldn't let addicts get away with anything. They saw compassion as opportunity.

After an hour of shifting from one foot to the other to stay warm, a street rescue van came by and offered him a ride to the homeless shelter. He declined that offer but took a hot chocolate and a sweet bun from them. The calories helped to fight the cold. They also gave him a pair of mitts and a wool hat. They made a big difference. Oh, where was the soft embrace of that scented September evening?

Any other night, Arthur would have been well advised to accept the ride to the shelter. But tonight was different. In the city-owned apartment building across the road from the detox, a Christmas party was running madly out of control. The strains of heavy metal music mixed with the sound of riotous good living and spilled into the street. The rounders at the Eddington got wind of the free drinks and that made the line to get in out of the cold move a lot faster. Arthur found himself back in the bubble after dinner time.

The skinny old guy was still passed out. He needed a shave when Arthur left, and today he needed someone to comb his beard. He was still passing gas and resting up for New Year's Eve. The other bunk, previously occupied by Eric, was now full of an enormous South Asian man who was trying to shake himself to death. He was sweating and swatting bugs that only he could see. He kept looking at Arthur with his big yellow, bloodshot eyes, hoping for some kind of response, some kind of help or consolation. Arthur wanted nothing to do with him. He rolled over onto his bad hip so he wouldn't have to look at the man. After about half an hour, the nurse came in and took the unfortunate man's blood pressure. She frowned and they whisked him off to the hospital. Peace at last.

Dr. Dickens' hush money didn't smell quite so awful here in the bubble. *I should have taken a little start-up money.* He caught himself. *No, don't go there. That part of it is over.* He kept saying that to himself, as a way of keeping his pain at bay. The lie didn't work any better than the Tylenol #3s he had picked up at Linda's and had smuggled into the detox to put out the fire burning in his hip. He had forgotten about the smell of this place the moment he left. It had stayed forgotten while he was lined up outside waiting to get back in. But the stink had jumped out of the cake once more. *What awful combination of things has to happen before you smell the way these guys do?*

This was nuts. Was he the only person on the planet who knew who Linda really was?

Dr. Irvin sure as hell didn't know. Alice got paid to clean the house, not mind the mistress. She didn't know. Neither did Gina. Linda's whole family thought the real her was an aberration and a bit of an embarrassment. Linda had shown him, and maybe only him, her true self and in doing so had inadvertently liberated him. So why was she locked up in Kingston while he enjoyed the wind chimes here at the Eddington?

Eric had been promoted out of the bubble and into the stratified heights of the rooms. The staff had allowed him and some of the other young hopefuls to attend a Narcotics Anonymous meeting that met in a nearby church. Eric caught sight of Arthur in the bubble and waved to him as he and the other young Turks went rolling out the door. Arthur knew they would get a chance to talk at breakfast. He rolled over on his good side and drifted off to sleep.

———

Breakfast at the detox was a lively affair. The dining room resembled a family restaurant, albeit one with long oak tables all in a row. There was a living room behind the tables separated by a row of room dividers. It had couches and single chairs and even a radio that only the staff could turn on. It was a nice place to sit and visit after a meal. Half the guys who came down for breakfast were too sick to eat. They pawed at their plates. A lot of good stuff got left behind on the trays. The frequent flyers were determined to get as much of that picked over food into themselves as they could. They hung around like vultures when they had finished eating. They were broke, and this was how they stayed alive until the next cheque came. Then it would be millionaires' week again. Arthur found that the trick was to keep your eyes on the food, which was actually quite good. The thing to avoid while eating was watching some poor old schizophrenic with false teeth spoon in the eggs. Arthur was hungry in so many ways this morning.

Eric grabbed the seat next to him. "You fucked up, Arturo."

"No, I didn't. I was a good boy. You would've been proud of me. Besides, now I have a sad story to tell waitresses for the rest of my life."

"Well, my morning is pretty much free, as is my afternoon and evening, so I hope it's a long story. Are you still going to treatment?"

"Everybody but me still has their heart set on it."

"So why go?"

"It may be the quickest way out of this mess. Capiche?"

"Ah, my best student."

Eric was making short work of his bacon and eggs.

"Eric, I can't help but notice that you're eating and enjoying it. Aren't you supposed to be dope sick? I was expecting to see you push the tray away this morning. I had big eyes for your fruit cup."

Eric looked around the room to see who was in earshot. "Well then you're definitely smarter than the local Mounties. I got a little help from a friend."

"In here?" said Arthur with an innocuous smile.

"Arturo, you really need to take notes when I'm lecturing. Remember I told you that you have to play ball? If I went cold turkey, I'd be sick for two weeks and everything would hurt like hell. So I asked for some help and they gave me a little something to ease my pain. But it also covers my tracks. So they throw in, and I throw in."

"What did you bring to the party?"

"A dude here has some killer weed. It's not quite a banquet, but it's better than a snow cone. You want some?"

"No, I have to pass a piss test this afternoon."

"Where?"

"That horrible place that we're not going to talk about."

"Why so quick? You just got here."

"Carol in the office is a little annoyed with me and plenty annoyed with my mother calling. I think I'm getting some tough love here."

Two hours later, Arthur heard his name over the loudspeaker. When he went to the desk to find out what they wanted, Carol gave him two bus tickets and a four-hour pass; a much better deal than he got in Kingston. But the intent of the donors was identical: Get out of here and stop being a problem for us. As he left the Eddington, he felt a moment of despair. The guys hanging around outside pushing and shoving and smoking frightened him. This neighbourhood was full of unwashed, dressed-out-of-the-rag-bag discards. No sports cars. No hot tubs. No Linda.

Is that all I get? A quick look behind the curtain and then off to a factory job for the rest of my life? How could what we had end up here? He spied an old woman in a wheelchair smoking a cigarette toothlessly, and he flashed back to the chapel. His body convulsed involuntarily.

Chapter 20

Arthur found himself, in short order, back in the interview room at Punanai. They gave him the same paperwork they had given him twice before. He answered the questions fully this time and in some detail. Greg was pleased with the improvement he saw on the written page. He watched Arthur move through the living room and then out through the double doors onto the smoking deck. He wasn't using the cane anymore, but more than that had changed. Had the Eddington worked its intended magic on him?

It took a few minutes to score the test. When Greg was done, he invited Arthur and Reg back into the interview room. Both counsellors were in full regalia. Greg was wearing his best blue pinstripe, while Reg had on his three-piece with the bow tie. They resembled lawyers trooping into a courtroom and laying their case notes on the table. Greg took a moment to look at his young client, trying to see him as he was now and not how he had been the last time he was here. He noticed that Arthur had a death grip on the arm of his chair. "So Arthur, what brings you in to see us today?"

Arthur was taken by surprise. Surely it was painfully obvious why he was here.

Greg smiled. Mike Sage had taught all of his counsellors to start an interview with a question that everyone thought that they knew the answer to.

Arthur weighed the possibilities and started with something safe. "I'm in trouble at school."

"Trouble?"

"I didn't go to class."

"Do you mean none, or did you miss so many that now you can't do your papers?"

"I didn't go to any."

Greg smiled warmly at his young charge. This was a familiar theme. "So how did you spend your time?"

Arthur was wary. He looked back and forth between the two interrogators as he tried to make up his mind. Why was Reg sitting there? Why wasn't he talking? *They're going to sandbag me if I'm not careful. They don't need to know everything.* "I met a woman at school, and she and I stayed high all term. She had kind of a breakdown and now she's in hospital. Her family is taking care of her." Reg made a note on his pad.

Greg didn't take his eyes off Arthur. "Is that why you came home?"

Arthur looked pained, surely this part was self-evident too. "She didn't get sick until after I left for Christmas break. I had to come home otherwise the jig was up." It was safe to tell them what they already knew.

Reg finally piped up. "But you were going to hit them up for some more money."

"Exactly." In a perverse way, it was very satisfying to be able to own that. It felt very grown up.

Greg noticed that Arthur's stranglehold on his armchair was relaxing. "What I'm interested in is your drug use. I had a hard look at your paperwork before you came in. Did you answer all the questions honestly?"

"Yeah."

"I appreciate the fact that you're laying all your cards on the table this time. I'm going to respond in kind and tell you what I'm struggling with. Arthur, you're at the age when it's the most difficult to diagnose addiction and alcoholism. People who are away at university often drink like alcoholics and take drugs like addicts. But there's a difference. At university, people are away from their parents for the first time and they experiment."

Arthur was listening. This gave Greg some real hope for the first time.

"What Reg and I are looking for are signs of addiction. Most of your classmates will get tired of the booze and drugs in about a year's time. There's a logic to these things. In elementary school, the big deal is cigarettes. In high school, you smoke pot. In university, you drink alcohol. These things are fads. They don't become the centre of your world. Most people say, 'Okay, that was fun, I enjoyed that, but I don't see how I could do that every day. There's so much more I want from life.' They listen to that quiet voice calling them. They find that they want to explore their world, go to grad school, get married, or start a career. Do you see what I mean?"

He checked out Reg for a reaction. He was happy to remain silent, waiting and watching.

Greg soldiered on. "Two young men are drinking and using drugs at about the same rate. One of them is going to crash and burn, but the other one isn't, and we can't tell which is which simply by counting the empty beer bottles. How much they drink is not the issue, it's how they feel about it. There's an underlying force that drives the one fellow but not the other. Do you get my drift? Arthur, were you satisfying your curiosity about all this stuff or was something more sinister going on?"

Arthur sat up in his chair. "I don't know what to do. I don't know who to turn to. I sure as hell can't talk to my parents about what's going on. The problem I have now is wondering if I can trust you. So let me put this right out there before I answer that. Does what I say stay in this room?"

Greg leaned into Arthur's personal space. "We'll say as little as we can get away with because we really do want to protect your privacy, but since the courts are going to be looking at your file closely, you might want to be a little circumspect."

I knew it! All I have to do is start a sentence and they'll finish it for me. They have their marching orders. They're as bad as those nurses. They need me in a lab coat with a stethoscope around my neck.

A look of sly satisfaction crossed Arthur's face, one that Greg misinterpreted for trust. "But before we start talking about other things, let's get the addiction piece settled as best we can. Arthur, do you crave cocaine?"

"Yes."

"When was the last time you used it?"

"I don't know. The last night Linda and I were together."

"Linda is...?"

Arthur's delivery of the line was slow and deliberate. "She was my girlfriend."

Reg's curiosity was piqued; that answer screamed falsehood and vulnerability. He flashed on Bill Clinton talking about his relationship with Monica. The trail started here.

"Someone you met at school?"

"Yes."

"Did she do drugs with you?"

"Yes."

"She's the one in the hospital now?"

"Yes, but not for drugs. She had a breakdown of some sort."

"Was it caused by the drugs?"

"I don't know."

"Who used first, you or her?"

"She got me going on the stuff. But we're right on the edge of what I'm prepared to say about that. Let's just worry about me."

Reg had the wind up. He was at his best when he knew that the truth was being used to hide the truth. *Oh, you'll be telling me all about this girlfriend, long before you tell anyone else. You can count on that.*

Greg felt Arthur's back go up, so he tried a lighter touch. "So you were using pot, alcohol ... but the main event was always cocaine. You snorted right?"

"Sometimes we freebased."

"Did you do any Oxys?"

"No, we couldn't get them very often. Otherwise, we might have used them more. They're good."

Greg looked at Arthur's assessment. "You didn't drink much in high school, did you?"

"No, I was trying too hard to get into med school. The competition was brutal. I was one clean-living boy back then." Arthur enjoyed retelling this part of the story. He looked relaxed for the first time.

"So getting high is not your usual thing — was this just a very long binge?"

There it was. The lesson to be learned. The life raft back to sanity. Youth and promise and foolish choices, that's what they landed on every time, exactly as the prophet Eric had foretold. They had taken the bait. A gentle tug would set the hook. "Well, I wouldn't have put it that way, but yes, that might be right." He was smart enough not to check them out for a reaction.

"Since you left Linda, I know you dropped some acid, but have you used any cocaine?"

Arthur thought about the square brown box in Linda's closet. About how it had felt in his hand. How it had made his heart race. How it had made his spirit soar. He heard her whisper: *Don't interrupt these clowns when they're making a mistake. You may have wanted to use, but you didn't.*

"No. I couldn't make a connection. I didn't have any money." Arthur's face told Reg that that wasn't true either, but it couldn't tell him why.

Arthur reflexively reached into his pocket and touched the bottle of T3s. He felt better knowing they were there. He listened for the sound of them rattling when he walked.

"But did you want to use?"

You don't know the half of it, you burned-out old bastard. "No, the using was kind of something I did with Linda. It was our thing."

Reg made the connection. *She's the trigger. Sex and drugs together. That's why he's keeping her safe and sound, tucked away for when he needs her again. He's not going to let us anywhere near her. Now it makes sense. He's going to use again. He doesn't even know it yet, but the decision has already been made.*

Greg kept probing. "Now I'm going to ask you an impossible question. If you hadn't screwed up your academics, I know that you did, but say you didn't, could we send you back to school for your second term? Would you be able to stay away from Linda and the drugs?"

Arthur felt let down by the question. It was clear now that Professor Moriarty had failed English in high school. These guys were poking around in the dark. Some experts.

The best lies are all but indistinguishable from the truth. A curious confusion had come over Arthur, it was an intuitive thing, he kept forgetting that Linda was indisposed. He was continually listening for the sound of her voice. Waiting for her to show up in a preposterous disguise. He still had a faint hope of heaven — one that would materialize with a single whiff of her perfume. When he searched his tormentors' faces, he saw the truth. They had nothing.

I can't trust these guys. They said so themselves. I know what they want to hear. Not an addict — a user that's all. No deep underlying trauma, just a bit of fun that got out of control. I can sell them this the same way that Linda did in — holy shit — the way she did in the chapel. Of course, that's the only way out for her. She got caught too. She's walking this damn thing back. Oh, you wonderful bitch. I love you!

Arthur's head went back and tilted to his left. His eyes lost their light, and his face became blank. He was oblivious to his companions for almost a minute as this latest insight rewrote his software. Reg and Greg exchanged a look that said, *Are you seeing this too?*

Arthur, being Arthur, remembered the last question he had been asked when he came to himself again. "Sometimes I want them both pretty badly."

"But not all the time?"

"No, it comes and goes, only sometimes now."

"How is it different? What's changed?"

Arthur didn't answer. That line had been drawn.

Greg tried for an easier piece. "What about med school. Do you still want to go?"

"Well, that ship has sailed. But if it were possible, I wouldn't say no."

Greg took him at his word and spoke from the heart. "You're in a tough spot here. If you'd only been smoking pot or drinking for the last three months, I wouldn't touch you as a client. I would've written the whole thing off as a binge and sent you back to school. It takes time for some drugs to become a problem." He gave Arthur a sideways look trying to work out how his words were being received. *He's listening but that's all.* "With pot and booze, it can take years. The difficulty is, you've been using cocaine and Oxys. Everybody who tries them ends up in trouble and generally sooner rather than later. Based on what you've told me, I don't think that you're as far gone as most of the clients I've seen, but I still think we need to address this now." He turned to Reg. "What do you think?"

Reg straightened his bow tie and sat up in his chair. "Well, I agree that we need to do something right away about the drugs. What I find a little disturbing is the girlfriend piece. I'm always wary of what I don't fully understand. Arthur, cocaine blurs the distinction between sex and drugs. That's why we have a righteous interest here. Where there's a cocaine addiction, there is always a sexual problem. I know you want to protect Linda's privacy. That's fine. We don't need to know her last name. But we do need to know the role she played in your life. How old is Linda — is she a kid? Is that why you're embarrassed?"

Maybe I should say yes to that … no … say nothing. "I'm not going to answer any questions about Linda."

The pit bull slipped his leash. Reg leaned into Arthur's space. "Is she the wrong colour? Is she your dealer? Why do you need to protect her? Can't she take care of herself? What does she need protection from?"

Arthur's face said *omertà* as powerfully as if drops of his own blood were boiling off the burning image of a saint cradled gently in his hands.

Greg knew they didn't have to get this solved today. "Since you're not going back to school this term, would you be willing to come in for four weeks of treatment?"

Arthur and Doc mulled the offer over for a moment. This would do the trick. The bloodhounds had let their hope get the better of their judgment. Why not let them have their Munich headline? Let them proclaim peace in our time.

"Whatever you say, Pops."

"Is that a yes?"

Arthur shook his head as he spoke. "You can take that as a yes."

Reg heard the voice of protest from deep in Arthur's psyche. *That remark has an edge sharp enough to shave with.*

Arthur knew the drill. He got to his feet, nodded to his examiners, and took a slow walk out to the smoking deck. When he left the room, both men listened for the sound of his footfalls to cease. Greg went to the door and looked both ways down the hallway before closing the door and resuming his seat. He pulled his electric guitar out from its place of concealment and leaned back in his chair, letting his fingers dissipate the tension from the interview. "That went a little bit better," he said as he loosened his tie.

"If we want the truth, we better break out the sodium pentothal," said Reg as he carefully got to his feet and stretched his aching back muscles.

"So you don't think we got to the bottom of this?"

"No, but we're maybe starting to get some of the good stuff."

"What do you make of the mysterious girlfriend? He handled all of that in five-point type."

Reg looked at his notes. "It's funny. He made two slips. He referred to Linda at first as 'a woman' he met at school, which would be an odd way to describe another student, and I assumed that she was a kid he met in the dorm, but then he makes it sound as if she was older than him. But maybe that's not right. I also noticed that his face coloured a little when he heard himself say that. Then he said, 'She used to be my girlfriend,' which suggests to me that it's over. I wonder who dumped whom? He looked incredibly sad when he said that. As if he was being noble. That relationship sure as hell wasn't over the last time we talked to him. He was desperate to get back to her then."

"What else have you got, bright eyes?" asked Greg as he happily fingered the fret board. "I thought you were asleep in that interview."

Reg smiled. "The hospital piece is interesting too. *Breakdown* is an odd word to use to describe the crash after a three-month coke run. It's a jargony way of hiding the truth. I would expect more precision from a med student. They love showing off the fact that they know the secret language of doctors."

Greg was impressed. Reg, as always, had a wicked set of eyes. "Arthur was much less guarded this time." He gave his colleague a playful punch in the shoulder. "Well, at least he was until you started to badger him. Why do you suppose he was different this time, Reg? The trip to the detox?"

"Possibly, but remember he didn't stay there very long."

"Even so, he's not the same fellow we sent to detox, so something happened. The thing that struck me was how calm he was this time. Last time he was panicked. He needed to get away from us because he had something important to protect. I still get the sense when I talk to him that he's smarter than I am and far more linear in his thinking. Arthur is a good choice for medical school. He thinks three moves ahead. His composure tells me that he's changed his mind about what's happening. He has a plan now. He's back to the game of treating us like stupid babysitters who don't know the rules."

Reg thought about what Greg had said then replied, "What I saw in Arthur was a new understanding of how to deal with his problem. I agree that he isn't spooked the way he was last week. He's repaired his delusional system, he feels safe and back in control, and because of that he feels confident about coming into treatment. He's confident that he can outsmart us and get what he wants. This is exactly where we want him. Let's run him through the car wash and let Punanai work its magic. The Lord has prepared a table before him in the presence of his enemies. Let's see if he can chow down on what we put on his plate."

Chapter 21

Gina and Linda found themselves alone in the chapel. An old woman had been saying a rosary for a while, but she finally finished and left. Gina slid up closer to Linda, took her hand in hers and looked into her eyes. Linda was so heavily sedated that she had been reading the same book for a month.

"Linda, are you feeling any better today?"

Linda responded with a wan smile. A small tear formed in her eye, but like a dark cloud on a sunny day, it only threatened. She felt its wetness and brushed it away. "I can't remember where I have been," she began and then halted. "I remember being excited about getting back to school. I ordered all the books for my students and I had planned the whole semester. I even joined the gym…"

There was a long pause. She looked as if she wanted to say more. Her head turned slightly to the left and she looked out at the horizon. Something internal prompted her and she shook her head and said, "No!" with considerable force. Her head bowed and she started to cry. Linda held up her hand as if she were pushing someone or something away. Gina gently took her outstretched hand in her own. A minute of quiet sobbing gave way to another short nap. Gina waited for her to come around again. In the silence she thought about Arthur and the role he had played in her life. Linda stirred.

"Is there something you want to talk to me about? You look so sad. Talking about these things always makes them better."

Linda looked around the room. Her energy rose when she had satisfied herself that she and Gina were alone. "I feel empty. I've never told anyone this before. I'm awkward around men. They frighten me. I think about being with them, but they always rush me and it feels wrong. That's why I loved teaching and being with young people. That's what I'm supposed to be doing. I get such satisfaction from my work."

"Is it lonely?"

"Often it is. During the term, I was always frantically busy, but when school was over, especially if I couldn't teach summer classes that year, I would go home and read and feel sorry for myself. Maybe that's why I rented the room to Arthur. Yes, that must have been it. He would have brought some sunshine back into that cold empty house." Her voice brightened. "And of course…" — she beamed — "of course … that's so strange. My head went empty there. What were we talking about?"

Gina prompted her ever so gently. "You were talking about Arthur making you happy."

"Yes, Arthur," she said, hoping that her thought would return. "My mother used to say that when you feel sorry for yourself, what you need to do is clean house. Make the place shine and soon enough you too will be right as rain." Gina knew this was going to take some time.

Chapter 22

Arthur tried to sleep in his old room without success. The head that lay on the pillow was not the same head that had last graced this space. Was he even the same person? He doubted it. The room had been preserved as faithfully as a display at the Smithsonian. He was that one-in-a-million kid whose shuttle had blown up on the way to the space station. This was his memorial. All that was missing was a velvet rope and a few stanchions.

This was the first space that he ever got to control. His model airplanes still hung from the ceiling, suspended by invisible fishing line. His faded and curling posters looked down on him from the wall. His baseball glove still clung tenaciously by its strap to the bedpost. Nothing had changed in here except him. Any bed felt ridiculous without Linda, and he shuddered when he thought about what she would say if he showed her this room or the pyjamas he was wearing.

Dale had been the real shock for him. His kid brother had been very carefully prepared for their meeting. Instead of running at him like a bull, Dale had approached him calmly and with a look of something dire in his eyes. What kind of story had they told him?

The whole family was behaving as if he was going to prison tomorrow instead of treatment: They were stiff, formal, uncomfortable, and desperate.

Arthur rolled over on his side, hoping to change something. *Am I going to feel this way for the rest of my life?* He still cared about his parents, but this new tough love bullshit they were trying wasn't working. He saw right through it. They needed to stop. He wanted to scream, *Dad, I'm your son! You're not training a puppy.*

The only other time he could remember feeling this way about his family was when Grandma died. That was a whole week of wading through a swamp.

Why are they doing this to me? What have I done that's so friggin' bad? I didn't kill anyone. I didn't steal any money. Was it so very wrong to want to be happy for once in my life and to try to make that happen? He felt his eyes welling up with tears. *Is it a crime to even imagine a life far away from this suburban bullshit?* That thought had an edge that cut. *Yeah, well what about that tough guy? What about Linda? Where is she right now?*

When he tried to reconcile the two images he had of her, all he could do was roll over again in the bed. What does sexual, smart, crazy, and free have to do with fragile, frightened, doped, and deluded? How do you move back and forth between those two solitudes? He felt an invisible hand grip his windpipe. How had she ended up in a wheelchair?

Maybe I should go to med school. It's the only way I'm ever going to figure out what happened to her. Her family sure isn't going to tell me. Those pricks wanted to whisk me up and get me out of town PDQ. I guess I'm a threat to more than one dynasty — or am I an embarrassment? I should have taken her old man's money and scooped the dope.

His spirits rose when he remembered doing a line of coke off Linda's lap. His head jerked back when he landed on the stain on her housecoat. He tried to remember her the right way, dressed to kill with a she-devil smirk on her face, but he couldn't filter out that broken look in her eyes. He rolled over violently onto his bad hip and cursed. *Which one is real?*

He wanted to punch something. *Family. That's supposed to mean something. A cord that can't be broken. That's what they said. Well, it's starting to fray, that's for sure.* Arthur remembered his dad saying that no matter what he did, no matter how high or low he landed, he was his son; he would always love him. Arthur shook his head. Square that with the look on Dad's face over dinner tonight. Chewing each mouthful of food four hundred times so he wouldn't have to say a word. As beaten down as a vagrant sitting on a park bench with the ass out of his pants and a bottle of cheap wine on his mind. *Should I have read the fine print? Was the "one exception" going on a coke run with a lunatic bitch? Was that the one thing beyond the pale? Or is it the medical school thing that has you bugged? You told me a hundred times I could kill someone, and you'd still love me. Well, here's the corpse, where's my hug?*

He rolled over on his bad hip again and felt another surge of pain. *Crap! How many times am I going to do that?* He didn't look at the clock radio. He didn't want to know what time it was. Now was horrible and later would be worse.

His dad only pretended to give a shit. He wasn't always there. He had secrets and dark places. *I think I understand that a lot better now that I have a few of my own. Is that how he deals with these tomcat feelings?* Arthur wanted to ask him, but he knew what his dad would say. He would get that uncomfortable look on his face and say something that made him sound as if he was running for school trustee.

His mom wasn't that way. She remembered holidays and birthdays long before they happened. She was there to talk to in the evening. When he was hurting, he could sit next to her and watch her read the newspaper. At dinner tonight she had looked sad and afraid — the way that people at church looked when they were sweating the results of a medical test. It hurt him deeply to be the cause. He loved her and yet there was still that siren song he heard, the song that emanated from Linda's lips. *How can Mom and Linda even belong to the same species?* For a second, he tried to imagine them in the same room. What would they say to each other? Two women, one looking concerned and hurt, the other impatient and disdainful, and both of them looking at him, expecting him to ask the other to leave. That image popped both his eyes open in the darkness.

What is wrong with me? Eric was right. I got to see the big smoke and live the high life for a while and now … there has to be some way out of this mess. Something better than beating the rap. And tomorrow the Marx brothers get to have another go at me. I hate those guys.

Chapter 23

The ride to the treatment centre was made in a pelting silence. Arthur sat in the back seat with his brother. He wanted to say something memorable, but he couldn't because Dale wasn't doing so well, the little boy was frightened. Arthur wasn't feeling much better. This trip was more painful and pointless than the ride to Queen's had been. He was having a hard time pushing his anger back down the rat hole. There wasn't much room left down there, what with all the expectations, opinions, and lies churning around and festering in this silence. Gerry was driving and concentrating on that task to the exclusion of everything else. He looked almost peaceful for the first time in days. Sally was easy to read. She looked calm but her eyes were distant and distracted. She kept playing with her hair, giving it first a twist and then a tug.

Why did they all have to come? A fight would be a better send-off.

The SUV pulled up in front of the treatment centre, and Gerry popped the tailgate. The sound of the latch releasing was more than Dale could stand. He reached out for Arthur. Arthur gave him a hug and then looked into his eyes. There was a depth of sorrow. Innocence put to the test. He couldn't work it out. The image couldn't land. But the horror in his brother's eyes was the most genuine thing he had ever seen. He sat there looking at the boy in wonder. Gerry lifted Dale out of the back seat and took him for a walk up the street trying to calm him down.

Sally took out her purse and slowly opened her wallet. She took a long time sorting through the folded bills. She was fighting back the tears and trying not to show it. She pressed a hundred dollars into Arthur's hand. "They told us you'll need this for coffee and bus fare."

The words *bus fare* did the job. He swallowed hard and said neutrally, "Thanks, Mom." In his heart he felt the sharp edge of betrayal and a savage pulse of anger. Another bus ticket out of town. Is that all he was to everyone now? He stuffed the bills in his shirt pocket and his feeling of despair even deeper. Dale wiggled out of his father's arms and came running back to give Arthur a final hug. But try as he might, he couldn't pop the demon loose.

———

Arthur was at best a middleweight about to face a heavyweight for the first time. He had never been in a fight that someone hadn't broken up. He had never traded insults with a peer and come out on the losing end. He had never faced an adversary who knew more about him than he knew about himself. No one had ever dared to audit Arthur's books. You don't do that to a prodigy. But that all changes when you arrive at the entrance to Punanai House and stand in the bright circle of light that marks the entrance into the future with a hockey bag slung over your shoulder.

Kaiser was an obvious choice for the task of setting the tone with young Mr. Cardel. He was to spend the morning with Arthur and become the human face of the institution. Kaiser was impeccably dressed in a dark wool suit, and his impressive mane of blond, curly hair suggested an athlete getting off the team bus for a playoff game. There was a touch of majesty about Kaiser, one that he cultivated with great acuity. Unlike the other counsellors, Kaiser had more than one watch, a supply of handkerchiefs, and a different belt for every pair of pants. But the thing that made the whole ensemble sing was the way he walked. He didn't swagger. That would send the right message, but it would be cheap. Kaiser moved the way that all big cats do. His tread was sure and firm, and it communicated purpose and power.

Kaiser held all the important cards. He'd studied the assessment prepared by Reg and Greg. He had enjoyed a brief phone conversation with Jan Smith about the family and how they did their business. She had a lot to say and all of it was useful. No one had doped out yet what Arthur was hiding. To know the whole story at this stage was far too much to hope for. What mattered was the addiction. Everything else was a distraction that would come out in the wash.

Arthur was lying to himself and to the people he loved. Mixing truth with lies and wishful thinking and then using the admixture to confound his critics. It worked because they were afraid to confront him. His potions wouldn't work here. Arthur was certain he could control his drug use. That was the delusion that had to be corrected. That was the reason why he was here.

Arthur had the problem upside down. He was certain that if he was simply given enough time and space, he could solve all the problems in his life. What he needed was privacy. He didn't need any more advice from the self-serving fools who had landed him in this mess. They had tried to hijack his life and he wasn't going to give them a second chance. All the failures he'd endured had come about because of other people's meddling. They were the problem.

The staff would chip away at that delusion for as long as it took. In the educational sessions they would explain the science that underpins addiction. In the counselling sessions, they would encourage a new culture of truth telling and accountability. The goal of treatment was to help the client hear the lie on their own lips for the first time. Nothing else worked.

Arthur and Kaiser walked through the house together doing the orientation tour. They were sizing each other up the way that boxers do. Arthur looked at Kaiser and saw a fraud. A paid flunky. He would be an easy fix.

"Are you the young fellow who was playing dodge cars on acid?"

"Yes, I'm afraid that was me." The patrician tone of his response spurred Kaiser on.

"Is your hip any better?"

"I'm on the mend." Arthur's tone suggested that he was expecting someone to shine his shoes overnight if he left them in the hallway.

"The good book says a broken hip is the beginning of wisdom. Did it smarten you up any?"

Arthur looked at Kaiser disdainfully. He wasn't going to trade scriptural references with this ham and egger. Arthur was expecting to make Kaiser feel uncomfortable with his silence. He wanted him to go away and stop bothering him. He wanted to take the measure of this place on his own.

Kaiser judged the distance between where Arthur was now and where he needed him to be by lunch time. He took out his nine iron and lined up his first shot. *You think I'm a boring old duffer, do you?* "Are you going to be a doctor when you sober up?"

"That's an odd way of putting it."

"Not as odd as the way you're going about it." Kaiser punched his line. "Well, it's true, isn't it?"

"I think I messed that hope up pretty good." Eric would have stood and applauded the delivery of that line had he been in the room.

"I love it when you do that aw-shucks thing."

Arthur's head came up and, for the first time, he looked Kaiser in the eye.

Kaiser moved one floorboard to the left and took dead aim at the head pin. "What is it about me that repels you?"

Arthur felt the heat. He tried to put Kaiser off the scent. "I'm a little stunned by that remark."

"Well, you've been here an hour, we've done the paperwork, taken a tour, made your bed, and I still don't know anything about you. I don't know who you are, what your reasons are for being here, or how to help you. What I do know is, you're answering my questions like you think I'm wearing a wire."

"I'm a little nervous. I don't really want to be here."

"Now that wasn't so hard, was it? You told me the truth and the world didn't end. Tell me about not wanting to be here."

"You remind me of a cop on TV telling a handcuffed prisoner that you want to know the whole story, and the first one to squeal gets the deal." *You look the part in that suit too.*

"Who are you going to rat out? Your addiction? Fat chance."

"You're trying to provoke me!" That usually put the fear of God into them.

"Let me tell you what I do know about you: Your mom packed your suitcase. It was beautiful. Everything was clean and folded and I could see these were all high-end clothes. Dad drove you to treatment in a Lexus. Your family gave us a cheque for the whole amount and didn't even bat an eye. You're no Chucky."

"Who, the crazy guy?"

"Young dude, Chucky is you in fifteen years' time. Cocaine psychosis."

"We don't even breathe the same air."

"The first time the Chuckster came to treatment he was all decked out too. Of course, it was bell-bottomed blue jeans and construction boots back then. His mom and dad are church people. They live in my neighbourhood. United Empire Loyalists or so they tell me. Came to Nova Scotia after the American Revolution. They took a mortgage on the house to get him in here. He was a good-looking kid with a future back then. He was going to be the next big thing in aeronautics. He did something important in college about a wing for a fighter jet. That's where the Chuck came from originally … you know, Chuck Yeager. That was in my rookie year around here. Yup, the Chuckster made a lot more sense back then. He's a shadow now. Not much left. He's one of our profound failures."

"You're trying to scare me."

"No, I'm trying to educate you. The fact that you don't want to be here with your life hanging in the balance tells me you're clueless. You don't even know that you're dying yet. You're still unpacking your suitcase. I've been here for fifteen years. Which of us is more likely to be talking crap?"

Arthur was forced to turn and face his accuser. *This guy isn't so much. Halfway between a vice-principal and a registrar. Not like Linda's old man.*

Kaiser spoke into the silence. "The client I want to see has to try five credit cards before they get the bill paid. He's lost his business, his family, and his self-respect and has the tax people and the bank calling him once a week."

"People like that are bums."

"The problem is that you have no pot equity here. Your money is still in your pocket, not on the table. You know that your parents are going to bail you out of any scrape you get into. They want you to be a doctor. Maybe they even need you to be a doctor. You know that. You use that. You want us all to know that someday you're going to be the top dog, and if we're smart, we had better make your path to the top an easy one."

Arthur glared at him. That wasn't the truth, but it was a near miss. No one had ever dared talk to him this directly. He was back on his heels. *How much does this guy know?*

"My favourite client of all time had a much better story than yours. He told everyone that he was the much beloved and doted-upon grandson of the wealthiest woman in South Africa. He and Granny had been inseparable when he was a boy. She'd taken him in and raised him herself when his mother left town unexpectedly. She was eighty now and in failing health. He never said it, which made it all that much better, but his meaning was clear: If you sucked up now and covered the short-term expenses, you'd have a seat at the table when the main course was brought in on a platter ready to be carved up."

Arthur mustered his forces and attempted to dismiss him with a look.

"And now you're making a face. Is that the look that sends your parents into a panic? Well, that won't work here. We're going to tell you the truth about *you* while you're here. No one else in the world is ever going to talk with you the way we do."

"How dramatic."

"You beat up on ladies with baby carriages."

"That wasn't my fault."

"That's right, the kid had a gun."

"This is bullshit!"

"You take your parents money and then bail on school for a whole term and lie about it."

"That's not what happened."

"And, of course, you can't even sit down and have an adult conversation with me about it. Why is that?"

"I don't trust you."

Kaiser watched the mental gymnastics play out across Arthur's face as all hell broke loose behind the young man's eyes. They sat staring at each other for a full two minutes. Arthur gave Kaiser his best John Garfield impression, perfectly replicating the actor's look of pure defiance and contempt. Kaiser smiled as he turned on his heel and left. *I'm starting to like this kid. He's got topspin.*

Chapter 24

Arthur headed for his room because he didn't know where else to go. Every place was the wrong place this morning. Every person was bad news and everything that could go wrong had gone wrong in spades. He had spent the whole morning barking his shins. This was new territory, and he desperately needed some time alone to regroup. When he got to his room, he was surprised to find that he now had a roommate. There was a tiny man on the other bed. He was a perfectly developed adult male human but done on a one-to-two scale.

"You Arthur?"

"Yeah." He was annoyed, the room had been empty when Kaiser had watched him unpack. This was his room; he didn't want to share it. This new guy was intruding.

The little man got up off the bed and offered his hand. He couldn't have been much more than five feet tall and maybe a hundred pounds soaking wet, but he had an iron grip. "I'm RK, and no, you don't get to ask what RK is short for."

Not surprisingly, Arthur missed the joke.

"Not much of a sense of humour, huh?" RK made himself comfortable once again on the bed.

Arthur felt as if he should say something, but words failed him, and that left RK in charge. Arthur governed by fiat. He had no idea how to negotiate with people, so he went to the dresser and needlessly rearranged the contents of the top drawer waiting for his moxie to return.

"They put you in here with me deliberately. I'm supposed to be a good influence on you. But that has set me to wondering ... what have you done that's so bad, son, that you need me to be a good influence?"

"I'm at the top of everyone's list today," said Arthur.

"Oh, I don't know if you got the top spot all to yourself. I had some fun with the boys down in the office. I've been here before. So I know how this works. When I slung my kit through the door, they asked me if I was sober. A mighty dumb question. If I wasn't sober no one would need to ask. I tend to be a little loud and uppity. So anyways, we dance through that part and they ask me how

I'm going to pay. So I zip open my kit and take out a bale of twenty-dollar bills all tied together in elastics. It was beautiful. It was the size of a football."

Arthur moved to the adjoining twin bed and took a seat.

"The fellow behind the desk looked at the bale with this priceless look on his face." RK laughed.

"Which counsellor was it?"

"The fella with the canes. He told me the only other fella to pay cash was a bookie. Reginald was a little afraid that this was ill-gotten gain. He got on the phone and the managers all came running to have a look. Why are people so suspicious of cash? They weren't going to accept it. That made me laugh. 'It's all there,' I said, 'you don't need to count it.' I could've written a cheque, but what fun would that be?"

Arthur thought this was a great joke. "Where did you get all the twenties?"

"Well, it wasn't selling drugs if that's what you're thinking. That's where that Kaiser fella went with it. No sir, I earned every one of them fair and square. Do you know what a racehorse is, son? Sure, everybody does. Ever been within five feet of one?"

"No, but I took a few riding lessons when I was a kid."

RK took out a bale of tobacco and started to roll himself a cigarette. "Well then, you'll understand what I do for a living. I'm an exercise rider. I work at Belmont and Saratoga. A racehorse needs to be exercised every day. The top jocks will sometimes ride a good horse in the morning, to get the feel of it, but, more often than not, they don't have the time.

"I start exercising horses before the sun comes up, and I keep at it till about ten in the morning. I used to race at all of the tracks in Florida when I was younger, but I got to be too heavy. One hundred and twenty pounds is pretty light for a full-grown man; too heavy for a jockey, but it's the ideal weight for an exercise rider. Depending on the track you get paid twenty or thirty in cash to exercise a horse. It don't take long if you're not lazy to get yourself a hatful. But that's not how I got that money."

Arthur was feeling a connection. "I don't understand..."

"Well, if I'd used my American money, they would've robbed me with the exchange rate." He finished rolling his cigarette. "Let's go outside and spark this." The two men walked down the hallway to the fire doors. "One of the owners down at Belmont had an Ontario-bred mare he wanted to run at Woodbine. When he found out I was coming to Toronto to get sober, he took me aside and put a proposition to me."

They passed through the living room and out into the bright sunshine. "He had this five-year-old mare that was a little difficult to get along with. Not unlike the missus when the rent don't get paid. They needed someone to stay with her twenty-four seven to keep her calm, otherwise she wouldn't run a lick. So he paid my way north, and me and Morning Star set up housekeeping in one of the stalls in the back stretch at Woodbine."

The other guests were smoking and exchanged friendly nods with the two newcomers.

"I walked her, groomed her, exercised her, and then sang her to sleep at night. When race day got close, I bought a racing form and I realized that Morning Star was going to wallop the local talent. In her last three races she'd been pissed off at the way she was treated, and she hadn't run a lick. When I galloped her that morning, I knew she was ready to roll. She went off at a fat twenty-to-one and I had my bottom dollar bet on her."

"That must've been sweet." Like all young people, Arthur was fascinated with stories about big scores and easy money.

"There's something to be said for being the only guy in the stands hollering and hooping as your horse runs past the wire. It was beautiful, but I had to get my picture taken with Morning Star and then get her back to the barn.

"So the next day I went around to the front side to cash my ticket. It took the clerk quite a while to count it out and that suited me just fine. If you want to be the centre of attention stand by the payout window while they count you out a hatful of cash. They had it all neat and tidy with little paper sleeves, but when I got home, I mashed it all up and put it every which way to make it tougher for them to count downstairs."

He snorted again. "A fella has to have his fun. Security asked me if I wanted to be walked out to my car. I told them I didn't have one but that they could walk me back to my horse if they wanted to. So this morning I said my goodbyes to Morning Star, put her on one of the trucks heading south to Gulfstream for the winter, and then all I had to do was pack up my kit and come here."

Arthur felt a little tug somewhere. "That's a great story ... but is any of it true?"

RK loved to tease. "Well, there is a racetrack in Saratoga."

Chapter 25

Robert Dickens hadn't become a multimillionaire by chance. The lavish lifestyle that his daughter, Linda, and her young paramour, Arthur, had enjoyed was the result of his personal dynamism. He was an efficient and ruthless capitalist and innovator. He found himself taking a meeting in the same building that housed Linda's doctor, and he decided on the spur of the moment to drop in to see his old friend Ted Irvin; they had been friends and colleagues since medical school. Gina, who was Ted's general factotum, greeted him with a huge smile. The waiting room was finally empty, and the staff was busy finishing off the paperwork generated that day.

"Bob! Merry Christmas! What brings you in to see us?"

Dickens adored Gina. "I came in for my annual hug."

"Done and done," said Gina, giving him a big, affectionate kiss.

"Any chance of seeing the boss?"

She glanced down at her phone. "He's on the line, let me give him the high sign." She opened the door that separated them and gave him a wave. He nodded and went on with his conversation.

"How's Linda doing?"

"Have you been to see her?"

"Yes, several times, but she's always asleep when I get there, or so groggy she has a hard time talking."

"Well, that's the major tranks. Ted cut her dose to thirty mils two days ago and she's slowly coming out of the fog. We're hoping she's had enough time to find her focus again."

"Are you still working with her?"

"Every day."

"Do you notice any changes, for the better that is?"

"Something is happening. She's reading the scriptures."

"Oh, that's usually bad, isn't it?"

"Depends which part they read. She's been reading Ruth, and she's been talking to me a lot about forgiveness and reconciliation."

"Is she making any sense?"

"Not yet, but that's the direction that her mind seems to be going in."

"I want to take her home for Christmas. Do you suppose his nibs will give me the green light?"

"Worst-case scenario is he makes you hire a nurse. She's coming along. Sometimes what happened is clear to her for several hours at a time, and then when she gets tired —and you know how tired they get on that medication — she drifts off and forgets everything. But she is slowly making sense of what happened. I have some hope for her."

"It really is a rotten disease."

"What about you? How are you holding up?"

"You know me, I do the invincibility thing."

The light on the phone display went out. "Quick, in you go, before he starts another call."

Chapter 26

When the lunch bell rang, RK and Arthur followed the crowd down to the dining room. Reg introduced them to the other guys and they very soon found themselves sitting in front of a bowl of world-class chili. It was made with equal parts of love and fire at Punanai.

RK took up his story. "I was here five years ago, and these boys did me some good. I need to be in tip-top shape to do what I do. Horses are sensitive creatures, and they don't want to have anything to do with you when you're hungover. They'll make it tough on you if they can, and they'll never forgive you for puking on them."

"You threw up on a horse?" asked Arthur in a fit of giggles.

"Well, I didn't run down to the barn to heave on him. I just happened to be riding him when the blessed event occurred."

"You know that never happened to John Wayne."

"Lots of things that aren't supposed to happen in this life do. When I got back from treatment last time, it took the trainers a couple of weeks to realize that I'd changed. They gave me better mounts to exercise in the morning. The horses liked me a damn sight better. Some of that old magic started to come back. Pretty soon one of the big outfits was asking for me again. It was a wonderful feeling. Because I wasn't drinking, I lost some more weight and one day the clerk told me I was only five pounds away from riding weight. That got me thinking about a comeback. I was thirty then, and that's not so old for a jockey, but losing five more pounds and keeping it off is hard to do. Lots of great riding careers end because of five pounds."

From the back, RK resembled an adolescent. He was long and lean, even if he was only five feet tall. He looked every inch the skinny young kid who could eat a tray of roll-up sandwiches at a funeral and still be looking for meat and potatoes two hours later. A young man on the edge of a growth spurt that never came.

When you turned him around and looked at the front of him, you could see he had muscular arms and some formidable-looking tattoos. Like a lot of exercise riders, he favoured the cowboy look, but unlike real cowboys, his clothes fit him, and they were always clean and pressed. It was his face that made you take a third look. It was a sun-baked man's face that didn't belong on that youthful body.

RK took up his tale again. "Besides, riding is a ruthless business. There are only so many spots, and the competition for them is fierce. I wasn't sure I wanted to do that again. I had a fairly good career, and I hadn't ended up in a wheelchair. I was still riding horses, which is what I love to do, and I was happy. But still there was that old dream. I met this girl and she got me going to a yoga class. I had to do that on the down-low, I can tell you. It helped me a lot. I got a little more strength without bulking up and the next thing you know, I have my paperwork in order. That first year, I got ten mounts at the end of the season and I won on two of them. That's unheard of."

The chili was gone, and the room was starting to empty out, but Arthur didn't want to be anywhere else. He was loving this story. Finally, there was someone he wanted to talk to. "Well, the work always goes to the hot hand, so the next year I did even better. It all should've ended in a Breeders' Cup win, but it didn't. One night I had a young colt I'd been working with, and he was entered in his first race. Young horses hate wind, and it was blowing up hard in their faces that night. My horse behaved himself, but the horse next to him reared up in the starting gate and got his blinkers pushed up over his eyes as the gate opened. He panicked and dumped three of us in a spill on the back stretch. Nobody got killed, but I got my ribs cracked and that's a bad injury for a rider. There's nothing they can do for ribs except tape them up."

Arthur was all ears. It never occurred to him to ask himself why.

"The boys all said I had to take six weeks off and let the ribs heal. But I didn't want to take the time. I was somebody again and I didn't want to give that up. That's where the alcoholic brain took over. We were only about six weeks away from the end of the season, and I didn't see why I couldn't take my time off then. So I taped myself up and tried exercising a horse. When he bucked, my ribs shot me full of pain and my jerking around set the horse off. He threw me and I punctured one of my lungs and that's how my season ended.

"They fixed me up lickety-split and gave me a big jar of painkillers. Now I'm not stupid. God knows, everyone at the racetrack has seen firsthand exactly what painkillers can do for a fella. So I bought one of them pillboxes with the days of the week written on it, and I set myself up as the veterinarian's mate. I took those pills exactly when I was supposed to, and I never abused them. I was able to get a job as a hot walker after about a week, and while it hurt, it wasn't earth shattering. I've been through worse lots of times. It never occurred to me that the pills would make me want to drink again."

The guy who had to clean up the tables was giving them the eye. "That fella wants us to hurry up. C'mon, let's get a smoke."

They found a quiet place on the patio, out of earshot of the others. "Some of the boys were smoking something you don't pay taxes on outside the shed row one night, and when it came around, I took a pull of it. I hadn't done that in years. It was a little spicier than the last batch I sampled. I kind of liked it. Old Eddy rolled me one and told me I could have it. I should've known. Eddy has the heart of a snake. I kept it wrapped up in my sock drawer for a week before I gave in and smoked it. It was special. It took all the pain away. I felt really relaxed and calm.

"Now that's where I should've come to with a start and screamed for my mother. People in my profession are always hurting. Not enough food, flipping, broken bones, and sore muscles are all absolutely normal. Feeling relaxed and comfortable is something that happens when the season is over. I got an awful case of the munchies from the dope and some of the guys were going to Church's Chicken, so I jumped into the back of the pickup with them and off we went. There we were all laughing and sitting around the big booth. I forgot who I was, and I ordered a glass of red wine with dinner. It was the most beautiful feeling in the world. Percs, pot, wine, and a gutful of rich food. When we got back to the track, all I wanted to do was sleep."

Arthur remembered that September night. Evenings with Linda always ended that way. Fading away into sleep.

RK noticed the thoughtful look on Arthur's face. "Has anyone shown you where to get the real coffee?" he asked as he ground out his cigarette on his boot heel.

"I thought we had to drink the decaf?"

"Only if you're lazy or broke. Come on, let's get our coats and I'll show you the town."

The two men went back to their room and got dressed for the pleasant winter afternoon. The air was cool and still, but the sun still kept its power until about three in the afternoon. It was a wonderful day for a walk through the stately old neighbourhood. They checked in at the office and got permission for a twenty-minute walk. They walked south on Madison until they came to the Granite Glen Nursing Home. RK stopped to admire the building.

"Finish your story."

"I thought I had."

"No, that was a happy ending. Something else had to happen."

They started walking again, past the Buddhist temple and the school of philosophy until they found themselves outside the pub. It was delivery day and there was row upon row of aluminum beer barrels piled on skids and ready for a trip across town. RK had been mulling over how to say what came next. Arthur was a nice kid who badly needed to be wised up.

"I was as happy as I ever get that night. I fell asleep as soon as my head hit the pillow. Next day was a problem though. I woke up afraid. All of a sudden, I was worried about what people were going to say about me. I didn't want the guys talking about me having a drink." He looked over at Arthur trying to figure out how he was taking this. He seemed to be listening. "In my mind's eye I could see them exchanging looks and nudges around the booth when my wine came. I was praying they would know to keep that quiet when the boss was around. My hope was they would just torment me with it for fun. So I dragged my sorry ass into the shower and gave myself a good talking to and got myself over to the backside for four a.m., trying like hell to look as if nothing had happened."

RK fell silent. Arthur wanted more. He needed a different ending. He gave his new friend a nudge. "Nothing had happened…"

RK smiled. "Nothing had happened, all right. The same way that nothing happens on the first day of a pregnancy: You can't see anything being different but, oh brother, it is."

"What do you mean? You're making this sound ominous."

The two men stopped at the black iron fence at Madison and Bloor and helped themselves to a seat on the bench. It was a great spot for people watching. The business of life, commerce and education were going on all around them. RK was astonished that Arthur didn't know what he was talking about. *He really is new. Why not? He's young enough.* He chose his words with great care. He reached out and put his hand on Arthur's sleeve. "It was back. That urge. It was wanting a cigarette when you're out of smokes. Needing to piss when the elevator is stuck between floors. It keeps working on you. People talk to you and you don't listen. You move your eyes over the newspaper, but you're not reading. You're a cat watching for a mouse to run out from behind the refrigerator. Nothing else matters. Nothing can break your concentration. Wanting to drink and knowing that I couldn't made me angry. My ribs hurt. My conscience was screaming at me and I couldn't stop it. I knew if I took a drink all that stuff would go away. But I also knew it would be back a few hours later, madder than hell and ready to kill me. That night I stood in the liquor store for twenty minutes looking at the bottles. The fella behind the counter thought I was going to pick one up and run with it. He kept saying, 'Can I help you sir?'"

Arthur's mind flashed to turning the key in the brown lacquered box in Linda's bedroom. How it felt in his hands. How it had made his heart race.

"'Yeah,' I told him as I put the bottle down on the counter. 'You can help me. I need something real special. Have you got a bottle that will make me drunk tonight but not make me hate myself in the morning? Cause that's what I really need.'

"The guy looked over his shoulder to make sure the boss wasn't around. 'Buddy we get a lot of calls for what you want, but we don't carry that brand. All we got in here is poison, heartache, and pain.'

"I knew he was right, and I left. I'd planned to take the bus back to the track, but I walked instead. Walking was good. I wasn't drinking. I wasn't eating. I was exercising and staying strong. I should have walked to Siberia. But I didn't. I went back there the next night and I bought a bottle. The same guy was at the till but this time the boss was around. The look in his eyes said it all. We both knew I'd already jumped off the cliff."

RK got up from the bench and started to walk again. Arthur stayed at his side. They were both thinking about wanting. How that felt. How it consumed them. Where it took them and how it made them dance.

A skinny old guy with a very deep dent in his forehead stopped RK and asked him for a smoke. "Can you roll one?"

"Sure."

RK gave the man a pinch of tobacco and a paper and watched his practised fingers find the mark. He took up the story again as they turned to go. "A couple of days later, Eddy startled me for fun when I was schooling a horse. My ribs burned so bad that when the horse spooked and I couldn't hold him, he ran down the tunnel all the way back to the barn. Everybody started laughing at me. I always hated that bastard, and I was mad at the whole world, so I gave him a wedgie. Right there in the paddock with the public watching. I tore the top of his shorts right off. It damn near killed me to do it but I got it done. Everybody but Eddy thought it was long overdue. The stewards all thought it was hilarious. They laughed like hyenas when they saw the tape. Then they wiped their eyes, took out the rule book, and slapped me with a fine and a good long suspension. It was by way of being a bit of a hint. And that, Arthur, was the precise moment when I realized it would be a good idea to head north and have a cup of coffee with you."

Chapter 27

John believed that the most bothersome parts about being dead were the relentless cravings: cigarettes, food, booze, even women. It was agonizing to be surrounded by things he wanted but wasn't able to enjoy. Why did he still want them? He often wondered why he couldn't get past these temptations. The look of them set him off. When he was a boy, he would look at pictures in a magazine and wonder what it would be like to smoke a cigarette or eat a lobster or even have a glass of wine.

Chasing the good life was what turned ghosts into poltergeists. Ghosts could last for a good long time, but not forever. Sooner or later, they ran out of steam. If they moved around a lot, they could wear themselves out in six months, Peter had told him. Which was all about wanting things. That's what happened to Walter down the street. He was a poltergeist now, and he wasn't old by any stretch of the imagination. He was a lecher at one of the sorority houses. He stood there all day ogling the teenage girls and making himself miserable. The other ghosts thought he was drawn to the girls' energy more than it being a sexual thing. The girls were so alive. He wanted that, but that was as far as he could take it. He stood there day and night rocking back and forth, acting every inch the demented psycho. Poor old sod. Full of pain and sorrow.

Peter used to hang around him before he met John. Peter had told him that, in the old days, Walter was full of life, running here and there, talking a blue streak non-stop, seeing shows, and burning the candle at both ends.

Walter took the view that the afterlife was to be lived and enjoyed, not spent in philosophical despair. Some ghosts who mind their p's and q's last for centuries. Not Walter. He was demented now. He couldn't speak. He tried to talk and reach out, but nothing happened. His eyes had a funny dull look. What used to work for him no longer did, and he got so frustrated that he would bang pipes and walls trying to make his point or get someone's attention. Ghosts couldn't mess with the real world that way. That was as bad as taking your parka off in the arctic. It was a calorie burn. Eventually the light would catch up to him.

He couldn't dodge it any longer. Just another piece of dried gum stuck to the terrazzo.

Chapter 28

On the way back from the coffee shop, the two new friends stopped in the park in the shadow of Walmer Road Baptist Church. It was a beautiful little island with mature trees and park benches. There was a schoolyard nearby where the kids were enjoying the last of their lunch break. The church towered over them all, ready to either impart salvation or resist cannon fire. Arthur sipped his coffee as he watched the hardcore Toronto cyclists wheel through the neighbourhood at speed.

RK had been chewing on Arthur's latest summary of his troubles. He saw a solution. "Be a vet."

"What?"

"Don't go to school for twenty years to be a doctor. That's stupid. As dumb as being a teacher. Do you really want to spend the rest of your life in high school?"

"You're not making sense here, RK."

"Sure I am. Do you like sick people and hospitals?"

"Well no, they scare me a bit. I hate the smell most of all."

"Well then, follow your nose."

"Horse shit doesn't smell any better than hospitals. RK, you're a cowboy. What do you know about medicine?"

"College boy, I'm a student of life and I know people. Look at you. You remind me of some of the horses I gallop in the morning. I look at your pedigree and I see the royal family of stretch-running racehorses. I look at your body and I see power and grace and natural athleticism. I look at your past performance in the Daily Racing Form and I see nothing at all. No horse, no run, no hope, no way. Son, some horses don't want to race. It's not in them. They go through the motions. The same way you do. But lots of horses who wash out at the races at three go on to be really good dressage horses or show jumpers at five. My point is, horses have an aptitude. Part of my job is to figure out how to get the best out of a horse. But you can't get a horse to do something it doesn't want to. When you try, they get stale. Eventually they turn nasty. But mostly they make everything such a chore that you lose heart and want to quit. You can see a little smile on their face sometimes when they buck off their jockey or refuse to come out of the starting gate. Horses know how to get their point across."

"So how would being a vet change anything?"

"Son, you are plain dumb. Who wouldn't want to be a vet? Up early, watching the horses work out. Imagine being the only fella at the track who's seen all the X-rays before the horses run. They get paid a fortune and they never have to do anything for pay that they wouldn't do for the love of it."

"Was that your dream, RK?"

"I never had the schooling."

"But if the cards had been dealt differently, would that have been what you wanted to do?"

"That's a tough one. At sixteen, I was so full of energy I wanted to take on the whole world. Winning a Breeders' Cup race didn't seem that hard. I couldn't imagine how it wouldn't happen. I did really well as a jock the first couple of years but then I got in trouble with the weight, and that's the one thing there's no appeal from."

Arthur smiled. "Things started to slide?"

RK shook his head and then took a big sip of his coffee. He put it down on the bench beside him and reached into his over coat pocket to get his bale of tobacco.

"So you do know about that. Yeah, they started to slide. I could've used someone to talk to. Should've been my dad but it wasn't. What about your dad, Arthur? Could you talk to him?"

"Nope, he wanted a low-maintenance son. Someone he could turn loose in high school and say, 'Go get 'em kid.' He used to pretend he gave a shit about me. But he could never remember the names of my friends or keep up with my life."

"Do you suppose his dream went sideways?"

"He never told me much about himself…"

"My old man was that way too. We'd go fishing and I'd feel like a million bucks, and then six months would go by before he spoke to me again. I guess I thought that winning a horse race could fix all that. That's why I love horses. People are awful. They say one thing and mean another and get offended when you call them liars. I can tell what a horse is thinking by the look on their face. They want to be safe and loved and cared for. Then they want to run a hole in the wind. I don't know if humans ever get to the same place that racehorses do."

"I want to run a hole in the wind, RK."

"I know that, Arthur. The question is … which track are we going to run you at?"

Chapter 29

It was Sunday. Peter spent the whole day in church, perhaps trying to cut a deal. It's a rare event when Flannerman's had a funeral on the Lord's Day. John hung around Punanai and pursued his own interests. The guys there enjoyed Sundays. They got a half day off and a homemade meal fit for kings. Norma was doing the cooking, and she had big plans. She could put everybody's mom right to shame. Salad, fresh rolls, soup, roast beef and potatoes, with a piece of pie and fresh coffee for dessert. The homeless guys loved the kitchen staff. They didn't get food this good anywhere else. Thank God the charity paid their way.

While Norma was rattling the pots and pans, John would be sitting in on the Straight Up meeting. He called it the shucking-and-jiving hour. It was good practice for him. He loved to play the colour man — the guy who comments on the personalities and backstories of these troubled souls.

John waited for the meeting to begin. He thought that grown men should know better. If you want to make an ass of yourself in public, he thought, then do it right — put on a wig and get a part in an Ibsen play. *When he listened to these men, he felt the same angst that the conductor of a middle school orchestra felt listening to a pack of ham-fisted kids club a classic to death.* The counsellors are asking these guys to do the unthinkable. Where else in the world is anyone required to stand up in front of a group of men they just met and tell the truth? In a courtroom, maybe in a documentary, but more likely nowhere, because no one wants to hear this stuff. *John squirmed. He believed that private matters should remain private. In his experience, the only time a human told the truth was when they were blasted out of their minds and didn't give a rat's ass what anyone else thought or felt.* Truth-telling is the cherished weapon of last resort. Well, it is until death — then it becomes a matter of sport.

Chapter 30

Greg Bass had the guys rearrange the furniture in the dining room for the Straight Up meeting. This meeting was pivotal. For many, it would determine whether they would recover or not. The men enjoyed taking the heavy tables out of the dining room through the double doors and out onto the lower patio. This is where the barbeque and the gardening shed lived year-round. The patio was poured concrete, but it was surrounded on two sides by a wonderful granite brick wall that formed the base of a garden. In the summer, the slope boasted hundreds of wildflowers and flowering shrubs. In winter, it was preened with love and looked as cared for as Edwards Gardens. The slope that got the afternoon sun was the first place in the city where green shoots appeared in the spring. Fitting, really, for a place of new growth. A set of stairs with a sturdy handrail led up to the upper deck where the guys in treatment smoked and gossiped.

The guys didn't mind moving the furniture. It felt good to feel their strength return and to have a chance to move their bodies in a good cause after the delicious lunch they had eaten. They arranged the remaining chairs in a circle. One chair for each participant, plus one that would remain tellingly empty.

It took the usual five minutes to chase everybody down to the dining room. The guys all knew how this meeting worked, and most of them looked forward to it. But in case someone was still unclear about what was about to happen, Greg took a moment to refresh their memories and help them settle in. He was dressed down for the occasion, trying to look relaxed and casual in the hope that this would make it easier for the reticent to speak. He had his clipboard so he could make notes and a large cup of real coffee that he pretended was decaf. He was good for the next two hours.

"All right, guys, everybody settle down please." All the eyes in the room came to bear on him. "Have you ever noticed how the counsellors around here talk too much?"

The guys all laughed. They felt safe with Greg.

"Well, now it's your turn. You're going to talk, and I'm going to listen. But there are some rules. I need you to talk about one of two topics. You can talk about the moment you realized you had to come to treatment. It's what my old professor used to call the 'Oh shit' moment. Do you follow me? That horrible moment when you know you're caught and you say the two magic words." There was a resounding silence, the guys loved playing this game. Greg gave them a hurt look and then continued, "The best story I ever heard was about this guy and his wife who agreed he had to come to treatment if she found him drunk one more time. So one afternoon she goes out shopping. He was drinking in the garage and he ends up passed out on the floor. When he wakes up, he thinks, *Hey this isn't so bad. I got away with it.* But then he realizes someone put a pillow under his head. Busted!"

Greg began to move around the room and wave his arms. "So that's when he said…" There was a long silence as the guys looked at each other in bewilderment. They loved teasing him, it was fun to pretend they didn't know what he was after. Greg beamed goodwill at them and kept pumping positive energy into the room. "Come on, fellas, work with me here. So what was it the fella said?"

A tentative voice offered up the magic words, "Oh shit."

Greg roared at them. "Say it, damn you!"

It was a wonderful feeling to have everyone roar it out at once. "Oh shit!"

Greg held up his index finger and shook it. "Okay, you seem to have a good grasp of that horn of the dilemma. So moving on, the other thing you can talk about is the 'Say now' moment. Everyone say it…"

They played along again, but this phrase wasn't nearly as much fun. "Say now…"

Greg kept whipping them up. "You got off to a slow start on this one, but you found your voice in the end. The 'Say now' moment is when you see the problem for what it really is. It's when all the mumbo jumbo starts to make sense. It's when recovery stops being a theory and starts to become something you can feel happening in your own body. It's when you stop doing what you're told to do and start doing what you know is right. So are we straight about what we're doing? You can talk either about the 'Oh shit' or the 'Say now' moment."

Greg had a school bell in his hand. "What I don't want to hear are war stories that glorify your addiction. If that happens, I'm going to try to pull you back on course once, but if you still can't do it then you get the gong. He gave the school bell a little shake. This means you have to wait till next week to try again. The bell tells you that you're lying to yourself. We all do it at first. It's a hard habit to break. You need to really listen to yourself when you talk to make sure that doesn't happen.

"Now here's another tricky point. Most people hate speaking in groups, but others, well they can't. Fair enough. But you're in treatment and you need to try. You might surprise yourself and find your voice. Lots of people do. So everyone in this room has to make an attempt. No exceptions. But, if you're one of the people who finds this difficult, then stand up when it's your turn, tell us your name and say, 'I have a "Say now" or an "Oh shit" moment, but I'd be more comfortable talking about it with a counsellor.' Got it?" Greg looked around the room trying to work out where they were from the looks on their faces. About half the guys looked ready. A few more looked as if they might find their voice once the meeting got started. Not wanting to go first was always top of mind at this point.

"But now, the final piece. I hope all of you have noticed the empty chair. That chair is symbolic. It's there to remind you that you owe yourself the truth. What gets said here is sacred. This is a special opportunity, maybe even a once-in-a-lifetime chance to speak from the gut about what's killing you, in front of a room full of men who are all in the same mess and who understand. Where else in the world are you ever going to get a chance to do this? I'll tell you: nowhere."

Arthur felt the hairs on the back of his neck stiffen. *I'm not telling these guys anything.*

Greg went over to the sound system. "So I'm going to play some beautiful classical music and, while it's playing, I want you to gather your thoughts and think about what you want to say." Greg selected "Lent et douloureux" from Satie's *Gymnopédies*, performed by Pascal Rogé. The music transformed the moment. It said what was in Greg's heart.

William Sonora had made up his mind that he was going to speak first this week. He recognized "Lent et douloureux" as the music from a movie score, but he couldn't remember which movie it was from. He liked it, but other than that he didn't know anything about it. William wasn't thinking about the "Say now" or "Oh shit" moment particularly. He was remembering something that had happened to him before he came to treatment.

He'd spent a Saturday night in the psych ward at Humber River Hospital. William had been sitting with a group of dispirited big-bellied men in the TV room, watching the Leafs lose badly to the Buffalo Sabres. William hated to see the Leafs lose to the Senators or the Sabres more than anything else in the world. He always felt let down and betrayed. The Leafs hadn't even worked up a sweat in this seven-to-one mismatch.

He had grimly watched the massacre to the very end because, as painful as what he saw on the screen was, it was not as bad as the scene that was going on at the other end of the room. A group of old, worn-out women had gathered at the far end of the common room, all of them wearing the tear-soaked housecoats they had been wearing for days. They sat in the big plastic covered chairs commiserating or blowing long slow sad breaths of air at the ceiling.

There were some cold, picked-over trays of food, which said all there was to be said about hospital fare, cluttering the coffee table in the middle of the room. The florescent lights gave everything a pathetic sheen that sucked the energy out of living things. It made him want to take his cue from the roaches who fled the poisonous light. To say the mood was blue was simply to not acknowledge the half of it. If you were not already depressed when you arrived in this space, being here amid the smells, the racking smokers' coughs, and the escalating despair would soon enough make them a fellow traveller.

William fancied he could hear the voice of the old nurse saying, "I can't stand you people for one more minute. You're so miserable, you're starting to kill me. I'm telling you: I won't have this! Everybody up and on their feet."

No one moved.

The old nurse was up on her feet clapping her hands as she spoke. "Are you deaf? I said, everybody up and on their feet. We're going to have a party."

Everyone looked at her blankly. She triumphantly produced a boom box that started to play some retro dance music. It was obscene. People looked stunned, most of them thought this was a bad joke or a hallucination. She went around the room physically dragging people out of their chairs and getting them to their feet.

"Okay," she yelled, "everybody, grab a partner. No, don't just stand there. You dance with him and you dance with her."

The pairings were grotesque. Old people had young partners and skinny toothless men were dancing with full-figured grandmothers. It was as bad as online dating. But the nurse kept blasting energy into the room with her voice.

"I said dance ... DANCE!"

The responses were lame: "This is stupid," "You can't make us do this," and "My stitches hurt!"

The nurse was yelling now, a maniacal smile on her face. "I SAID, DANCE!"

The classical music stopped William's reverie.

Greg began to look around the room as the music finished, looking for an eager face, someone who could get them off to a good start.

William seized the moment. He felt an icy stab of fear in his gut, but he ignored it. "About two months ago, I was in a psych ward. I'm not crazy, but I got so bent out of shape on the booze, I needed to be somewhere safe. So my doctor put me there for a week while I dried out. When I get going on a binge,

I don't want to eat. Then, when I stop drinking, I'm so sick, I can't eat. By the time I got to hospital I hadn't eaten in a week. I was starving, but all they could give me was liquids. I couldn't keep anything else down. I was all wrapped up in a bathrobe and feeling about as miserable as I've ever felt. That made me a fit for everyone else in the TV room. They were all depressed. If you showed any signs of life, the doctors sent you home on weekends. So you can imagine, Saturday night was the worst. All the sickies in one room. I remember thinking, *If I look as bad as the rest of these mutts someone ought to shoot us all.*

"On top of that, the Leafs were stinking the place out. None of the women cared about the game. They were huddled together in a group on the other side of the room, crying and examining wet handkerchiefs. They probably had husbands as bad as the buzzards I was sitting with. Everyone was waiting for the medication cart and oblivion. It was unbearable. So the old nurse gets to her feet and starts hollering at us to dance. She was a big Jamaican woman. She took no nonsense from us. She started to yell, 'DANCE ... I said, DANCE ... YOU DAMN WELL BETTER DANCE!'

"So we paired off and started to sway to the music. It felt really stupid. I hated it. Worse than high school. The woman I'm dancing with is close to sixty and she has no teeth. I'm actually starting to feel creeped out when, suddenly, I get this rush of pure pleasure and well-being. I don't know about pills; I'm a boozehound. But I think we had so much medication in us, we got used to it. Dancing did the same thing as shaking a bottle of warm beer. It suddenly comes to life.

"Well, that's what happened to all of us. It took a minute or two but suddenly we all felt wonderful. We were laughing and dancing and having a great time. I looked over at the old nurse and she was beaming and grinning from ear to ear. 'I told you,' she said, 'dance.'

"Well, we carried on for about half an hour. The party broke up when the medication window opened. We all lined up and got our fix even though we didn't feel the need for it at that moment. I smoked a cigarette and went to my room. I was lying in bed when the thought hit me: That was the best I'd felt in twenty years. How pathetic is that? No wife, no life, but there I was dancing in the nut house, having the time of my life on a Saturday night. I felt so empty, so lonely. I knew I had to do something, anything. Dancing wasn't going to do it for me."

"Oh shit!"

Chapter 31

John helped himself to the empty chair while the beautiful music played. The men were oblivious to him although one of them did see a small whirlwind out of the corner of his eye. He ignored it and went back to organizing his thoughts. The thin ghost was working out a few of the finer performance details for a character he was developing. He had an alternate agenda for this meeting. One that served his singular artistic vision. He used the weekly meeting as rehearsal time for his play-within-a-play.

John looked around the room at the faces of the meditating men as he ruminated. They've come here this afternoon to tell the truth. But it's a fine, fat, false version of the irrefutable they're pedalling. They push a chubby, clueless boy to the front of the room and proclaim him warrior king and emperor while he plays with the ruffles on his shirt. The old emperor is dead, and the job needs filling, but this child is not the ruthless calculating killer that the empire requires. They live in the hope that he might grow into the job.

John's artistic vision was to accomplish in the hereafter that which he had been unable to bring forth in life. Bad breaks and ruthless rivals had undone him. He fancied himself a virus. The ultimate predator. Forever floating between life and death. A cunning, ruthless agent intent on inserting himself back into being, in order to supplant reality and undo death. A force capable of straddling every line ever drawn. Something immoral and immortal that showed shabby humanity the awful truth about itself. They wanted the truth, did they? Very well. He would give it to them.

He wanted his new character to deliver his instructions to the men dressed as a ringmaster but so far, he had failed to obtain a top hat. He knew that the opening he had in mind would be so much more dramatic if he could begin by pulling back a handkerchief to reveal and release a dove from a champagne glass. No way to bring that about so far.

He stood quietly and allowed his thoughts to inform his character before he turned to address the men in a blistering parody of Greg's instructions. "Addiction is the art of misdirection. Those who want to continue to drink have to distort reality in order to win arguments and maintain social and financial control. If you lose even one argument, that's the end of your dynasty. It's that simple. A bigger dog should always shoulder a smaller one away from the kill — but an aggressive dog is another matter."

He struck a thoughtful pose. "It's hard to justify buying a case of beer when the kids are hungry, but it's not impossible. It calls for a judicious application of truth. Some yelling to put the opposition on the defensive, a few thematically appropriate threats, lots of blaming and shaming, and the next thing you know you're sitting in your favourite chair with your feet up watching the game, while the kids get a good meal, and mom gets a shoulder to cry on at Aunt Sherri's. Truth telling is politics and abrasion. Our fear of losing the little moments of peace and connection in our lives makes us so vulnerable." He looked over at Greg as if to say, So there, chump.

"When the music stops a few of you are going to try quite unwisely to reinvent yourselves. You will take a lot of borrowed words and phrases that you have picked up during the week and try and cobble them into a philosophy. Greg would have you believe that it's no different from the free clothing line at the Good Shepherd: Drop the rag you're wearing onto the floor and put on something new. In my view that is a naive and altogether improper use of this resource.

"This time and space would be better used as a symposium on prevarication. Who doesn't love to lie? How many of you are here simply to wait out the heat of the day? There is no fooling me. I see what you get up to. I listen in on your calls. The ones you make on the phones that you're not supposed to have. I hear you talking to your dealers and drinking buddies and sly pieces on the side.

"Ask yourselves the fundamental question. If you know that you're going back on the sauce the minute you get the chance, why do all the stupid things that they want you to do in treatment? Tell the truth, clean house, and try to make it up to the people you hurt. No one who still has the big thirst is going do that." He paused and held up his forefinger as turned his head to the side and smiled. "But they might want to appear as if they had. That is why it is imperative that you develop a story that contains both Greg's 'Oh shit' and 'Say now' moments."

John was feeling big energy coming from the ringmaster. He left his chair and leapt onto the serving counter where he began to walk back and forth. "Then there is the tactical situation to be considered. The lynch mob has gathered. You're in the pillory — and in their power. Courts have oversight; wives and employers are watching; hell, everyone who has never known an hour's bliss has come to see you crawl. They would never admit it but that's what they want to see. Blood — yours and lots of it. They need that. They lost a lot of arguments that they should have won and now they want to see you pay through the nose. This is Dr. Schadenfreude's waiting room. He's booked you in for a double."

He took a count of twenty for dramatic effect. "Can I help you see the problem through veteran eyes? The role that misdirection must take in your life. This is where you learn to play the double game. This is Nixon's Checkers speech. Can you say the words, without faltering, that you need to say when hostile eyes are upon you? If you get enough practice, you can win the doubters over.

"You see, they want to believe; they need to believe; they're dying to believe — after all, they've waited so long. There's something so mind-numbingly satisfying about the sinner repenting or the prodigal son returning home. It tugs at the heart strings. But why? Because it says to the outraged and put upon — see you were right all along and who doesn't want to be right all along? It can overwhelm our sly side if we're not careful.

"A few guys here are beginning to understand. They know what the lynch mob wants to hear but it's hard to get it said without getting all red and flustered. You need to hone your skills in front of a live audience. This is where you learn to say the right thing when all the money is on the table. Get it right, and you get to have a good chuckle over a couple of drinks when you're done. Get it wrong and you'll be right back here with a black eye and a new court date in a month's time."

Chapter 32

Greg had a difficult choice to make. The meeting was off to a flying start. William's story was perfectly timed and right on the money. The unhappiest face in the group belonged to Enzo. He had been scowling and arguing with everyone since he got here. Greg didn't want to change the tone, but something told him that maybe, just maybe, Enzo might be ready to give this a try. Greg went over the empty chair and stood behind it for a second as he looked around the room. If Enzo bombed, he would go straight to Dusty the Postman, who always had something good to say.

"What about you, Enzo?"

RK nudged Arthur. "Pay attention to this fella. He'll have something interesting to say."

John walked behind Greg and rested his chin on his shoulder while he gave him a big smile and a hug. He didn't want to miss one moment of the Enzo show. He had big eyes for Enzo. He would be a lovely addition to the cast.

Enzo had been thinking about the worst day of his life. Bad things shouldn't happen to a guy who had worked around the clock. The first shift had been at regular time, the second at time and a half, but the third one was in a different truck and he was getting straight cash. He was still working for the same company, but this run was off the books. Provincial law said he was supposed to be home sleeping. According to the paperwork, a guy who retired three years ago was driving this rig. It was business.

The sun had come up and the morning promised to be clear and hot. There wasn't a cloud in the sky, and the world looked new and fresh on that fine June day. Enzo had been hauling lumber to a construction site in Pickering from the company's yard in Woodbridge. This load was definitely funny business. Even the paperwork was the wrong colour.

The amphetamines had helped pass the starlight hours, but they had worn off. That was a good thing. Enzo knew he was going to crash but he didn't care. He would have a pocket full of cash that his wife, Debbie, didn't know about and a weekend to put it to good use.

The rush hour was starting to build. Edgy drivers were on their way into work. Some damn thing up ahead had slowed the pace to a crawl. Enzo shook his head and advanced in low gear at a steady pace. He left an enormous distance between himself and the car ahead but, of course, the other drivers took advantage of this and zoomed into the space he created. Getting this baby rolling from a dead stop was hard work. It was so much easier if you could keep rolling.

The traffic paused, lost interest, and finally gave up altogether. Enzo saw the guy ahead of him get out of his car and start walking toward the trouble. He couldn't keep his eyes open. He shut them for an instant and felt a moment of blessed relief.

A blast from a car horn behind him jolted him back to consciousness. The traffic had started to move again. He lurched forward 500 metres at a snail's pace before all hope petered out again. Enzo was southbound on the 427-ramp heading for the eastbound 401. He turned on the traffic report, hoping to find out what was happening, but they were busy selling dignified cremations. He turned off the radio in disgust.

Without something to focus on, all the bills came due. He dozed off a second time, and this time he actually fell asleep. He was awakened by a large angry man with a beard who was pounding on his window. Enzo didn't want to talk to him. The fellow looked angry enough to throw a punch. Enzo didn't dare roll down the window. He waved meekly and put the truck in gear. The man hopped off the truck's step as the big machine began to roll.

Enzo kept watching the man in his rear-view mirror. The guy was furious. He was still standing in the middle of the highway, shaking his fist and making faces at him, as the other cars tried frantically to move around. In the heat and the traffic, everyone was getting crazy.

Enzo was glad that the traffic was moving. He didn't want to call attention to himself. He kept watching the guy in his mirror, trying to figure out what he was going to do next. If the guy called the cops, this could be bad. He was too tired to work out all the implications. He wanted to move. To get away from here. Get his money and get home to see his little honey. His foot pushed harder on the gas pedal than he intended.

He accelerated and was rounding the turn and making his decent on the ramp to the 401 when his attention was drawn from the side mirror to the sea of brake lights ahead of him. He jammed his foot hard on the brake pedal, but it was hopeless. He was going way too fast. A construction fence had obscured his view at the crucial moment. It was an optical illusion. A second before, the curve of the ramp had perfectly hidden the stopped cars; the way ahead had looked wide open to his blistered tormented eyes.

He instinctively slammed the cab into the concrete wall in the hope of coming to a stop, but he misjudged the speed and angle and ended up jackknifing. The cab rolled over onto the passenger side, and the heavy load behind him broke loose as the trailer mounted the cab. It wedged its way skyward and began raining lumber down on the highway below.

The sound of the crash went on forever. Enzo thought for sure he was going to be crushed. When the roar stopped, he took a quick survey. Everyone had gotten out of their cars and was milling around. He gathered up everything incriminating, including his drugs, and squeezed painfully out of the driver's side window. He ran for a mile along the side of the road until he got to Weston Road. He trotted up the off-ramp and, as luck would have it, he was able to hail a cab. He took the cab to Yorkdale where he got out, paid the driver in cash, phoned his boss from a payphone, and jumped on the GO Bus.

The westbound GO Bus passed the scene of the accident as it made its way west along the 401. Traffic was backed up for miles and there was lumber all over the road. There must have been a hundred vehicles with their lights flashing. Enzo looked out the window as if none of this had anything to do with him.

From the bus station, he went straight home and got into bed. He was going to get away with this. He wasn't supposed to be in that truck. He was supposed to be home asleep. Let them try to prove that it was him driving. He was so exhausted that he did sleep. The kids woke him up the way they always did when they got home from school. He turned on the news as he drank a coffee and discovered to his horror that the crash was the lead story. The accident had closed the highway for a whole day. There was an interview with his boss and some lawyers who said that the truck had been stolen. There was even a grainy video of him taken from behind, trotting along the side of the highway. He felt his heart pounding in his chest. Would they be able to tell it was him? When he saw the face of the angry bearded man come on the screen his heart broke.

Greg's disastrously timed question brought Enzo back into the room. "Enzo what was happening for you when you got caught?"

"I wasn't caught."

That got a rise out of the guys.

John smiled broadly. "This is what I'm talking about, fellas. This is how it's done."

"Please, fellas, that doesn't do any good." Greg looked over at Enzo and despaired. The poor man had his head down and his chin touched his chest. He was red in the face and talking to himself under his breath.

Before Greg could speak again, Enzo got to his feet and started to jab the air with his finger. "I'm here because of a bunch of liars!" He looked around the group, aching to see a friendly face. All he saw were heads shaking and eyes turned politely away. "Oh, so it's that way. Give it to Enzo. Yeah, well, join the line. I already have cops and wives and judges up my ass; a few more fools won't make any difference. You guys all need to be here. I get that part. You're pussies. I didn't do anything wrong. My boss and the insurance company needed someone to take the heat. That's why I'm here."

John stood on the empty chair and applauded his man. "What did I tell you! Crashin' 'n' drivin'! Shuckin' 'n' jivin'! That's what I'm talking about. Look them in the eye and say, 'Prove it!' It doesn't get any better than that! This boy is ready for court!"

Enzo dropped his eyes to the floor. The group vanished from his thoughts amid the familiar roar of disapproval, leaving him only with his memories. Tina from next door had met him at the smoke shop that afternoon. She looked hot in her pink tank top and short shorts. They pretended they had met by accident at the variety store, and he was giving her a ride home. The old guy behind the counter didn't seem to care one way or the other as he endlessly fed cash, tickets, and dreams into the lottery machine for a line of hopeful lottery losers.

Enzo drove Tina to the industrial plaza that housed the ZiggZagg. That's where all the action happened. They parked and rolled down the windows so they could hear trouble coming.

Enzo was gunfight scared. All afternoon he'd been waiting for a knock at the door. When it didn't come, he almost lost his mind. There was this pressure building up behind his eyes, the kind of desperation you feel in a hot-air balloon broken loose from its moorings.

He handed Tina the pipe and helped her take a big hit. She slumped in the front seat beside him. He fondled her breasts as he watched her eyes lose contact with the world for a minute. "How does that feel?" he asked. She didn't even know he was touching her. He lifted her onto his lap and pulled her tank top up around her neck. He undid her bra and threw it in the back seat. She let him touch her for a minute and then said, "Not here," as she pulled her tank top back down to cover herself.

As she smoothed out the wrinkles, he took a hit and felt all of his doubt and despair disappear. He would make short work of all those morons on Monday. They went to the motel on Airport Road, the cheap one where the TV doesn't work even if you put money in it, and they smoked the rest of the drugs. Tina left to get cigarettes and never came back. In a day or two, the cops did. The manager let them in. Enzo was too drunk to even stand up. Then there was jail, the hearing, and the final evening at home. Everyone sitting around the table. No one talking. Just sad eyes looking at him. The same eyes staring at him now.

Screw 'em all.

Chapter 33

Greg had gambled and lost. After the brilliant beginning made by William's story about the psych ward, Enzo's rancid denials had left a bomb crater in the middle of the room. The meeting was only ten minutes old, so he couldn't send them for a smoke. He thought about putting the music back on but that wouldn't work any better. He had to go to his bullpen. He looked around the room for a face that wasn't embarrassed, and he landed on Dusty the Postman. He gave Greg a little wink that said he knew what to do.

Dusty had a story that would turn things around. He let his thoughts wander back to the fiasco that had landed him here. He saw himself once again on the video, watching himself try to open the door to what he thought was his car. The real owner was startled to see someone trying to steal his wheels but, once he got a look at the state that Dusty was in, his mood lightened. The man gently took Dusty by the elbow and showed him which car was his.

"I got nailed fair and square. They got me on a cell phone camera. One more reason to hate those things." He was expecting a laugh but didn't get one. He realized that he had gotten ahead of himself. He needed to explain what had happened. "Look guys, I'm not going to candy coat this. I'm a postie. If you're not sitting in the pub at lunchtime with an empty mailbag, then there's something wrong with you. We work as hard as we have to and drink as much as we can."

The men all laughed. This is what they wanted to hear.

"You see … you're all laughing, so you know what we get up to. It was a Friday, and the mail volumes were unbelievably light. It happens in the summer. We had a real chance to finish early for a change. So while we're shooting out the door, one of the guys says we should all meet at the Army Navy Club for lunch. Shit, we're all there at twelve-thirty; done for the day and the weekend's coming up. Pure bliss. I hadn't been drinking for a while, so I didn't even bother to change out of my uniform. They were practically giving away chicken wings so we loaded up on them. Then we played some pool and I won, and someone bought me a beer. I didn't think that one would hurt. Next thing I know, it's five o'clock and I'm drunk and still wearing my uniform."

Dusty shifted in his chair. "That's a definite no-no. The other posties have all left. I'm pretty blasted, so I decide it's time to leave too. So I go out into the parking lot to get into my car. The problem is, it's a grey Toyota and there are a lot of them in the parking lot. So I try to open the door to my car but the problem is, it's not my car. The key fits but it won't turn. I'm so blasted, I'm slow to catch on. So I fiddle with it forever."

He smiled and shook his head. "What I don't know is that there are two postal supervisors from my station who got wind of where we were and what we were doing, and they came by to keep an eye on us. They got me on the cell phone camera. Anyway, after a couple of minutes of me stumbling around, the owner of the car comes out and we have a short conversation. He flicks my keys and lo and behold ... there's my car. So I thank him and go on my way. But I'm too drunk to drive. So I open the door and get inside and well ... I decide to have a little nap. I put the seat back and turn on the radio and roll down the window and the next thing you know I'm fast asleep. I figured I'd feel better when I woke up.

"But the next thing I know the cops are there poking me with a nightstick and I'm under arrest. Care and control of a motor vehicle. I'd forgotten to disconnect the battery. I was too drunk. I consoled myself while I was being booked with the thought that this wasn't too serious, there was no crash, no moving violation. I can explain it to the judge, how things took an unexpected turn, maybe make up a story about the brother-in-law coming to drive me home. I wasn't worried about the post office, but I should've been; they had me on a no drinking agreement. The famous last chance clause that I'm sure all you fellas are familiar with."

The men roared with laughter. They knew all about that piece of deviltry.

"I was grateful they hadn't blabbed to my boss. The cops played it straight. They never let on. But it was the post office supervisors who had called them. So on Monday I go back to work. I'm sorting my mail and keeping my mouth shut and my head down when I see the big union guys and zone manager start to show up. That always means someone is toast. So to make this short, they take me into the office and show me the video. There I am. Drunk and in uniform. Busted. They have a copy of the police report and a signed copy of my no drinking agreement. Even the union guys couldn't think of anything to say. What could anyone say!"

The guys chimed in with a rousing "Oh shit!"

William was fully enjoying the moment. He shouted over the laughter, "Maybe in this case it should've been *no* shit!"

Greg nudged Dusty gently. "How did you feel about what happened?"

Dusty's face was untroubled. "Look I'm not going to bullshit anyone in this room. Out there, bullshit works great, but not in here." That was for Enzo. But it wasn't a put-down, it was an offer of support. The only guy who missed it was Enzo. A couple of the guys looked over at him to take a reading, but he was still wrapped in the flames of rage.

"You guys know me as well as I know you," Dusty said. "Look, I'm all over the place. I'm here for my job, my wife is furious with me, I keep getting grief from my doctor. I know I have to quit drinking. But I still want to drink. Not always. But there are days. I don't know what to do with that. I'm hoping you're going to be patient with me. I can see how what we do here is working for some of you guys. I'm hoping that at some point it's going to work for me too."

Greg was feeling better about the meeting. Somehow Enzo's defiance had given the group some kind of unity. Maybe even purpose. It was fragile. He needed to make another good choice. As he looked around the room it was clear that Enzo had left the building in all but body. The new guys all looked a little perplexed but that was okay.

"Thank you for that, Dusty. I appreciate your honesty." Greg's eye landed on Arthur's old friend Andrew. It was funny that they weren't sitting together. No matter. He invited him to speak. "Andrew, what's happening with you? Say, you're going home tomorrow."

Andrew Medved had been fidgeting and trying to dry his palms on his blue jeans since the meeting began. He hated being the centre of attention. That had never once in his life gone well for him. But he was resolute. He was going to tell the truth this week if it killed him.

He was a rail-thin young man with a long, thoughtful-looking face. He was tall, but there was no heft to him. His body language said awkward, preoccupied, and self-absorbed. The kind of teen who needed a hug so badly that they were bleeding inside. Andrew had an inner calm when he was alone that failed him when other people were around. It was one thing to grow up without a father. It was quite another thing to grow up with a madman living in the basement. But to have everyone know about it and use that as the basis for rejecting him, was Andrew's special torment.

Arthur was suddenly afraid when it was Andrew's turn to speak. He didn't know why. He hadn't worked it out yet. He would in time. Andrew was a threat. A witness to events. One of his early victims. Lying about the past was going to be much more difficult with him in the room.

Arthur had been trained since elementary school to cultivate people who could advance his career. He hung with the cool kids as a matter of right. That left Andrew out. Now a second barrier had arisen. Andrew had taken to telling the truth. Twice rejected, Andrew was now a dangerous loose end.

"This is hard," said the badly stressed young man as he looked around the circle for a friendly face. The guys liked Andrew and they wanted to see him do well. They were all listening and giving him gentle, silent encouragement. Their looks said, *You can tell us.* It was the kind of support that Enzo didn't know how to ask for.

Andrew was so gratified by the men's response that his words got jammed and he first laughed and then had a coughing fit. No one said a word. They waited patiently until he found his voice.

"Last week I chickened out. I thought if I did a one-on-one with a counsellor it would be easier. Wrong. Reg and I had a long talk and he told me I had to tell you guys the truth this afternoon. My drugs are pot and ecstasy. You older guys probably don't know much about ecstasy. It doesn't land me in the same kind of trouble that your booze and cocaine do. People don't often die from taking this stuff, but they do ruin their lives. I've seen that myself. A lot of time can pass between the knowing and the going."

His words were coming from a deep well and the fidgeting stopped. There was power in his voice. "There was no big dramatic thing. No drug bust. No overdose. What I do know is, I can't go home anymore." He sighed and took out a letter.

"My dad is an alcoholic. Worse than anybody in this room. For as long as I can remember he's been a big, fat, dirty lump sleeping on a cot in the basement. Mom won't let him come upstairs. We would hear him down there, tearing the hell out of the place at night when we were kids. Yelling at ghosts and telling off the dead. He scared the hell out of me. I would jam my eyes shut and pray that he wouldn't come upstairs and kill us.

"My sister Karen hates him, and she hates living at home. She goes out with this big dumb prick named Herbert. She feels safe with him, but everyone in the world — everybody that is but her — knows that he's a bum. My mom doesn't function anymore. She looks shell-shocked. She sits in her chair and rocks, watching her shows on TV until it's time to put on dinner." His head went down.

"I swore to her that I would never drink." He blew out a lungful of hot choking air. "You guys can see why. But I thought it would be okay if I did pot and ecstasy. And at first it was great. I'd go to these raves and I'd feel absolutely amazing. And there were girls and they were all hot and sexy. We'd dance until the sun came up.

"But you can only do the ecstasy once a week. If you do it more than that, it doesn't work very well. So the other days I would smoke pot. I ended up taking a summer job after high school. It was a great job. I was driving the auto-parts pickup truck. I loved it. But at the end of the summer, I still didn't have enough money for tuition, so I decided to take a year off and work. That was the ticket. I had time to study, and the bankbook kept getting fatter, and it was nice to have a job and be responsible. My mom was so proud, but then the dealership closed. One of the managers was stealing. You got it: He was using the powder."

There was a change in Andrew. He was telling a familiar story, one that he had told before, but this time it was different. He was listening to his own words in public, not inside his head. His words were being respected. He felt positive energy and encouragement coming from the men around him. These guys were honest. They could talk about themselves and not feel the need to lie. They accepted themselves for what they were and hitched their hopes to what they might become. For a second Andrew dared to hope too.

"I got unemployment for a while and so I wasn't worried. Until the day came when I woke up and I didn't know what day it was. How could I? Every day was the same. Get up at eleven. Smoke a joint. Listen to music. Eat. Smoke a joint. I wasn't studying. I wasn't looking for work. I hadn't even applied to a school or for a student loan. Where the hell had the time gone? No wonder my mom was rocking harder in her chair." He hung his head in sorrow. That was too tough a hurdle to get over.

The guys all gently intoned, "Oh shit." But even that didn't restore his energy. His feet were hopelessly tangled in a past that was as hateful as barbed wire.

Greg prompted his young charge, hoping he could take the battle one step further. "Can you read them the letter?"

Andrew couldn't look up, he tried, but he couldn't sustain it. "No ... I can't do that."

"Do you want me to?"

"Yes, let's do it that way ... I couldn't ... not in front of everyone."

Greg took centre stage and took a minute to open the letter and find the paragraphs that he wanted to read. "This is from Andrew's mom, Rose. Andrew shared the letter earlier with me. I'm not going to read all of it. But here is the part I want to read."

Andrew could see his mother sitting in her spot at the kitchen table writing this out and agonizing over the words. He choked.

"Your dad has been sick for as long as you can remember. You never saw him when he was well. Karen might remember it a little bit, but she was pretty young then too. That was when we all lived in Montreal. We never told you what happened. We didn't want you to know. Your dad had a store. He was in the plumbing business.

"We were doing all right. He worked hard and he made a surprisingly good living. We were happy. My brother Murray, who you never met, did the books for your dad. But he was a gambler. He started keeping two sets of books. Murray was stealing from the business.

"He stole so much that the suppliers cut us off. Murray panicked. One night there was a fire. The business burned. Murray got caught at the scene with his pants half burned off. The only bill that had been paid in the last six months was the fire insurance. Probably your dad could have lived with that. But there was a young family living over top of the store. Your dad had rented them the room that afternoon. Murray didn't know they were there. At least that's what he said at the trial."

The men in the circle were awestruck. Even Enzo was listening. *How the hell would that feel? To be his father. Sitting there in court. Guilty of nothing but having faith in the wrong guy.*

"They died in the blaze. The newspapers were howling for blood. No one helped us. No one believed us. We lost everything. After that, your dad was never the same. The man I loved vanished. They put him in prison for a couple of months and then they had to send him to the hospital. They gave him shocks and pills. They'd send him home, but it was hopeless. He didn't have a home anymore. He had a wild look in his eye, then he'd break something and he would crawl inside himself and try to die. He got better and then worse. Finally, they gave him a small pension and sent him home. That's when the drinking started.

"You kids were starting to know who you were and look forward to school. We moved to Toronto, to get away from the past. I'd grown up here and the story hadn't made it this far. Your dad tried to get a job, but he would start to shake and sometimes he would even cry for no reason. He kept getting let go.

"After a couple of years of this, I knew he wasn't coming back. He got violent a couple of times and that's when I banished him to the basement and nailed the door shut. He didn't ask for what he got. I couldn't leave him in that state, but I had to protect you and Karen. So I stayed and did the best I could. I couldn't save your father, but I thought I could save you. But then you started to use drugs."

That line tore Andrew's flesh. He instinctively drew in a breath waiting for a heavier blow to fall. Arthur was horrified. He didn't know anything about this.

"At first, I thought it was an age thing. When you didn't go to university right away, I had to agree that it wasn't your fault that I couldn't afford to send you. It was only going to be a year and of course you were working. But then you didn't go back to school the following year and you stopped working and looking for work and studying, and the next thing I knew, when I talked to you, I had this eerie feeling that I was talking to your father. The thing that made my life bearable was the hope that you and Karen were really going to do something with your lives. Now everything is coming apart. Your dad has lung cancer and he's in palliative care at St. Joe's. He doesn't have long to go. I'm getting out of here. I can't live in this house for even one more day.

"Karen and Herbert are going to be married this spring. So that pretty much leaves you on your own. Andrew, I love you, but if you ever want to see me again you need to get over this drug business once and for all. My brother Murray did the crime, but I ended up doing the time. I spent a whole lifetime watching your dad die for your sake. I can't do this anymore."

Chapter 34

On Monday morning, Reg met RK in the living room. It was too early for breakfast, and Reg was intrigued by a note that Greg had left about the Straight Up meeting. Arthur had been visibly moved by Andrew's story but had declined to speak when it was his turn. Reg wondered if he could find out which way the wind was blowing from his roommate. "RK, why don't you get a cup of coffee and join me in the office. I want to talk to you."

That sounded ominous to RK but he knew Reg wasn't the guy who handed out pink slips.

"What's up?"

"Nothing's up. I wanted to talk to you and see how you were doing."

"Oh good. I thought I was on somebody's list."

"How's your new roommate working out? Does he snore?"

"No, he's a nice young fella. Even his bedbugs say please and thank you."

"I'm glad to hear you say that. We deliberately put him in with you. You know that, right?"

"Somebody said something about me being a good influence on him. I find that a highly dubious prospect."

"It's not all that hard to be a good influence around here. Seriously, this kid doesn't know what he doesn't know, and we want to keep him alive until he figures out whether he wants to stay sober or not."

"Why do you think I could help him with that?"

"Because you care about people."

"Me? You think I care about people?"

Reg had to smile. "You're the only one in the world who doesn't know that about you."

On Monday morning, Paul Bethune and Kaiser were dispatched to speak with Enzo and Arthur. Their task was to find out which way the wind was blowing.

Kaiser needed a smoke and so Paul went with him to keep him company and give him a hard time.

Paul was a well-built man of forty. He had a thick mat of brown hair that was only now starting to show a little patch of grey around the temples. He saw right through Kaiser. He was actually quite fond of the resident bad boy. They both spoke the lingua franca of addiction, but when they were alone, they favoured the tell-the-truth-and-call-bullshit-when-you-hear-it world of twelve-step meetings. They were old school.

It was hard to say who would come out on top if the two men decided to brawl. Kaiser was taller and looked fleeter of foot, but Paul was solid. The kind of guy who would pause after taking your first punch to put away his glasses before he broke your leg. But Paul was never violent. No need. His sense of humour was his sabre. He observed people thoughtfully, explored their interests and perceptions carefully, and when they annoyed him called them on their nonsense unerringly. Kaiser called him the sniper. Apt description.

Kaiser sparked up a smoke. "So what did you do on the weekend?"

"I thought about you."

"What got you going on the subject of me?"

"Lily and I were speculating on your name."

"Oh … that again. Remind me, why do you care?"

"I don't. I just want to embarrass you and be the first one to be able to spell Rumpelstiltskin. Which, by the way, is Lily's guess. She has it in the pool."

"Lots of people only have one name."

"Showbiz types, thugs, tyrants, and mass murderers, but not you, my friend. No, you have a guilty secret. You're not defined by the single name. You're hiding behind one. That's where *Kaiser* is misleading. It suggests noble origins, royal authority, all kinds of things that you plainly lack."

"Can I shut you up by growing a man bun?"

"You have a fruity first name. I suspect it's either a girl's name — the two leading contenders are Liza and Billy — or, and this is my favourite theory, you have a ridiculous name that a drunken parent gave you. Viscous or Iditarod."

"Have you speculated about middle names yet?"

"No, but we'll get there, monoboy. But while I have you here I have to ask … what in the world are you going to say to angry Enzo?"

Kaiser shook his head. "The boss told me I have to spend some time with him. So that's what I'm going to do. I plan to ask him a question and then endure his abuse and accusations for a count of five hundred, and then I'll thank him for his time and find something more useful to do."

"Not even going to try?"

"Not today. Greg pushed him pretty hard in front of the group. He'll be days getting over that, if he ever does. I'm going to let him vent. What about you?"

"Arthur has had enough time to get comfortable. Who knows, maybe he's had enough time to start being honest."

"That's what I admire about you, Paul. You're a cockeyed optometrist."

Paul wanted to infiltrate Arthur's space rather than invade it. To prepare for the role, he took off his suit coat and rolled up his sleeves. It gave him a much more informal and relaxed appearance. He approached Arthur and led him upstairs to the reading room A quiet, beautifully decorated space that was designed for reading but which could serve other purposes equally well. "Arthur, you didn't say anything at the Straight Up meeting. Greg said you reminded him of a smuggler going through customs."

Arthur had a ton of energy for this topic. "That was awful. Why do you make us do that?"

"Doesn't your family talk around the dinner table?"

"Never. We all grab something to eat when we come through the door. After school is for homework, and homework is sacred. My dad hates unorganized time. That's what he calls it. What kind of idiot would want to hang around playing baseball with their friends when they could get shipped off to math and science camp instead?"

"Didn't you want to go?"

"I hated every minute of it. One summer, Mom and Dad both got sick at the same time. They had the flu. They were too sick to do anything but wear pyjamas all day and blow their noses. I got sent to stay with our Aunt Melba and her family for a week. Can you guess why they sent me? Well … can you? They didn't want me to get sick before I went to camp. That would have spoiled everything. Well, their plan backfired. Melba let me hang out in the garden, go for walks, and play Monopoly. I didn't want to go home. It was so cool to be able to do what I wanted to do when I wanted to do it."

"Did you tell your parents how you felt?"

"My mom heard what I said, and she and I kind of started to talk about it, but then my dad came into the room." Arthur remembered the look on his father's face. He couldn't make sense of it as a child because it was more than one thing. There was anger, that was a given, but there was also hurt and maybe some shame but mostly good old-fashioned puzzlement. His skin colour had changed in an instant, and his body language became wary and defensive. "He got really mad and shouted at both of us. He'd never gone that far before. Told me, as a kid he would've killed for the chances I was getting. So I told him he should quit his job and open a science camp if he felt that way."

"How did that go over?"

"He had a change of heart and chopped off one of his fingers. I have it here in a box. You want to see it?"

That explains a lot. Paul tried to look a little sad when he said, "It's hard when you tell them and they don't hear." Then he subtly changed gears. "You grew up with Andrew, didn't you?"

"We went to the same school and we knew each other from church. My dad told me to stay away from him. Now I know why."

"Andrew knows how to say what's bothering him."

"That was the worst part. That letter was horrible. I could never talk about my stuff the way he did and certainly not in front of a group."

"That's interesting. I would've thought you'd be good at that."

"Paul, I was the valedictorian in high school. I'm comfortable speaking in public and I speak very well in front of a crowd. But when I do, the content of what I'm saying is also completely public. What goes on in my private life stays private."

"I don't want to make this point a battleground, but what Andrew did yesterday is likely going to be the turning point in his life. Telling the truth is what stops an addiction."

"I thought you boys had it that God stops addictions."

"Do you ever pray?"

"No."

"You wear a silver cross around your neck."

"Vampires. You got to watch out for vampires."

"Would you pray if your brother Dale was dying?"

There was a pause. That almost got through his defences. *Even if I do, it's none of your business.* "Yeah, I would. But he'd still die. Prayer is something you do when you're trying not to piss your pants."

"So who is God for you?"

"The guy you try and cut a deal with when the canine unit shows up to search your car. Trust me — the colour of your socks matters more."

Paul smiled. "Who was it exactly who told you that you were bright enough to go to medical school?"

"Funny…"

"Would it be fair to say that you don't trust anyone."

"Certainly not you, but I do trust people, people who make sense to me, people who listen to me and try and understand me, the ones who are not crazy and who don't believe nonsense."

"I see. I didn't know that about you. So answer me this: When you got in trouble for the first time with the drugs — you know … when you realized that you had blundered into something destructive, maybe even something you couldn't control — which one of those people did you talk to about it?"

Arthur jumped to his feet. "I don't want to talk to you anymore."

Paul let him go. He had made his point. Watching Arthur take the stairs three at a time confirmed it for him.

Arthur was glad to find RK in their room. He flung himself down on his bed and groaned.

"You look a little down in the mouth," said RK, looking up from his novel.

"Paul had a go at me."

"What did he say?"

"He pretty much said that if I didn't start talking to them about my private stuff there was going to be trouble."

"Did he really say that?"

Arthur felt betrayed. "Don't you believe me?"

"I wasn't there of course, but Paul is one of the good ones. Seems kind of out of character. I'd expect that kind of shit from Reg or Kaiser."

It took a few minutes for Arthur's thoughts to coalesce. "RK, I'm never going to be able to talk about myself the way you do. When you tell stories, you take the most outrageous things you've ever done and you don't spare yourself, but somehow in the telling they become kind of warm and funny. Even the worst stuff you do seems like it's an extension of you. My shit is dark. It's shameful. There's no way to make a good story out of it."

RK put down his book. "We do things drunk that we can't live with sober. You haven't figured that part out yet. You're still afraid of what people think of you. You're running the wrong way around the track. When you don't tell people who you really are, they might be intrigued by you for a while, but before long, they get to seeing you as one more bullshitter. Did it ever occur to you that we might still like you, even if we knew everything there was to know about you?"

"Not in my world. Never. No way!"

"It's not everywhere in my world either, but there are spots and people I can go to and be real. There's not many, but there are some, and that's enough. This place is one of them."

"You make it sound like everything else they say around here. But what if there is no happy ending?"

"Being real doesn't mean you're going to get off easy. All the awful shit that happens to other people happens to us too. But if you don't believe in yourself, if you can't trust another person, you're going to be alone when the bad stuff does come down."

"RK, do you pray?"

"Is that what we've been talking about?"

———

At 7:00 p.m., the counsellor opened the front door and turned them all loose. The guys milled around the door trying to decide what to do. Then, like a flight of birds, they found their leader and their direction and took wing. Most of the guys went down to the corner for a coffee and a half hour of horseplay. Enzo hurried directly down Spadina toward the subway. He had an appointment. He blew through the entrance without paying his fare and headed down the escalator toward the coffee kiosk. Halfway down, Enzo's face lit up. Mad-dog was sitting on a bench looking impatient. He had a sour expression on his face that suggested he was on the way to the dentist for a painful extraction. "Why the hell are we meeting here?"

"I'm in treatment … I got eyes on me."

"Treatment? That shit doesn't work."

"Don't I know it."

"I got what you need right here. Do you have the money?"

"Maybe."

"What do you mean maybe? If I came down here for nothing, I'm gonna bash you."

Enzo had a full head of steam up. He spied the bank machine and took the virgin credit card he had hidden from Debbie out of the deepest recess of his wallet. He kissed it and stuck it in the machine. It worked. He pulled out two hundred dollars.

———

The first light of dawn broke in the east. A finger of pink smudged the black ink of night and turned the tinge of the buildings on Madison Avenue first to grey and then into orange. A shaft of morning angled through the stained glass of the huge oak door that guarded Punanai and pooled in a tear-shaped circle five feet inside the door. No one was stirring. The men were abed, and the night man, Maurice, was perfectly balanced in a swivel chair with his feet up on the desk. A small whirlwind circled fitfully around the edge of this lake of light. Like a match not quite up to the task of igniting kindling, it reddened the edges of the wood shavings for a second before it petered out. It was gone, but then it came again. This time it prospered. A very young girl in a summer dress stepped out of the whirlwind and into the solitude of the sleeping house. She moved through the living room and into the big office where she found John, with his back turned to her, sitting at the conference table and looking out the window at the wonderfully gnarled old maple tree. He was ranting and giving shapes to shadows that only he could see. She crept up behind him and stilled him by placing her middle and index fingers lightly over his temples. The effect was immediate. A small bright spot of sunlight appeared on his forehead just above his eyebrows. She leaned forward and spoke softly into his ear.

"A single tree in a field is always a glorious symmetrical creature. Its branches reach out to soak up the sun in an orderly and graceful sweep. It is a creature that does not know the horrors of crowding or shade. Sometimes an injury below ground damages a root and causes a branch to wither, but other branches are quick to rush into the space the sunlight graces. The patches restore the even finish of the tree. With the deft stroke of a painter's brush the blemish is hidden from the eye.

"Trees that grow up in a city full of buildings and shifting shadows are different. On a winter's afternoon, you can see their twisted frames, their perilous slopes and the certain disaster that gravity and erosion have in store for them. In June, when the canopy is full, you can't see the imperfections, the overreaching, or the peril. The leaves make it all seem graceful and eternal.

"Trees make the only choice they can. They follow the light. Accidents, injury, and competition are not on their horizon. They can't avoid what they do not comprehend. Light is life, and they send their leaves where the light is brightest. Branches twist and turn in their deeply entwined battles for life. Trunks angle backward and forward to find a fulcrum to leverage the pivoting limbs. Wooden sinews twist, first right and then left, as an opening disappears, or another opportunity arises. The history of hope and defeat, and reaching out again, is recorded in the gnarled, twisted, often self-contradictory careers of the limbs. Plants love symmetry, and geometry is their poetry, but sunlight is the lens that allows humankind to make sense of their choices."

John was asleep with his eyes still open. The first sleep he had experienced as a ghost. The first moment of peace in a very long time.

"Ah, my poor Prospero. How am I ever going to get you back to Naples?"

Part 2

Chapter 35

Andrew Medved had scored a bed at Baker House, just down the street from Punanai. The accommodation wasn't fancy, but it was clean and, most importantly, everyone in the house had to be sober. If you missed curfew or came home drunk, you were out. No exceptions. They wouldn't even let you back in to collect your toothbrush. If you came back the following morning, your estate would be neatly packed up for you on the table outside the big door. Most guys didn't bother. There were lots of clothes for free on the skids.

Andrew was travelling light these days. Two pairs of jeans: one blue, one black. A pair of brown Dockers. A red, heavily lined lumber jacket. A stack of Ts and four dress shirts, along with assorted boxers and socks. Not a designer label in sight.

Gail, who ran the place, had made him put his clean clothes in the dryer when he arrived. The staff at Baker House had a long association with, and a deep understanding of, the life cycle of the bedbug. They were having none of that jazz on their property.

From his new room he looked out over the heavily shaded backyards and dormant gardens. The lots in the neighbourhood were ridiculously small. Only enough room for a bed of flowers and a patio. The window in his room had a diagonal crack in the bottom right-hand corner that drew his eye. Someone had tried to fix the crack with an adhesive. It had discoloured and yellowed along most of its length. An unfortunate blue bottle fly was caught in the fissure. Not exactly a fly in amber, but a remarkably close modern example of the same principle. The poor little bastard had made it halfway out before he had become hopelessly mired in the adhesive.

You couldn't navigate the human world, but then neither can I.

Andrew felt sorry for the fly. He could see where he wanted to go but he couldn't get there. That one little hole was his only chance, and some idiot had filled it with glue. So there he was frozen forever with his nose in hope and his tail in failure.

Andrew made his way into the kitchen and brewed himself a cup of coffee. The other guys were all out during the day, so he had the whole place to himself.

He looked around and found a chair and a desk that would be perfect for studying.

Gail came bustling into the kitchen. "Andy, you're work ready, aren't you?"

"Yeah, I would love to get a job."

"The Handy Market down the street called a few minutes ago. One of our guys, who is unfortunately no longer with us, was doing casual labour for them. Have you ever worked in a supermarket?"

"No, but I'm strong and I learn fast."

"I'm not supposed to let you do this the first day you're here, but these things don't come up very often. Grab your coat and I'll walk you over there and introduce you."

Andrew was moved. "You'd do that for me?"

Gail had a big heart. "I'll pick up a few things while I'm there so you won't feel awkward, how's that?"

———

Rachael Dunning had come to see Andrew Medved on visiting day. They had known each other since childhood. For Rachael this was a duty call. She knew that she would eventually bump into Andrew at church, or else on the street, and that it would be awkward if she hadn't come to see him. She really did want to support him after all the horrible things his family had been through — especially in the last month. The real connection was between her mom and Andrew's mother. They had been at school together. Andrew was an acquaintance. She didn't feel close to him. She would have frowned had she known that he had repeatedly bragged to the guys that she was his girlfriend. When Mike told her politely that Andrew had gone off to transitional housing that morning, she took the news in stride.

Arthur was sitting in the living room reading the paper when he looked up and saw Rachael. He hadn't seen her since the graduation dance at North Toronto. He felt a rush of joy rattle through his frame, and then he pulled the newspaper up over his face. *What is she doing here?*

Arthur had paid scant attention to Rachael in high school. Back then she was one of the cool kids who did drugs, so he had no time for her. But now, today, feeling the way he did, he wanted to revisit that decision. The light beckoned and he was drawn. Mike was no fool and he was keeping an eye on things. When Rachael asked to use the visitors' room before she left, Mike deferentially showed her the way. When she disappeared around the corner, Arthur tugged on Mike's sleeve. "I'm going for a coffee; do you want one?"

Mike looked both ways. "That's against the rules, so make it a large double-double." He had a prepaid Tim Card in his shirt pocket that he handed to Arthur.

Arthur walked down to the corner so that he could be out of Mike's line of sight. His brain was spinning furiously trying to come up with a way of approaching Rachael. There was no cool way to do this. He decided to sit on the stone wall at the corner and say hello as she passed. She was only a minute behind him. No time to work out the details of a story. In desperation he tried the truth.

"Rachael … it's me, Arthur."

She looked up from her phone and gave him a smile. "What are you doing here? Are you on campus?"

"Did you come to see Andrew?"

That insight gave the whole game away.

"You're there too?"

"I'm afraid so. I had to bushwhack you this way because Mike would freak if he knew I was talking to a pretty girl, especially one who came to visit Andrew. But I couldn't resist the temptation. I wanted to talk to you."

Rachael was still sorting through the high school version of Arthur. "But you don't even smoke dope. I thought you were going to be a doctor."

The door to the old hustle had opened up once again, but this time Arthur didn't let Doc step through. He took a breath, smiled, and turned on his innate charm. "No, I completely blew that chance." He could tell Rachael was surprised. "I wasn't sure that I wanted to do it, and when I got away from home for the first time I got scared. Then I started to do some drugs and the next thing I know the term is over and I haven't gone to any classes."

Rachael was stunned. This was the last thing she ever expected to hear from the superstar. "Is that why you're here?"

"Pretty much. My parents are yanking back the power. I'm on a short leash these days." His face softened and he looked in her eyes. "They're scared."

Rachael looked ready to bolt and that put Arthur into a full-blown panic. He started to talk very quickly. "But this is a bump in the road. I'm not an addict or anything. This is a prank gone bad. A year from now, no one will even know it happened." He desperately wanted to avoid talking about himself. "So how about you? What are you doing these days?"

Rachael could hardly miss his rawness. "I'm studying film at Ryerson. My class finishes early on Saturday and my mom asked me to come over and visit with Andrew."

The subject of Andrew was of no interest. "What kind of film are you studying?"

"Everything. It's so cool to be in a class full of other nerds. Everyone there is smart, and they all work hard and love what they're doing. It's so amazing. Film is like nothing else. It consumes you. And it's madness. Everyone has a project and the only way to get things done is to swap favours. One day you operate the sound, the next day you're an extra, and the day after that you edit. I live for this. It's a dream come true. No money yet, but if I wanted that I would've gone to work on Bay Street."

Arthur was enthralled, completely caught up in her energy. When she talked about film, the whole world changed. He wanted some of that. He needed her to keep talking forever. "What are you going to do when you graduate?"

She smiled and shook her head. "Who knows! That's years in the future. For now, I'm out on my own and doing what I want to do for the first time."

A cozy domestic scene was beginning to take shape in his head. "And you have your own place?"

That line was pushing it. Especially coming from a guy who used to ignore her and who was now in a treatment centre. "Sort of. My mom lost the argument about me staying in the residence but she makes me come home on the weekends. I suppose it's best. I miss my family. But all the parties are on the weekend, and I miss a lot of the fun. But it's only for this year. Next year I'm going to share an apartment with two of the girls."

Arthur wondered if his idea of fun could exist in her world. "I'm not going to be here forever. Maybe I could come and hang out with you sometime?" Arthur cringed when his voice lost its power on the final two words.

"Let's do that. Let me give you my number."

Arthur started to write it on his arm. Rachael gave him a quizzical look.

"They have my phone in the office. I'm living in the nineteenth century until next week."

"Nineteenth century?"

"No phone, no TV, bacon and eggs for breakfast seven days a week, and we go to church twice on Sunday. Oh yeah, and we talk a lot about horses."

Rachael laughed and the world tilted on its axis from winter back toward spring.

Arthur looked up to see Mike walking slowly down the block. He had spotted Romeo and Juliet from his perch on the sun porch. "I think we're done here. Mike's going to yell at me for talking to you."

"Do you want me to explain things?"

"No, that'll make it worse." *He'll fall in love with you too.* He looked deeply into her eyes. "Call me. I really want to see you again."

She laughed and began to walk toward Bloor Street. *Oh how a kiss would have sealed the deal.*

Mike was calm. He sat down next to Arthur on the stone wall. He saw the eternal triangle in the young lover's face. "You said you wanted a coffee, not to hit on Andrew's girlfriend."

"I'm sorry, Mike. I went to high school with her. I couldn't let her go. I had to talk to her."

"Telling lies is not the way to do it. Arthur — I wrote the book on chasing girls. Don't try to Bullwinkle me. Button up your fly. If you start obsessing about girls, you'll be obsessing about girls and cocaine before the sun goes down. So here's what we're going to do. You're going to go and get me that coffee, and while you do that, I'm going to put you on toilet duty. That'll give you something positive to think about."

"What's positive about cleaning toilets?"

"It's a problem that can be solved. That's a rare thing in this life. To be able to do something simple, perfectly. I take such good care of you. You should think about leaving me a big tip when you leave. Now go get that coffee."

Mike shook his head. Arthur would have plenty of time for romance. He would get his chance. Mike watched him go. *Kids, what can you say? They work so hard at messing this up.*

Chapter 36

Rachael put the kettle on for a pot of tea. The other girls were out, and she had the kitchen to herself. It was nice to be alone with her thoughts for a few minutes. *Well, that was certainly a surprise! Not about Andrew — he was doomed from the start. Everyone knew that. Dropping out and driving that truck. No, that's not right. He wasn't always that way. Back in junior high he was the star, not Arthur. He was nice back then. He always tried to make me laugh. I liked that about him. But after a while, the drugs made him so dark and depressed. All wrapped up in himself. So secretive. It was just so much easier to stay out of his way. I don't want to be around anyone like that.*

Now Arthur is headfirst into it. How did that happen? Arthur swam in a different pool than Andrew. He had some life to him. The smartest kid in high school and not hard to look at, either. He always dressed in that cool and edgy way of his. Neat but defiant. Maybe not such a big surprise that he screwed up. What does he know about life? His parents turned him into a study monster.

She smiled when she remembered how vulnerable he looked when he asked her out. She could get used to that. Him chasing her. The more she thought about it the clearer the picture became. It was only natural for him to kick up his heels once he got free. She felt deeply for him getting busted and locked up. How humiliating.

But he had found the courage and an ingenious way to talk to her, and he had told her the truth. He said he wasn't like the other guys. She could see that. From what she had seen, they were more like Andrew; all of them pretty far gone and maybe even a little bit creepy. Arthur was a guy who could really go places. She felt good about herself. The thought struck her that this made her the prom queen, even if it was six months after the dance.

There was a message waiting for Rachael on her landline when she got back from the kitchen with her pot of tea. It was from Arthur.

"I know I just talked to you, but … I don't know, I had such a good time seeing you again. Well, it brought up all kinds of good feelings I haven't had for a while and I wanted to call and say thank you." You could see Rachael softening around the eyes. She started to sway ever so slightly as she wrapped her index finger with the phone cord.

"Mike was so pissed with me for talking to you, he put me on toilets. He told me I could meditate while I did them. 'Very zen,' he said. I don't think he knows much about Buddhism." There was a pause that was more horrible for him than her.

"Could we meet up at the Second Cup at Spadina and Bloor at say seven? I'd be breaking some more rules, but I gotta tell you, I haven't felt this real and alive in a long time. I don't care if Mike makes me tar the roof barefoot. I need to talk to you again.

"So I'll wait for you at the coffee shop and hope that you decide to come. But even if you don't show up, the sheer possibility that you might is giving me some hope, and that is making this a very good day for me." The answering machine beeped to tell him he was out of time.

Arthur felt a warm sense of well-being. He didn't want to put the phone down. He hung on to it, still feeling a connection to Rachael. One of the new guys in the house was glaring at him. He wanted to use the phone. Arthur smiled at him and offered him the receiver. The new guy looked at him suspiciously. Arthur, still smiling, hung up the phone, and bounded up the stairs to his room.

RK was doing his calisthenics when Arthur entered the room at a gallop. He flung himself into the air landing with a thud on the bed. The floorboards rocked.

"I'm in love."

RK couldn't resist. "Who's the lucky fella?"

"You're ruining the moment for me."

"Well, I walked through the whole house an hour ago and the only female I saw was the cook, and she has three grandkids so, pray tell, my young friend. Where are you hiding her?"

"Her name is Rachael, and she's the most wonderful girl in the world."

"Where did you meet her?"

"Downstairs. She was here to visit Andrew Medved."

"Oh, so you claimed a filly, never a bad move. How does Andrew feel about this?"

"He's a Leafs fan. He's used to a lot of disappointment. This will give him something else to talk about in group."

It took RK a moment to put a name to the face. "Wait a minute. Andrew is the young fella with the letter."

Arthur wanted to really go places with this idea, and he felt kind of brought up abruptly, having to stop and answer RK's questions. None of this trivial stuff mattered. He was in love.

"I'm meeting her tonight."

RK could see now why they had put him in the same room as Arthur. This kid was a little impulsive. "You think this is a good idea? Your last girlfriend didn't work out too well."

"RK, that was different. Besides, all we're going to do is have a cup of coffee."

"Let me tell you something about yourself that you don't know, Arthur. If you were my age, I'd believe you. But you're a young buck, and no cup of coffee, no matter how good, is going to scratch the itch you're feeling. But let me ask you one question: This girl, does she go to meetings?"

Arthur looked at him for a second. He knew she used to do a lot of drugs in high school, but he had no idea if she used anything now. It hadn't come up. But he was fairly sure she didn't go to meetings.

"That awful silence hanging over that question tells me either you don't know, which is pretty bad, or you don't care, which is even worse. Well, the first thing you do when you claim a filly is to run her by the vet. I'll have a look at her tonight and tell you what I think."

"You're going to ruin this for me."

"No, you're going to ruin this for you. You're no judge of horse flesh. Your last filly broke down in the stretch when the serious running started. But let me give you a choice. It goes without saying that you're taking a chaperone on this date. The only question is this: Do you want to take me or Mike?"

"You are not going to sit at the table with us."

"Nope. I'll be reading a newspaper nearby. You won't even know I'm there."

"You're going to love her."

Arthur bounded out of bed and grabbed his shaving kit. He headed off to the showers.

Two showers in one day. This kid really does have the bit between his teeth.

Chapter 37

Arthur was desolate without his cell phone. How was he supposed to reach out to his new life on a house phone that wouldn't take incoming calls? It was so frustrating, trying to sound cool and in control without the technology to back that up. On a whim he decided to call Eric to tell him the good news about Rachael.

"Arthur, how you doing?"

"I'm all right. I'm staying at a dude ranch."

"In Toronto?"

"It's a very *in* joke … it's good to hear a sane voice. How are you doing?"

"I'm doing all right for an aging sinner. They still have me in the detox, but I can't stay here much longer."

"They going to throw you out?"

"Well yeah, they're counting up the days, but that's not the major malfunction. You remember I told you about the night I got thumped?"

"Yeah, I remember the story."

"A couple of guys from the college came by to visit me this afternoon. At first, I was really glad to see them. But they didn't really care how I was doing. They wanted to know what happened to their money. They're taking the attitude that the money they gave me has to be repaid. They didn't feel I'd done the right thing by them. Apparently, I violated their trust."

"Dude, you almost died."

"Almost isn't good enough. I'm not really too concerned with those chicken shits. Them I can handle. But after I told them I couldn't pay, they phoned me back and told me they'd sold the debt to some bikers. Them I can't handle. So I'm going on a low-profile tour of the new frontier. I thought Alberta might be better for my health."

"How much do you owe?"

"They want five thousand."

"But, you only had two."

"The vig and the nut. These new guys are charging interest. I can't pay the vigorish, let alone the nut, so I have to go."

"Eric, would they take drugs instead of money?"

"You know they would."

"Do you remember me telling you about Linda?"

"The unbelievably beautiful and crazy older woman who screwed you until you started to stutter?"

He dropped his voice. "Sh-Sh-Sh-She has a stash."

Eric was a little shocked. "Dude, that's cold."

Arthur looked around to make sure that no one was in earshot. "No, you need to understand. When I was at her place last time, I looked around to see what happened to her drugs. She has a Japanese box she keeps them in. She bought a shitload of cocaine the night before her doctor put her in the hospital. I don't know if there's five grand, but there's something pretty close to that."

"But she's your girlfriend. She'll know it was you."

Oh crap, how the hell am I going to tell him about Rachael?

"No, she's out of it. Look, I didn't tell you the whole story." There was a pause. This didn't feel right. This was Linda they were talking about. But now there was Rachael to be considered and this new problem with the bikers. He wanted to do the right thing, but then it all started to run together in his mind.

I can figure this out. Just one thing at a time here.

"She doesn't remember me or what we had together. She's in a psych ward, and the last thing in the world she needs right now is to come home and find enough cocaine to get her a federal address for a couple of years."

"Tell me more…"

"Getting there is no problem. We can hop on the bus. The problem is, I gave her father my key, and for sure he's changed the door code by now."

"Well, if it's a vacant house I can get us in there real easy."

"There's an alarm system."

"Dude, dopers growing up in Woodbridge know more about alarms than the guys who work on them. You smoke dope with the right people, you find out things you shouldn't know. Life is all about learning. Capiche? Alarms are designed to keep the suckers feeling safe. They don't actually work."

———

Mike did his hourly walk through of the house. It was almost 7:00 p.m. and he needed to chase the guys out the front door to their meetings. They got stale very quickly when they were confined to the barracks and it was good for them to go down to the corner as a group and hang out and have some fun. It took them back to a simpler time in their lives, a time when it was possible to have fun without taking drugs.

When Mike opened the door to the third floor, he was struck with an overpowering cacophony of conflicting and competing men's grooming products that had combined and refined each other until they greeted his nose with a mad rush of sensation. This scent was a new creation, the result of a hundred random variables coming together — it might never be experienced again in his lifetime. Mike had smelled its forbearers, and as he inhaled the stewing, boiling vapours, he shook his head and smiled. "Someone is in love, and he stinks real good."

Chapter 38

The Second Cup on Bloor Street was an astute choice for a chance encounter. It was a very public space where people came and went at all hours. Who could say, without fear of contradiction, that two young people who both resided in the neighbourhood hadn't happily bumped into each other here by accident?

When Mike unlocked the big oaken front door at 7:00 p.m., Arthur bolted. Mike watched him sprint down Madison Ave. It took all of two seconds for Mike to work out who he was going to see. He let it go. Arthur was finished this week.

After a two-minute-and-twelve-second quarter mile, Arthur was fogging up the plate glass window of the Second Cup. If he had known for sure Rachael was going to be there early, he would have taken a chance and snuck out the side door ahead of the mob. But the precious moments with his lady that he had hoped that his speed could buy came to nothing. She wasn't there. Her absence was felt as a kind of sadness and self-hatred. Why should she bother with him? He had no chance, he was dreaming. A minute of *she is not coming* changed the focus of the day from triumph to tragedy.

He furiously began to run a series of plausible explanations through his head. *Maybe she didn't get her messages. She didn't actually agree to meet me. Maybe she has a date — no don't go there. Maybe her mom is dying.* That felt better in a twisted way. *Late, that has to be it. She's running late.* It wasn't cool to show up at a dead run for a lovers' meeting the way he had. She was cool. She would make an entrance.

But then another agonizing minute passed. RK finally caught up and led the distraught Arthur into the coffee shop. This horse needed schooling.

"We can still have a brew even if she is a no-show."

RK selected a table for the two of them and then joined the line-up for coffee. He could see the dramatic possibilities of the evening playing out on Arthur's face as he went rapidly from joy to despair, and back again, every time the front door opened.

RK made it to the front of the line but his mind was still on Arthur. *If I saw a horse look at me that way at race time, I'd book off my mounts for the rest of the day. That's crazy looking for a place to happen. This colt is going to be a puddle if his filly doesn't show.*

RK was trying to think of something soothing to say when Arthur's face abruptly lit up. He was on his feet and moving toward the front door in a second. Rachael was looking very smart. She was wearing jeans and high boots and a navy peacoat, all set off by a knitted wool hat and scarf. She was an original. From his perch RK could see that he was not going to be needed. This girl was no druggie. Her eyes were clear, and they sparkled when she smiled. Her hair was fashionably cut and looked strong and healthy. The young couple made a handsome pair.

Someone had discarded the *Hockey News* at the next table and RK slid over to take possession of both the table and the tabloid. He figured he had half an hour to kill before it was time to make their way to the meeting. There were two other guys from treatment in the coffee shop and they were watching Arthur with great interest, but RK shot them a conspiratorial look. Any conversations about what was happening would be strictly limited to the smoking deck. This was highly classified.

Arthur was smiling and bouncing in his chair. So much for cool. "I was so afraid you wouldn't come."

"I had to leave the workshop half an hour early to get here."

"Oh no…"

"Well I knew you'd be suicidal if I was late. Not having a phone really makes this difficult."

"Do you want a coffee?"

"No, I'm coffeed out. Maybe a soft drink."

They took their place in the line. Arthur wanted to throw his arms around her and had to fight the impulse to do so.

"So what's up … you left a really intriguing message."

"I'm missing a word to describe what's happening for me."

"When that happens, I keep talking until it all comes clear to me. Words are the most magical little nanoprobes. They gather up all the loose ends of feelings and impressions and knit them into something useful."

"I'm not sure I follow you."

"Tell me what you're feeling and then let's see if we can pair it with something that's going on in your life."

Arthur knew that it would have been much smarter to let Rachael speak first, but he couldn't contain himself. His dopamine was running the show.

"I couldn't believe my eyes. There I was sitting in the living room reading a newspaper and when I looked up there you were. The sunshine blinded you.

Everyone who comes through that door stands in that spot until their eyes get used to the light. I knew that while I could see you, you couldn't see me. I watched you take off your sunglasses and check your phone. You had this peaceful look on your face. The way the sun puddled at your feet made you look like an icon. I had this feeling you were going to be someone huge in my life. That we were connected somehow. I wanted to jump to my feet and run to you, when suddenly I was filled with the most awful sense of being a fraud. I pulled the newspaper up in front of my face and hid from you. That's crazy, isn't it?"

They reached the counter and got the soft drink. Rachael's unspoken thoughts transcended the silence. They made their way to the table where Arthur's coffee and coat were holding a place for them. Once they settled, he looked into her eyes. The words kept coming. He couldn't hold them back.

"Rachael, I don't know what's real anymore. My whole life, people have told me who I am and what I'm supposed to feel. I went along with it. I trusted them. But when the time came to stop talking about it and start doing it, I was empty. I didn't know what I wanted but I knew what I didn't want. So I did something unforgivable, something so bad that they could never take me back. That was a good move. I felt alive for the first time in my life. Now here's the weird part. All of those great feelings and possibilities are coalescing around you."

Just inside earshot RK was cringing. *A broken-down quarter horse running in the Preakness has a better shot than you do, son. Slow down!*

RK and Rachael were of one mind. "You didn't date much in high school, did you?"

"No, I studied all the time."

"You missed a lot."

Arthur owned up. "Did that sound as awful to you as it did to me?"

"It was honest and kind of adorable, but Arthur … you're talking smack."

"I know, I have these feelings inside me and they're coming from someplace that's special and kind of sacred, but I can't ever seem to get them to make sense in the real world. It's all still kind of elusive and shadowy when I need it to be real. When I try to talk about them, my words get all messed up. I sound idiotic and I can't stop talking. Maybe this wasn't such a good idea."

Suddenly Rachael's eyes lit up in a moment of inspiration. "Well, this sucks as a romance, but it might make a good documentary."

"A film?"

As she started to work out the intriguing puzzle of how to do this, her energy spiked. She looked at Arthur as if she were seeing him for the first time. She reached across the table and caught his chin between her thumb and index finger. She turned his head ever so slowly to the right. "I always want to make a film. That's how I make sense of the world. Turn on the camera and let the story tell itself. It always does. Voices and points of view you never even suspected of existing make their way to the surface, if you give them a little time and a bit of a push. No documentary ever ends up telling the story it set out to tell. It's always something better." She reached into her handbag and extracted a notebook. She began to scribble feverishly into it while she spoke. "Have you ever wanted to do a film?"

It was fortunate for Arthur that Rachael was writing her inspirational thoughts in her scribbler. The innocent question she had asked was full of dark and sinister implications. Had Rachael been looking at him she couldn't have missed the look of deep shame that crossed his face. *What am I going to say about the video? Sooner or later, she's going to find out about Linda. About what we did.* Arthur took a severe pull on his coffee and burned his tongue.

Rachael looked up when he winced. "Are you all right? You look a little waxy."

From his duck blind behind the hockey news, RK was carefully following the conversation. RK was the master of pace, both on and off the racetrack. Arthur was running sprint fractions in a route race. He was going to propose before the coffee got cold. *Oh to be young again*, RK thought as he observed the young lovers from his perch. RK approved of Rachael. He could see that she really was something special. She was the kind of girl that Arthur should be chasing. He got to his feet and intruded on the conversation. "Good evening young lady, my name's RK and I have to drag this young fella off to a meeting."

Arthur was dumbstruck.

"Meeting…" said Rachael as she looked over at Arthur for a reaction.

Arthur's horror-stricken face was pleading with RK. *What are you doing? She doesn't need to know this stuff!*

RK soldiered on. "In treatment, we need to go to the meetings with someone and come back from the meetings with the same person. You can see how that's a good safety precaution. The meeting is around the corner. Why don't you walk us over there to make sure we get there safe?"

RK had a way of putting things.

Arthur and Rachael got dressed and headed out into the wintry night. They walked ahead while their minder hung back out of earshot.

"Is he your roommate?"

"He is until I smother him tonight with a pillow."

"What's wrong? He's sweet. He's obviously looking after you."

"I wish he hadn't talked to you about that. It made me feel awful."

"That strikes me as being both odd and interesting. I already knew you were in treatment. Why is this so embarrassing for you?"

Arthur tried to connect the pieces. She was right, why was he embarrassed? Suddenly his head was as empty as the Grand Canyon. He couldn't for the life of him remember what they had been talking about. It was something deep and deadly. Damn it … they had just been talking about it.

His uncertainty set off the torrent words again. "High school for me was all about pretending. Pretending to be real and grown-up and interesting. I think that they made me valedictorian to find out if I really had anything to say."

"Quickest way to expose a bullshitter … hand him a microphone."

"In the meetings, before I speak I have to stand up and say, 'My name is Arthur and I'm a drug addict.' The first time I said it … it was so horrible. Worse than any high school nightmare. The first time those words came out of my mouth, I felt this rush of red-hot blood to my face. The words physically hurt me. I was as embarrassed as if I had opened my valedictory address by saying, 'My mom picks my clothes and my dad picks my friends.'"

She had to laugh because that was so close to the truth. "So you're in a tough spot…"

"When I say, 'I'm a drug addict,' it confirms that voice I've been hearing all my life — do you know the one? The one that says, 'You're a phony.' Well, this meeting stuff confirms it. I am a loser now. I can see now why they tell us not to talk to women while we're in treatment. I feel so low right now. I kind of feel like using."

Rachael took his hand in hers and gave it a reassuring little squeeze. But it was the director in her and not the mother. "It's only a feeling, it's not destiny calling, it will pass."

Arthur beamed with satisfaction at the touch of her hand.

"But these meetings are private things, aren't they? That must help."

"No, this one is an open meeting. Anyone can come to one of these. The real nasty stuff gets talked about in the closed meetings. You have to be a self-confessed type to get into one of those."

"Will I get you in trouble if I come in and sit with you?"

"I don't care if they skin me alive, I'd love to have you with me."

They arrived at the front steps of the church. There were twenty people visiting and laughing outside, all of them smoking.

"You can always tell it's CA night," said Rachael as they edged their way through the crowd toward the door. The air was thick with the smell of tobacco and vaping.

"How's that?"

"The smoking. Christians don't stand outside a church and smoke."

RK caught up with them as they mounted the steps. "Really? What's wrong with them?"

As they entered the building, the night supervisor waved at Rachael.

Arthur looked at her quizzically. "How do you know him?"

She smiled her Mona Lisa smile. "This is my church."

RK poked him in the ribs. "The vet says this one wants to go long on the lawn."

Chapter 39

Arthur didn't hear a word that was said in the meeting. His focus was Rachael. What was she thinking, what was she feeling, how was she reacting to what was being said? Did she think he was as crazy as the rest of this bunch? Not knowing was painful. He daydreamed about being a pirate chained to the wall with a treasure map one inch beyond his reach.

He came to, painfully, as someone with a racking cough unloaded a salvo in his left ear. What had he been thinking? It was madness to bring her here. She was going to think that he belonged with these mutts. He kept looking at the side of her face. She was so beautiful. Could she love a loser? No way, not her. He needed to do something, anything to put some distance between himself and this pack of morons.

"Well, what did you think?"

"It wasn't awful. It looked a bit like a game show that's about to get cancelled."

"What did you think about the God stuff?"

"They didn't explain that very well, even though they went on and on about it."

"I don't know if anyone really understands that part of it. I kind of feel like I'm Mormon and you're Catholic, and I have to convert you before we can go out together."

Rachael wanted to smack him. But only for a second. She put herself in his shoes. It didn't take long to suss out what he must be feeling. *Save it for the lens. That's where it belongs.*

She gave him a kind answer. "We're not Montagues and Capulets. This isn't an issue for me. The thing I got out of that meeting was some hope. There's no doubt in my mind that these guys all belong here. The fact that they're sober tonight and not off in an alley somewhere tells me everything I need to know."

"So you're okay with me going to the meetings?"

Rachael was surprised by the depth of his neediness. There was no way she was going to be his dutiful girlfriend and attend these silly meetings to support him. She had lived a lifetime of that kind of pious devotion to the less fortunate under her mother's direct supervision. She had a life of her own to live. She wasn't going to waste her chance at real happiness by babysitting Arthur. But her voice did not carry her agitation. This would all be explored later and in the greatest detail. "You're an adult, do what you need to do to take care of yourself. You don't need me to hold your hand."

That stung. He did need someone. He couldn't bear the thought of being on his own. Somewhere in the backroom of his mind he was working on a way to deal Rachael into the game. He would turn her on to the wonders of twelve steps. They would grow their hair and wear bedsheets if that's what it came to. She would become the centrepiece of his new life. He looked up into her untroubled dark eyes and he paused. She would never go for something that crazy.

The wheels in Rachael's imagination were turning too. That speck of fire in her eyes was back again. "I want to do a film about this."

"About recovery?"

"About changing. TV is full of images of angry desperate addicts and sobbing incoherent relatives. But the thing they never get to is this — what goes on inside a person as they change. How does it feel to get hijacked by a substance, and what has to happen before you finally break free again? The camera always shows people hugging children, storming out of rooms, starting fights, and threatening to kill themselves. That's what addiction looks like from the outside, but that's not what it really is."

She was fully in the moment. She reached out her hands and grabbled Arthur's biceps as if she intended to initiate a dance. She flashed him a smile. It was all so perfect and all so clear. "I want to know what's really going on. I want to know what goes on inside your head. I want to know what goes on inside your heart. You're the valedictorian, hey … that would be a great title for the film. Let me point a camera in your direction. You want someone to love you, well here's your chance, tell the whole world who you really are. Be the first one ever to look them in the eye and give it to them straight."

Arthur looked Rachael in the eye. "I don't care about the world. I want you to love me."

Rachael was more than a little taken aback. How could the outside and the inside of this guy occupy the same space? They were made of contradictory material. Cool and slick on the outside and reactive and clingy on the inside. His face would work so beautifully if she shot it in the right light. The director's voice in her head told her to speak with authority. "Then you know what we have to do. I'll pick you up tomorrow."

In his mind's eye, Arthur had a vision of leaving Punanai for the last time with Rachael on his arm. He could see RK smiling and waving goodbye to him while Mike stood there sadly shaking his head. The face of his beloved was happy and accepting. They were going to make a film together.

Oh shit. Did she say tomorrow?

Arthur heard first one, and then two, cyanide pellets drop into the sulfuric acid. A cloud of choking lies began to fill the sealed gas chamber as the sad old padre and the warden looked on helplessly. He thought about the lacquered box and the mad promise he'd made to Eric. *Oh crap, why did I say I'd do that?*

He tried to push the feelings of panic down. He was praying that his face wasn't giving him away. A presence tapped him on the shoulder and cut in. The wooing of Rachael was in his hands now. Doc made the contradictions disappear and the bullshit slide down easier. He knew that she didn't need to know the whole story. There was a lot that she didn't need to know. He would tell her the truth. Not everything … but enough. They would make her film and then they would be done with the past.

Doc had a lovely speaking voice. He could have read the news on the radio. "I have something to do with my buddy Eric tomorrow. I don't know how long it's going to take. But the day after tomorrow is free. I'll have my phone back then. I'll call you and we can set the whole thing up. I won't plan anything else for the rest of the day."

———

It was noon and Millie and Norma had outdone themselves. They had put together a plate of chicken wings and salads that called forth the glutton in all men. There was even a bread pudding for dessert. As the happy staff tucked into this treat around the conference table, Reg took the opportunity to ask for a few impressions. "Arthur 'the bullet dodger' Cardel is leaving us today. I have to do the discharge summary. So far it resembles a eulogy. What do you guys make of this brat?"

Paul spoke up first. "I think we did a fairly good job on him. His next coke run is going to be a big improvement over his last one."

Kaiser predictably had something acidic to share. "I don't buy this kid, either. I think every time he tells a lie, he finds a stolen American Express card under his pillow."

Greg weighed in: "I want to see a little more suffering before I make up my mind. I haven't seen him sweat yet. He's still in control. He needs to get slapped around good before he'll take this seriously. It's a shame we won't be there to see it happen."

"He has a pretty girlfriend," said Mike. "When he messes up, it'll be up to me to console her."

"Ah hell," said Doug, "you guys are betting the over-under on this one. Did we ever get to the bottom of what happened to him at school? No, we didn't. Did he ever come clean about his mysterious girlfriend? No, that's still a big secret too. Did he ever let his guard down and have a good cry with a staff member? Nope. All these things say 'blockbuster summer sequel' to me. But he still has fifteen weeks of aftercare to look forward to. Maybe they can sort it all out there."

"This is a job for sodium pentothal," offered Paul with wink. "It's hard to make a stone speak."

———

Reg was ready to give this one more try. He wanted this to be a conversation between two friends. He removed his tie and offered Arthur a cup of real coffee from the counsellors' private stash. Arthur had a smug look on his face, and why not, he had outfooted his pursuers over a long course on difficult terrain, and he wasn't even breathing hard.

"Who would have thought after our first interview, you and I would be sitting here talking over coffee."

"Are you going to read my coffee grounds?"

"That's exactly what I'm going to do. I have to write up your stay. Here's an idea: If you could hijack the report, what would you write?"

"That would depend on who gets to read it."

Reg thoughtfully stroked his chin as if he were seriously considering Arthur's suggestion. "Good point, you have to know your audience — colour the story to appeal to their prejudices, that works way better than the truth."

Arthur didn't react to his provocation. He was home free, and he knew it.

Reg was feeling let down but hoping not to show it; a fight would have been progress. "Arthur, the courts are going to read this, and what they want to read is remarkably simple. They want to know that you now realize there's a problem and you're trying to solve it. My hope is that we've made three points clear to you. The first is the identification piece. Have we described the nature of your addiction in such a compelling way that you now realize you have a problem? The second point is the agency piece. Now that you know how your disease works, can you see how abstinence and going to CA meetings is your best hope? The final piece is about deciding what you're going to do. Are you going to bring the time and resources necessary to this problem? Are you going to give this a fair chance to work?"

Arthur had spotted the weak point. He always did. "You guys are telling me I have to stay off the coke and go to meetings. How is that any different from my parents picking out my friends and choosing a school for me? I'm changing one set of bullies and their opinions for another."

Reg knew now that it was hopeless. The ones who were going to recover landed on emotion. The ones who weren't done yet always landed on logic. "I wish you were going to the meetings because you wanted to, because you saw them as your best shot at a real life." Reg closed the folder in front of him with a sad look on his face.

Arthur had developed a sneaking fondness for Reg and while he thought his performance was up to par, he wasn't fooled by it for a minute. He knew that good looks and bright prospects kept young asses out of the slammer. Still, it didn't hurt to ask. "So where am I?"

"This is still a theory for you. You're playing with this. You're not feeling any real hope or despair yet because you still think that you can control events."

"You're not going to put that in the report…"

"Not to worry. I'll put it all into the proper doublespeak, because, Arthur, what I say in that report won't mean very much by this time next week. What you do the first ten days you're out of here will tell the tale. The judge will know what to do with you when you show up in court. He'll know simply by looking at you."

Arthur was unmoved. He set his face like a flint for Kingston. In one decisive act, he was going to put everything right. He was going to save Linda from her demons, Eric from his creditors, and liberate himself once and for all from his meddling parents' dreary vison of what his life should be. These clowns were all wrong about what to do — the solution was at hand, and it wasn't going to happen in a church basement. The future belonged to the bold. History needed a little nudge in the right direction and then all the dominoes would fall in the precise path that he had chosen for them. Game, set, match, Cardel.

Chapter 40

The bus ride from Toronto to Kingston was a time for reflection. Arthur needed to get this chore out of the way so that he and Rachael could get down to the serious business of falling in love. He still felt everything under the sun about Linda. She kept going in and out of focus for him. He couldn't get his brain around the idea that she wouldn't be at home waiting for him when he arrived. *Did we really love each other? Is this how loving and losing feels?*

He looked across the snack table to the window seat. His new best friend, Eric, was at his side, someone else who had been through the wars. He had a happy self-satisfied look on his face. This was a magic moment. Arthur had found within himself the will and the insight necessary to put things right. A task that only he could perform. It was a shame he couldn't tell anyone.

Southern Ontario in winter was a beautiful place. It was fun to look out the bus window. Farmland and pasture gave way first to scrub and then to the southern end of the boreal forest. The miles rolled by.

"You catching a little nap there, Arturo?"

"No, I was praying."

"Don't worry, this is going to be a cinch."

"That's not what I was praying about."

"Oh dude, you drank the Kool-Aid."

"Maybe just a sip, don't you believe in God?"

"No, he's an underachiever. But now I'm worried about my mission partner. This next question goes straight to the state of your mental health — When did you start praying?"

"In treatment. But I go back and forth on this stuff. Sometimes it makes me feel better, but most of the time, I feel like I'm kissing a cabbage."

"There's always a girl behind it."

"Well actually, I met a girl named Rachael, and she goes to church. I want to get close to her and it just kinda happened. I just do it sometimes. I don't know why."

Eric put his seat in the upright position. "They made me meditate in detox too, but I kept thinking about this girl who was in my self-esteem group. She was so beautiful. She had brown hair and sad eyes. She could've talked me into praying."

Arthur brightened. "Do you know about Pascal's wager?"

"Nope, in Woodbridge, we obsess about Pro-line tickets, not philosophers."

"Well, you must know something about it, you know. Pascal was a philosopher. Listen, dude, this is cool. Reg Topping talked about this one afternoon in treatment. It's what got me thinking about this. Pascal wanted to work out a way for a regular guy to decide if God existed or not. You know ... prove it to yourself. He thought theology and reason were bullshit. What he came up with was so simple. He said, 'Go to your room. Close all the blinds and shut the door. Don't tell anyone what you're up to. Then in the privacy of your own thoughts, ask the God of your understanding to help you with something that you know you cannot change on your own.' Pascal figured one of two things was going to happen. Either this would work or it wouldn't. So if there is a God, which is one question, and if that God cares a rat's ass about people, which is a separate and distinct question, then he may choose to help you. The point is, what does it cost you to try?"

As Arthur made his point, his energy crested, but as Eric listened, his face became more and more concerned. A burglar on his first job needs to stay focused. Eric needed this score. For that to happen he needed Arthur on the right page. He went exploring.

Eric took a can of cola out of his bag and offered it to Arthur. "I'm so glad we have an hour to talk about this. Arturo, you're chasing your tail. People under stress make up games like that. They come up with rules and insights, but it's all make-believe. All the bullshit does is make them feel safer."

Eric had Arthur's attention. A bus trip is the perfect backdrop for a long, satisfying intellectual conversation about the way that the world works. A topic of endless fascination for young men on the cusp of adulthood. Eric helped himself to a can of cola. "In my history class, we read a book about Auschwitz. Everyone who went into that camp, both guards and prisoners, were doomed. Everybody knew it, but nobody could let themselves believe it. The guards told themselves that what their officers had told them was true. That what they were doing served a higher purpose. Batshit crazy. They knew it wasn't true. But still they clung to it.

"The prisoners had a different problem: They couldn't get their heads around the idea that they were going to be gassed, shot, beaten, or starved to death, and there was nothing they could do about it. They were used to the world being cruel and unfair, but this was three steps beyond that. They needed to have some hope. So they found some. A few of the prisoners pretended that the decision about who lived and who died was rational. They persuaded themselves they would not be killed as long as they could stay healthy enough to work. These guys would go out into the cold without their coats to prove to the guards how fit and tough they were. They would trade their rations for cigarettes, which were the official currency of the camps, and build up a store of wealth for a rainy day. They were survivalists. But here's the thing. If they were right about how the camp worked, then they were pushing the sick and the weak ahead of them right into the ovens. This made them no better than the kapos who brutalized them in order to survive."

"What has this got to do with Pascal's wager?"

"The connection is in mistaking depraved indifference for anything else. But let me finish my story. When the Americans interrogated captured guards after the war, they all told the same story. There was only so much room in the camps. When a new shipment of prisoners was on the way, the guards had to make room for them, and the easiest way to do that was to push the ones who were too sick and weak to resist you anymore into the gas chambers.

"The prisoners always knew that something bad was coming when the guards started to drink with both hands. That was the tell. On the third day of the drunk, the train arrived. The guys in the barracks were separated into two files: the ones who'd been starved and worked to death went one way, and the rest went the other. The selection, that's what they called it, was done by glancing at people as they walked naked past a fixed point in the exercise yard. There was no calculation. It was random and inhuman. It was done by drunken, brutalized, frightened, shame-driven, hell-bound men. But here's the point. A few of the prisoners who'd underdressed and traded their food for cigarettes managed to survive. They did all the talking when the slaughter was over. The fact that they survived was a kind of half-assed proof that they were right."

"You don't believe in a damn thing, do you?"

"I believe in holy mother dope."

"That makes me sad when you say that. Do you think it's possible to recover from an addiction?"

"If you want to, yes, I've seen guys do it, so I know it's possible. But here's the thing, seeker-after-truth, Do you want to? Is it worth the price you have to pay? Apparently, some people survive lung cancer. Is that the life you want, walking around with an oxygen bottle?"

"Narcotics Anonymous is a much darker fellowship than CA."

"Heroin is a much harder dance partner to give up."

"So what, are you and Nietzsche on the same page? Is this all about will?"

"No, I believe in luck. Pop could have wasted his life praying for dead people, but he got a break, he met my mom and boom — suddenly he has a life. Pascal's wager is as goofy as selling your food for cigarettes and going out without your coat in the dead of winter. If you survive, even for a short time, you get to pretend you know what you're doing. But that's it. That's all you have. You don't get to look back at the camp from outside the wire. You're still in a death camp watching the searchlights go round and round. All you've done is make yourself feel superior. They were no better off."

"But even the bullshit gave them some hope. People can't live without hope!"

"People can live without hope. Dope trumps hope. Look around you. How else would you explain the twenty-first century?"

"What?"

"Everyone is on some kind of dope. Everyone's cheating and pretending."

Arthur hadn't given up on life yet. He agreed with Eric about some of this, but he knew he wasn't right about all of it. There was more to life. There was Rachael — but there was Linda too. He couldn't name what he was feeling. His silence brought Eric further into his personal space.

"Arturo, your motives here are abundantly clear and they do you credit. You're doing the twelve-step thing. You're cleaning up the mess you made. And I say … good for you. I think being clean is the right choice for you.

"But you and I are different creatures. I'm on a dope diet. We're both doing the same thing but for quite different reasons. I'm cleaning up the mess I made so I can rest up and get ready to make a bigger mess next time. I'm going to stay off the stuff until my tolerance drops low enough for me to order my smack off the kiddies' menu."

"Eric, you're talking crap. That's no kind of life."

"Is it my fault that history's screw-ups are always variations on the same theme?"

"What's the theme?"

"Narcissism."

"That's rich coming from a dope fiend."

"That's how I figured this out! Dope is the only reliable lens to see the world through. If you want to do dope, you need to let go of what your parents taught you. There's no God and there's no such thing as right or wrong in my world. There is only the here and now — and today is always about dope. I'm one of those survivalists. I'm never getting out of this camp. I accept that. But I'm not going to die easy. If I have to hurt people to get what I need, then that's what I'm going to do. That's the price of survival. You don't have it in you to do that yet, Arthur. The darkness hasn't got its shithooks into you yet, but it will if you give it a chance. That's why you should quit and stay quit."

"Do you ever take your own advice?"

"Arthur, take this to heart. You've been using with some pretty gentle and civilized people. Lots of fast cars and hot tubs. That can't last. Remember the guys from detox?"

"Hard to forget that smell."

"After a while you get used to that, even when it starts coming from you, and the next thing you know, you're sharing needles."

"No way. Couldn't happen. The guys there are roadkill. I say, let Darwin do his work. You could pour cocaine into me for a hundred years and I'd never behave that way. It's not in me."

Chapter 41

At the bus station, they grabbed a bite to eat and then took the local bus to Linda's. Eric parked Arthur on a bench a block from the house and gave him his instructions. "Listen, these guys know you, so I'll do the break in. I don't want them seeing your face or a familiar walk on the video camera. You stay here and when I have the back door open, I'll come get you."

It was almost dark and the perfect time to do this. As Eric walked calmly out of sight, Arthur's mood became giddy. He thought of Robert Service and started to laugh. *There are indeed strange things done 'neath the midnight sun by the men who moil for gold.* They were moiling all right. But they were not panning a frozen stream. The gold they were after was in a lacquered box. *What's worth more, a pound of dope or a pound of gold?*

Eric was back in less than ten minutes. Arthur panicked. "What's wrong, was somebody home?"

"We're in."

"You did that in three minutes. You said it was going to take half an hour."

"I prayed."

"Very funny."

"I said half an hour if the system was up and working. It's hard to know exactly what to do from outside the house. But, and here's the serious teaching point, my friend, it's all a lot easier if the back door is unlocked."

"You're kidding."

"You always check that first. All I had to do was punch in the service override. Look, there's a way to get into the backyard from the walkway behind the house. No one will be able to see us. We'll slip in that way. Are you ready?"

"My heart is hammering. I've never done a break-and-enter before."

"A serious hole in your resume, if you ask me. Come, mungie cake, we have long nights of abstinence to avenge."

As they walked through the darkened laneway, Arthur started to lose his resolve. This was betrayal. It felt wrong. Worse than theft. Arthur took a hit of adrenalin when the house came into sight. He felt empty and afraid, but in spite of that, he flipped himself over the fence as easily as a cat.

"I see the hip is feeling better."

"Yes, I guess it is."

Once inside, Arthur made a quick reconnoitre to make sure everything was as it should be, and then he entered the bedroom. It was exactly as he remembered it but with one exception. The housekeeper had been busy packing up his things. All the clothes Linda had bought him were now neatly piled in boxes in the corner heading for the Goodwill. It felt awful to see his stuff getting boxed up that way. It was so final. There was some nice stuff there too. He was tempted.

Eric read his mind and shook his head. "Dude we leave no sign of our passing, right?"

"I should've taken her old man up on his offer. She bought me some nice clothes."

"The drugs my man, the drugs. We need to focus."

Arthur went to the closet and put his hand on the drawer. He took a breath. A lot was riding on this. What if Alice was way ahead of them? Did she know about the drugs? *Well, duh. How could she not know now? Maybe she'd gone looking after he left. Maybe Linda's dad had helped her.* They would think nothing of flushing the accursed powder down the toilet after what it had done to Linda.

Arthur took a breath and felt around in the darkness with his hand. There it was. The lacquered box. He closed his hand on it. It had some heft. He smiled and felt an overwhelming sense of relief. He waved the box under Eric's nose, and when he tried to touch it, he yanked it away and put it in his pocket. It felt good.

There was fat wad of cash and some rings lying around but he left them. That would be stealing. What he needed now was Linda. Not the cripple, but the awesome, intoxicating woman that he loved and missed and would remember forever. *I can't let that memory go.* Inspiration struck him. He went to her dressing table and pocketed a bottle of her perfume.

Eric disapproved; souvenirs were deadly, they had talked about this. "What are you doing?"

"Sorry dude, I have to have something of hers."

"I would've thought the video of you on the web would be a great reviver of memories."

"That's not the part I want to remember. She was special."

"I thought you were all about Rachael these days?"

Arthur stopped dead in his tracks. He had completely forgotten all about her.

How the hell did that happen?

Eric noticed the change and sensed danger. Thinking about women always landed on thinking about drugs. It was time to cue the getaway. "Give me the dope. It's your drug of choice and maybe not such a good idea for you to have to carry it."

"But you're a bigger addict than I am."

"True, but it's not my brand. You sit here and bask in the glow of your memories. I'm going to take a tour of the house to make sure there are no cameras. I didn't see anything that looked suspicious, but they make them so small these days."

Arthur sat in the armchair in the bedroom. He took the bottle out of his pocket and squirted some on his wrist. He inhaled deeply. There she was. He had come into this chamber for the first time a naive and idealistic young man. He had done a lot of changing in this room. Some of it was good, some terrible, but all of it was him now. He felt as if he was sitting on the stage after the concert was over and the sound guys were packing up their gear.

Eric was the tour guide now. He hustled Arthur to his feet and gently pushed him toward the rear of the house. "We're okay, no cameras. Let's get the hell out of here." They retraced their steps and soon found themselves back at the park waiting for the bus. Arthur plonked himself down on the bench and took in the cold night air. It still held the faint undertone of Linda's cologne. He felt immortal. "Most housebreakers don't rely on public transit for their getaways."

"Maybe they should call us the low-carbon-footprint gang."

Arthur was still excited. "Let me hold the dope. I still can't believe it's real. I can't believe we pulled this off."

Eric was wary. He'd seen this before, and he knew what it meant. "Sure, but only for a second. This isn't a very private place." Eric reached into his pocket and produced the box of powder.

A wave of dopamine rushed over Arthur's face. His hand was hovering over the moonstone. He was all about wanting now. "Oh man. That is a lot of dope. I can't believe we pulled this off. This is so cool."

Eric was desperate to put out the fire while there was still a chance. "That's a lot of pain and trouble struggling to get out of that box. Give it back to me before you faint. We have to follow the plan."

"There's a restaurant around the corner. I need to take a dump."

Eric knew what that meant too. Coke addicts always need to go when the candy man shows up.

Oh shit. He's triggered. I should never have brought him along. Now he's going to be twitching and whining all the way home.

Eric waited on the park bench while Arthur ran the errand that no one else could run for him. He looked upward into the cold, crisp starlit sky. This was such a beautiful score. He lit a cigarette and inhaled the wonderful combination of winter air, nicotine, and success. There was a lot more dope in that box than he expected. This score was one to brag about for years to come. Eric was beyond pleased with himself. It's not every day that someone hands over twenty thousand dollars in dope simply because you asked them to. Usually, you have to wave a pistol.

Eric became aware of a familiar drumbeat in his own chest. His palms were sweating. He felt cold dead hands from beyond the grave embrace his forearms. It creeped him out. His flesh was all goosebumps. His breath came to him in short sharp bursts. His brain started to revolve like a water wheel. He willed it to stop, if only for a few more minutes, until they could get out of here and back on the bus. That's all they had to do. This would be so much easier if he were walking. But he wasn't. He was sitting. Where the hell was Arthur?

He took another breath. *We're going to be all right. We're going to get on that bus and go.* But each repetition of that mantra added fuel to the fire. *Get back on the bus. How do I change this coke into smack? Get back on the bus. Who do I know who can do this for me? The bus. The bus. Think about the bus.* Ah, the eternal verities of addiction.

Arthur was hanging on by his fingertips too. He looked at his image in the washroom mirror and cringed. Until this very minute, he didn't think that this was possible. He had never wanted anything more than he wanted what was in the box. When he got back, he sat next to Eric on the bench and pretended that what he felt was going to pass. All they had to do was make it to the bus terminal. The fear of relapse and beatings by bikers still had a kind of deterrent effect. His idealism allowed him enough perspective to keep the cravings at bay.

He fought back by shining the positives. His thoughts turned philosophical. Linear, goal-related thinking was the answer. He had shown those dumb bastards at Punanai a thing or two. They didn't have all the answers. Now Eric was out of trouble. They had made a score they could brag about forever. He had saved his friend from a beating and stopped Linda from coming home to something she couldn't handle. It was a masterpiece. All they had to do now was get on the bus and stay sober for a few more hours and then everything would be back to normal. This was exactly what happened in sitcoms. No matter what happened, everything had to be back to normal at the end of the episode. But there was an emptiness now. It went directly from behind his eyes to his gut.

Knowing that the box was within reach … it was too much. He could see the outline of the dragon creeping slowly through the vegetation. The flowers and the smell of the wood. *We should sell it here and take the money back with us to Toronto. Money is clean. It has no power.*

The dope sang a siren song more persuasive than the ring in Tolkien's trilogy and as seductive and inviting as the Horcruxes in *Harry Potter*. The powder was imbued with a manic energy. It spoke to him. The shepherd was calling his flock. The dope pulled at him as powerfully as a black hole in space.

Arthur knew what was happening. But he might as well have been on ketamine. He was aware of the danger, but he didn't care. The word *wanting* didn't and couldn't carry the meaning of what was happening deep down inside him. He was being held underwater by powerful hands intent on taking his life. Yes, he needed a breath and wanted a breath, more than anything else in the world, but the harder he struggled to escape, the more oxygen he used and the closer his final breath came.

He was fast approaching the moment when he would breathe in the water and drown. That instant in which he lost voluntary control of his diaphragm. As the carbon dioxide built up, the urge to exhale became the fact of exhaling. Beyond a certain point, your conscious will doesn't matter anymore. A primal voice says, *Breathe!*

He didn't notice in the moiling waters of wanting and fearing that his connection to Linda had been supplanted by his friendship with Eric. Arthur suddenly needed Eric to make everything right. The whole conversation that should have happened between Arthur and Eric never took place. There was no need. When they looked at each other they both knew what was going to happen next. Two lovers who had run out of words. They were committed.

"Check out the crack whores." Arthur spotted them first. Arial was nice. Thin with a full bosom and a head of girl punk rock band hair. She smiled at Arthur warmly as if she had known him in elementary school. Her friend, Dara, was dark-haired, and she was nice-looking too. Older than Eric and Arthur and a bit more jaded, but still a fine-looking cat.

Desire was piling on top of desire. There was too much weight on the floorboards. The planks began to sway before they cracked and gave way underfoot. Arthur felt a giddy sense of relief as he fell.

What had he been thinking? He couldn't go on feeling this emptiness for another minute, let alone the rest of his life. And why should he? Having the drug and not using it was madness. Something purposeful popped and whirred inside his head. He detached as the free fall gave way to a firmer footing. Arthur suddenly felt shouldered aside by a more powerful and ruthless version of himself. The master was home from the hunt. Barking orders and beating the sleeping servants. These were not Arthur's words, and neither were they his actions. Even Doc was incapable of such cunning and resolve. Arthur found himself standing a short distance from himself taking in the scene from a time portal. There but not there. He looked meekly at Eric who also knew it was over. They nodded.

The girls had a warm spot around the corner. They had planned to go to Toronto for the weekend, but they were willing to put off their trip until tomorrow to help out two stranded travellers.

Eric came up with a very reasonable suggestion. They would get the girls to swap some of the coke for some heroin, and then when that little chore was done, they would all give themselves up to a single night of debauchery to celebrate their good fortune, and then it would be up early, out the door, and on the bus back to Toronto by 11:00 a.m. at the latest. On that point there was universal agreement.

The new plan lacked the nobility of the original essay, but it accommodated a more complicated understanding of the human creature. One where the desire to do the right thing and the desire to take care of oneself fought continually for dominance. This would be the farewell tour for a much-beloved rock band. A chance to feel all that love and connection one last time.

To give the dope to the bikers would have been all right. It would have solved the debt problem, but it would have been a betrayal of the self. A kind of soul murder. This was his dope now. It was a legacy. Linda bought it for them. She wasn't going to use it, so really if it didn't belong to him, who did it belong to? This was his inheritance. Hush money from the Dickens that didn't have a stink.

This dope was a sacrament. It would connect him one last glorious time to the memory of Linda. He would get Arial to wear her perfume. She would be a surrogate. He would tell her the things that were locked in his heart forever. It wasn't as good as telling Linda, but he knew somehow in this great jumble of a universe that she would feel his love and be satisfied in a way that defied human logic. Intimate feelings of love unseen animated his bursting heart.

Besides, at the end of the day, what about me? What about what I want to do with my life? I can't be out there for the other fellow all the time. I have to take care of myself. This will run smoother than the burglary. In and out in a flash and no one the wiser.

Chapter 42

The accommodation wasn't fancy. The furniture had all been moved away from the walls to allow the exterminators to spray for the cockroaches. Ideally, they should have stayed out of the unit for another hour, but what the hell. The place was supposed to have been cleaned and dusted before the exterminators came — that's what the instructions had said, anyway — but Dara and Arial were party girls, not Molly Maids.

Where the furniture had been moved, you could see half an inch of dust, crumbs, and lost change all held together in a lattice of cat fur. There were bits and pieces of dead bugs everywhere. That's why Dara and Arial had been at the bus station. They were clearing out for a couple of days. But in the initial excitement of making friends, they had forgotten to tell the boys about this. The smell of bug death was everywhere.

"Is it safe to be in here?"

"Oh yes," Dara said looking at her watch. "We had to be out for three hours and they said it was best to leave everything pulled out overnight. It was awful, the filthy beggars were everywhere. Look … there's one dying there in the corner."

"Euthanasia!" cried Eric, as he mashed it flat with his foot.

Arthur dumped an armload of clothes off the La-Z-Boy and made himself comfortable. Dara was smoking so he lit one up too.

Eric was a crafty bastard. He went to the washroom, and when he came back, he threw a baggie of white powder onto the table. It really amounted to a drop in the bucket. But the look on his face credibly said, *Look, this is all there is.*

He began to shine them on. "Here's the problem girls. This is coke, and I need heroin. Do you know someone who could do a little transubstantiation for us and change the one into the other?"

Dara was the take-charge girl. "I know someone. Why don't you guys order a pizza and I'll do the rest." She got on her cell phone and disappeared into the bedroom. Arthur speed-dialled the local pizzeria he and Linda used to order from and then settled in on the big chair in front of the stereo.

Arial had a definite preference for Arthur. She knew a good thing when she saw one. This kid was bent enough to be interesting, but not so twisted that he was going to get rough with her or give her a dose. She had been slapped around once or twice in her time and survived, but she wasn't going to let that happen again. She got gonorrhea one time from the guy who Dara said had been a friend of hers in high school. The high school for the damned. The bastard was on his way back to jail and well … she went to the clinic and got it cleared up, but she hadn't been happy about it.

Arial still wanted to get married. This was something to do while she was young and could still have fun. She had seen enough of family life to know how hard it was going to be. Party while you're young. That was the answer. She loosened the buttons on her blouse and sat on Arthur's knee in the big chair. She was his choice too. She had dark red hair and fiery black eyes. She would have made a fine vampire bitch. He nibbled her ear a little bit. He hadn't been with anyone since Linda and he was ready for some romance. Arial's skin was marble in the sun. Warm to the touch and smooth and beautiful. This was going to be great.

———

The dealer Dara summoned was a well-dressed Hispanic man named Mickey. He wore a business suit that would not have looked out of place in a lawyer's office, but which looked ridiculous there amid the pizza boxes and dying bugs. His dark, curly hair was trimmed close to his scalp and his eyes had a mistrustful way of constantly scanning the room for things that irritated him. Everything irritated this latter-day Aztec. He treated Dara and Arial as his property — he paid the rent, and they did what he told them to do, or they did without. He eyed up Arthur and Eric and saw intruders. He didn't allow people he didn't know on his turf. That was dangerous. He had no illusions about two cops being able to put one over on Dara and Arial.

"How do I know this is real dope?"

Arthur poured out a line for him. "There's only one way to find out."

"You being a little cheap with it?"

"No, dude, this stuff is pretty much uncut. A little goes a long way."

Mickey did the line and sat back in his chair. His eyes registered mild surprise and then deep satisfaction as his face went asymmetrical from the jolt. "Man … that's good blow."

"We were lucky to get it. Can you do a swap for me?"

"Yeah, I'll set you up." He reached into his pocket and took out a small bag. Eric's eyes were focused now. He took his kit out of his pocket and started to prepare the dose.

"It's not as good as your stuff," said Mickey.

"It's good enough," said Eric, with a happy smile on his face.

Mickey enjoyed wheeling and dealing. Maybe these guys turning up could be turned to his advantage. "Can you get some more?"

"No, dude. I lost the connection."

Eric looked up at Mickey trying to appear as if he cared about what he was saying. He needed his services and he didn't want to be rude. But there was the matter of shooting up that needed urgent attention.

Arial broke off her lingering kiss and pointed to the coffee table. "Mickey's taking a business course," said Dara proudly.

Arthur looked up from the table where Arial was preparing the cocaine. *I don't trust this prick. He's dropped off the shit. Why is he hanging around?* He was about to say something when he saw Eric pulling out his needle kit. His thoughts turned darker still. *Why did he bring that along? He's been lying about using. He said he was only taking pills and smoking weed.* Arthur's anger at both Eric and Mickey was short lived; it was overwhelmed by his desire for the cocaine. This was only for one night; he'd straighten those pricks out tomorrow. Besides, he needed someone to watch his back tonight. *Who knows what Mickey is capable of...*

———

Ten o'clock had come and gone with no phone call. Rachael's creative juices were really flowing. The shape of the project had pretty much crystallized in her imagination the moment she first proposed it. Of course, the fun of filmmaking was all about making the plan and then watching it dissolve under the duress of truth and lies pushing to the front of the stage. Her professor had told them all on the first day that you always go into a shoot with a plan, but that you never get a chance to execute it. Something always goes wrong. A star, for example, who was absolutely smitten with you last night, not calling today.

Chapter 43

The Holt Renfrew display window had been decorated for Christmas. It had a fifties feel to it. The ghosts of the Grand Council jostled around before finding some old cross-country skis and wooden boxes with the 7 UP and Orange Crush logos on them and using them for chairs. The floor was covered in minced Styrofoam that looked, even to Canadian eyes, like genuine snow. The mannequins in the scene were young and fit and they were all wearing high-end knitwear and sitting around a wooden stove. It looked quite homey.

It was a lovely counterpoint to Barry. He stood facing his nearest and dearest, worn weary with the heavy burden of administration the group had thrust upon him as leader. He looked put upon and underappreciated. John wanted to yell, "Show us your ass, you bony old poser," but he decided against it. He would have to save that gem for another occasion. He did give Barry some credit. He tried. God knows he tried. Until he tried John's patience to the breaking point.

"Good afternoon, everyone," Barry had started. "If you could make yourselves comfortable, we can begin. The Bailey brothers aren't here yet but I'm sure they will be along soon. The executive met at eleven, and it was decided that since there was no new business that we would..."

There was no holding it in. John blurted out, "Executive? Executive! For the love of God man there are only eight of us. What do we need an executive for?"

Barry shot him a fearsome look, seconded by Peter. "John, this is what happens when you peevishly refuse to attend meetings and shoulder your share of the burdens. We think it is disgraceful that you leave all the work to the rest of us."

"Work you say? What work do you do at these meetings?"

Barry hovered into John's personal space. "That is none of your concern. If you can't behave yourself and allow us to conduct our business in a civilized way, I will instruct the sergeant-at-arms to remove you."

"Bullshit heaped on bullshit."

"Oh, this is outrageous!" said Barry, throwing up his hands.

"I couldn't agree more. But I tell you what ... since you have made such a fine beginning, why don't you carry on? I'm desperate to know what you think about the light," John begged.

Barry's face was molten with rage. At that moment, John was pleased that he had come. Then dear, sweet Maddy did something curious. She went over to John and put her arm around him. It was mysterious and sweet and made John wonder if she was the real sergeant-at-arms.

Barry had an inexhaustible supply of bluster. He stood foursquare in front of the assembly and called out for order. "My friends, I have been charged with the responsibility of chairing the working committee looking into the properties of the light. As chair, I have been working in tandem with the Bailey brothers and our own dear, sweet Rosa to try to articulate some kind of working theory about what the light might mean to us and for our hopes for the future."

That's when John realized why the Baileys weren't present. The rehearsal must have been enough for them. Peter was all ears, as were the rest of them, and he started to lean forward, as if he was trying to physically attach himself to Barry. Witticism after deadly witticism kept popping into John's mind but he dared not speak. It was the tone of the thing that he was trying to preserve with his silence — it was precious.

John pondered what he could possibly say to disparage this idiot that would be more damning than his own empty-headed prattle. John looked down at dear, sweet, vacuous Maddy and wished for a moment that he could be gulled by this crap. To happily believe that simply saying something would make it so, or that the act of wanting something amounted to anything more than inflicting sorrows on themselves. John had felt for some time in his heart that they were all like coffee beans, inexplicably caught between two rivets in the metal flume of the grinder; they could hang on for a good long time, but their end was certain.

Barry had the rhetorical training. The same gift as all the classic old windbags John had to endure in his youth. Barry loved to ask himself questions, like they had. "What is the light? How often, my friends, have you asked yourself that? Well, nobody knows. A better question is this: Does it have a purpose? And if so, whom does it serve and what end does it hope to achieve? If we knew that we could orient ourselves to the light. Is it from heaven or hell? Does it come to save us or damn us? We go back and forth on these questions, but we can never attain clarity."

John raised his eyebrows and admitted to himself that, if Barry had stopped there, he would have won the day. John would have been the first to say that it was a nice review of the fire regulations for children. But no...

Barry's head dropped ever so slightly. He took off his glasses and held them up to the light. "I wanted to share some of our recent insights with you. Rosa told the committee that years ago, way back when the war was still on, some of the older ghosts laid traps for the light. They thought back then that it might have something to do with the Holy Ghost, so they would meet in churches when communion was being served or go to evangelical churches when there was an altar call. The idea was to see if the light was predictable and to find out if it served more than one purpose. Another faction that used to meet at Delany's Steak House tried using the standard weapons of black and white magic to see if garlic, salt, or pentagrams had any effect of the light."

Everyone looked at Rosa who was playing with her hair and looking out the window.

"But she couldn't remember what the outcome of all that was."

John could see why Rosa was a fit for the committee.

"Some of us were kicking around the idea of trying some of these experiments again. Maybe even improving on them. It would be interesting to find out if the light responded to microwaves or high-frequency sound. It would be a lot of work, but I think we could make some real progress if we all came together and formed ourselves into a task force."

The thrust of his narrative overwhelmed John. He had to speak, for he couldn't hold it in any longer. "Barry, would you be willing to provide the leadership?"

Barry had a moment. He fogged up in his deepest and tenderest parts. "If I was asked, I couldn't say no."

A whole room full of people running off in the wrong direction. If the Grand Council had had a national anthem, John was certain that it would have been sung lustily at that moment — a cappella. Peter hugged Rosa, and Barry shook hands with Jack, while John slipped out the side door and grabbed the first fur collar that came to hand. He didn't care where that lady was going, so long as it was out of there.

The whole business put John in mind of a story his grandfather used to tell. John grew up hearing about the grocery store he ran in eastern Quebec early in the last century. There were a lot of people in those days who never learned to read. A couple of times a year some poor soul would arrive at the store dusty and hot from a long slog up the road. They would hand his grandfather a note that said only SEND FURTHER THE FOOL.

The idea was that the grandfather was supposed to direct the person somewhere else. It was cruel and pointless. Who knows how many people were involved in this prank and how hateful it would be for the bearer to find out what the note said? The jokes on a farm tend to be a little crude. His grandfather never played along. He would read the note with great solemnity and thank the courier — usually asking them to stay and have some refreshment against the long journey home. He never told them what the note said. He spared them that dose of venom.

The old shopkeeper had better manners than his grandson.

Chapter 44

It was all so close again, that feeling of being fully alive, and once again at the centre of the universe. The smell of freshly mown hay mixing with the bitter afterburn of the coke. Arthur knelt down in front of the coffee table. He did a big line of the powder. This really was the most unbelievable stuff. Linda had spoiled him. He wiggled to the side to make room for Arial at the altar. She caught a scent. "What's that you're wearing? I smell perfume." She thought it was very funny. Arthur had forgotten that he had sprayed himself. He felt foolish and exposed. She took his place in front of the coffee table. He moved in behind her and put his hands on her hips as she bent her head forward to do her first line. Her body felt good to his touch. Without even being fully conscious of what he was doing, Arthur reached for the bottle in his pocket and sprayed some on the back of Arial's neck. She giggled. "That smells nice." She bent low again and made another rail disappear. When she had finished, she arched her back and rested her head on his shoulder. A silly satisfied look stole across her face as she pawed at her nose. Arthur moved his hands from her hips to her breasts. She purred and swayed to an unheard melody. It was good. That was the missing ingredient. The connection to Linda.

I can catch lightning in a bottle any time I want to.

———

The last voice of protest was spoken early Saturday morning. No one was making any sudden moves. Arthur looked around the devastated living room with an amused look on his face. "Are we going to get on that bus at eleven?"

Eric was still in his bathrobe. Dara was resting her head on his lap. "Dude, it's Saturday. We need a day to recover. We were doing some heavy shit last night. I can't go back to Toronto looking this way. Is there a gym around here where we could go for a workout?"

Arthur approved. "I still have my card for the YMCA. But I don't have any exercise stuff."

Eric shined him on a little bit. "Maybe we should go for a run. That would help."

Dara knew they didn't mean it, but it irked her. After all, she was the hostess. She sat up on the couch and took a sip of her tea. She put her mug down on the table and started to chop up some powder for Arthur. "That's okay," said Arial. "I can do that." The boys stopped talking. Dara moved aside to let Arial finish the chopping.

She lit a candle. "Better to light a candle than to curse in the darkness."

With that she began fixing Eric a persuader. "You're not going anywhere today, you big stud. You're going to spend the whole day with me in bed." She looked up at him from the floor and took the drawstring off her bath robe. Her teddy fell open revealing her considerable charms. She tied the drawstring around Eric's forearm and teased up a vein. Eric was mesmerized. She injected him, with no more fuss than a flu shot.

———

This wasn't a party. Parties start at twenty minutes past the hour. People dress up and show up, they flirt and boast, there's finger food, someone takes a phone call and everyone else gets annoyed, the room gets hot until the smokers leave the patio door open. When someone finally looks at their watch, the spell dissolves. Children and sitters and work and the morning come back into focus. Everyone sighs, "It's getting late," as the dishes pack themselves up by the sink and the wine bottles, now grown tired and empty, make their way to the floor of the garage. The bright lattice of light that illuminates the possibility of eternal youth and connection in the evening sky falls gently back to earth and flickers like a swarm of fireflies until it is extinguished by the rising moon.

The lacquered box inverted that tarantella. The dancers no longer moved in response to the music. The movement of the dancers called forth the tune. Feet and arms moved unseen valves and keys conjuring the music of the spheres. Arthur was suspended outside of time, rolling in the primal surf of a new kind of musical ocean. The universe had drifted for eons with no hand on the tiller: waiting, waiting, always waiting for the touch of his hand. The movement of his wrist brought everything into being as surely as a conductor raising his baton prompts the inhalation of breath. In that instant the silence exploded into consonance. It was permanent and perfect until it was gone again without a trace. Had anyone ever felt so low, so empty, and so completely alone?

At this ebb tide, the dark, stalking predators would move in to devour him. He heard their footfalls and smelled their acrid scent. Another line of powder kept the savage pack at bay. He wasn't getting high anymore, but he wasn't getting sick either. Arthur was ruminating about Linda, even if it was Arial who was next to him on the floor uncovering his nakedness.

He ached to consummate his relationship with Linda. How does one restore a goddess to life after her season in hell and darkness? He was mad to have her again. The way she was meant to be. The way she had been when he loved her. He held Arial in his arms and smelled the essence of Linda that clung to her. He could liberate the gold from the dross. It was so simple. He would inhale this woman like a fragrance and, holding her safe inside himself, take her deep beneath the waters to the place of perfection he went to. At midnight, they would surface and swim ashore. On that far sandy beach, they would look up and be the first to see her outline in a new constellation of red giants rising majestically for the first time two degrees below the pole star. Linda would rediscover herself in that light.

In the throes of this metamorphosis, Linda danced, grinding her body against his. The music unstrung every living heart. She gloried in him and he in her. She held him in her hands as certainly as he held her in his heart. Their dance was life and harmony and perfect accord.

No poet or philosopher, no matter how skilled or wise, could ever do justice to this insight. Theirs was a love that had its roots in this world, but which could only flower and bear fruit in a far nobler space.

Then in an instant the drug would fail, the insight was lost, and there was only him and Arial hunched over a coffee table.

Dara rolled over on her side and looked at the nodding Eric. She was coming down a bit. She had never skin-popped heroin before. She took him in her arms, but he failed to respond. He had mainlined so he was still in the ether.

"Eric…"

"What up?"

"Eric, hold me."

"Sure, baby." They snuggled up. "What are Sid and Nancy doing?"

"They're still hard at it."

"Are they ever going to stop?"

"Nope, not till they run out."

Dara was worried now. "Are we going to run out?"

"Not till long after they do."

"This stuff really is better."

"Ah, my best student."

There was an awkward conversation about current events on Sunday. Eric knew that the riptide was taking Arthur and Arial out to sea where they would drown. But the conversation was abstract. The words belonged to a world that neither of them lived in any longer. Yes, they could stop, yes, they could get on the bus back to Toronto, but nothing happened. They would talk about doing something for a while, and then Eric would go into the bedroom and come out with another full baggie claiming, as he always did, that this was the last one. The words didn't change anything. The subject of diminishing supply was the new global warming. It was inevitable, and it was coming fast. Nothing to be done about it though.

Even with four people bailing it took a long time to empty out the box. But empty it out they did. It happened at 4:00 a.m. on Tuesday. The last of the powder shaken out of the baggie made a pitiful line. Eric was almost comatose in the bedroom with Dara who had now completely switched allegiance and gone over to the heroin full-time. Mickey, who looked in on them from time to time, was not pleased. He wanted these guys out.

Arial and Arthur were shivering, shipwrecked survivors on a stony shore. It went without saying that the cops had been watching the house for days. The sound of the wind moving through leafless branches filled them with fear and dread. They hadn't slept in forever and they had nothing but a bottle of Tia Maria to come down with.

Arthur hated Eric more than he had never hated any other individual in his life. That selfish prick was getting his rocks off in the bedroom while he and Arial were suffering the agonies of the damned on the floor. Arthur would have given anything to be asleep. To be out of it for eight hours and to wake up feeling normal. He was a hungry cat in a cage, pacing back and forth, looking out the window, drawing the blinds, making himself a cup of coffee, and then pouring it down the sink. Everything was wrong. Everything was out of place. He looked at the apartment and he despaired. He was one more dying roach, hip deep in the powder.

They were living in a gypsy caravan that had overturned on the highway. His nerves danced and screamed. Arial was frantic, running her fingers over the filthy carpet. A woman searching for a lost contact. She kept her despair at bay, convinced that she would find some more cocaine on the floor. Arial had deep black furrows under her eyes and she looked all of her thirty-five years and twenty more, to boot. She had been quite good-looking when they started. What had happened? More ideas swept these away. Was he a panther in a cage dreaming he was a man? Was he a man? Was a panther dreaming he was man?

When he had been with Linda, this never happened. They would do the cocaine until the predators arrived. Make no mistake. Even the gods have enemies. You could feel them moving around in the darkness — circling, endlessly circling. They were never far. Unseen eyes in the forest, scenting the air, licking and watching. But Linda knew the trail home.

They would smoke a joint, take a pill, and mellow out over a drink. Yes, they felt edgy, but not this ragged. They would fall asleep in each other's arms and awake feeling more or less human.

Why hadn't he bought some pot and pills from Mickey when they were still flush? Yeah, and what about that Mickey? Mickey had been robbing them from day one. He was next in line for a good thumping after he finished with Eric.

Once Arthur had lost control of the cocaine to Eric … well, Eric had used it to get the heroin he craved. He didn't give the coke away, but he didn't grind out the price that they needed from Mickey. It all still would've run out, but it wouldn't have run out this morning. Now all was desolation and loss and counting and despair. Would that accursed sun never rise again? Were they trapped in the blackness of a winter's night as surely as Inuit north of the tree line?

He heard Dara moving around in the kitchen. She had fried up some bacon and eggs. It was hard to say what looked worse, her or the food. She found some bread, but it was mouldy. She toasted it anyway and put grape jelly on it.

"Eat this."

Arthur could smell the mould even over the bug spray. The food stuck in his throat. He had no appetite even though he hadn't eaten in days. He drew his energy from the drugs now. He was no longer mortal.

Dara thrust a second plate at Arial. "Even if you don't want it, you have to eat this. You are going to eat and then sleep." She reached into her pocket and took out a vial of pills. Oxy — eighty milligrams of love. The most precious substance on earth. The very thing.

"Eat up, lover boy, and mama will lay a couple of these on you."

Arthur knew they were going to be all right. He looked at the eggs the way you look at two acres of wet lawn that need to be cut, and he did what he had to do. He didn't chew. He swallowed as quickly as he could and then washed it down with a glass of Tia Maria. It was drinking chocolate milk with breakfast all over again. The alcohol and sugar went straight to his head and he felt a bit lightheaded and giddy. Dara handed him the two precious pills.

"Down the hatch, lover."

"You are good to me."

"Yes, I am," she said. "You need looking after."

Arial was too sick to eat. Neither of them had showered in days. Arthur grabbed her by the wrist and took her with him into the shower. The hot water was a violation, as if reality and responsibility were lashing out at them from the darkness. The dance was over. The sun was coming up but that was neither here nor there. They no longer worshipped the sun. Arthur and Arial curled up in their vampire bed and drifted off for twenty-four hours of exhausted sleep.

By chance, it was morning again when they awoke. Arthur felt damaged. His lungs had crystallized while he slept, and his heart was beating through his chest. He was full of fear. They were watching. Mickey wasn't to be trusted. He had known that all along. But what was it he had said? He practically admitted that he was working for the cops. Arial was missing from the bed too. She and Mickey were in this together. A child could see that.

Arthur looked around the room and his eyes fastened on a ball-peen hammer that was sticking out of a toolbox. He put it under his bathrobe and made a quick reconnoitre of the apartment. Eric and Dara had gotten more mileage out of their heroin than he and Arial had gotten out of their coke. Maybe smack really was the better drug. The smackers looked pretty much dishevelled, but they were up and taking mouldy toast and tea. The crackers looked like they had just chopped up the corpse of a clergyman. Even after a twenty-four–hour sleep, they looked infected and fevered. Their eyes were full of pain. The dark circles cried out a warning to the living.

The furniture in the apartment was all still pushed away from the wall. The mountains of books and clothes that had been piled neatly on top of the furniture had found their way to the floor where they had been trodden upon. The centre of the room was impassable and so people used the periphery as a jungle trail to get from one room to another. The air in the room was too hot and far too close. The social contract had been abrogated by a more potent understanding of need.

There were rules about how to behave but they had nothing to do anymore with mutuality or respect. There was only the dope, the getting of the dope, the using and then the whole thing again and again, until something broke and darkness descended. Arthur and Arial were shaking with fear. Eric and Dara were infuriatingly calm, and rather matter of fact, about how to spend the morning.

"Dude, you look terrible," said Eric, who was sitting in the one comfortable chair in the apartment drinking a cup of tea in his bathrobe. "We were beginning to wonder if you were ever going to wake up. You were out for twenty-four hours."

"I don't feel good," said Arial. "I need a wake-up."

"Lady, the reason you went to bed is because we're out of dope. Sleeping for a whole day didn't do anything to change that."

"What are we going to do?" she asked.

"Steal, deal, or quit."

Arial lost interest. She was too sick. She didn't want to hear it. There's nothing worse than dope fiends looking for a way out. Everyone talking at once. Everyone talking over everyone else and all of them talking about something different. Him on about robbing a filling station, her all for breaking into the pharmacy, and the other wanting to kidnap dogs. She quietly got to her feet and moved away back into her bedroom. She closed the door behind her and lay down on the bed. When she looked up at the ceiling fan, her head began to spin and she had to close her eyes to keep her sense of balance.

Arthur wasn't buying the official history. Eric had been saying they were out of dope for days. There had to be more somewhere. "I can't believe we went through five thousand dollars' worth of dope."

"Dude, that was way more than twenty. That was a big box. You should keep it as a souvenir. Old Linda loved you. But that doesn't matter anymore. It's gone."

Arthur couldn't fight his way through all the clutter. He shut his eyes hard and pressed his fingers forcefully against his brow trying to strangle a migraine at its birth.

It was Dara's meeting. "The question now is, how do we get some more?"

Eric asked a question he already knew the answer to: "You got any money?"

Arthur shook his still aching skull. "Only enough for a bus ticket home."

"Well, you're twenty bucks ahead of where I am right now. Dara came up with a great idea."

Arthur hated that. Since when was Dara in charge?

Dara spoke up nervously. "I was talking to Mickey. He said if we liberated some of the stuff from your lady's house that he would give us top dollar for it. He knows somebody with a van who could meet us over there."

So it is true! Mickey and Dara are in this together! "No, we're leaving that place alone."

Eric had the inner calm of a man who knows his next three meals are not going to be a problem. "Okay, fair enough, what's your plan?"

"I'm going to get on a bus and go home."

"Think about that for a moment, mungie cake."

"I gotta go. I can't stay here."

"Shut up with that shit," said Dara. "You promised your mom you'd be home for dinner a week ago and you haven't even phoned her. Oh, and your parole officer was expecting to see you too, but you had better things to do, and you couldn't pass a piss test right now if your life depended on it."

Arthur started to think about what was happening. Lots of things weren't right here but there was one heap of rubbish that stunk much worse than the rest of them put together. Eric wasn't in a panic. He was relaxed and letting Dara do all the talking.

"Why aren't you worried? You look very calm for a man with a bunch of bikers on his tail."

"Worrying about that isn't going to help. What we need is more dope."

"No, something isn't right here. Why aren't you all bent out of shape? I feel like I've blown my whole life but, really, it's not my ass on the line. I can lie my way out of this no problem. You're the one both sides of the law are looking for. Why aren't you sweating?"

The images in his mind shifted and formed a convincing new pattern. Eric had brought his needle along. Eric had triggered him by letting him hold the dope. This wasn't an accident. This had been deliberate. He had been betrayed. This dope was never going to go to the bikers. Eric had feathered his own nest. He and Mickey and God knows who else. He rounded on Eric.

"We were home free! We were out of trouble. Why the hell did you throw us back into the lion's den?"

"Whatever you say, Pop. Put it all on me. The rest of us stink to high heaven from this stuff. Why doesn't it stick to you? It's because of that bitch's cologne. That takes the stink out of everything. Who are you going to spray it on next, Rachael?"

"You bastard."

"Don't land your shit on me. You did this. You came up with the plan. You organized the trip and you got the friggin' girls at the bus station."

"You betrayed me."

"Are there bikers looking for your ass? No there are not. You get to go home and suck up to mommy again and say nothing happened and you can prove it. You're a fuck-up, you never deliver the goods, and I gotta say I agree with you about one thing. I hate you too."

"There never were any bikers were there?"

"You finally got there. I had your shiny Boy Scout ass figured out the first time I talked to you. You're a near-zero hero. You're the next big thing that's never going to happen. You never deliver, and when that spotlight starts going somewhere else, you shrivel up and die. You needed a sidekick. Someone to tell you lies. You're too arrogant to know when you're being played. There now, how's that for some truth."

Arthur was stunned. He couldn't take it in. "So all this was shit from the beginning."

"Nice recap. I was hoping to score fifty bucks off you that's all. But no, you decided to take on the project and save me from myself. My own personal Bob Geldof. They really got to you in that treatment centre, didn't they? They fucked you up. You've lost your edge. So what are you going to do about it? Thump me good for wising you up? Go back to church with that bitch, Rachael? Pray about it? It's not like you had to reach into your own pocket to pay for the dope. I may not be much but I'm the closest thing you have to a friend in this whole world right now."

"We're done. I'm not mad at you. I'm not even coming after you. But when you see me on the street, I won't see you. Got it. You're a ghost."

"Cakes, you can't do a damn thing with them."

Dara jumped in. "You fucking guys need to shut up. We need more dope. We're all fucked, and we're all going to jail, but maybe not today. So quit the Woody Allen shit and get on your coats. We're going for a walk."

It had snowed overnight. A fine powdery dusting of the white stuff. The weather had cleared, and a bright sun was scattering perfect light in all directions. Arthur remembered the story about Peter hearing the cock crow for the third time. He had abandoned Linda; he had robbed her and now he was going back again. This was beyond betrayal. *Why do my feet keep moving?* He was a perjurer in a cardboard suit standing in the witness box at a show trail. A liar, known to be a liar, perfectly coached and prodded to deliver. His bent words bearing unfaithful witness to an even more brutal untruth. *I really am a monster now.*

Eric had left a basement window unlocked. He had known they would be back. That explained his lack of panic when the dope ran low. How could Arthur not have known? Arthur didn't want to be there, but he was afraid what these animals might do to the place if he was not there to restrain them. This was such a mad, desperate venture.

Before, they had gone on tippytoes at night, sober, full of caution and with a plan. Now they were pillaging in daylight. Four lunatics, all of them looking as if they had spent the night in a parked car, walking down a sidewalk in an upscale neighbourhood where everyone else drove. Why Dara and Arial had to come along he didn't know. He didn't want to know.

He caught a glimpse of the future, of Dara and Arial touching Linda's things. Making jokes about her clothes and calling her a whore. The coke wobbles hadn't gone away. He was waiting to feel a hand on his shoulder. The cops had to be watching. How could anyone not know exactly what they were up to simply by looking at them? Dope fiends. The living dead. Preying on the helpless. He was walking around with a ball-peen hammer stuck in the waistband of his pants.

His phone rang. It was Dale. He stopped dead in his tracks. He remembered for a second how it felt to be a kid and watch the adults do incomprehensible things.

Chapter 45

Mike and Kaiser were taking a breath of fresh air on the sun porch. Kaiser noticed Arthur skulking along Madison before Mike did. The body language spoke volumes.

"A little warranty work coming our way."

Mike turned and looked. "Oh, he's gotten himself sorted out properly."

"Who's he going to ask for?"

"He'll want Reg. Nice soft shoulder to cry on."

Kaiser pursed his lips and shook his head. "I'd say either Greg or Paul. This is confession time."

"I don't suppose you have twenty-five cents to back that up?"

"Betting is not allowed on the premises."

"Taking money from a fool isn't betting — ante up, blowhard."

Arthur stood at the bottom of the front steps with his hand on the railing. He looked winded but he wasn't. Had these been the thirteen steps that led to the gallows, he could not have feared them more. At least that ascent brought a resolution. This was pulling a panther's tail.

When he looked up and saw Kaiser, he faltered a second time. He was back to staring at his image in the bathroom mirror. But this time it was not about finding a face to stare down the world. He had been supplanted in that glass. There Kaiser stood in his place — tall, ramrod straight, with a shock of blond curly hair. His features were sharp, and his emotions damped down. A sentry guarding a public building. He looked right through Arthur and saw everything. Every putrid, disgraceful, soul-rotting thing. All of it visible. None of it hidden. The how and the why and wherefore laid bare. Kaiser knew, and knew that he knew, and Arthur hated him. He hated Kaiser for being inside his head, under his skin, and behind his eyes. The face of his enemy stared back at him where his own reflection in the mirror should have been. He despised himself for his weakness. He mounted the stairs until his eyes came level with the two counsellors. That was as far as his courage could take him.

"You look a little rough," said Mike.

"I am. I went nuts."

Kaiser stepped in front of Mike and right into Arthur's personal space. "When did you use last?"

Arthur took a step back and almost tumbled down the stairs. "A day ago. I spent an awful night sleeping in the bus station. Look, I really need to talk to someone." Arthur didn't take his eyes off Kaiser. He kept waiting for the scorpion to strike. Why didn't he strike and be done with it?

Kaiser delivered the needed counter poison in a soft and measured tone of voice. "Does it strike you as kind of odd that you've won all the arguments so far and yet here you are back on our front step bleeding to death? How do you explain that? Why did you come back?"

Arthur didn't respond. He couldn't. He was holding on by a thread.

Kaiser offered him the poison chalice a second time. "So you thought you'd swing by here and bullshit us again? Is that the plan?" That comment tightened Arthur's gut even further, but he held his tongue.

The interview was over. Mike gave him a faint look of support and pointed to one of the deck chairs. "Have a seat, General McArthur. Let me go talk to Doug."

———

Doug was wrestling with what to do with Eustice Czombo. Like Kaiser, he was mononymous but unlike Kaiser, his reasons for going by the single name were obvious. He had showed up for treatment with his shoulder-length hair dyed green and a bathtub plug on a chain hung around his neck. His attitude was even worse than his personal grooming. He had showed Paul a card that he claimed allowed him to smoke medical marijuana for his fibromyalgia. The staff wanted nothing to do with him.

Doug looked down at the assessment. *We can't put up with that. He's going to be nothing but trouble. It's going to be one damn thing after another until he pisses off everyone and I have to throw him out.*

Doug was hesitant because of Czombo's age — he was only twenty. Doug understood teens. He put up with a lot from them because he realized that even a disastrous stay at Punanai could take ten years off the time they spent in active addiction. The problem was that they disrupted the house. It was always difficult to weigh those two perennial issues. What was right for the house and what was right for the client.

When Mike knocked on the door Doug was grateful for the interruption. "Our boy is back."

Doug smiled at him. "Ours is a large and dysfunctional family. Which boy?"

"Arthur Silver Nose Cardel."

"Why Silver Nose?"

"He won the silver medal at the world coke championship."

"Has he talked to his mom? She's been phoning."

Mike pointed to the door. "I don't know. He's outside, beat up as all hell. I left him sitting in the cold with Kaiser for company."

"This could be our chance," said Doug with a gleam in his eye.

"Who do you want to talk to him?"

Doug bit his lower lip, something he only did when he was about to tell a lie. "Let's shuffle the deck and make him do the work for a change. Let him talk to whoever he wants to."

Mike was intrigued. "That's generous. Why are you letting him choose?"

Doug stepped out from behind the job for a second. "He's a good kid from a decent family and I want to nail this thing if we can. If he gets to choose the counsellor, maybe we can avoid one of his legendary pissing contests."

Mike smiled with his eyes. "That is so sensible."

Doug put his game face back on. "That's why they put the extra zero on my cheque."

Mike was certain now. "You're up to something, you conniving old bastard. You never could tell a lie. Out with it."

Doug gave him an embarrassed grin. "Body language is hearsay and therefore inadmissible. You can't convict me for either colouring or twitching."

Mike smiled. "Where there's smoke, there's fire insurance."

"I'll say this much: I badly overstepped the boundaries with his parents. I guessed in the heat of the moment and I guessed spectacularly wrong. If I get a chance to put things right, I'm going to take it."

"And if you guess wrong again?"

"Then it'll be your job to bring my successor up to speed."

———

Reg wished that he had brought along his Urim and Thummim. This kid lied at the best of times. What would he be capable of now desperate and reeking of shame. He put his misgivings aside and led Arthur into an interview room. "Grab a pew, sinner" was all he said by way of an introduction.

The look on Arthur's face was one of genuine humility. "Thank you for seeing me."

"We sure do a lot of interviews with you," said Reg, placing his canes out of his way on the chair beside the desk.

Arthur put his head down. "I feel like the Manchurian candidate."

Reg understood why he did, but he needed to get him talking so he played dumb for the moment. "I don't know that one; explain it to me."

"He was a guy in a movie. He was programmed to be an assassin, but he didn't know it. Someone would say the secret word and he'd turn into a remorseless killer."

Reg leaned back in his chair and opened his arms. "This is getting way too serious. Let's do a line." Reg punched the words and then made a show of patting down his pockets searching for a bag of powder.

The offer jarred Arthur to his bones. He felt as if his face had been slapped hard enough to break his nose. He responded with an inane "What?"

"The secret word." Reg had him. "You should've seen your face. I bet your heart is hammering too. C'mon, admit it. I triggered you simply by saying the word."

"That wasn't a fair test." Arthur's look dared Reg to disagree. "I'm not that bad."

Reg slammed him again without raising his voice. "Actually, you are. You're a friggin' blood-splattered, brain-munching monster."

"You saying it doesn't make it true."

"That's what my eyes and nose are telling me. You smell worse than a polecat and you look like you live out behind the 7-Eleven. Not looking down your nose at Chucky today? Are you and the Chuckster finally getting on speaking terms?"

That stung. Arthur had wanted to tell Reg the story very badly, but now he was having doubts. He didn't know it, but what he really wanted was for an adult to make sense of what had happened. He wanted Reg to explain this whole mess to him and then fix it. That's what adults were supposed to do.

There was suddenly an urgency to his words, one that would not have been out place in the back seat of a police car. "I met this guy in detox. He said he was in trouble over some lost money. My girlfriend had a big stash of dope at her place, and Eric and I finagled our way in and took it. We were going to sell it and use the money to pay off the bikers."

Reg was thinking about how this would go down with a judge. Arthur had done more than enough to get himself some provincial time. He wasn't a jaywalking wannabe anymore. "Does she know it was you?"

It was easier to tell the story now that the spell was broken. "No, she's in a psych ward. She doesn't know what happened. I'm nothing to her." He started to choke up. He had never verbalized that before. "She screwed my brains out for three months, got me thrown out of medical school, and now she doesn't know who I am. She was never going to use that dope. I couldn't let her come home and find it."

He imagined the scene in his mind's eye, her reaching into the drawer and finding the lacquered box. Curiosity giving way first to surprise and then to confusion, until it all leapt out from the darkness like a sharp-fanged predator in a moment of dreadful insight. Over the edge she would tumble. His head went down as he went with her into that pit. *Oh shit, Linda. How did this happen?*

Reg started to pick up the pieces of broken glass before Arthur could cut himself. He started with an easy one. "Have you talked to your mom yet?"

"No."

"Couldn't face her?"

His back went up. "You remind me of Kaiser when you say that."

"Is that a no?"

"Look. I didn't know that was going to happen — everybody knows, I'm not like that."

"Bullshit. You are lots of things, but you're not dumb. Did you finally do something so absolutely friggin' awful that you can't live with it? That insight alone would make all this pain and destruction worthwhile. Did you at least get that done?"

"No, I messed up — but I'm not a monster. When the dope ran out, we were going to break into Linda's house again and loot the place. We had to walk there because we didn't have enough for bus fare. It was a long walk. I couldn't do it. I can live with taking the dope. But they were going to wreck Linda's place. I couldn't let that happen, not to her. Not the way she is now." The image of her vulnerable and broken in that godforsaken wheelchair had him clubbing the side of his head with his fists. His fit passed and he became silent once again. He sounded finished but he wasn't.

"My brother called. He'd been calling every hour. The same way I'd been calling Linda. I did that to him." There was a gasp and a groan as his head went down, but when his head came back up, a terrible resolution had replaced his sorrow. "I told them to stop. We weren't doing this. They freaked. Dara spat in my face. She asked me if I was a man. Arial said, no, because I couldn't get it up. Eric stood there, nodding his head, looking vindicated, as if he'd known all along I couldn't be trusted. I was so angry. I hated them. I tried to dial the cops. I was going to tell them junkies were on their way to rob Linda's house. That's when Dara knocked the phone out of my hand and stomped on it." His arm went up over his head. "But I pulled out a hammer and I backed them all up. They were pissed."

Reg's face seemed interested, but he was not buying a word of what he was hearing. This was bullshit writ large. The noblesse oblige sunk the story faster than a sack of rocks.

Arthur's energy faltered for a moment as he considered the implications of what he had said. He was waiting for Reg to contradict him. He started speaking faster and faster, fearing that he had to say everything that there was to say before he was inevitably told to shut up.

"I walked to the bus station and panhandled until I got enough for a ticket. The bus was full of students. I couldn't look at them. If I could've pulled my coat over my head on the bus, I would've done it. No one wanted to sit next to me. I didn't belong with them anymore. They were all happy and excited about going back to school. I kept my head down and felt inside my belt for the hammer. Knowing it was there helped me stay still."

Reg had to ask. "You tried to protect her ... do you still have feelings for Linda?"

"Yeah, in spite of everything, I still care." He sighed and put his head down. "She took me places I didn't even know existed. Having her attention made me feel worthwhile. I'd been pretending for so long and hating myself for it. I had feelings locked down deep inside me that I didn't know about, but she did. I was so afraid. I couldn't even speak the words ... let alone ask for what I wanted. She came along and before I knew it, the words were there. I adored her."

He checked out Reg for a reaction and got none. Reg had his game face on. The look of disapproval Kaiser had administered on the sun porch leapt off Arthur like a bed bug and landed on Reg. It shook the anger loose. "Do you understand, Reg? Well, do you? Can I even talk to you about this if you don't know? Linda was a goddess when I left for home. I couldn't wait to get back to her. Then something crumpled her up and threw her away. She's old and broken now. The way she looked in the hospital creeped me out. I couldn't bring myself to touch her." There was a long pause. Arthur's head went down and his lips pursed in disgust.

"This is the part you wouldn't tell us about earlier."

Arthur's answer had nothing to do with Reg's question. "I don't know. I don't know. Leave me alone." In his mind's eye, Arthur scrutinized Linda's face in the wheelchair. Waiting, hoping, and praying for the wink that would tell him that none of this was true.

"I figured Linda was a guy."

"What?"

"The reason you wouldn't tell us who Linda was. I figured Linda was a guy."

"Linda is no guy."

"Yeah, but do you see my point. Linda had to be someone you were ashamed of. Someone who had to be kept hidden."

"So you think I'm a fag?"

"Try to listen to what I'm saying. Why were you ashamed of Linda? When people feel shame it's a sign that something is wrong."

"It was her age…"

"The way your voice trailed off there tells me there's more."

"She made me do things…"

"Things that could come back and bite you?"

"I don't think so. Well, it might. She made a video. Linda was like a dominatrix. She told me what to do and I did it. It was fun. I really enjoyed that part. The dressing up. The acting. Rehearsing the scenes. Meeting the girls. Suddenly realizing that what we'd been talking about was going to happen. It made so much sense when I was stoned." There was a pause, and his voice dropped. "But then she put it on the web." He looked up at Reg as if he could put it all right. He was a kid holding a bird with a broken wing in his hands.

"It was supposed to be only for us — private. When we were high and together, I was okay with what we'd done. We showed the world what we thought of them and their rules. We put their shitty little lives under the microscope. We did what they didn't dare. It was insane — immoral and magnificent."

This time saying it didn't make it so. His gut got there first. Sending him a message of disgust. Telling him to turn away and clean himself. His heart grew heavy and he despaired. In his mind's eye he saw Doc sitting in the wheelchair in the same stained housecoat sneering at him and making faces. He shook his head violently. Words started to pour out of him like dark blood from a deep cut.

"When we crashed, I wondered what my mom would feel when she saw it. I thought about the look I always get from my dad. I started to think about all the kids who ended up killing themselves when their friends saw them in videos. I tried watching it when I was straight, but it was too raw. I hated what I was saw."

Reg felt heartsick. "Well, every sick son of a gun is doing a porno these days. Maybe it'll get lost in the pile. Is that the whole story now or are we still hunting snipe?"

"Sort of." He didn't want to talk to anyone about Rachael. If Reg said something toxic about Rachael, the way he had about Linda … that would be too much and a half. He couldn't risk that.

Reg felt Arthur slinking away. He was wounded. He tried to keep him talking. He wanted him to spill everything. He circled back to a safe question. "You said Linda was in hospital. Is she still there?"

"As far as I know." The evasive answers were creeping back into the conversation.

"Have you been to see her?"

"Yeah, that didn't go so well."

Reg tried to rekindle his anger, to get him to speak without thinking first. "Did the drugs you gave her make her crazy?"

That question hurt. It made it sound as if he was to blame, that he was the one who got this whole thing started. Arthur was fully engaged once again; he wasn't having any of this. The wounded animal turned and committed the last of its strength to the fight. "No, they think she has something wrong with her." His anger toward Linda finally showed its head. "She's straight to the point of being boring when she's in her right mind."

Reg now had the game pieces on the board and for the first time he understood how they had ended up in these positions. "Why didn't you tell us?"

"I don't understand."

Reg switched his tone from grand inquisitor to doting uncle. His voice said that he understood now what had happened and he was back on Arthur's side. "We don't care who you sleep with, especially on a drug run. What did you think we were going to do with that information?"

There was a long silence. Arthur had to think about that. "If I told you the truth, you would've stopped me."

Silence. Reg needed an answer. "Stopped you how? What could we have done?"

Arthur's answer floored him. "You would have told my parents."

Reg reacted to this badly. He went from confidant to accuser in a breath. "You're looking at jail time and you're worried about me telling your parents? How old are you? Cut the crap! You wanted it to continue!"

"God, yes! The drugs, the sex — all of it. It was perfect. I was happy there, for once in my stinking life. I'd go back there in a second if I could."

His mind flashed on what happened in the chapel. He couldn't bring himself to say, *Just to be with Linda one more time ... the way it was* — because he'd tried that with Arial and it hadn't worked and because that desire separated him in perpetuity from the possibility of Rachael.

"That's all we wanted to know. Arthur, you didn't want to stop. We get that. So what do you know now that you didn't know before your road trip?"

"I thought I could be around the cocaine and not use."

"This look on my face means I think you're telling me what you think I want to hear. Don't do that. So straight up, the first time, why did you really come back here?"

Arthur was so hung up on the juxtaposition of Rachael, Arial, and Linda that he forgot to lie. The news went out without a tweaking from his now-disgraced spin doctor.

"When I'm out there, I want to use. I don't mean to, but it happens. It comes out of the blue." Arthur was stunned. He didn't know that about himself a minute ago. The first fruit from the Punanai talking-to. Hearing the lie on your own lips for the first time. "When I was here, I could stay sober. I felt okay. I want that feeling back."

Arthur really had Reg with that answer. That was precisely what he wanted to hear. Reg was still wary. It was all too pat and easy. Not enough pain to make him feel certain. Arthur was experienced enough now to know what to say, so Reg cut a little deeper, he needed to be sure. He wasn't going to waste his ace of trump on a trick that wasn't decisive.

"Mr. Cardel, you're a full-blown addict. You'd say that in a second to get in out of the rain. Maybe you're not as sick as some of the other guys, but so what? How far gone do you have to be before you say, 'Okay, I got it'? A hundred pounds? Seventy-five? Two teeth gone? Two teeth left? Are you going to kill someone or watch someone die before you own this?"

Arthur was squirming. Kaiser's disapproval was seeping in everywhere now, as surely as sea water finds a path through shattered planks. It had taken up a new station behind Arthur's eyes and found congruence with the words excoriating him from both within and without. The harmony was physically painful. He would have willingly slithered through a narrow pipe to escape this close confinement. He needed to breathe fresh air again. He needed to wash the corrosive sounds out of his consciousness. They clung to him like sand fleas. Arthur stared to yell, trying to beat down the chorus inside his head. The nascent truth that had stuck its head out of the burrow and scented the air ached to be gone — longed to be down deep inside the earth for another season of sleep.

"You're killing me with this."

Reg was back to calm. He started to gather up his canes pretending that he was getting ready to go. "Until you burn down the orphanage with the kids locked inside, it's hard to believe you're a monster. Until this happens to you, in your own body, there's no way you can imagine it. You can't explain this to anyone who hasn't had the experience. It's off their map."

"Is there some hope ... some hope for me?"

Reg struggled to find his feet. "I don't feel any hope for you. I know you're lying to me and I'm quite sure you're lying to yourself. You keep trying to control something that can't be contained. I don't know which of your many faces is more ridiculous. Who do I throw my support behind: the cougar's plaything, the smart self-destructive young fellow who never quite gets to medical school, the slippery young cokehead learning the ins and outs of addiction at detoxes and crack houses, the guy who steals dope from his girlfriend? Not one of those faces has a soul. When I line up all your masks and look at them as a group, I ask myself, what are all these false faces hiding and what are they pointing to? Is there a mastermind behind this or is the tail really wagging the dog?"

"You make this shit up. You can't know all the things you pretend to know."

"Let me show you how I do it." Reg took off his glasses and leaned into Arthur's space. "Look at my face, Arthur. Take it in. But concentrate mostly on my eyes. This is the way a healthy face looks. When I don't see one of these staring back at me, I get curious. You see, there has to be a reason. Faces change for a reason. Your face speaks volumes. I've seen your face many times before on other young men. I'm not fooled. I'm not afraid. They all eventually told me the truth because they had to. We do things when we're stoned that we can't live with when we're sober, and we can't stay stoned all the time."

Arthur sat with his head down. He was out of words. Emptiness had him by the throat.

Reg drew the Urim out of his breastplate. "The thing that's going to keep you out of medical school is your character, not your drug use. You're at the point now where if you don't quit, you're going to die or go to jail and then die. Either way, the cocaine is on the verge of solving the Arthur problem."

Chapter 46

John knew that Peter was angry because he had missed two sessions at Flannerman's. He was waiting for John on the third morning. That was the tell. John was usually the first to arrive. Peter's body language was rigid and ill-tempered. There was no doubt about it. The Grand Council of the Undead had sent their ace trouble-shooter to get this wretched sinner back in line.

Peter looked up at John in sadness. The odd white patch that showed from time to time was back on his forehead. John tried to say something to him about it so that he could look in the mirror before it vanished again, but he was not there to listen.

"Are you insane?" Peter stammered.

"No, I didn't listen to shit-for-brains long enough for that to happen, but another five minutes of Chairman Barry and I would have been nuts."

"Don't be flip with me. Do you have any idea the danger you have placed us in?"

"Ah, no," John chimed back.

"The council wanted to excommunicate you."

"Really? That would be swell. Do they have a ceremony for that?"

"I don't know why I bother with you — you treat everything as a joke. When they do excommunicate you, I can have no more to do with you."

"That sounds bad. What else did they say?" John prodded.

"That is privileged communication. I am not at liberty to say. But what I can tell you is this: This is your last warning, John. You have tried the patience of council once too often. If I hadn't used my influence…"

"Peter, there is one thing I have to know. Oh, Peter — we used to be friends."

There was a horrible silence until Peter drew out, "Well…"

"Can I keep the decoder ring?"

"Naff."

Chapter 47

After lunch was finished and the dishes were cleared away, Mike communicated that he needed a few minutes alone with Doug. He did this by saying the magic word. "Backgammon?"

"One won't hurt," said Doug, eagerly rising to the bait. Mike watched Doug set up the board. In the old days when Doug still smoked, he could always be corralled for ten minutes with the offer of a cigarette. It was a very efficient way to get things settled. It gave Mike ten minutes of the boss's full attention without interruption. In the post-tobacco era, he had learned to approach Doug in one of three ways. When Mike needed to say something unprofessional about a colleague or something libellous about a superior, he suggested that he and Doug go for a walk. When all hell broke loose, the preferred venue was the bagel shop at Wilson and Bathurst. This conversation fell halfway between impertinence and catastrophe and so backgammon gave them the time and space necessary to clear the air. Mike knew something was up, and Doug knew that Mike had rumbled him.

"Did you get your compassion booster shot?"

Doug tried and failed to look surprised. "What do you mean?"

"You're acting guilty. First you drive Chucky to the detox for old times' sake, then you let that horrible little airhead Czombo, green hair and all, into the house, and now you're mulling over bringing Cardel back in. Are we sweating the results of a colon-cancer screen?"

Doug laughed. There was no fooling Mike the Nose. It was time to come clean, but not before a few playful equivocations. "No. My health is good and everything is fine at home. My subscription to *National Geographic* is up next month and I *am* wondering if I want to renew it, it's a big commitment, two years. Otherwise, everything's Jake."

"So you're not trying to get into heaven? Say, you haven't been reading books on counselling again have you?"

"Alas, there is never enough time for that. No, my friend, I am in possession of secret knowledge in this case."

"Well that all sounds very mysterious. What can you tell me?"

"I had a visit from Dr. Robert Dickens at my home."

"House call?"

"Hardly, he's not that kind of doctor. He's the father of the mysterious Linda Dickens."

Mike was furious with himself for not being able to work it out on his own. "I'm not with you yet."

Doug was enjoying his confusion. "Arthur's older, storied girlfriend."

"Oh, what did he want?" In his excitement Mike missed an obvious move.

Doug pounced on the misstep. "Well he has a bigger mess to clean up than we do. His daughter was Arthur's teacher when she boinked him. Arthur is old enough to follow where his heart —or any other organ — leads, but she was in a position of trust with him. There's no doubt she went way over the line. She made an intimate video of their time together and put it on the web. She even sent the dean a copy, in case he missed it, along with a bottle of red wine and a rather saucy note. She's lost her tenure."

"She's lost more than that."

"The problem is, she doesn't remember most of it."

Mike thought about Arthur's tortured face as he stood on the steps. "Most of it…"

"Dickens couldn't get the whole story out of his daughter, so he had some detectives look into things. They have pretty much tidied up the mess. But Dr. Bob is one of these characters with a conscience. When he met Arthur at the hospital, he figured he was a hustler and he offered him some money to blow town. He was getting ready to write a hefty cheque when the kid surprised him by asking for breakfast money and a bus ticket home."

Mike couldn't believe his ears. "Arty the coke monster turned down the money!"

"Yup. Dickens didn't think that would be the end of it. He thought Arthur would have some sober second thoughts. He said he was expecting a letter from the parents or a lawyer, and when that didn't happen, he got even more curious and he turned the detectives loose on Arthur to see what he was up to, and they tracked him down here."

Mike shook his head. He was only half paying attention to the game and he rather unwisely employed the doubling dice. "Normal people can't do that…"

Doug was delighted by Mike's lapse in judgment and he doubled the stakes again. "This guy isn't normal. *Uber gelt.* He feels bad for Arthur. Middle-class parents, smartest kid in school, works his ass off to get into university, and ends up getting his ass spanked in frosh week by his psychology professor in an all-girl gangbang video."

Mike recognized that his position on the board was hopeless. "I will never be able to look at Arthur again without feeling enormous respect for his contribution to the visual arts."

Doug made a face that said, *that's not the half of it.* "I phoned downtown and talked to the big brains about Dr. Dickens. Bill Parks predictably claimed the pressures of overwork and went to ground. Erin Fogbriar took up the challenge and has taken it upon herself, in Bill's absence, to personally oversee every aspect of the case. So we'll have to work around her. The most interesting reaction was from Jimmy the fundraiser. He wet his pants when he found out who we were dealing with."

"So that was the big meeting yesterday?"

"It was."

"So when Cardel showed up, you started to break the rules because the big boys downtown want to hit a financial home run."

"It's a shame your smarts don't run all the way to backgammon. Another?"

"You said just one."

"Anyways, the good doctor wants to borrow the keys to the time machine and go back to the night Linda and Arthur met and send the kid off to the movies instead."

"Time machine on the fritz again?"

"You know it. Every time you pop the clutch, you find yourself ten years older. So here's the problem, my dear friend. The doc wants to put things right. He's willing to pull all the strings necessary to get Arthur back into medical school and on a full scholarship. Arthur impressed him when he turned down the money. But the good doc didn't get to where he is today by being dumb.

"We spent two hours that night trying to work out if helping Arthur this way is the best or the worst thing we could possibly do. Dickens made it clear that nothing would please him more than having this all pass for good fortune. He wants to put things right, but from behind the scenes. But more than that, he wants this settled. If there's going to be expense and name-calling, he wants to deal with all the bad news at once."

"Did you talk to the Cardels yet?"

"Nope, only you. But they're on the way in."

"So we're not sending Arthur somewhere else?"

"No, I'm going to keep him here."

"Is Dickens paying for his treatment?"

"He wrote us a cheque for a hundred thousand dollars. For a sum that handsome, he deserves a miracle, but he may have to settle for a happy ending. So the poop from on high is this: If we disappoint Dr. Idi Amin Dada, our next gig will be at the two-for-one Polish sausage booth on Richmond Street. But hey, no pressure, eh?"

"No, simply turn a youthful porn star into a surgeon and all will be well."

"How much can we tell the staff?"

"Unless you yearn for the smell of charcoal and burning bratwurst, not a freaking word."

Chapter 48

Reg and Kaiser were having a smoke. The wobbly ceasefire brokered by Mike was holding exactly as it had the time before and the time before that. The winter air was cold and dry. The endless cloud of December had given way to the bright, sundrenched blue skies of January. At midday, you could feel the sun's power on your face. The axis of the earth would soon tilt, and North America would slowly move back toward spring and new life. Reg and Kaiser resembled two world-weary crows waiting for something to succumb to the cold.

"Kaiser, what do you really think is going on with Cardel?"

"I got bigger problems to worry about."

"Such as…"

"I got another box of dead bees this morning."

"Again? Who's sending them?"

"No return address. Only a name. Chester. Who names their kid Chester? Got to be a serial killer. What did I ever do to deserve this?"

Nah too easy. "Answer my question."

"Queer as Dick's hatband. Closet case. Can't get the job done with women unless they're dressed like plumbers."

"Paraphilia?" asked Reg as he turned awkwardly away from the rail to look at Kaiser.

"Who knows, you could talk to him about this in therapy for years and he'd never tell you a thing. But change the scene, meet him in a bar and buy him two drinks, and he'll take you home and show you the sick shit that floats his boat."

"I think this kid has been smothered. Stifled initiative. A young man needs to smoke weed and follow a punk band for a while." Reg recalled his own youth. "Growing up is still all about rebellion. He told me he never dated in high school; he spent all his time studying."

"Ah, the breeding ground for a serial killer. Say, you don't suppose his middle name is Chester, do you? Yeah, of course it is. It's all starting to make sense — Arthur Chester Cardel."

Reg wasn't finished. "I figure, if your sexual feelings get repressed, they still find their way to the surface but in distorted ways. They get twisted and compressed and bent out of shape. When you can't express yourself sexually, things get weird. That's what paraphilias are all about."

Kaiser smiled from ear to ear. "Still can't bring yourself to call this kid an asshole?"

Reg felt Kaiser crowding again, only one opinion: his. "My guess is that he's furious with everyone for jerking him around." He looked at Kaiser for a reaction.

Kaiser appeared to be rapidly cooling to this subject of conversation. "He's a dumb kid."

Reg didn't agree. "Nope. I get the sense this kid is smarter than me. He makes connections in his head at lighting speed. It's hard to keep up with him sometimes, but then he always trips himself up by saying something stupid."

Kaiser nodded in agreement. "He's kid dumb. He buys a dodgy car from a curbsider. He can't afford to insure it or even find a place to park it, so he leaves it on the street. He laughs at having a glovebox full of tickets until he discovers he can't get his driver's licence or plate renewed until he pays the fines."

Reg stubbed out his cigarette and took up his canes. "Ah, adolescence. I remember it well. Thinking that the end of the month was such a long way off."

Kaiser brightened as if an unexpected cheque had providentially shown up in the mail. "Take heart, my quadrupedal friend, there is going to be a moment of retribution."

"Really? Are you going to lop off one of his ears, Kaiser?"

"Nothing so pedestrian. No, they're putting Slippery Cardel in the same room as Eustice the Green Menace Czombo."

"Whose twisted idea was that?"

"The evil Mike. He had to stifle a chortle as he did it."

"This is one up on the time he put a cop, a bank robber, and a judge in the same room."

"All our bad eggs in one basket, is that the plan? Let them kill each other off?"

"No, this is a change of tactics. We gave him RK as a good example last time. Let's see how he fares with the bad example. Maybe looking at brother Eustice will put him in touch with his own shadowy self."

"Say, you don't suppose anyone ever called him 'useless Eustice,' do you?"

"I hope not. I want to be the first."

Chapter 49

Sally and Gerry made the drive to Punanai for yet another meeting with Doug. That man sorely tried her patience. Sally imagined herself a prisoner sentenced to life with no possibility of parole, and this car ride her last look at the world she loved.

Gerry might as well have been some grim, burned-out policemen. A poor old plodder praying for the passing of days, aching inside for the end of work and a new start in life, away from all these pathetic toxic people so unfairly placed in his path.

Sally sighed and looked out the window. Resigned to the horror of it. Nothing to be said. No point of law to be disputed. No evidence to be tested and decried. Only the hopeless footfalls of the damned. Going to a place where dreams are taken away from you as easily as wristwatches from prisoners, a place where everything you once were, or ever hoped to be, is tagged, and placed inside manila envelopes and stored along with the clothes you were wearing on the day of your arrest.

Like fossilized footprints or leaves pressed in a book, we leave a desiccated signature of our passing. But these tokens only show that we once passed this way, they offer no path back to where we long to be.

"Gerry."

"What is it, my love?"

"You look so lost."

Gerry exhaled. The image was in his mind.

Sally felt a nascent tear in his sigh, but an invisible, reflexive hand snatched the blessed tear back from Gerry's eye and dragged it, screaming, back into his hot, angry, boiling gut. The moment of vulnerability passed as it always did.

She tried again. "What do you want to happen today?"

He twisted the steering wheel as if he was trying to braid a rope. "I want this to be over. Every time we talk to Doug, I get so angry I want to hit him. Arthur makes me angrier still. I can't stand to look at him. Everything about him annoys me. At lunch, he leaves the knife in the peanut butter jar. Pre-schoolers do that, not grown men. I'm sick to death of this kid. This whole addiction thing is killing me."

Gerry pulled the Lexus over to the side of the road. He undid his seat belt and turned to face Sally. He took a deep breath and reached out to take both of her hands in his. "I'm angry at Arthur for trampling the chance I worked so hard to get for him. I'm furious with myself for not knowing how to fix this. I ask myself why God has abandoned us. I can't put up with this anymore. I'm a man. I have to have what I want. I have put everything on hold for my family. I work for assholes. I cozy up to people I despise so I can get ahead. I take money from gullible people and then lie to them. I told myself it was just business. All of this seemed, if not worthwhile, at least bearable because it was going somewhere." He paused as if the horror of it all was coming clear to him for the first time. He looked out the front window a hundred years into the future. "I'm one of the people you see after a tornado has touched down, looking at what used to be their house. The only thing I really know this morning is this: We have to get this settled. I can't live this way."

Sally started to cry. Gerry regretted both his outburst and his honesty. He had said the wrong thing again and still didn't feel any better.

She looked up at him. "Why did it take you all these years to say that?"

"What?"

"Did you think I didn't know?"

"Know?" Gerry felt the edge of a blade at this throat.

"There has been no joy in you for years. I thought it was me."

Chapter 50

"There's something I've been meaning to ask you for some time."

Peter was wary. John could be so difficult. "Ask whatever you want. I don't have any plans for the rest of the day. Would you mind coming with me to the lobby? I have to keep an eye out for my ride."

John hated being one down to Peter, having to ask a question diminished him, but he needed to know. "The other day you were talking about people believing in God…"

"Were we talking about that?" responded Peter.

John prompted his aging memory. "You were telling me a story about being in a deserted town and seeing a sign that said Cool Water."

Peter brightened. "Yes, we did talk about that. Don't you believe in God, John?"

The thin, restless ghost was having a hard time keeping still. "I don't know what to believe. I was expecting to live a long time and then die and well … be gone. Being stranded here for my sins makes a brutal kind of sense if you believe in heavenly bookkeeping. That's got to be a point for your side. But here's one for mine. You still attend church, Peter. Why are you still here?"

"Naff."

"That's the second time you've used that word. What does it mean?"

"It's a nicer word than fuck, but it means the same thing."

John was starting to enjoy himself. "Have I offended you?"

The larger ghost got to his feet. John thought that the answer to his question was a resounding yes, and that this was the end of the conversation. He was mistaken.

"Not in the least, but look, I need to get to the lobby. Walk with me. You and I keep diddly dicking around with this damn light we're chasing. I feel as foolish as a child chasing a falling star. We're wasting a lot of energy and we have nothing to show for it." Peter pressed the button to summon the elevator. "John, I have no doubt that there is a God. But I don't think God is particularly interested in us. For me, God is someone who is far away and doing important things, spinning out new galaxies and presiding at the demise of stars. Someone who makes a sport of black holes and dances, like a sandpiper on the curving edge of a singularity."

John turned to look at Peter expecting to see a smile, but the big man was in earnest. "What the hell has a sandpiper got to do with this?"

Peter reframed his argument. "The serious point for me is that I never got my chance. My parents took it in the teeth during the depression. They lost everything but their lives."

The infuriatingly slow elevator soundlessly opened in front of them. Peter waved his companion ahead of him and then entered the car himself. Neither ghost pushed the button. Peter had pushed the button in order for the car to come to the basement. There was no reason for a living oldster to ever go down there, and the car would not come unless called. But neither ghost was willing to waste the additional energy required to push the button again when they knew they didn't have to. Like pious Jews on the Sabbath, they would ride the elevator until it opened on the floor they wanted. It gave them time to talk.

"When we were young, I didn't have a dime. I tried dating girls, but I couldn't afford decent clothes or even a haircut. No one wanted a poor boy, especially one with buckteeth."

"You had buckteeth?"

Peter showed him his gleaming smile. "Lots of people did back in the day. Mine were huge and yellow with brown spots. My breath stank too. They all had to come out when I was thirty. It cost a pretty penny to have the falsies put in, but what a difference. I could never have gotten a job selling real estate looking that way."

"So no girls, eh?"

Peter ignored the provocation. "In those days, we worked hard and saved our money. But the years got away from me. I was always winning monthly awards and getting sent away on trips. After a while, that became my whole life."

My God, he never had a girlfriend, John thought.

The door to the elevator opened and two ladies on walkers cautiously entered the car.

Peter didn't want to talk to John about anything that personal. John would find something to twist and then torment him with, simply for the fun of it. The way he did at council. Ridiculing Barry and Jack and disparaging the work. What have you ever done, you skinny little bastard? *thought Peter.*

"Only fools settle for any woman. I knew my day would come. God would send me someone special and that would make the wait worth it." *Peter checked John out for a reaction.*

"Didn't happen though, did it?"

You could see Peter sag. His shoulders rounded and his head went down. "I ran out of steam. I got so used to looking at women the way a wolf looks at a sheep, *it never occurred to me that someday those feelings would vanish. But go they did. I lost interest and before long I started to dislike most women."*

"Oh dear, did you putt from the rough?"

"Let us simply say that I found men to be easier companions, but I still need a special woman to complete my happiness."

John could see Peter looking to his defence. The poor man was on uneven ground, facing superior fire power, with the poverty of his position exposed to hostile eyes. Knowing that Peter was at a disadvantage, John decided to play a trump card. "So why did you have yourself freeze-dried?"

Peter stood up to his full height and glared at John. "That is a very ignorant way of talking about a stupendous process that enlightened people put great store in. Cryogenics is the best investment I ever made. Scientists are now starting to unpack the secrets of the universe. Cloning has been done on animals and will shortly be done on humans. If only I could have lasted a few more years. It has to be easier to prolong life than to start it from scratch. I know they can recreate my body, but without my mind — well it would be a cruel passage."

His bluster took John by surprise. "There's a contradiction for you. Believing that the God who gave you life can be cheated."

"It's not a contradiction. Who would want to go blindly to heaven and take the chance that eternity wouldn't be dreadful? I want a second chance in the body I was born in. This time I won't be some dumb, bumbling, bucktoothed kid stumbling through life without a clue. I know how the world works and I keep up on what's happening, even in death. I read the papers every morning and watch the real news. When this old head is put back into a young body, look out, mister. I will finally be able to do what I never got a chance to do. I'll have the bucks and the smarts to rule the world."

"So this isn't all about romance and love."

The door to the elevator opened to reveal the lobby, and Peter strode manfully out into the sunlight. He turned to address John, who remained in the elevator while the two women took their time getting out.

"Some of us have greatness within," he declared.

John had to say it. "So for you, a longing for belonging becomes a longing for belongings."

The fire passed from Peter's eyes. "Can you say that again? You're confusing me."

John moved closer and got right into Peter's face. "What do you think the light is?"

Peter stood his ground and glared right back. "It is how we perceive something that we don't understand."

"The way a deer standing on a highway perceives oncoming headlights?"

Peter took a step back and considered the possibilities. "That is an apt image. That light might be the very thing we need to find our way in the darkness or the very thing we need to avoid at all costs. It may have a use that is beneficial, but maybe not for us, and I'll be damned if I am going to step into its path until I know what I'm getting." With that, Peter took a seat by the window.

John threw his hands up over his head. "Peter, you have to know that's nuts."

"As we are taking turns pissing on each other's freshly laundered sheets, tell me, John, my cynical, easily satisfied friend, what do you think it is?"

He slowly turned and took a seat beside the larger ghost. "I don't know, either. If I had to guess, I think ghosts have some kind of charge. Maybe electrical or chemical in nature. I think we need to be attached to something. I have fancied myself like DNA in a virus, floating around looking for a new place to live. The light comes looking for us, but I wonder sometimes if it is intelligent. It might be drawn to us the way that dust is to a magnetic field."

Peter rubbed his face with his massive palms. "There has to be a better way for us to figure this out than hanging out in display windows or going to the ZiggZagg Club."

"I'm not sure which group is more annoying." John looked around the lobby for something, anything, that he could distract himself with. "Well, if there is another way forward, old pal, you're going to have to come up with it because I'm out of ideas. I'm sick and tired of following halfwits around in the faint hope that they are going to be snatched by the light."

They left the matter hanging between them for quite some time until they heard the sound of footfalls and polite leave-taking coming from down the hall. Peter stirred at the sound and got to his feet.

This left John alone with his thoughts. All this effort and nothing to show for it. Do we have this thing backward? What if the light isn't looking for the dying? Maybe it's only interested in the dead. The ones who didn't show up at the train station when they were supposed to.

He was about to say something to Peter, but Mrs. Zinder at 32 Madison had finished her visit with her husband, Earl. Peter hopped onto the front of her walker as she passed, and John watched both of them vanish out the front door. She was in a hurry. Her show came on at three o'clock.

Chapter 51

The mood in Doug's office was vastly different. The last time Gerry and Sally were here, their young man's life, while in peril, was far from lost. There were facts to be unearthed and alternatives to be weighed. The clock was crowding them but had yet to have the final say. They had such hope.

It's hard to stake your life savings on the turning of a roulette wheel. But that all changes when your reason for getting out of bed in the morning vanishes. After that, it's a simple matter to lay down your coins. They mock you. Money doesn't matter much when your dreams are gone.

Sally and Gerry had their heads around the problem this time. They were resisting the horrible feeling that this was their new normal. They felt like Arthur was already in custody and serving a life sentence. Their beautiful baby boy, so young and full of promise, was dead to them now. The boy they loved was inexplicably gone, and in his place stood a malevolent stranger. A heartbreaking twister of words, thoughts, and emotions. A predator with mayhem in his heart had made a home in their flesh and blood.

Sally spoke first. She always did. "Why do you want to put Arthur back into treatment? He didn't last a day."

Doug had changed his mind about the Cardels. They really were a little different from his regulars. But his heart was heavy with double-dealing. He knew things that he couldn't share with them, and it was this secret knowledge that was colouring his choices. He didn't know if he could get through the next hour without getting caught in a lie. A voice from deep in his gut whispered to him, *Don't do this*. It cost Doug a night's sleep to push that voice back into the unconscious and play the cards he had been dealt. This was the right thing to do, even if it didn't work. How do you explain that to a parent?

Doug stuck to the truth that was available to him. "We're bringing Arthur back in because it's the right thing to do. He told us this is the only place in the world where he feels safe enough to try to get sober again. That is sacred for us. We're not going to charge you for this. And I want to acknowledge, too, that I said some things last time that I regret saying now. Most of the people I deal with need that kind of talking to. I misread you and I apologize."

Gerry surprisingly offered Doug his hand. "We are where we are."

"What about you, Sally? How do you feel about what's happened?"

Sally had a distant look on her face. Her brow was deeply furrowed and little lines around her mouth and her eyes deepened as she stared at the top of the table, as if somewhere in the wooden grain the memory she was looking for could be found. She clenched her right hand tightly and spoke clearly, taking great care to enunciate her words. "The only note I heard in the whole symphony is this one: To be of any use to Arthur, I have to stay sane while I watch him struggle for his sanity. This feels so wrong. But I'm trusting and praying that this the right thing to do."

———

The telephone lobby at Punanai was hardly the place to make this call. But Arthur only had a few minutes to himself before Kaiser returned to show him his room. Arthur briefly considered calling from the corner, but he couldn't exactly call his dream girl from a payphone on the street to tell her he'd relapsed. *I need to talk to you* couldn't help but be heard as *I need a place to stay.*

He had rehearsed the most dignified way to say what was in his heart, but really, at the end of the day — no amount of polish could put this one over. A degenerate gambler asking to borrow money for his mother's heart medication had more credibility. Doc couldn't let himself sound needy — and this conversation stunk of desperation — but maybe Arthur could. He had picked up a bug and it was rewriting his software.

He took his calling card out of his pocket and stabbed it into the phone. When he heard the dial tone, he pulled it back out. He had a feeling that the end of the world would begin with a put-down from Rachael. He felt a rush of fear. He had to force himself to take a breath and stay near the phone. His feet wanted to take him places. He put the card back into the slot and dialled the number.

What an irony. Now he wanted to hear the voice mail. He was praying for the machine to pick up. If she answered, he was going to have to hang up. He couldn't say what he had to say to her in person. It was still too tender a root to support that kind of weight.

When Rachael heard the message after her class, she had to listen to it twice to make sense of it. The voice sounded lost. "Rachael, it's Arthur. I'm back in town and I'm all right. I got messed up but good on my errand. Could we meet for a coffee? I'll be at the Second Cup at seven. I need to talk with you."

Arthur looked at the telephone after he had hung up. He was expecting something to happen. Any act this brave and necessary couldn't simply pass between a disinterested piece of aging technology and the dead air of an institutional hallway.

He walked into the living room and picked up a magazine. He didn't want to read it, he didn't want to be here, and he couldn't bear to sit quietly and wait. Had anyone on this godforsaken planet ever let go of wanting and needing? *What kind of asshole lets things happen?* There had to be something that he could do to make himself feel better! He started to rock in his chair.

Inside he felt old and disfigured, as if he had been chewed up in a fire or an industrial accident. He looked around the room and wondered. *Are any of these guys going to get well? Is getting well even in the cards? Does anyone really give a rat's ass about what happens to drunks and junkies?* He couldn't figure it out. There was no way to know. What he did know was that he needed to talk with Rachael.

Chapter 52

The task of getting Arthur settled into his new room fell to Kaiser. Arthur had only been out of the house for a short period of time, so the two men flew through the paperwork. As they revisited their previous conversation, the unresolved tension between them had the time and space it needed to ripen. Arthur had no use for Kaiser. His overtures of friendship repelled him. Kaiser, for his part, was developing a sneaking fondness for Arthur. He saw in him a simpler version of himself. Not wrestling in his weight class, to be sure, but trying with great vigour to overthrow demons that he did not know how to master. That suited Kaiser. He saw that his role with Arthur would be to provoke. One of the softies could clean up the mess he was about to make. Kaiser had been looking forward to the next introduction all morning. As he showed Arthur his room, Kaiser was delighted to see his new roommate, green hair and all, sprawled out on his unmade bed with his suitcase standing open in the corner. The room smelled of socks, strong aftershave, and defiance. Arthur froze in the doorway not wanting to enter and trying not to look fussed. Kaiser squeezed to get by him. "Mr. Cardel," he said brightly, "this is Mr. Czombo. You two will be sharing a room."

Arthur felt let down as he moved past Kaiser to get a look for himself. He didn't want a roommate. The fact that Czombo was here first made him the intruder. The final irritant was the smug look Kaiser had on his face. There was a hidden hand at work here. This was some kind of payback.

When Arthur saw Czombo's green shoulder-length hair and the bathtub plug on a chain around his neck, the magic happened. This jolly green indigent was no RK. This clown was an embarrassment, drunk or sober. If Rachael saw them together, he'd be sunk. Arthur stuck out his hand to make the mandatory introduction with a rising sense of panic.

Czombo had lived on the streets for fifteen of his twenty years, even if he had slept at his mother's townhouse most nights. He counted on people not giving a shit and delighted in them refusing to see what was right in front of them. Affectation and indifference were the meat and potatoes on his plate. The look on Arthur's face told him that his charms and crystals still packed a disorienting punch. This poor boy was one more doomed stag beguiled by an orange spotlight shining from the back of a pickup truck. "Call me Czombo," he said with a smirk.

Arthur's face had lost even the pretense of interest. Czombo noted that his new wingman had gotten around the course in near record time. *Wouldn't throw me a brick if I was drowning.*

He watched the dominoes continue to fall behind Arthur's eyes. He was being written out of the script. Of less interest than either Rosencrantz or Guildenstern's livery men.

The look of satisfaction and superiority on Kaiser's face was only a little bit tougher to crack — that smirk told him that the staff had deliberately put Arthur in his room for some nefarious purpose. But whom was the joke on? Was Arthur supposed to be a role model for him? An inspirational figure to make up for the father he never had, or wanted, or for the big brother who should have taken his part, but who beat him instead? If that was the con, it was lame.

The three men stood there sharing a pregnant moment. Each had an agenda. Each certain they could jam the other fellow's radar. All fully invested in the forlorn hope of garnering some sort of advantage even if it had to come from someone else's storeroom. After the mandatory handshake Kaiser left the two new roommates to the silence. Out of sheer embarrassment and frustration, Arthur set about unpacking and setting up his side of the room. It gave him some time to think about this latest catastrophe. *What am I going to say to this moron?*

Czombo had seen a lot of clueless weaklings in his travels. The treatment centres and detoxes were full of them. Young men who couldn't quite put their finger on what was killing them. The street punk in him hated the little prince in Arthur. Pampered and preposterous, no imagination whatsoever. It was going to be as annoying as hell to watch Cardel sleepwalk with his eyes wide open. Just going through the motions and passing the time. He could feel his pain, it was palpable. What the poor mutt needed was a good blast of the shit. But that was a short ration around here, and not one to be offered freely with no hope of some kind of a substantial return.

Most of all, Czombo hated Arthur's face. He was the one. When the two of them got hauled into the cop shop, the sergeant would take one look at Arthur and know who to offer the deal to. Pretty boy looks said soft and gutless. They would put the questions ever so respectfully to Arthur in one room while they heartlessly put the boots to him in the other. They would ply Arthur with a cup of coffee and a biscuit and ask why he had ever listened to his evil companion while he enjoyed a cold head soak in the American Standard.

That was the way the world worked. It was also why it was so easy to stay one step ahead of these guys. Dye your hair green and wear a bathtub plug around your neck in place of a diamond pendant and you have created an indelible impression. Then when they look at your file and see you left school in grade eleven, their brains become paralyzed, and why not, surely it's a law of nature. If you look stupid you must be stupid. Maybe not to the point where they spoke pig Latin to each other while they discussed how to abuse you, but the basic contempt was there. It would never occur to any of them that you were far too smart for school.

———

There was a tradition at Punanai about taking care of your roommate. You were expected to take him to a meeting the first night he was there. What Arthur needed was privacy. He had pressing business. He had confided in RK the last time he met up with Rachael on the down-low, and that had actually worked out well. But not with this deadhead. The other guys had taken to calling him Zombie. Arthur couldn't dump the dude. That would be suspicious. So he went along with him to the coffee shop trying desperately to think of some way to ditch him. When Czombo muttered something and didn't follow Arthur inside, his spirits soared. Apparently, he had a few errands of his own to run.

Darlene had caught his eye standing outside the 7-Eleven. She had taken up a station in the alley behind the drugstore. After her fortnight in custody, she was determined to regain her lost market share with her always popular cash-in-your-stash suitcase sale. Someone had made a point rather forcefully with her. She had a dark bruise on her cheek, and it was clear that she needed cash badly enough that she was willing to sell to complete strangers. Czombo liked that about her and put her on his speed dial.

Later, when he had a moment alone, Czombo would push up a tile in the ceiling of the shower room and stash the dope there. The room had a lock, and no one was going to take any notice of a young man who spent a lot of time in the shower. He had worked this angle out to perfection in his last treatment centre.

Treatment centres always test for pot in their urine screens, but most places didn't get too fussed if the reading stays high for the first couple of weeks. Most places tested for a range, not an exact number, because it's cheaper. Besides, the quicker they threw him out the better. There was always a glorious, three-month wait before they could find some other hellhole to shove him into. Sooner or later, his Employee Assistance Program was going to tire of this treatment nonsense. Until that happened, he had to look to his own comfort and well-being.

The trick he had found was to shower immediately after smoking. Nothing gave you away quicker than the faint smell of hemp. Sunglasses and patchouli oil would never work here. If there was one counsellor on duty, you could stay out of his way. But the do-gooders were everywhere and saw everything. They spend their days gossiping worse than any murder of crows. Ratting him out would make their bones. So in a way, a disdainful roomie was a bit of a break. Artsy Fartsy had his beak so far up his own tail that he didn't even know anyone else was in the room. Even so — he had to go when a way could be found.

Chapter 53

Rachael hadn't been impressed by Arthur's phone message. *Someone has a nerve. What does he mean? Messed up and back in treatment? Mr. Hasn't-called-in-two-weeks! He'll be lucky if all I do is throw a shoe at him.*

She'd put her things away and put on the kettle before she returned to the phone to listen to the message again. She was surprised by the depth of her feelings. She thought she was over this guy. But she found that her fury turned rapidly to hurt and finally dissipated into a kind of vague disappointment. But she had to admit she was curious. *This could be one hell of story.*

Arthur waited for Rachael three nights in a row. The coffee shop was a bad place to wait for a lady who didn't show. The shop was full of smart looking young people going about their business with energy and purpose.

Why can't I be one of them? They were shining. He was dull and listless, watching the front door and counting minutes that seemed as heavy as overdue bills. The coffee in his hands went cold. The sweetener he had flavoured it with began a slow rancid decay on the back of his tongue. Each night he stayed till the last possible moment. Arthur was beginning to feel the kind of despair that rooted the homeless in addiction.

———

Rachael was watching him through the lens of her camera from the park across the street. The documentary had begun. She was sitting on one of the benches making sure that all the technology she'd brought with her was working. She looked every inch a one-woman band.

In the good weather, people competed for these seats but tonight it was far too cold. There was only one other person, an older man wrapped in blankets and a fur hat, sitting across the square from her. He looked far from well. Her voice filled the silent square as she said, "Welcome to my world. My name is Rachael and this is my mini-doc. I don't really have a script or a plan. I am hooked up to record sound and images, but I really am flying by the seat of my pants. My professor wouldn't approve. He wants to see structure. What I'm doing is beyond unethical. I hope it doesn't end up being ridiculous. I am sitting in a park across the street from a coffee shop." The image of a male figure sitting alone by a window came up on the screen. He was too far away to recognize. "Do you see the young man sitting watching the door? That's my subject. His name is Arthur. I am calling this documentary *The Valedictorian*. That title needs a word of explanation. Arthur and I went to the same high school. Good old North Toronto. He was the best student in the place. I took a walk over there this afternoon. Let me put that footage up on the screen for you. You can see all the academic silverware here in the showcase. He got it all. Best in math and science. No film credit though. I guess no one is perfect."

The bright lights and shiny surfaces of the display case gave way to the film noir image of Arthur sitting alone by the door. The image moved back to the interior of the school. Rachael was walking the halls.

"Arthur stole the show in high school. I had a serious crush on him, but he was out of my league. I was one of the stoners. All us slackers used to hang around here. This is the reading room." The camera panned around the space revealing twenty-five teenagers sitting on the floor playing with their hair and phones and talking non-stop. "We never read here, either. This was our space. I did a lot of learning with my textbooks closed." The image switched back to the solitary Arthur. The contrast suggested loss and maybe even pain. Rachael's voice grew reflective. "That was something Arthur's mom was never able to pack into his *Sid the Science Kid* lunch box. Which is probably why he's chasing it so hard now."

The camera moved to a stock image of a university building. "Arthur was going to medical school. Everybody knew that. The teachers used to beat us up with it, 'Why can't you be like Arthur?'"

The camera found the roundabout of an emergency department with lots of people dressed in scrubs coming and going in a hallway. "Do they make doctors from a recipe or are they born that way? Was Arthur's very public dream carved in stone, foretold in prophecy and enunciated by fawning angels and math tutors?"

Back to the shot of Arthur in the window. The image that whispered *lonely* the first time it was seen, now said *loser*. Her voice prodded your curiosity and made you wonder, *Who is this mysterious girl? How do these two fit together?*

"That plan miscarried. There's been a major script revision. Which is why we're here tonight, seven months after graduation, wondering how all of this is going to end."

The camera zeroed in on Arthur. "Now about that funny look on his face. I have some critical insight into that. Arthur has been waiting for me to meet him here at this coffee shop for three nights in a row. I'm torturing him. Not for fun. My cruelty serves my purpose. He's in treatment down the road, and if what he told me earlier is true, he's taking a chance trying to meet me here. I think that might be important. But what is his motivation? What does he think I can bring to the party?"

The image shifted again. "The reason I'm over here — hang on a minute, while I turn the camera around so that you can see my face. There, now that's better. I don't want to be too mysterious. The reason I'm here is that in a minute I'm going to keep rolling film and go across the street."

The face matched the voice. What a perfect pairing. The image on the screen was grainy and the lighting was far from ideal, but the effect was breathtaking. Rachael was still young enough to have flawless skin and hair. Her teeth had been sculpted from pearls and placed lovingly in a timeless arrangement. Her face was dominated by her large, inviting eyes. Her nose, though slightly broad, especially at the base, gave way to full rich lips and a dominant chin. She wore her thick brunette hair cut short. No longer a child but not yet a woman. Her appearance was so stunning that for a moment the focus left Arthur.

"Arthur agreed to do a documentary about recovery. We were going to meet and talk about it but then he vanished. I thought he was just one more stuck-up guy not calling, but he eventually did phone, and when he did, he hinted darkly about messing up, which to my way of thinking must mean a relapse. That and the fact that he's back in treatment pretty much says it all. So I'm going to stick a camera in his face and follow him around this evening to see what there is to be seen."

The screen revealed Rachael getting to her feet somewhat clumsily as she was overburdened with gear. As she closed the distance between the bench and the coffee shop one couldn't help but wonder. Were they a pair? Was romance in the air? Rachael came through the door of the coffee shop holding her laptop in front of her with what appeared to be a miner's lamp on her head. Every eye in the place landed on her.

Arthur had not expected to see the love of his life arrive in the equivalent of a hazmat suit. This was the hippest part of Toronto, so a university-aged girl walking around talking to herself with a lot of video equipment wouldn't prompt a 911 call. But this was an odd angle of entry into a serious conversation.

Arthur rose to his feet to greet Rachael but she motioned frantically for him to stay still. She wanted to keep him at arm's length, to better keep his face in the frame. This was an odd courtship dance. The movements were as clunky as a submersible filming a shipwreck. Rachael quite cleverly gave Arthur his cues with her free hand, as she made herself comfortable.

"This is Arthur. He's the subject of this documentary. Say hello, Arthur."

Arthur's face worked very well on the screen. His short black hair and muscular shoulders suggested youth and health and vigour. Somewhat out of step with the talk about him being an addict. You wanted to hear what he had to say. Arthur thought this was pretty funny. "Hello," he said to the camera with the same little wave and a silly grin that the Beatles had used to infatuate his grandmother. The students in the coffee shop were loving this. A couple of them started to gather around to watch the fun.

Rachael kept moving forward. "Arthur and I agreed in principle to do a documentary film together, but then he disappeared. Isn't that right, Arthur?"

The camera panned briefly around the coffee shop so that the viewer could orient themselves, then came to rest again on Arthur's now-troubled face. The move from smile to frown was intriguing. It suggested that he really didn't care for the direction in which this was going. You could see him puzzling it out as he stared at the camera. He was obviously here to beg for mercy, so he went along with what she wanted. "Okay, Rachael, you sure have me there. Can we turn this thing off?"

She adroitly moved the camera until her face came into the frame. "You can't turn off a documentary any more than you can turn off your conscience. It follows you around and sees everything. It gets into all the dark crevices of your mind. Ignore the camera. Try to pretend that it's only you and me, getting to the bottom of things."

Arthur wanted to do that very thing. Sure this was goofy, but wasn't that really where he wanted to go with this woman? It was kind of playful too. Not too serious. A wonderful piece of improv. But this was still dangerous. The down-low meeting was profoundly incompatible with the ethos of Lights, Camera, Action! If any of the guys saw this, he'd be sunk. They'd talk for sure. He had to figure out a way to make her to stop without seeming to.

"Can I get you a coffee?"

"Do we have time?"

"I have to be at my meeting at eight o'clock."

Rachael took a bearing. "With all this stuff to worry about, I don't think I could manage a hot drink."

Rachael found a more comfortable position for her laptop. Arthur started to look for something to work with, some lever, anything would do.

"Are you broadcasting this?"

"No, Arthur, this is a documentary. We're rolling tape. Well, in a post-tape-rolling sort of way."

"What do you want me to say?"

"I think it's fair to say I've engineered a unique and maybe even an original situation here. I've never heard of anyone having the kind of conversation I hope to have with you this evening in exactly this way."

Arthur settled in. This was the most fun he'd had in ages. Rachael made everything all right, simply by being there. "Go on, you have my rapt attention."

"Arthur, who are you?"

It was a sound question. "You have no idea how many people have asked me that lately."

"How did you answer them?"

Arthur looked into the lens, as if it was an eye that could reveal the hidden intentions of its owner. "Sometimes I lied, but more often I told them what I thought they wanted to hear, and sometimes I went back and forth between the two. It worked pretty well for a while, but then they caught me at it. It turns out they're better liars than I am." He had a moment. He hadn't known that the second before he spoke. You could see a change, or maybe it was simply discomfort, steal across his face. He bit his lower lip. That insight, sensing that it wasn't wanted, slid back beneath the waves. An opportunity lost for a young filmmaker who was for the moment smitten with the image of her star biting his lip. *How perfect is that?*

"Arthur, you and I live in a world where most people pretend to care about what other people think or do. There's no such thing anymore as real community for most of us. We've lost the ability to be intimate in anything other than a sexual way. We eat alone at breakfast, we sit silently on the subway, we work in a cubicle, and live in fear of the office politics that rage like civil wars all around us. We go for drinks after work in a desperate attempt to connect with the people we work with, only to find that *after work* is the same dance they do in the office Monday to Friday, set to a new tune." Rachael's eyes gleamed with power and authority when she spoke. This was coming from the heart. She meant every word of it and it showed. The camera moved back to Arthur for his reaction.

"So we type our hopes into handheld devices as we sit around the table listening to the boss waxing humble and then finally, exhausted from a day of working for a wage at a job we hate, we go home to some computer dating and television shows about make-believe people who have the kinds of friends and human connections that we would kill to have."

The horror of what Rachael was saying rendered Arthur's face immobile. This wasn't the conversation he hoped to have. His image on the screen changed as he reacted to her words. His face looked as if he had suddenly become aware of a pain in his innards. His face went blank for a second time as he tried to regain his balance. The camera caught his eyes this time.

"Rachael, I'm trying very hard these days to get over my drug addiction and get a real life going. I'm sort of looking at other people, the people in this cafe for instance, as models for what my life could be. Are you're telling me that their lives suck too? Is that what I heard you say?"

The Mona Lisa spoke. "That is exactly what I said, and that is precisely what I meant."

Here was a pungent truth. This woman had an edge to her. Arthur imagined Eric grinning as he watched this. Maybe he had been right all along, maybe the only worthwhile comfort in this world did come through the point of a needle. Could he get from where he was to where he wanted to be in light of her last remark? It seemed doubtful.

Rachael was a good interviewer and let the silence work for her. She waited as patiently as Penelope for her true love to come home. But Arthur still couldn't make the connection she wanted him to. So she shuffled the deck and dealt a new hand.

"You know from personal experience that drugs don't work. Getting high is bullshit. It can change the way you feel in the short term but that's all. It can never make you happy. Now I've given you a second piece to chew on. Living a lie, whether you do it sober or drunk, is almost as bad. It may turn out that this world is so screwed up, there's no possibility of ever being happy. Or it may turn out that being happy has always been a myth we use to dull our pain and give ourselves some hope..."

Arthur was quick to take her point. She thrived in the ambiguity of dialectic. He dared to hope again. "So if that's the case, this documentary could end with us going off the Bloor Street viaduct."

"Precisely. With the camera on a long lingering kiss of despair all the way down. But let's struggle for our sanity for a few minutes. You were the valedictorian once. Looking at you now, I wonder — did you tell us the truth that day? Well, life has presented you with a second chance. Can you tell us the truth, Arthur? Can you screw up your courage, look the camera in the eye, step into the light and say what's on your mind and in your heart?"

Doc pushed Arthur to the side and bullied his way into the conversation. You could see the transition on the screen. The deep lines in his forehead and the hypervigilant eyes. Not the kind of face you need to play poker.

But what a voice, all oil and ball bearings. "You make it sound like psychotherapy."

Rachael laughed with delight when she saw the transition. "With you involved this might develop into *psycho* therapy."

"Do you think I'm nuts?" He gave her a playful, come-hither smile.

She leaned back to show her disapproval. "Ask me at the end of the film."

"All right, but let's talk for a second about the format. Why stick a camera in my face? It's original, I grant you that. I'm enjoying it … all this attention is fun. But this is hardly the way to have a serious conversation."

She gave him a little half smile. "You don't understand documentary makers. Our art is our truth. We try very hard to avoid doing documentaries. They're dangerous. They cost a lot of time and money to make, and they always put a hurting on your soul. They mess you up by calling your whole world into question, and they point to things about us and our world that are deeply disturbing. Arthur, you only make a documentary because you can't stay away from the magic mirror."

Arthur hadn't known that. He looked surprised. Did art and film go together for Rachael in the same way that sex and drugs did for him? Rachael was making sense of the world in a new way. He understood the focus of her questions for the first time, and more than that, he knew something else — he wanted this woman. For the first time in his life, he wanted to be real with someone. Rachael was offering him much more than a chance to tell his story on camera. Was this the moment everyone talked about? When you knew for the first time? The alarm on his watch went off.

"It's five minutes to eight. I have to go."

"Where's your wingman?"

"I snuck out tonight. I'm not supposed to be here."

"I want to film you from behind, walking to the meeting."

"But we won't be able to talk."

"Oh, we're going to talk, but not on the way to the meeting."

Arthur walked the long block to the church that housed the meeting. He was cutting this pretty close. The last smoker was putting out his cigarette and entering the front door when he mounted the stairs. Arthur turned around to smile at Rachael, but she was gone.

Chapter 54

Arthur walking alone along Bloor Street toward his meeting was a perfect backdrop for Rachael's next narrative move. She was back in her kitchen, warming up with a well-deserved cup of tea. The other girls had gone to the late movie, so she had the place to herself. She watched the silent figure of Arthur walking alone several times before she decided what she wanted to say in the voice-over. The image spoke to her of perseverance.

"Arthur is going to his twelve-step meeting. Self-help groups always meet in church basements. I call the people who attend them pilgrims because they travel endlessly from holy place to holy place. He's at a treatment centre down the road. I won't tell you which one because they're more secretive than the Vatican. Every night of the week, they send their guys out to a meeting. But unlike Chaucer's pilgrims, these guys are not looking for remittance of sin. These guys are looking for release from an addiction." The camera moved back to her face. This time it was well-lighted, and she wasn't packing technology. She held an oversized teacup in both hands as she peered into the crystal ball. Her wool turtleneck made her look soft and inviting, but also durable and aware.

"Of course, the part I don't get is the struggle. Why is this so hard? It's so obvious — the drugs messed up your life, so drop them and move on. Find something that works. We all smoked dope and did pills in high school. It was a big deal for six weeks, but nobody wants to do that stuff now, except for these guys. Dope is their golden age. There's a mystical bond that keeps them connected to it. I wonder if I can get Arthur to describe that for me? How would it feel in your body and your mind to be in the middle of that? That's where I hope to go with this." The next image on the screen was taken from a distance. It showed shadowy figures leaving the front door of the church. They all milled around together smoking and then the camera looked skyward and faded to black.

———

Arthur was the first one out the door when the meeting ended. He sprinted up the long staircase and burst through the heavy door hoping to see Rachael waiting for him. But there was no light shining in that patch of darkness. His mood crashed. He had a lot invested in his next conversation with her. He would have given anything to be on the inside, to feel settled enough to call her a friend, or a girlfriend. That somehow the inevitable rebuke was not coming. *Who do you think you are?* looked him in the eye and stared him down while *How dare you presume?* looked on disapprovingly and jabbed a thumb into his breastbone. The silence of the winter sidewalk echoed the cold empty feeling behind his eyes. He was swimming alone and a long way from shore. He found himself instinctively looking around for RK. But RK had moved on, finished treatment, stayed out of trouble, gone back to work, back to sanity, maybe even back to a life he wanted to live.

———

Arthur's seven-day assessment fell to Paul, who had no idea what his young charge was getting up to instead of doing treatment. Doug's decision to use him was driven by the logic of depletion. Doug was running out of counsellors. In the classroom, the staff had closed down the avenues of thought that made continued use seem viable. Day after day they hammered home the themes: No, you couldn't smoke pot. No, you couldn't just drink on weekends. Pills always lead to trouble. The big prize was the crazy idea at the centre of it all, the delusion that held the addicts' world together. Every man Jack of them believed that, someday, when all the money was on the table, when it was their good name, their family's well-being, and their very lives hanging in the balance, they were going to come up big. They were going to find a way on that fine morning to untangle the Gordian knot. Pretending they could control the whirlwind was the problem.

All four counsellors had called Arthur on his nonsense in their own inimitable ways. But they knew that was only one half of the job that needed doing. Arthur had yet to experience despair, that final irrevocable surrender to the true nature of his situation. He was still rolling out schemes. The four horsemen were obstacles in his way, standing between him and what he wanted. He didn't trust them. Which was very odd because they were the ones he turned to when he was in trouble. They'd heard versions, and versions of versions, of the Arthurian legend. One of them, and it didn't really matter which one of them it was, had to be in the room when the words failed and the truth broke water again. Saying the words aloud wasn't going to be enough; someone who understood had to be sitting with him when it breached. Saying it, and then realizing that it could be strangled at birth was much worse than never saying it at all.

Arthur despised Kaiser, he avoided Reg studiously, and Greg was on vacation. That left Paul, the master of deadpan comedy and direct invective, but he wasn't in good odour with Arthur, either, after his crack about him not being smart enough to go to medical school. To the untrained eye, this series of adversarial relationships and impasses could not help but appear to be flailing and failure. Mike and Doug knew better. They weren't bothered by being on a war footing with a client. One-word answers and evasions told them that they were getting close. They knew that you can't tell a lie unless you first know the truth. Every day that Arthur was in their care, his delusions about himself and his addiction were taking a pummelling.

Arthur had made a face when Paul told him he wanted to talk to him. As they took their places around the big table in Doug's office, Arthur was radiating disdain. Paul settled himself in his chair and with a look on his face worthy of the Buddha he swung for the fence.

"You don't like me."

Arthur wasn't prepared for that. His voice cracked when he tried to deliver a rebuttal. "Do you even care what I think?"

Paul kept his tone of voice neutral. He refused to answer adolescent complaints about fairness and caring. "About me personally? No, I don't. I don't even think you know who I am. I think you see me as an obstacle, something you need to get around in order to get wherever it is you think you're going."

Arthur knew the outline of this game, lots of teachers had tried this. "Is this the building-rapport piece for you?"

Paul loved swatting flies. "It's how Hannibal got Starling."

"What are you talking about?"

"In the movie, the psycho killer gets the girl by being the only one who tells the truth. I grant you that the truth is pretty awful, but, what the hell, it's only fiction after all."

The contempt for all things adult crept back into Arthur's voice. For a second, he thought he was back under the bright lights with the camera rolling. He instinctively leaned over the table hoping to intimidate Paul. "So what truth are you tempting me with?"

"Why, the truth about you! The masked chameleon!"

Arthur's face froze with his eyes open wide. Then he got to his feet, he didn't know why, and, feeling exposed and foolish, he sat down again before Paul could insist that he do so, only to find that he felt even worse. "That's stupid. A chameleon can blend in with its environment by changing its colour. It's a master of camouflage. Why would it need to wear a mask?"

Paul smiled. He'd made his point. "Well there's fooling the world but there's also fooling yourself. You wear a different mask for everyone in your life. I don't think even you can keep them all straight."

That's where you'd be wrong, my smug, self-satisfied friend.

Chapter 55

The two detectives had been a little surprised when Rachael showed up at the coffee shop impersonating a TV studio. They had noticed her presence in the park on the two previous evenings but hadn't connected her to Arthur. But then that was the beauty of their craft. People behave one way when the camera is on them, and sometimes in another way when they forget that it's there — but how do they behave when they are reasonably certain that the cameraman has gone home? That is what made sneaking around after dark worthwhile.

Shakespeare would have cast their work as a play within a play. Rachael would eventually see it as the first big revelation in her documentary. Passive surveillance is what the two pensioned policemen called it.

Fred and Allan assumed that Arthur was waiting for his dealer. He certainly looked the part. Alone when he wasn't supposed to be, waiting until the last possible minute before bolting out the door to his meeting, watching the comings and goings in the coffee shop with fanatical interest —none of that said happy things to them. This man wanted something. He looked, to their experienced eyes, a desperate junkie on the hunt.

Rachael's intrusion made this a much more interesting problem. The whole idea of this gig was to make sure the young man was doing what everyone, minus himself, wanted him to do — to stay off the powder and keep his yap shut. A guerrilla documentary was a possibility that had never occurred to them. This was the last thing in the world that their employer wanted to see. The mess they had so very carefully cleaned up and bagged had now soaked out of the garbage bin and back down onto the clean floor.

It was easy to get a microphone into the coffee shop. The kids all crowded around Rachael and Arthur to watch what was going on, and Fred joined that happy throng. One more face in the crowd. Allan followed Arthur out the front door and into the church basement, while Fred discreetly followed the preoccupied Rachael to a vantage point she had chosen about a block away from the church. Allan waited until Arthur found himself a chair and got himself settled at the CA meeting. He sat behind him and waited for his chance. When Arthur got up to get himself a coffee halfway through the meeting, Allan knocked Arthur's coat off the back of his chair. He nonchalantly picked it up and secreted a microphone in the lapel of the jacket.

The image that Fred captured of Arthur emerging from the meeting was hard to read. He looked dope sick to the former policemen. Dr. Robert Dickens had gotten his money's worth.

———

Dr. Dickens read the transcript and watched the video in his office. It was heartbreaking to see all his efforts to contain this mess come to nothing. *A bloody documentary, about this little shit? Young lady, what are you thinking? What is it about this kid that makes all the women crazy? Even Gina and Alice, all of them bitten by the same bug as Linda.*

He dialled the phone. Fred picked up on the third ring. "Fred, it's Bob."

"Mr. Dickens, how you doing?"

"You and Allan sure did a bang-up job last night."

"I suspect you would have preferred something a little tamer?"

"Deadly dull would have suited me. My hope was you would show me stills of him reading *Gray's Anatomy* by flashlight in his room after lights-out."

"How do you want to handle this?"

"Fred, the ethics of this thing stink to high heaven."

"Well, they bother me a little bit too."

"I read your report and I can't see my way clear to doing surveillance on Miss Dunning. That wouldn't be right. But stay on Arthur at least for the next two days. I have a meeting with Doug Moore over at Punanai. He knows a little bit about what I'm up to. I think the only way to get this settled is to bring everyone into the room, Charlie Chan style. But I want to know everything that can be known before that happens."

"So then to be clear, you want us to follow Arthur, get whatever we can by passive means but stay out of sight."

"Yes, we're on the wrong side of the line here. Our intentions are good, but we have no legal reason to be doing what we are doing."

"I'm glad you see that … it makes this easier for us."

Fred hung up the phone. He felt bad for the Dickens family. They were the kind of clients he enjoyed working for. Fred ran everything he'd seen through his brain one more time, trying to give the kid the benefit of the doubt. *Why do you sit there night after night looking so desperate? What are you up to? Sound clips and cameras don't lie. You shouldn't be there. You shouldn't be doing whatever it is that you're up to. Kid, don't you know that once an image hits the screen it becomes the truth?*

Chapter 56

Rachael was very pleased with her work. All told, she had fourteen of the thirty minutes she needed in the can. The picture quality was less than ideal, but given the camera she had to work with, and the sensitive nature of the conversation, well, dark grainy images suited. She was both surprised and delighted by the way her voice came across. It sounded ominous coming from behind the screen, confident and a little edgy, hinting that she knew everything and was simply biding her time. This was going to be the doc that made it to the top of the pile. She fixed the camera on herself and let the lens explore her face.

"Narrative is the hope of the world. It's what allows us to make sense of our lives. Words and reflection are what separates us from the animals, well at least most of the time. Get a human mad enough, drunk enough, or scared enough and they will show you how our species did their business two hundred thousand years ago. That savage wiring is all still there.

"Animals are driven by their instincts. They follow their noses and take their pleasures without remorse. That's what I'm seeing in Arthur. Cocaine is a time machine for him. It drags him back into a preconscious past. The problem is that the human part of him remembers his savagery when the drug wears off. If the coke changed him forever, if it tore the conscience right out of him, why, his problem would be solved. He could beat and rob his way through the world and never give it a second thought."

She brought up some images of a younger version of Arthur. "I stole these off his mom's Facebook page." The screen explored a series of slow-moving photos taken when Arthur was about ten. "Hard to see the savage in these shots. He was happy to have his picture taken. Looking at these photos, it's hard to imagine him turning out the way he has. I can't help but wonder what's missing for him, what isn't he getting?"

She stopped the carousel on the one dark picture that had found its way into the collection. It wasn't a profoundly dark image. It showed Arthur at about the age of sixteen. It was his eyes that told the story. The bright eyes of his youth had been replaced by sad eyes. It was so easy to overlook this one image, to put it down to a curiosity of the lens or a quirk of the material, or to simply disregard it and move on to one of the many happier, brighter images.

After his sixteenth birthday Arthur had become camera shy. There were no more close-ups of him. The camera only ever caught him around the edge of groups. He appeared infrequently in family photographs, always with a forced smile on his face. What was this young man trying to conceal?

Those eyes pointed to the truth. Those eyes showed the pain. Those eyes spoke into the silence with a veracity that his words could not. She kept the image on the screen and moved the focus around in a way that made the image seem alive.

"This is the one that's different. Whatever was in his heart when the camera clicked was caught forever in this frame. When I find out what that look means, I'll know what's driving this man."

Chapter 57

Arthur heard Rachael's voice call to him as he walked along Madison Avenue. She pulled her father's Buick up to the curb and reached across the front seat to fling open the passenger door. "Get in."

"I can't — it's against the rules."

"You're a drug addict — you paper your ass with the rules."

"Someone will see."

"We're doing a documentary; everyone is going to see."

"I can't…"

"Arthur, get in."

He balked. Everything he hated about himself told him that he shouldn't while everything that he longed to be insisted that he must. Were a few minutes of Rachael's undivided attention worth getting kicked out of treatment? He thought so. Rachael had combed her hair back and put something in it that made it slick and shiny. She was wearing a black leather beret, that would not have looked out of place on the head of one of the earliest film directors. She was irresistible. Playful, sexy, and quirky, all of it without effort. He wanted to get in, but he couldn't. When she smiled and tilted her head slightly to the left, he found himself headfirst halfway down the waterslide.

The front seat was noonday bright. "Why all these lights?"

"We're filming…"

"But you're driving."

"The camera is on the windscreen and the mike is taped to the dashboard. Put it on."

Arthur struggled to attach the device to his coat.

"Oh merde," said Rachael with a scowl on her face. She was using her index finger to poke and prod an earbud. "There's a funny feedback sound. Put the mike back on the dashboard — better yet, hold it in your hand. It shouldn't be doing this."

Fred, who was back at the office recording this conversation via the bug that his partner Allan had secretly placed in Arthur's lapel at the CA meeting, dropped the power to the listening device by half. Feedback was a dead giveaway. It meant there was another microphone nearby. Better to lose one conversation than be discovered. They could always try to amplify the signal later.

Arthur playfully palmed the microphone that Rachael had provided, pretending to be a Vegas performer, hoping to earn a smile.

"How's that?"

"Oh, that's much better … look in the camera and say something adorable."

"Such as?"

"I don't know. Pretend we're two young people driving around town in a stolen vehicle looking for a place to score some powder. You know your regular midweek errands."

"Do you really think that kind of stuff makes a gripping documentary?"

"Start talking or hit the bricks, babyface."

Arthur wasn't feeling the magic. She threw him another bone.

"So what happens if you get caught driving around in a car talking to me?"

Arthur saw Kaiser's face light up as if had won a lottery. He had to smile. "Kicked out, no hope of a reprieve. Stern faces, hurt eyes, and the low steady hum of remorse. Then a long silent drive home with two broken-hearted antecedents."

"But they're going to have to let you go sooner or later."

"You might want to tell them that."

"How did you end up back in treatment?"

Arthur fidgeted as he tried to work out what to say. He bit his lower lip. "Do you remember me saying I had to run an errand?"

"Etched in my memory."

"That was a funny sort of lie. I was telling you something I hoped would turn out to be true. I wanted to impress you, to show you and everybody else that I'm not … that I don't belong here." The words stopped. He couldn't tell her. She'd never speak to him again. If he told her the parts that he could tell her, she would know he was leaving something out. That he was cooking the books. Omissions leave muddy footprints that always drag the truth back into the light. He looked over at her as she drove. She deserved the truth.

She was patient. "Not too much detail, Arthur, don't get tangled up in the small stuff."

He tried again, determined this time to get it right. He looked the camera right in the eye. "Okay, I met a guy in detox. He lied to me about being in trouble with some bikers. He was … he *is* a heroin addict. My girlfriend … that's not the right word … she and I … well we were … she had a lot of dope that she was never going to use, so I went to her place to steal it so we could get my friend out of trouble with the bikers. But there were no bikers. He lied to me about that and about a lot of other things. And my girlfriend was way older than me … she was my teacher … she doesn't even know who I am anymore … she made me do some crazy shit." The camera watched the brazen rinse off him like street salt in the carwash.

The silence and the lights defeated him. He couldn't go on. Why couldn't he make his stories dance the way RK could? Whatever made him think that sharing this stuff with Rachael was going to make her love him? He felt absolutely ridiculous. His words, his back story, filled him with a kind of disgust. *Why am I trying to talk to her about this? Shut up!*

Rachael frowned. His feet had almost left the ground.

Chapter 58

The Chamber of New Life — that's what it was called it in the brochure — was a thick, grey cryogenic tank that stood in the basement of the Granite Glen Retirement Home. The bronze faceplate on the door bore the inscription: NEW LIFE INSTITUTE.

Peter had already read the morning papers, standing awkwardly over the shoulder of a retired economist who had a suite of rooms one floor above the cryotank. Professor Danby was a man of regular habits who had the grace to read all the major papers at the same time every morning at his dining room table. The professor had a tendency to speed-read, which often annoyed Peter, but, as a good researcher, he always read everything from cover to cover, and his saving grace was that he always laid the paper flat on his table while he read. That is why Peter joined him every morning.

When Danby finished and put the papers in the recycling, Peter made his way downstairs to see his sweetie. Terri was much easier to manage now than she had been in real life. He knew that she was sample forty-eight, row six, tank three. Peter was sample forty-nine, row six, tank three. She had been here since 1979. Seeing her name on the brass manifest and touching the tank made him feel a connection.

Peter caught a glimpse of himself reflected back to him by the manifest's shiny surface. It wasn't a sure image. It was distorted and imperfect owing to the cylindrical shape of the column. He actually preferred that. Seeing his face in small segments allowed him to remember the way he used to be. Thin as a rail until he was in his middle years, and then portly for a decade, and after that, well ... it comes to us all in the end. Romance and adventure give way to more sedentary pursuits until all that we have left to look forward to are the things we consume and which, in turn, consume us.

I was handsome once, *thought Peter. He recalled the wonderful picture of himself that was put on real estate signs around the city. All teeth and hair and muscles. All of it glowing with good health. Where did it all go? Twenty-five thousand of those flyers were sent out every week for over twenty years. They never changed. They made Peter rich and famous. But he dared not show his face. The lens caught him that day in a moment of perfection. It became the truth and he the lie. It's funny what people believe about a person.*

Peter thought back to the day he first heard that she wouldn't be buried or cremated. The emptiness that that memory occasioned pushed the words out of his head and into the room. He needed to talk to her, about what happened after she had gone, and how things were going to be when she awoke and they could finally be together again. "None of us had ever even heard of cryogenics until you died. We were appalled at the idea. I remember the whispering voices at your funeral. Just as well that you didn't have to hear it. Crackpot, they said. Proper Christian burial and the hope of the resurrection not good enough for Barney. Dreamer, they said. Foolish indulgence. Can't let go. Not man enough to take the loss. And what about those poor kids? Trying to get on with their lives knowing that their mother is inside an ice cube tray somewhere. Well say what you will about Barney. He got some of it right.

"But you were more than that to me. Damn the luck anyway. I remember when we were only kids. Our first kiss. I had never kissed anyone before, well at least not in the way you kissed me. And I must say, no one has ever kissed me that way since. Your kiss was as gentle as a butterfly; it was soft and unsettling. It wasn't one of the wet messy kisses I got later. It was pristine and ladylike. I still think about it all these years later and what should have happened.

"Damn the luck. Who knew that the first girl who ever took an interest in me would be my last chance at happiness? What are the odds of the kid next door being your one chance at love? We were twelve years old, for heaven's sake. We were looking at military school and the convent if we got caught doing anything more than holding hands. But that was enough. How I wish I could hold your hand in precisely that way this morning.

"When you married Barney and had your family, I just, well I just kind of drifted. Without you to hope for, nothing made sense. I followed you into the church and kept a respectful distance. I lived for our chance meetings and infrequent conversations. So many times, I wanted to bellow like a bull and take you in my arms and tell you how I felt. But you had a family and that simply wouldn't do. So I lived on crumbs of hope.

"But that was then, and this is now. Today is our anniversary. We've been together for ten years. Yes. I imagine you had forgotten. You know, you present quite a problem in terms of a present. There's what you can use and there's what I can get and that doesn't amount to much. The book I read suggested tin or aluminum as a gift. They're chosen because they're flexible, which is what a ten-year marriage requires. Hardly the thing to give a woman in cryogenic suspension. You are surrounded by the stuff. So I brought you your favourite — cashews, but I had the very good sense to get them in a tin. Impractical yes, but there must be some measure of consolation in knowing that at least one other person remembers that you love them."

Peter sat down on the marble bench and listened in silence as the cryotank gurgled. A patch of white appeared very briefly on his forehead and then vanished. He didn't see it, but he felt it. His hand instinctively rubbed the spot. "There was so much I never got to talk to you about. I built my career and saved my money and planned for a future with you that never happened. I remember praying on Sunday mornings, sitting right behind you in the pew, that one day you would wake up and look at Barney and say, enough. I secretly hoped that you were only staying with him because of the kids. How often did I imagine a scene where you dispatched your youngest child off to university and then packed your own bag and left. But then you got sick. At first it didn't look too bad. You were so beautiful and alive I couldn't imagine you any other way. But the mischief was running wild out of sight. You got this funny otherworldly kind of look. Sometimes I swear you were crying in church for just a second. I wasn't too worried when you started to lose weight, I was expecting that. But then your hair went limp and mangy, and I knew in my heart this was bad. You looked so different, so sad. Then when you died, the hope in me died too. Nothing was ever the same after you went. I thought I might as well die, too; I wanted to.

"Then a few years later I was reading in the paper that they had found a cure for the very leukemia that had taken you from me. That's when the idea of cryogenics stopped being crazy and started to make sense. Of course, back in those days, the idea was to revive dead people and then cure them — but now we know that is not how this is going to work. Who would have thought that God would give us bodies that could be cloned? It was all so perfect. This was the one way you and I could finally be together again. When the idea struck me, I was so overwhelmed I was teary for a week.

"The last time I checked, your kids are all grown and moved on. They don't need you anymore. Barney got busy with other things and lost interest in cryogenics. He got himself cremated. You would have been booted out years ago if I hadn't paid your bill in perpetuity. Every month the payment comes out of my account. Keeping us alive, waiting only for the coming of a new kind of spring. A spring in which you and I can finally be together.

"Sometimes when I'm talking to John, I want to tell him about you, about what we had and what we are going to have again soon. But I can't. He's coarse and common. He's just about the only person I have to talk to these days, but this is too special. If he said a word about this, I wouldn't be able to contain my anger. Maybe this is never going to happen, but this is the closest I have ever been to what I really want out of life. I won't be fobbed off. Nothing but this will do. And so, my love, I will take my leave. Until tomorrow, sleep well in your bleak midwinter."

Chapter 59

Arthur forgot about the camera and slid sideways in his seat so that he could look at Rachael's face. She was calm, and oh so very beautiful. There was no hint of trouble or judgment. She was enjoying the drive and the day and the conversation and she was ... well ... so perfect and at ease. She was doing what she was born to do and that made her irresistible.

What was he going to say to her? How could he make her understand? What did she know about being driven and doing terrible things? He knew now that they were terrible, but at the time they hadn't seemed so awful. He felt as if he had sung a full octave above his natural range and now, his voice stricken with fatigue, he was incapable of carrying a tune.

The camera on the dashboard caught the look of desperation stealing across his face. His eyes were wide and white. "Everything that happened sounds so stupid now. I had to put things right. I had a plan."

She nudged him in the right direction. *Maybe beating up on his parents will get him talking.* "It's an awful thing to realize that the people who know you best and love you the most, the people who would take a bullet for you, misled you."

Arthur sighed. "They made me one dimensional. I had a purpose, and everything followed from that."

She smiled wickedly; apparently, she had a horse in that race. "Except for that one little sharp edge you kept cutting your finger on?"

He paused for a second, trying to work out the implications of what she had said, but he couldn't stop the flow of words. They were pushing each other as desperately as panicked theatregoers heading for an exit. "One day, the idea was just there. I was going to be a doctor. No one ever told me why. I invented reasons: An older cousin had died and passed the expectation on to me. There was a secret codicil in my grandfathers will. The family stood to lose a duchy and four vineyards in the south of France if I didn't come across." His words slowed down again.

My God, he's still working this out.

"It was always there. I could play with something and put it out of my mind or make fun of it, but then I would look in the rear-view mirror and there it was. The expectation. It followed me around as faithfully as the drug squad.

"My father taught me to play the power game. My mother showed me how to dress. I learned to choose my friends with an eye to the future and for no other reason than that. My father picked my school, and Mom screened my tutors. I learned to speak the language of privilege. I went to camps I despised, and always at my elbow was some adult or another giving me that little wink, the one that said, *Go for it, kid, make us all proud*. I got hooked on that. I needed something. I guess I wanted to make them happy. I thought if I did what they wanted me to do, it would make me feel all right too. It was a lot of work, and that kind of kept me too busy to really feel about what was happening."

Rachael couldn't hide her surprise and delight. "Who taught you to feel about things?"

"It's a treatment thing, they make us do it. I hate it most of the time."

There was a silence as Arthur searched Rachael's face. He desperately needed a wink. She still had her director's hat on. She decided to ask her next question after considerable thought. "Insanity always has a goal, and the closer it gets, the more momentum it has. When did you know for the first time this wasn't going to work?"

This answer was easy. "The day we loaded up the truck and went off to Queen's. It was awful. I knew from the minute I laid eyes on the campus, I couldn't do it."

"The promised land was a dump?"

"No, it was really nice; but it was wrong. I loved Sarah, and I was about to marry Jane. It was an arranged marriage."

"Perhaps the word is *deranged*."

"The worst part was the looks on my parents' faces. They were so happy. They'd given up everything to get me there."

Where did that come from? What had they given up? "Did they ever tell you that you didn't have to do it, that you could choose something else?"

"Yeah, but I knew they didn't mean it. They always had this look of desperate pain in their eyes."

Her tone was Girl Scout–bright. "So you were pretty much free to choose…"

Arthur turned his head and looked out the passenger window. The look of shame on his face explained his choice of words. Ridicule was all he had left. "In my family this is the Holy Grail. You know, for the first time in my life, I'm wondering who didn't get the chance to live their dream. I guess now the crown gets passed to Dale. I can no longer carry on in my duties without the love and support of the drug I love. The king is dead, long live the king."

"Was it your mom or dad?"

"They were both bright enough, but it had to be my dad. He's the driven one. The one who can't ever say aloud what's always written on his face."

The camera caught the moment when he made that connection. As telling as the image of him when he was sixteen and camera shy for the first time. Arthur saw his aunt's living room. From that happy summer when he was there because his parents were sick. He had come running in for a glass of water and seen his father ... looked at his father ... seen his aunt ... watched her step back and flush ... the inexplicable things that adults do ... something was so very wrong. He had surprised them. But he couldn't remember what happened next. An opium cloud hung over that moment. He had awakened from a compelling dream whose theme he could no longer remember, although the bitterness of something lingered. The camera saw it all. A full minute of horror, then a look of confusion and finally the face of an innocent child. He turned to Rachael. "What were we talking about?"

Rachael brought the Buick to a stop a block from Punanai. Arthur still had one foot tangled in the barbed wire of the past. She reached across the seat and opened the door. Arthur got out without saying a word. He looked back into the car from the curb, as if he had left something irreplaceable there. Something was missing. He couldn't remember exactly what had been said, but he felt very strongly that what had passed between them had deeply offended her in some way, or worse still, disappointed her. It felt over and too embarrassing to ever speak of again.

Rachael didn't say a word, she pointed at her wrist. They had been gone exactly twenty minutes. He had to get back. He picked up his feet and dogtrotted the two blocks back to the house. He could have used a real coffee from Tim's but he didn't want to press his luck by asking to go out again.

Rachael watched Arthur disappear from view. When her hand came away from her hair, it was oily with product. She looked around for a tissue. *What did I just see? What the hell just happened to him there? Am I playing with fire?* She pulled away from the curb and headed south on Madison overtaking Arthur as he was mounting the front steps of Punanai. She watched him open the front door as she passed.

He hung up his coat and sat down in the living room. The knife edge of fear give way to the deeper cutting thrust of panic. He had finally blown something that mattered. He had to move. He ran up the stairs to his room hoping for some privacy, but the jolly green nuisance was sprawled all over his side of the room. The floor was covered in misplaced potato chips and discarded packaging. A wave of ill will swept through him. Life was not about hope. It was about being annoyed and putting up with other people's crap.

Why am I doing this? Why do I keep letting it all hang out with the camera running? I'm going to lose Rachael if I don't shut up.

He choked on that thought. He felt a shudder in his core. A line of coke would put an end to all this gut-wrenching shit. He shut his eyes and rode out the storm with the bitter tase of powder on his tongue and the familiar feeling of numbness running all the way up his throat and into his sinuses. *Please help me. I don't want to use today.*

Chapter 60

Bloor Street United Church was constructed in the nineteenth century. Quarried fieldstone was used to construct the basement and the boiler room. The walls and stairwells that lead down to the lowest level are structurally sound and well maintained, even if they have a wonderfully uneven handmade feel to them. Time and gravity have dragged the walls ever so slightly out of true. The beams are rough cut local wood, full of knots and coarse grains, that have weathered magnificently into dark bands of sinew that gird the building together.

The mortar was applied in great haste without much thought for its appearance; after all, no worshipper was ever supposed to see this part of the building, and it had been repointed several times down through the years. The resulting chinks and crevices made it look and feel a bit like the Wailing Wall in Jerusalem. The space felt anachronistic without seeming distant or inhuman. It was here that Rachael laid her final scene, in the hope that she could graft a shoot onto this gnarled old root.

The church rented this space out to a CA group on Tuesday nights. It was the same night that the church ran its Out of the Cold program. At 8:00 p.m., the two groups simultaneously occupied opposite ends of the same floor. The only point of contact was the washrooms where the showers were located. Volunteers from the community shepherded pyjama-clad street people to and from the showers while the twelve steppers drank coffee and told stories before their meeting. The two groups, by mutual accord, pretended not to notice each other.

Rachael had grown up in this building. She attended Sunday school here. The basement had been where she and the other kids had run and laughed themselves into squealing hysteria while their elders prayed. This place was special for her, full of happy memories.

The church secretary was only too glad to give her the keys to the boiler room and permission to film in the basement. "Why do you want to make a movie down there?"

"It's the walls, they're so spooky, and it's the perfect backdrop for a close-up."

"If you say so. I could let you have the stained-glass windows, you know, or the brick in the sanctuary. They're aching for a camera."

"They're nice, but it's too much light for what I have in mind. The shot I want has to be dark and a little dangerous looking."

"Go nuts. I get a credit for this right?"

"You'll be the first person at the top of the We Want to Thank list."

"Finally, my name on the big screen."

Rachael wasn't telling the whole story, but then, she didn't have to.

———

Arthur had to come to this meeting — it was mandatory. Rachael's plan was to waylay him in the hallway and then drag him down to the boiler room. A perfect ambush. With all the comings and goings of the homeless and addicted, no one was going to notice one cigarette missing from an open pack. Her drive-by had caught him off guard, loosened his tongue and stirred up a hornets' nest. He'd gone wide eyed with horror in the car. The camera caught it. *Inchoate* was the word that came to her mind as she looked at the image. Whatever it was that he saw was toxic. It blew a circuit breaker. He didn't even know that he had gone somewhere when he landed back in the front seat with a look of pure innocence on his face. He had to ask her what they had been talking about. That confused her. He knew something, maybe even everything. But he didn't know it all the time. That's why she chose the dungeon. No place to go. No distractions.

Her strategy was to deliberately blur the line between telling the truth because it needed to be told and telling the truth to impress her. This whole process worked because Arthur wanted her.

She set up her light in the darkest corner. The shot had a forsaken feel to it. She found some rusted tools and metal furnace parts that someone had been meaning to throw out for a hundred years and hung them on the wall behind where Arthur was going to sit. They gave an additional element of texture and depth to the shot. She set up her tripod and took the seat she intended to place Arthur on. She began to record her prologue.

The camera found her face shining in the darkness. "This is the final shot. This is where I plan to pop the big existential question. What I want Arthur to tell me is how it feels to be in the middle of a change, a change that you are not sure that you want to make, and maybe even a change that you don't think you can pull off. The drugs are killing him. So why doesn't he stop? If he hates his life, why doesn't he choose another path?

"When other people have tried to capture this on camera, they've let their subjects go over the top. They make threats and promises, but that isn't what I want. That's how people behave when addiction has them by the throat. That's the outer surface but that is not all that there is to be seen."

She got up from the three-legged stool and panned the camera around the room to allow the viewers to orient themselves. This was a spooky place. She then selected the picture she had taken earlier of Arthur looking back through the passenger side window at her with a tortured look on his face. She put that image up on the screen.

"My original thought was to ask Arthur to write his obituary. But he's so clever, he could spin a dozen stories that would leave me none the wiser. I need him to revisit the place that put that awful look on his face. That's where this story starts." The camera explored the deep shadow of the boiler room. "This is the place to have that conversation. There are no distractions here. Only light and dark. His voice, my voice, and the lens."

She brought up another image. This time it was Arthur running out of the church after the CA meeting hoping against hope to see her. She froze the image of longing and dissatisfaction on his face. "Maybe I'm the one being ridiculous. What could he possibly say that would satisfy my curiosity? I'm sitting here blabbing about truth and meaning, but is this simply me flapping my wings and hoping to fly? Is this some crazy dance I'm doing to amuse myself? I'm in the middle here too. Which is why I love this drug, with its carefully nuanced layers of curiosity, shame, and needing to make sense of ourselves, to be known and ultimately to be loved." The screen revisited the image of her walking the corridor at North Toronto.

"Arthur dropped some intriguing clues. Who is this girlfriend? He says she was older. How much older? She's hip deep in this mess. He looked so uncomfortable when he talked about her. And what about the mysterious friend who betrayed him? If the stuff he's sharing with me is this messed up, what does that suggest about his secrets?" The camera landed on a shot of the front of Punanai House. "Watch and see what happens when I ask him why he won't quit. He won't answer the question. He'll circle back to that first time he used. He'll sort through every idea that ever ran though his head. As if something that someone gave him or took away mattered. He thinks the answer is in that jumble of things somewhere. I can't believe he hasn't worked it out yet, but maybe that's exactly what we're doing."

Chapter 61

Arthur was taken by surprise. Rachael had left him sitting for another bootless hour in the coffee shop, another septic detention in which to obsess about the meaning of his life, another chance to miss her, an annoying space of time that fanned both his desires and his fears, but which brought him no closer to a resolution. His whole world spun as unloved as an empty Ferris wheel on a cold rainy night. His solemn feast unattended, his offerings of meal and flesh ignored, his household gods adamant that they would not and could not be appeased.

The lens of Rachael's camera had supplanted his conscience, a magic mirror that reflected his true image back to him, the sounding board for his changing perceptions about the world and himself. Rachael, that magical, mysterious figure behind the camera, had transcended reality, and had found a new life in his imagination as a sullen, intrusive goddess, one whom he could neither propitiate nor abandon.

One minute he was walking down a hallway toward a CA meeting he really didn't want to attend, and the next minute, he looked up and saw what he wanted with all his heart — Rachael, dressed in a black turtleneck and wearing thigh-hugging leather tights and high red leather boots that filled his sexually charged imagination with fire.

She coyly beckoned to him from out of the shadows. He glanced at his wingman, Czombo, and pointed in the direction of the washrooms. Doughhead grunted dully and obligingly went into the meeting alone. Arthur waited until he was out of sight before he followed her down the hallway. Rachael grabbed Arthur roughly and hauled him into the boiler room. She shut the door behind them. A single lamp provided illumination, etching a tear-shaped puddle of light around the three-legged stool.

"What is this?"

"Judgment Day," she said as she stepped into his space and grasped the hair at the base of his skull. She gently pushed his back against the wall. Her lips were on his and her tongue was exploring his mouth. He stiffened for a second and then relaxed.

Without saying a word, Rachael miked him and then led him over to the three-legged stool. His head was spinning — no surprise there. He opened his mouth to say something, but Rachael silenced him by holding her fingers to his lips. He could smell her body powder.

What is she doing? This is so erotic but, my God, it can't be happening again. I'm going to get caught. He felt his breath coming hard and short and he was acutely aware of being aroused with no way to hide it. A rush of blood coloured his face. When Rachael took up her station behind the camera, he felt as if he had been fixed to a slide and placed under the microscope, where a blinding light hurt his eyes. Judgment Day, indeed. He was aching for the touch of a human hand.

Her voice resonated in the silent room like the crack of a whip. "I see now how the older woman and the kinky sex fit in. The rough stuff appeals to you."

Arthur felt a drop of perspiration run down his ribs. *Is it hot in here? Maybe it's the lights? Crap, I'm pouring sweat.* He wanted to check himself out, but he knew he couldn't do that on camera. *I am not going to talk about Linda.* He hated sitting there drenched in incriminating sweat. He could smell his own fear and he knew that she could too.

That kiss had changed everything. That kiss had connected him to immortality. For an instant, that kiss had given him the courage to kill a lion. But now he needed another. This was his second time on camera. This time he got to keep his clothes on, but he felt even more exposed than when Linda was doing the filming. He ached to see a line that connected where he was to where he needed to be.

Rachael said she wanted to know, she said she needed to understand. But Doc's voice in his head shouted, *Don't even think about it!* He felt an impulse to tell all. He ached for someone to make sense of what had happened. He could take a beating if he had to. As long as Rachael was still there at the end of it with a cold compress in her hands. If this was over, so was he. He wanted to jump out from behind the barricade. But nothing happened. There was only the lens, the light, and his silence.

Then as if from off stage, he heard Doc again — the dotter of i's, the crosser of t's, the master debater and the valedictorian. A monster twenty years in the making. He was going to spin a version of what had happened until Rachael yelled uncle. "Explain your last remark to me," said the physician healing himself.

The camera caught a cold arrogant version of Arthur that it had not recorded before. Rachael sensed the change and felt the temperature in the room drop. His eyes were different, but she couldn't have told you how. There was no time to work it out. She went with her gut and made one of those connections that come from out of nowhere. She instinctively prodded him with a statement posing as a question. "How do you get out of an arranged marriage? You do something unforgivable. It's the only way, short of murder."

Doc's poised and self-possessed voice continued its studied betrayal and affirmation of all things self-absorbed and inhuman. "I don't follow you…"

With Doc doing the talking, Arthur was pushed into the background. An actor who had spoken his piece and now was only waiting for the lights to fade so that he could make his exit. He couldn't take his eyes off the leading lady. *How does she go from searing kisses to filmmaking in one breath? Is any of this real? Is her heart beating as hard as mine?*

Rachael recognized Doc's outline for the first time. He and Arthur were as alike as twins, but they were not one and the same. She hated Doc. Suddenly words were coming out of Rachael's mouth that she never intended to say. "You didn't want to go to medical school, but you were afraid to stand up to your parents, so you found a way to mess everything up, a way that made it look as if none of this was your fault. That's what this is all about. It couldn't be your fault. You were ready to do the right thing when it all got taken out of your hands. You were betrayed. They all let you down. It's the first lesson we learn as children. If you don't want to do something, make a fuss. If that doesn't work, why then, you break something and cut yourself. You set this whole thing up."

The camera caught the transition. The face on the screen moved from poised powerful Doc back to desperate and broken Arthur. He looked as if he was about to yelp in pain. The words started to pour out of him. "My teacher Linda invited me back to her home after the first class. She had some books for me to shift from her office at school to her study at home. She asked me to help her with that. She was nice. I saw an opportunity. It's good to have a friend on staff."

"When was this?" Rachael's tone was flawless. It said *you can tell me.*

"The first weekend. Everybody else from the dorm was out at orientation getting drunk. But I didn't want to go."

She blundered with her next encourager. "Still too good for the rest of us?"

There was a very long pause. She thought that she had lost him. Arthur's face changed again. He looked angry. "I did what I'd been trained to do. Find the kingmakers and make them your friends. I'd been doing it for years. It was all a part of the image thing, the power game."

He stopped for a second. He had drowned out the liar for a moment. He could feel his agitated presence deep in his gut. He and Doc were struggling for mastery of the microphone like two gutter politicians wrestling on a podium.

"The people on my floor came to my room to say hello and they invited me to go out for drinks. I wasn't in the mood. I didn't want to be there. They were over-the-moon happy, and I was miserable. I couldn't put up with them. Linda's invitation took me off the hook. It gave me an option. Getting on a personal basis with a staff member felt very adult and civilized. Linda and I chatted about absolutely safe subjects while we loaded up her car with the books and drove back to her place. I noticed her looking at me a couple of times in what I thought was a suggestive way, but she was so much older, and she was my professor."

Where in God's name is this going to land?

"She drove a Lexus. Better than my dad's. We listened to classical music all the way back to her place on this killer sound system. The drive took about twenty minutes. The air from the AC was cool and the car smelled new. The seats were leather, and the car interior was in showroom condition. For the first time since I left home, I was someplace I wanted to be.

"When we got to her place, she pulled out a beeper and this massive iron gate opened. There was a little shelter beside it, unoccupied, where a security guard could sit. I thought at first that it was a university building. She parked on the cobblestone roundabout and opened the garage door. There were ten high-end vehicles in that garage, most of them under tarps. Behind them was a wall of books in cartons. She wanted them all moved into her study. I saw an opportunity. It was great to have something to do. So I starting slinging the cartons. It felt good to use my muscles. I wanted to show off how strong I was."

He fell out of warp for a second. The silence could not be mistaken for anything else. He was working some kind of numbers in his head. He tried to look confused for the camera, but it didn't work. He was trying to catch lightning twice in the same bottle. His eyes changed as he worked out how best to start. "I wanted to take off my shirt."

"In front of your teacher?" said Rachael in a saucy voice that would not have been out of place in the foyer of North Toronto Collegiate.

Arthur blushed and smiled. A wave of excitement stiffened the hairs on his arm. "That kind of made it irresistible to me. I was feeling two things at once. A part of me wanted to play the power game but another part of me wanted to be … well sexual. After all, I was at university now. Linda kept looking at the books and pretending not to notice how awkward I was feeling, but I could tell, something was happening. She kept touching her hair and tossing her head. I'd seen girls do that before. I always thought they did it when they were nervous."

He doesn't know…

"She went away for a few minutes and I got brave. I took off my shirt. No … don't laugh, it really was hot in the garage. But then I felt embarrassed, and I was putting the shirt back on when she showed up with a tray of cold drinks. She had changed her clothes. She gave me a long look."

He blew out a stream of breath. He was feeling the excitement of that moment a second time. His head went down. "Something deep down inside me, a part of me I can't even name, let alone understand, was loving this. I was full of frantic energy. I wanted this to get way out of control and I wanted it to be her fault." He looked up into the camera lens and, after a second, he shut his eyes and said, "I wanted her to touch me."

There you are at last.

His head went down again. He regretted everything he had said. But he couldn't stop himself. The three-legged stool was uncomfortable. Rachael had chosen well. There was no way to change your position without looking as if you were squirming. He was. He knew it too, which made it worse. In a moment of recklessness tempered by desperation he decided to push all his chips into the centre of the table. "I don't know. All these feelings are so crazy and when I try to talk about them, they get tangled. Linda flushed a little bit and I thought I was about to get a time out, when suddenly she changed. One minute she was a perfectly respectful university professor, very much in control of herself, distant and aloof, but then in an instant … well, all of that changed, and that distance gave way and there she was … she was Linda, a new creation."

"How do you mean?"

Arthur's face glowed a deep hue of red. "She looked right through me. She was beyond being worldly. She knew exactly what I was up to." Rachael did a slow pan of the camera that landed on Arthur's profile. She slowly zoomed in the lens. He looked up in the instant that she found the focal point. He was talking to the lens now. His face on the screen looked as if he was six inches away.

"She looked at me and said, 'It's hot. I've worked you too hard. Let's go sit out in the garden and have a cool drink. Bring that tray along. I need to get my bag.'

"I took the tray of drinks and followed her out into a garden. My thoughts were running wild. My mouth was dry. I was so keyed up, I thought I was going to faint. I'd never been alone with a woman before. I had a hard time managing the tray. My hands were sweating and shaking hard enough to spill the lemonade. I didn't want that to happen. I didn't want to be clumsy in front of her.

"We sat down on the patio. It was all done in marble and teak. There were real couches and a bar and a stereo. There was a tarp you could roll out with the flick of a switch when the sun got too hot. It had the feel of a restaurant. But it wasn't. It was private. What I was feeling — well you would have to see the house — that would help explain it. It was a mansion. Everything was done to a standard. Her family had the kind of money that made everything possible. Things didn't have to be practical or durable. Other people worried about that. It was enough that they were beautiful and comfortable. That was the way she did things. This wasn't my world. My compass pointed due west here."

Holy cow, look at his eyes. He's forgotten I'm here…

"Linda got us settled under the umbrella and she opened her bag and took out her sunglasses and her cigarettes. I was surprised she smoked. It didn't suit her. It was then that I noticed she'd changed from her long skirt into a short one. Her legs were tanned and perfect. She placed her cigarette in a long elegant-looking holder and then looked first at me and then at a Dunhill lighter that was sitting on the table. As I lit her cigarette, she looked through me again in her cool, appraising way. It unnerved me. I could feel blood moving through my temples.

"Then I had a moment of pure horror. She got a funny look on her face. An expression I'd never seen on a human being before. She bit her lower lip. She was trying to make up her mind about me. I was waiting for a put-down — an adult woman telling a precocious boy that he was way out of line just as an angry husband came through the front door … something awful was looming. I could feel it coming.

"I couldn't stand the tension. I felt flustered. I stood up to put my shirt back on. I wanted to go home. I felt a static charge when my shirt touched my arm. The hairs on my body were standing on end. She smiled at me and said, 'That's all right, leave it off, Arthur.' She reached into her black handbag and took out a pair of handcuffs. She handed them to me. 'Put these on instead.'"

Arthur vanished through a hole in the ice. But thrash and struggle as he might, he could not find a purchase with which to lever himself out of the freezing water. If no one fished him out, would he perish there?

Rachael kept the camera on the back of Arthur's head and let the tension continue to build. She was terrified that any word she spoke or move that she made would break the spell. The moment at hand might be lost forever. *He's as good as confessed to murder. He's kept all this inside. Hidden maybe even from himself. Is this what he remembered yesterday in the car? This is where we're supposed to take them. To where it all comes out. To where they're defenceless and trembling. But now what?*

Somehow, together, they had brought a new consciousness into the world. She kept the camera running. Not daring to speak. Praying that he would forget that even she was there. She was a vet waiting to see if the newborn colt could struggle to its feet and nurse.

Arthur looked up from the stool to search Rachael's face for a clue. *She's going to listen and give me some hope, like that kiss on the way in, but then her face is going to change. She's going to hate me and try and hide it and then just give up trying to. I'll be a monster that she trapped on film. Just like Linda.* He wasn't ready to go there. *No, she wouldn't do that to me.*

Doc was down but he wasn't out: *She will if you tell her the whole goddamned story.*

The silence had given her time to think. She had to help Arthur untangle this knot without getting enveloped in his sexual fantasies. She was in line to take Linda's place. Arthur turned everything into a drug. Why not her too? She needed to keep him talking, waiting for him to blunder and say too much again. "What was going on for you as you stood there?"

Arthur's head came halfway up, he convinced himself that her asking the question meant that things between them were still all right. "I knew it was wrong. I didn't want to put them on. But I wanted her. She gave me a look that turned the world upside down and gave it a good shake. Everything awkward came tumbling out and she saw it, but it was all right because I was with her." He looked at Rachael hoping to see understanding in her eyes. There had been understanding in Linda's eyes as they stood facing each other that afternoon. Her prefect acceptance made everything possible. Rachael didn't give him that, but she did give him a nod.

She wants more.

Doc countered, *You've said too much already.*

He took a breath and stared into the luminescence at his feet. "What I really wanted was to say yes and do what she wanted me to. Listen to me … what *she* wanted me to do. It was what I wanted. But I was too ashamed to say it. I couldn't tell her what I wanted. I had a vision of myself running out of that house and then having to turn around and beg her to let me back in."

He tried to duck. "I was so awkward around girls that one of the guys in my class took me aside for a talk one time and asked me right out if I liked men."

She was on to him. "You're wandering."

"Sorry, this is a hard story to tell right to the end." The awful darkness of the furnace room with its old petroleum smells and mechanical clicks and whirrs were getting to him. As was the bright unblinking light from the camera. It occurred to him that he could stop here. He could try and walk some of this back. Thinking with your mouth open was bad enough, doing it on camera in front of someone you desperately needed to love you was madness. But he couldn't stop then, and he couldn't stop now. Arthur looked past the lens and into Rachael's face. The only way to get this said was to pretend that this was only for her. That telling her this would be the making of them.

"We stood there on that beautiful patio looking at each other. I didn't know what to do. I was too terrified to move. I was afraid to speak. My heart was going to break if this didn't happen. I was frozen in that moment, wanting and hating. I had never felt feelings that strong before. I wish there'd been a camera running that day. I must have looked like I'd been caught shoplifting. Maybe if I saw my face, it would help me understand what happened next."

There was a long pause. He frowned and wiped his brow with his sleeve. His shirt was soaked through. The sexual excitement that had been underpinning the conversation seemed to have passed. Arthur looked two steps removed from the story for the first time. The camera saw a faint softening around his eyes, but it was the quality of his voice that signalled the transformation.

"Silence is consent. Linda stepped into that silence. She pointed to the ground in front of where she was sitting. She was so calm that I lost my fear. It felt as if we were rehearsing a scene for a school play. I stood where she wanted me to. She took one the handcuffs and attached it to my right wrist. 'Turn around' was all she had to say. I did as I was told. She fastened the other cuff behind me. I kept my head down and my mouth shut. She was so close I could smell her perfume and her body lotion. I started to shake. I couldn't stop the tremors. I hated the handcuffs. I tried to speak but no words would come. I couldn't swallow. The best I could manage was a one-syllable grunt.

"Linda took off her sunglasses and looked me in the face. I turned away as best I could to hide my feelings. She put her hand on my cheek and brought my gaze up to meet hers. Her eyes were incredible, deep and alive and without fear or contradiction. I followed those eyes, and in that instant, we were one. I felt this incredible sense of well-being. 'Do you want to stay here for the weekend, Arthur?' I said, 'Yes, Professor Dickens.' And she told me, 'Call me Linda. Professor Dickens is for the campus.'"

His eyes turned inward as narrative gave way to soliloquy and the past and present merged.

"She moved effortlessly behind me and nudged me forward onto the lounge chair. I was on my knees and feeling a little unbalanced on the soft cushion. She steadied me from behind and stuck her tongue in my ear as she reached around to undo first my belt buckle and then the clasp of my blue jeans. I felt so vulnerable. What she was doing felt wonderful.

"She whispered in my ear, 'It's hard to concentrate when you're so pent up.' She jerked me to my feet and moved me over to the service bar. She brought out a lacquered box. It had a dragon on it. A dragon moving through thick undergrowth. In an instant she'd produced two perfect furrows of white powder."

"That was your first time?"

"My first communion. It blew the top of my head off. I heard bells. The sexual stuff was mind blowing but this was one better. The cocaine made me feel the same way that Linda did. After a while I didn't even bother trying to separate them. She kept pouring out the coke. She was standing behind me and laughing. She grabbed my hair and forced my head down to do another line and when I came up for air, she would kiss me."

Rachael was having a hard time taking it all in. Her face registered mild shock. "How did that make you feel?"

"I didn't want her to stop."

"You didn't feel used?"

The question derailed him. "I felt like the luckiest guy who ever lived."

A spark of middle-class anger flashed across her brow. *Is he getting off by telling me this story?*

He could see from the look on her face that she was struggling. The *with what* evaded him. "Coke is funny. The first time you use it is the best time. It's never as good after that. It really is the kind of thing you should try only once. But I didn't. I kept going back looking for the high I got that day in the garden. But it wasn't there. Not that that stopped me from chasing it. And after a while, it was kind of hard to figure out where the cocaine ended and the sex began. Then the bad stuff started."

Rachael gave him a little nod. He had gripped the edge of the stool with both hands as if he was trying to hang on to a swing.

"It took me a while to realize something was up with Linda. Something maybe not about the coke. She never stopped. She went around from thing to thing, talking a mile a minute, starting projects that she never finished, and always with this wild look in her eye. We kept escalating. More sex, more drugs, more crazy behaviour. She could make anything happen.

"I went back to the dorm on Monday to pick up my toothbrush. I never set foot on campus after that. Neither did she. She went to see her doctor one afternoon the following week and when she got back, she told me he'd put her on sick leave. We celebrated that night by having one of her girlfriends join us in the hot tub. We carried on screwing and using the drugs until the term was over. Sometimes I'd think I was going to be killed when I got home, but then it would occur to me that I wasn't going back, that I was home. I was finally doing what I wanted to do. I felt alive." There was a look of triumph on Arthur's face.

That can't be right. Rachael put some pressure on the idea. "But it was on someone else's dime. If you said the wrong thing, if you failed to please, if you said no, that would be the end of it."

"Linda wouldn't do that…"

"Not going to put on the handcuffs this time?"

Arthur groaned — the wind was knocked out of him. *She's been playing with me! I wanted her to understand. I needed her to.* He wanted to kick over the camera and throw the laptop across the room. He looked up at Rachael expecting to see a terrible satisfaction and judgment in her eyes. She wasn't fussed. She was working the camera, listening, hearing every word he said, extracting every subtle nuance of meaning from his speech and his face and his movements. But it wasn't mean spirited. It was loving. It was connected but not intrusive. She was there, available and fully immersed in what she was doing. She was irresistible. Linda but not Linda, different but the same. He could have sat all evening quite happily watching her do a crossword puzzle.

She walked over to where he was sitting. He was soaked in sweat now, his shirt clinging to his chest and arms. She put her arms around his shoulders and gave him a hug as she took off the microphone. "I'll take you back."

"No. Take me back to your place."

The camera was still rolling. The mike in her hand was still recording sound. "You have to get this drug thing settled and I don't know how to help you with that."

"That's under control … no really, it is."

"Let's leave it there for now. The meeting is over. I can hear people moving around in the hallway. You have to get back."

———

Mike Sage met Arthur and Rachael as they came out of the boiler room. Arthur was not entirely surprised to see Mike. Getting kicked out of treatment suddenly didn't seem important.

"Hey, Arthur, who's your friend?"

Arthur wasn't sure what to say. *This is the woman I love* was incongruent with the relationship as it now stood. It seemed much safer to simply say, "This is Rachael."

"Doug has called a meeting for tomorrow afternoon in his office. Everyone's been invited to a sit-down. We're going to try and figure out what to do about you. Have you been using today?"

Rachael jumped in. "No, he's been with me."

Mike smiled. "Good, I didn't want to send you to detox. You can come back to the house tonight and then we'll decide what to do with you tomorrow."

Arthur turned to Rachael. "I'd rather go with you."

"I know," said Rachael. "But I don't have any place to put you. Besides, I have to pack. I'm going on my placement next week."

"You didn't tell me that."

"I thought I had." She turned to Mike. "Can I come to the meeting?"

"I don't think they'll let you."

"If she can't come to the meeting then I won't be there either."

She turned to Arthur. "Help me pack up my stuff."

Chapter 62

An hour before the scheduled start of the meeting, Doug lowered the blinds in his office and selected the classic rock station on the radio. The kind of brinksmanship he would shortly have to display didn't happen in a vacuum. It was grounded in a greater truth, but not a universally accepted one, as had once been the case. His recent decisions crowded the statutes of both his employers and the fellowship of recovery to which he belonged. He had gravely offended both God and Caesar with his ministrations and that made him a candidate for either a lightning strike or an afternoon with the lions. He had some serious exposure and no realistic way to walk anything back. He had played the hand he had been dealt. He had first checked and then raised and called, and now all he could do was wait to see what would happen. He took a washcloth and a bar of soap from the shaving kit he kept stashed in his desk for emergencies. The water in the staff washroom was always scalding hot. The faucet there was the one closest to the water heater and so the pressure was good. He methodically washed his face, paying close attention to the sensation of water and soap moving across living flesh. When he had finished, he did it again simply because it felt good. Lemon Zest had been an excellent choice.

He looked at his reflection in the mirror. How could anyone fail to know who he really was simply by looking at this tired, old face? God knows, they all tried. This was the face that stood between desperate people and what they wanted. It had been slapped, punched, spit upon, and occasionally caressed. It had withstood tears and threats and ambitions and white-toothed flattery. It was going to draw more fire this afternoon. The right thing to do was neither safe nor certain. It was only necessary and as such it had no place at the table.

He thought about the hour ahead. Today's meeting wasn't being held in a railway carriage at Compiègne, but that wasn't a bad model for what was about to transpire. The exhausted armies of Europe had come to the end of their power outside his front door and now they were knocking. All that would be missing this afternoon were the dress uniforms, cigar smoke, and the instruments of surrender. These frustrated warriors had come to his conference table to accomplish the task they had failed to produce on the battlefield. Instead of redrawing the map of Europe they were here to remake a young man in their own image.

Punanai, his sacred place of self-discovery and healing was about to be hijacked by a military band intent on playing a new Marshall tune they had written for the occasion. Doug was damned if he was going to let that happen.

Nobody else seemed troubled by what was about to transpire when he proposed the meeting. They thought it was a great idea. In their rush to get this settled, they overlooked the very real possibility that they could perpetrate a monstrous injustice by being here and holding court in this way — using the promise of healing as a means of social control. What was that line that old Linton came up with? You can pay and pray but that don't give you the final say.

The post-modern hell is a room full of self-indulgent people. Doug tried to imagine a way out. A way back to sanity. Was there a winning hand for anyone in this horrible house of cards? And if there was, could he help them to recognize it? This was playing Russian roulette with two bullets in the chamber and one pull of the trigger already accomplished.

An hour later, with all of his doubts and fears submerged beneath four fathoms of showmanship and bluster, Doug stood at his office door and welcomed the delegations as they arrived. First through the door was the British delegation, Dr. Dickens and his entourage. First Sea Lord Admiral Rosslyn Wemyss was here to sign for the empire. He looked poised and magnificent. His two hired coppers flanked him at a respectable distance while a grim-faced nurse wheeled in his ailing daughter, Linda — the foremost casualty thus far in this great affair. He was here to put paid to his daughter's misadventures and malfeasance, and he'd brought his best ballpoint with him to sign the cheques. Why not? He could buy this place tomorrow if he didn't get what he wanted today. His kind of money and power bent people to his will. Doug knew that there was no point in talking to the man who was building the new Jerusalem about that old-time religion.

The French delegation was the next to arrive. Doug looked over at Gerry. Marshal Foch had watched his country bled white and he ached to paint this room red and blue with his disappointment and rage. He had demanded impossible sacrifices from his nation and now he would see his foe brought to book. Gerry finally had Arthur where he wanted him — he saw nothing wrong with the prince restoring order by demanding obedience from a recalcitrant at the point of a sword.

Doug saw Sally in the role of Marianne. She was calm and looked a little sad, but she was ready to hear the truth. She was ready to do the right thing, but she was feeling the pain.

The German delegation was the last to arrive. Arthur made a splendid Major General Detlof von Winterfeldt and Rachael an indifferent Matthias Erzberger. But were they here to sue for peace or play for time? Arthur did a double take when he saw Linda that left no doubt that there had once been some significant heat between them. For her part, Linda seemed largely indifferent to her surroundings and companions.

Doug looked around the table taking in all the faces, trying to gauge where they were, and more importantly, trying to work out how far they would be willing to travel with him this afternoon. Could he close out the carnage of the great war in such a way that they wouldn't find themselves right back here in twenty years' time, signing another instrument of surrender in the same damn railway car?

"Lord," he said softly to himself. "Put me in harm's way and keep me safe."

Doug's office was now familiar ground for most of the combatants. Doug placed Arthur and Rachael at the head of the table. His parents sat to Arthur's immediate right, and the Dickens family sat to his left. Arthur was grateful that his mother had taken the spot between him and his father, and he was more than delighted that Linda was as far away from him as she could be. At the foot of the table, three places had been reserved for Mike, Reg, and Doug. After the guests had taken their seats around the large conference table, Doug closed the door and seized command. "I've been working in this business for thirty years and I've seen thousands of people come and go, and, quite frankly, I thought I'd seen it all. But the situation we find ourselves in this afternoon is one in a million. For the first time in my career, I'm dumbfounded. Which is why I felt it necessary to call this extraordinary meeting."

Gerry was about to give Doug a tongue-lashing when he felt Sally's hand gently touch his arm. He looked at her for a clue. She gave him an ashen smile.

Mike as usual was sweating the body language. This group reminded him of nothing so much as a Swiss watch with the back taken off. All of these tiny interrelated and dependant parts crammed into this one space. He was surprised that Gerry's straining neck muscles hadn't popped off. *Maybe Daddy isn't going to play the blame game, explain how the world works, or offer up the threat of some legal action ... good, that might get everyone home in time for dinner.* Mike smiled and daydreamed a little more. *What would happen if we all took wing for an hour and gave up on wanting results? And instead spoke the truth as we saw it — no, more than that — actually listened to what everyone else had to say too. Where would we find ourselves when that flight touched down?*

Doug soldiered on. "I'm going to go around the room and make some introductions. Most of you know most of the people here, but I think I'm the only one who knows everyone. You all know Arthur, and sitting next to him is Rachael Dunning, who is making a documentary about Arthur." He omitted saying, *for which she should have to scrub out bed pans for the next six months.* "Arthur's parents, Gerry and Sally Cardel, are sitting to Arthur's right. Opposite them and to Arthur's left is Dr. Robert Dickens and his daughter, Dr. Linda Dickens. Fred Coles and Allan Busch are private investigators hired by Dr. Dickens. Flanking me are Reg Topping and Mike Sage. They are familiar with Arthur's case.

"The purpose of this meeting is to decide what, if anything, we can do to assist Arthur in his recovery. So far, we haven't done very well. I'm going to take the liberty of speaking first and laying out my understanding of what has transpired. It wouldn't surprise me in the least to find that I'm not the only one here with only a partial grasp of the facts." He looked over at Arthur trying to shake him up with a frown.

Arthur was certain everyone in the room could hear his heart beating. He was about to give way to a well-deserved coronary when the cavalry arrived. Rachael put her hand over top of his balled-up fist and gave it a little squeeze. Almost as good as that kiss. He turned to face the lions.

Doug continued in his role as host and moderator. "I'm going to invite everyone to introduce themselves and take a moment to explain why they're here and what they hope to accomplish. I trust that when everyone has had their say, we'll know what needs to be done. Is everyone in agreement with this as a format?"

There was an apprehensive silence reminiscent of the darkening calm before a summer thunderstorm. A day where suddenly the circling wind shows the underside of the leaves and the swirling breeze relieves the heavy dead heat of the day.

Out of the corner of his eye, Arthur saw a dust devil bounce around the ceiling for a second before it disappeared back into the plaster. *What are those things? I keep seeing them. I need to get my eyes checked.*

Doug, who talked better on his feet, began to move slowly around the front of the room. "Arthur has been in our care on and off for two months. We've had moments of great hope followed by stretches of disappointment. I think it's fair to say that Arthur has led us a very merry chase."

Arthur kept his head down and his mouth shut, but he was listening.

"Last evening, we discovered that Arthur was making a documentary with Miss Dunning instead of attending a twelve-step meeting. Fred and Allan tell me that this has been going on, undetected, for some time. This is where I have to take a stand. What we do here is life-changing, but only when it's given the time and resources it needs. We don't let people play at this. This institution saves lives and I won't let anyone discount what we do." There being no visible signs of rebellion, he moved on.

"I've been very carefully managing the information available to me in this case. I did so in an attempt to keep Arthur's focus on the business of treatment. But my plan has misfired and now it's time to own up." That got everyone looking at their neighbour. He noticed Mike smiling at him. He knew what Mike was thinking, *It's a shame Erin and Bill weren't here to hear you say that.*

On he went straight into the shield wall that confronted him. "Gerry and Sally, there's a reason why we didn't charge you to take your son back into treatment."

Dr. Dickens looked up at Doug. His brow showed a trace of concern. Putting this over would take a delicate touch. "Perhaps I could take up the tale at this point?"

"Go ahead," said Doug with a look that reminded him that this was still his meeting.

Dickens took his cue from Doug and got to his feet before he spoke. "I'm a stranger to most of you. My name is Dr. Robert Dickens." The well-tailored suit and impeccable haircut said that he was the real thing. "My daughter, Linda, was Arthur's academic adviser at Queen's." He walked over to her wheelchair and put his hands on her shoulders. Linda didn't respond. She was enjoying one of her frequent naps. She could have been mistaken for a well-dressed mannequin. There was no analogue in language that could express what Arthur felt for Linda in her current condition. Having his mother and Rachael in the room turned complicated feeling into chaos. There was a good fit in body language. Arthur was grinding his teeth. Mike smiled. He had always wanted to see poised and perfect Arthur squirm.

This really was the end of the world. Linda the walking corpse could testify to everything he needed to keep hidden — perhaps not hidden from himself anymore —and certainly much of it could be shared with Rachael. But the rest of these meddlers, well, they didn't need to know. He could hear the roar of the comet that promised extinction for his world coming, feel its onrushing heat on his face as it compressed the very air that he breathed into lethal fire. He couldn't stop himself from checking her out one more time. He was still expecting her to wink at him. She didn't and he moved on. *If they find out about the video or the break-in, I'm sunk.*

If his mom heard the whole story straight up, without an editorial tug here and there, would she still be on his side when the dust settled? Rachael was nowhere nearly as invested in him as Sally was, and he was doubtful that she would still be around if it all came out. For the first time in his life, he earnestly wished that he was dead. Arthur looked over at the darkening faces of his parents as the story proceeded.

"Shortly after Arthur moved into residence, he and my daughter began an ill-fated relationship that ended in disaster for both of them. Linda is bipolar and she had a manic episode that unfortunately went undetected. She's now under a doctor's care and progressing slowly. We're here because her relationship with Arthur was inappropriate. She was in a position of trust, and, because of this, the university reluctantly found it necessary to revoke her tenure."

A single tear of wonder came to Sally's eye.

Gerry saw opportunity and a way back to sanity.

Dr. Dickens looked over at his daughter and sighed. She was still somewhere else. "While I feel for my daughter and her circumstances, I have to concede that this is the right decision. What we're pinning our hopes on is the possibility of her being reinstated when her health improves. The university has some discretion in these matters." He looked directly at the Cardels. He was making his pitch directly to them. "I have taken it upon myself, in my daughter's illness, to bring this unfortunate chapter to a close in a way that alleviates the suffering caused to other people. I'm heartsick that Arthur has lost his year at Queen's. I have spoken with the dean and I'm prepared to undertake the costs of having Arthur reinstated. The dean was quite sympathetic when the case was more fully explained to him."

Gerry's eyes grew wide with excitement. All was not lost. He kept his mouth shut and his game face on. He had played this game oh so many times before. No one was going to give him hope and then take it away. Not this time.

"When I first met Arthur, I didn't know who he was and I needed him to sign some papers. I was prepared to offer him a sizable sum of money if he would sign a nondisclosure agreement, which he did. This was the one condition imposed by the university. I was astonished to find that all Arthur wanted in exchange for his signature was the price of a meal and a bus ticket home." He swivelled to his right and looked at Arthur with fondness. "Young man, that impressed me very deeply. That and the fact that you cared about what happened to my daughter." Arthur's squirm turned into writhing as the flop sweats returned.

"When I didn't receive a letter from a lawyer looking for money, I became even more curious about you. I had Fred and Allan track you down so that I could see how you were getting on and take your measure. I was distressed to find a young man of your promise in these circumstances ... circumstances that unfortunately involved my daughter. That's when I put myself in contact with Doug."

The Cardels were lost in wonder. *Why didn't he talk with us?*

"I was in a tough spot. I wanted to do what was right for everyone, and I had the means at hand to bring it about, but I needed privacy both for myself and for my daughter. My lawyers excoriated me for being reckless, but my conscience would give me no quarter. That is how I came to be in a conspiracy with Doug. We met and tried to work out how best to help you, Arthur, without being seen to be involved. We hoped that you would respond to a second round of treatment. Why not? Most people do. I thought our plan had a good chance of succeeding. But, alas, it has miscarried. That is why I am stepping out of the shadows and talking directly with you tonight. I admit that what I did was selfish, but as a parent I have no remorse for protecting my child and I can only hope that you will understand a father's pain and his love."

Doug looked at Linda who was stirring after her latest catnap. "Linda, do you want to say something?"

"I hope they find the men who robbed my house." She looked around the room in horror. "Oh, it was terrible; they wrecked the place." Linda looked at her father. "That wasn't the right thing to say, was it?" She tried again. She looked at Arthur as if he had just entered the room and needed to be acknowledged. "Mr. Cardel came to see me in the hospital. He is a fine young man, and I'm sure he'll make a wonderful doctor. Maybe he'll be in my class next year. That's something to look forward to."

Reg looked over at Arthur, who was frozen in fear. Truth blurted out by an innocent dissolves well-crafted bullshit better than turpentine. He recalled Arthur's initial description of these events. He couldn't help himself. When he caught Arthur's eye, he pantomimed pulling a ball-peen hammer out of his belt as Arthur had claimed to have done. The young man turned white.

Nothing that Dr. Dickens had said carried the weight of Linda's own words. This woman was too sick to be held accountable for anything. History had been rewritten in her psyche and all the interesting parts transmogrified into pleasantries. So much for legal peril, but what of the home front?

Sally's face was radiating sorrow and stupefaction. Try as she might, she couldn't fit Linda and Arthur into the same frame. What in the world had gone on between these two? She looked over at Arthur who had his head down and his eyes averted, as if what was transpiring was too painful to be taken in. *Oh God, Arthur, what have you done?* She looked around the room at all the faces. How had they become so involved in her family? Her sense of reality and her sense of competence were taking a pummelling. "I've been worrying about Arthur since he got home from university. I keep going over what's happened and what people are trying to tell me. But it spins on me. There's no sense to this. The one possibility I never considered was that Arthur wouldn't tell me the truth. Telling the truth is in his nature. But I see now that he's been lying and keeping secrets about a lot of things, and that hurts me. Arthur, these what-ifs and the half-truths are toxic. I don't want to be afraid of the truth ever again. So I'm going to sit here until we get to the bottom of this. Arthur, nothing you could have done is as frightening for me as what my terror has me imagining. Give me the truth straight up and let me make my peace with it." Arthur clenched his teeth in an attempt to maintain the appearance of composure. Things got worse.

Gerry looked neither left nor right. They were wavering, this whole pack of idiots. How could they not see what was right in front of them? They had Dickens at their mercy. All Arthur had to do was say yes. No one cared what a young man got up to at university. Christ, that's why you sent them.

He looked slowly around the room trying to gauge where everyone was. *I have to get these guys back on side. The past means nothing. The future is everything. I've seen this a hundred times with clients when the portfolio goes south. But this time it's not someone else's money on the line. It's mine.* "I'm sick at heart. I thought I knew what I was doing," he said. "I made a plan, drew up a budget, followed the advice of experts, and made it possible for both Arthur and Dale to do something they really wanted to do with their lives."

Rachael wasn't having that. "Whose dream are we talking about now, yours or Arthur's? Can we at least get that settled?"

There was murder in his heart, but Gerry sucked it up. He didn't care what the girlfriend thought. She would join Medved on the list before the sun went down. "I can own this. I wanted to be a doctor, but I never got the chance." There was a measured tone of bitterness in his voice.

Dickens had returned to his seat opposite the Cardels. You could tell that he was grateful for the civilized tone of the conversation thus far but wondering if this was about to become the tipping point. "When my dad died, I got sent to work in my uncle's brokerage firm. I've been there ever since. No one ever asked me if I wanted to go. I make as much money as a doctor, maybe even more, but it's not what I wanted to do. Maybe I should have quit the firm and gone to medical school in my thirties, other people have done that, but it wasn't only about me at that point."

He swivelled in his chair to make eye contact with Arthur. Arthur could see love in his father's eyes. "I met your mother and we got married, and you kids came along, and I simply couldn't take a risk that big. I had to think about what was best for you. I'm still thinking about that. Young people always think that they know how the world works, but they don't. That doesn't come until much later in life, and you pay an awful price to find out."

There was a pregnant pause. Doug and Mike exchanged a look that said, *Holy cow ... Gerry does know how to be a father*. Even Sally was a little taken aback. But better late than never.

"Arthur, there are a lot of days between blowing your chance and the grave," Gerry said. "Long lonely days to think about how it might have been different. I have no more power over your future than I have over my own past. But I'm your father. I'm still willing to do the right thing here, no matter what it costs, but, Arthur, I need to know what it is that you want to do. I can't look out for your best interests because you're not playing straight."

Reg was stunned. There it was. Someone had finally come right out and said it. And Gerry, of all people. No one would have bet on that.

Doug looked at Mike. He was still sizing up the room. His face was open and fully engaged with the conversation. He wanted to hear everything. Doug knew him well enough to know that the absence of a scowl meant he thought everyone was telling the truth.

Rachael leaned back in her chair and put her hands behind her head. An action deliberately out of step with the blocking chosen by the previous speakers. She had the chops to go a long way in any business. "My documentary is a school project. The only person I ever expected to show it to was my teacher. There's some very personal stuff in it and, I have to say, I'm proud of this work. I had no idea there was so much going on behind the scenes in Arthur's life. I wish I was rolling film right now." She playfully touched Arthur's foot with her own under the table. Even Mike missed it. "The reason I'm here tonight is to see how the story turns out and to support Arthur."

Fred looked at Allan and then Dr. Dickens before he introduced himself and explained what he and Allan had been up to. "The only reason we're here tonight is so that you can question us if you wish and see that we mean no one here any harm."

You could see that Reg was hard at work trying to harmonize all the new information with the remarks he had originally intended to make. He reached into his pocket and removed a handkerchief that perfectly matched his bowtie. He set to work polishing his glasses. Without the frames, his handsome face looked several years younger. As a disabled adolescent, he had been pushed around and bullied by the blameless and the just, and he still had it in for them. These bozos were about to crush the life out of Arthur for reasons beyond reproach. He wasn't going to let that happen.

"I want to share one insight with you. There's a cursus honorum that people go through in addictions. It's a timetable. They smoke cigarettes in elementary school, pot in junior high, they learn to drink alcohol in high school, and as undergraduates, they mess around with drugs. It's a familiar pattern. One of increasing dependency. People learn to lie, break the law, cover their tracks, and even steal or prostitute themselves to get what they think they need. It all takes time, usually a lot of time. That didn't happen to Arthur."

Sally's face showed her relief. She had an inkling that he was right. Gerry for his part was far too busy thinking of what he was going to say next to listen.

"Arthur's addiction started in September last year. Do the math. He has been in active addiction for fourteen weeks and in recovery for nine. If you're surprised and overwhelmed by the changes in Arthur, imagine how hard this has been on him. To say the very least, his case is atypical."

Reg finished playing with his glasses and returned them to his face. He had pulled the same move twenty times last year in his performance of the jury foreman in *Twelve Angry Men*. He couldn't wait to tell his director the new use he had found for his notes.

"Imagine going away to university and taking on life for the first time and having it all end so badly. Arthur is bright. What he needs is time to process what has happened. I think it would be a mistake to try to push him into anything right now. What he needs is time to heal." Reg smiled at them. "Of course, the staff minority view is that what Arthur needs is a good swift boot in the pants."

Mike had managed to lose his suit coat and roll up his sleeves. The casual look worked for Mike. "A good boot in the ass is wasted without the hug at the end. There are only two choices for you, Arthur. Keep doing what you've been doing or try something new. But you have to choose. There are only two teams in this league: the Montreal Canadiens and the Toronto Maple Leafs — pick a side, put on the jersey, and skate down the ice like you mean business."

Arthur once again found himself the focal point of the group. They had all had their say and now they were waiting for some kind of response. Doc went to the mat. He was on his hands and knees, begging for one more chance. It would be so much easier now that he knew exactly what everyone wanted to hear, what everyone knew, and what everyone was prepared to do. But when Rachael squeezed Arthur's hand a second time, she fractured three of Doc's vertebrae.

Arthur took a bearing of everyone in the room. "This is a lot to take in. I want a minute to pull myself together and think about what you've all had to say. Mike, is there somewhere where Rachael and I go to be alone and talk for a few minutes?"

Doug looked around the room. He was encouraged that Arthur wanted to talk to Rachael before he responded. "Okay, do what you need to do. We'll be here when you get back."

Chapter 63

John had had enough. He stood on the conference table in Doug's office and addressed the group as they milled around getting coffee.

"I'll tell you what needs doing here. When Humpty Dumpty sat on the wall, he was undeniably drunk and most likely feeling invulnerable, all and all. And maybe even in the mood to show off a little and stir up his audience by putting himself in danger. It's not hard to get inside his egg-head, and maybe even have a little sympathy for him. It must have seemed like a good idea at the time, getting up on the wall and acting the fool. But wobbly eggs and leaning walls are all about inevitable falls, not maintaining the status quo. The whole point of treatment is to get you up on the wall, high above the beckoning sidewalk below. All the king's horses and all the king's men can never put you back together again, and that, my friends, is what treatment is all about. A delusion is very much like an eggshell. You can squeeze as hard as you please and it will never break. It's a solid shape that radiates stress equally throughout the structure. But a short sharp rap from an unfriendly beak is a different matter, and there are lots of sharp edges in a treatment centre.

"I have been hovering over the comings and goings at Punanai for years. Throwing someone out of treatment is never a bad thing. It's pushing that chickenshit Humpty off the wall. Well, think about it. If they are not brave enough to jump on their own, or not careless enough to trip themselves up, what choice do you have? You gotta push 'em. More than one wretched sinner has finally despaired when the heavy door at Punanai closed behind them. The view from the sidewalk with a green garbage bag in each hand is telling. It can be more eloquent than sonnets and lyres.

"And who is this Rachael? I'll tell you who she is … another drug-crazed co-dependent in a short skirt who gets her jollies by stirring up the boys at the meetings. I've seen her kind before. She'll end up marrying some halfwit Romeo and living over a store. Bet you she ends up telling sad tales and waiting tables at the ZiggZagg before she's thirty-five.

"You can't pamper these punks. You gotta do what's right for the house. Doug has twenty-five other careening bodies in early recovery to worry about. Twenty-

five highly sensitive, disoriented, relapse-prone lunatics on the mend. That's a lot of eggs to brood over. And the thing the general public never gets is this: You can't let addicts get away with anything. You have to call them on their bullshit every time, and mean it, or there was no point in even starting down that road with them. They live to nickel-and-dime you. If you let them get away with discounting you even once, you become one more spineless bullshitter they can hustle."

Chapter 64

Arthur led Rachael into the interview room. He gave her a hug. It felt good to be away from the maddening crowd.

"What are you going to say to them?"

"Can you roll film in here?"

Rachael smiled wickedly at him. "If I can do it out there, you know damn well I can do it in here!"

"You said you weren't filming."

"Recording sound isn't filming. Neither is moving a camera over a still photograph to give the viewer the sense of movement and depth. Besides, being mysterious really helps sell these things."

"Was that what that little kick was all about?"

"Uh-huh."

"I loved the way you shut my dad up."

"That was the best part for me too. I could never say that to my own parents."

"I'm coming with you on your placement."

"I'd rather you stay in treatment."

"No, I've heard what they have to say."

"I'm going to Los Angeles."

"I have a passport."

"It's expensive."

"I can get the money."

She looked at him for a full two minutes while she made up her mind. "Then sit there and listen while I tell you what I really think." She turned the camera on both of them. "I've been wandering around inside your head feeling like a ghost in a train station. I don't know who you are, Arthur. There's nothing to hang on to. You go here and there, and you do this and that, but I can never figure out why. What I see on that screen is a man who denies his deepest feelings. There's a different you for every occasion. You're so busy playing everybody, it's become your whole life."

"But don't you see? I had to. The only life that was possible for me was a hidden one."

"Maybe, up till now, but not anymore, Arthur, not if you want to be with me. In Los Angeles, there's no more dope and no more lies and no more pretending. If you can't manage that don't get on the plane. I'm working hard to make my dreams come true. I'm not going to let you spoil my chance."

"You have me all wrong."

"No, I have you right. You're a man without hands. You've been playing a sick game. You manipulate people into doing what you want them to do in the hope that what they come up with will satisfy you. You told me this whole story to make me fall in love with you and that is precisely why I haven't."

"That's not the same as saying that you couldn't."

"You'd have to make a lot of changes for that to become a possibility."

Chapter 65

Mike was very curious about Linda. The last great unknown in this drama. What he had been told about her and what he was seeing for himself couldn't be reconciled. He sat down next to her at the table and tried to draw her out. "So you were Arthur's teacher?"

She looked at him as if she had been waiting anxiously for someone to ask her this very question. But as the first word formed on her lips, a funny look came over her face. She reminded Mike of an infant staring uncomprehendingly at a camera, too innocent to be aware of anything as complicated as a motive. The silence went on for several minutes. Her untroubled calm slowly gave way as she tried to work out where she was and what was being asked of her. She suddenly looked tired and embarrassed. "Who are you again?" she asked.

Dr. Dickens tapped Doug on the elbow. "Could we get them back? I have to take Linda home. She's fading." Doug nodded and pointed at Mike.

Mike walked into the meeting room to collect Arthur and Rachael. The room was empty. The kids had left a disc on the desk. A Post-it Note read: PLAY ME. That made Mike laugh.

"Where did they go?"

"I don't know. They left us this."

Mike set things up and hit the play button. Arthur's image came into focus. He looked into the lens and let it search his face for a full minute before he spoke. He seemed at peace.

"The conversation we've had reminds me of the Greek dramas I read in school. In those plays the chorus gave a voice on stage to both the voice we only ever hear inside our own heads, and to the myriad voices that surround us telling us what to think and how to behave. My first choristers were my mom and dad. They told me who I was and how the world worked. When I got to school, other voices joined the throng. Teachers and tutors shaped and sharpened my perceptions about myself and the world. I listened to them, but I never loved them. The other kids were busy tearing the ass out of the world. They were full of energy and ideas. They questioned everything with a righteous intolerance that I ached to possess. But I was set apart, destined for greater things. I'd listen to the factions as they went back and forth. Idealism and conformity locked in mortal combat.

"Then one day I was asked to be the valedictorian. That looks good on a résumé, so of course I said yes. What did I know? I was all about image and getting ahead. But as I worked through what I wanted to say, I hesitated. I realized for the first time that I didn't belong with either the kids or the adults. I wanted to talk about that and what it meant, but I lost my nerve. It was so much easier to read from the script they'd sent over. So comes the day and I put on a suit and get up on stage and I repeat everything the chorus ever said to me. I hated myself. I looked out over that audience and all I saw were blank faces. They knew I was lying. That was the moment when doubt got the upper hand. Maybe willing something to be true wasn't going to be enough. I had chosen conformity and I was choking on it."

Mike heard a groan come from Gerry. He snuck a look at the Cardels and saw shock on Sally's face.

Arthur continued, "Then off to university and suddenly the chorus went silent. New voices sprang up: Eric and Linda and Dara and Arial had a refreshing new take on things. And soon after that, there was another voice in my head. He knew how to talk to people. But more than that, he knew what they wanted to hear, how to slap them around and how to get things done.

"His voice was dark and daring and didn't care what happened to other people. That voice never lost its way. I can still feel him struggling to get back into my thoughts. I miss his certainty almost as much as I hate his lies.

"You guys are the latest version of my chorus. You sang all the classics off the greatest hits album. That's the problem with a chorus, no originality. The thing and the purpose of the thing are messed up. Are you educating me or trying to indoctrinate me? Am I a tragic figure? One doomed to disaster from the day of my birth?

"No, really, this is a serious life lesson. I get the part that you have moved heaven and earth to give me a chance to do something special. But at the end of the day, it's not what I want to do. Where does that leave me and where does that leave you?

"Rachael's documentary made me realize that I can't say no to you when I'm sober, but by being high, I say no more eloquently than any poet could manage. I wonder what's going to be harder for me now, saying no to the people I love or saying no to the drugs that are killing me. Doing only one of them is not going to be enough. I know now that I have to do both.

"This afternoon, my mom had to remind me that I don't tell lies. That is where the pain in my gut has been coming from. I can tell lies and live them and damn near come to love them. I didn't know that about myself. You see no one ever asked me the question directly: Arthur, do you want to be a doctor? Because the answer to that question is a resounding no. But I wanted to be loved and the only way to be loved was to answer yes. At least it was. Then I met Linda and she showed me another way. Then I came here, and now I'm with Rachael.

"In a few moments, you are going to be given the opportunity to watch Rachael's documentary *The Valedictorian*. It was only supposed to be something she was doing for school, but clearly it has attracted a wider audience.

"Mom and Dad, I don't know if you want to watch this. If you really want to know what I got up to at school, it's there in no uncertain terms. I'm sorry that your dream of medical school didn't work out. But I'm glad that the wheels fell off early rather than late. I love you but I can't do what you want me to do."

The camera caught his eyes as he paused to take a breath. They were clear and untroubled. The tension of the previous hour was gone. The duplicity too. Or perhaps it had finally learned how to throw a slow inside curve when all the money was on the table.

"Rachael and I have run away to Los Angeles. She has to spend a month down there working as an intern in the film industry. Rachael wants to see what her future looks like and I want to be with Rachael. I don't know if film is what I want to do, but I know that something has a hold on me. I'm going to use this time to figure out who it is I plan to be when I grow up. Oh and yes, I do believe they have CA meetings in Hollywood.

"Dr. Dickens, thank you for bringing Linda to the meeting. I really wanted Rachael to meet her. I can see now that if she and I had never hooked up the way we did, neither of us would ever have gotten into trouble. Alone, we were inert, too chicken ever to find out who we really were. It was only when we were combined that we became volatile. The explosion that broke us apart set me free. That hasn't happened for Linda. I wish it had, and I hope it will."

Rachael joined Arthur on camera. He put his arm around her and smiled. "The thing that Rachael and I feel bad about is that the story doesn't have an ending. We've written one, but we're never going to get the chance to film it. That'll be up to you.

"Andrew Medved is living down the road at Baker House, paying his bills by stacking cans and piling fruit at the market, looking for a miracle to get him into medical school. His family is a train wreck and they're never going to be able to help him. Dr. Dickens, you said you'd be willing to send me … send Andrew in my place. It would be a shame to waste that gift on someone who didn't want it with all his heart."

Gerry let fly with a barrage of obscenities, but the tape paid him no mind.

"Finally, to Mike, Reg and Doug, thanks for wising me up. I can tell when I'm kidding myself now. I guess that's a good thing, but it burns. We'll be back in about a month and I'll drop by and see you guys then.

"When I was writing my valedictory address, I came across a quote from the Gospel of Thomas that spoke powerfully to me. It was something I really wanted to use in my speech, but I lost my nerve because I was afraid it would offend the people who'd brought me this far. I wish I'd said it and wish even more that I'd fully understood it and lived it. Well, I'm there now. 'If you bring forth what is within you, what you bring forth will save you. If you do not bring forth what is within you, what you do not bring forth will destroy you.' I've had a near miss. One powerful enough to kill me, but perhaps badly aimed. I won't give the furies a second chance.

"So I'm off to Hollywood to seek my fame and fortune. I don't know how happy you would've been with a son who was a reluctant physician. I would've been plagued with psychosomatic illnesses. I don't even know if you can still love me now that I'm stark raving sober. But I do promise that when I get back, we're going to sit down; maybe after you've seen the documentary, if that is what you choose to do, and we're going to talk about this."

The screen froze the frame of his face reaching over to turn off the camera. The credits rolled and the music played.

Fred looked at Allan and shook his head. "They won't let him across the border. He has charges."

Dr. Dickens nodded. "I can fix that if everyone is okay with him going."

"How?"

"Don't ask."

Doug loosened his tie and put his hands behind his head. His usually implacable face boasted a little smile. He checked out Mike and Reg. They were happy too.

Sally looked at him in wonder. "Why are you smiling?"

"Why aren't you?"

"What did you see that I didn't? He's running away again, to Hollywood of all places, you can't run any further away from reality than that."

"Let's get out of here," said Gerry. "I can't stand looking at these people for one second longer."

Sally's voice was sharp. "Then go wait in the car."

Doug moved into Sally's personal space. "He's tuning the piano. Listening for the broken key. Don't you see? It's the great wheel of bullshit, it's come full circle. This happens in every recovery. When addicts and alcoholics crash and burn or when they are confronted with reality, they always spin whatever happened and explain it away. But there's an unconscious pattern to their denial. Every excuse and evasion is a retreating army, falling back and reforming along a new defensive line. 'I don't have a problem, but even if I did, it would be none of your business. If you hadn't interfered in my life, I'd be okay. This is all your fault. You let me down. I am not hurting anyone but myself. If I do have a problem, a big if, I'm still a better person than you are, you close-minded little cretin. I don't need your help to fix this. I don't need to go to any damn meetings either, thank you very much. I'm not that bad and if I ever get that bad, I'll kill myself. Stop trying to tell me how to live my life you pious hypocrite.'"

She was listening.

"But here's the thing, Sally. This is the wonder of it. Every one of those statements is a lie. But every lie in the sequence is an improvement over the previous one. All of those positions were attempts to explain and control his addiction. In his heart of hearts, Arthur was certain that he could make this right. He could outhustle and outmuscle any opposition. Each one of those statements was a bold idea that got tested by reality. He told the lie because he really hoped that it was true. The lying is over. It's served its purpose. It has finally collapsed in on itself to reveal, if not the truth, then at least a preference for the truth."

"Sally, the Dickens are leaving," Gerry said. "We have to talk to them before they get away!"

"So you think that's happened for Arthur?"

"Oh, he is so close. He may have figured this out. I need to see the video. The answer will be there."

"Turn it on. I'm not leaving here until I get to the bottom of this."

Gerry exploded, "That's it! I'm outta here, find your own damn way home!"

Fin